THE PYRATES

George MacDonald Fraser was born on 2 April
1925 in Carlisle. He was educated at Carlisle
Grammar School and the Glasgow Academy; he
served in the XIV Army in 1944–45 and was a
lieutenant in the Gordon Highlanders in 1946–47.
Mr Fraser has worked as a journalist in Scotland
and in western Canada. He frequently contributed
reviews to the *Glasgow Herald*, becoming finally
its deputy editor, and has been a contributor to
such periodicals as the *Economist* and *International Short Story* (US). He is married and has
two sons and a daughter. He now lives on the Isle
of Man.

George MacDonald Fraser is the author of the
series of books based on The Flashman Papers
and recounting the further adventures of that cad
and bully from *Tom Brown's Schooldays*.

THE
PYRATES

*George
MacDonald Fraser*

Pan Books
in association with Collins

First published 1983 by William Collins Sons & Co. Ltd
This edition published 1984 by Pan Books Ltd,
Cavaye Place, London SW10 9PG
in association with William Collins Sons & Co. Ltd
9 8 7 6 5 4 3 2 1
© George MacDonald Fraser 1983
ISBN 0 330 28390 1
Reproduced, printed and bound in Great Britain by
Hazell Watson & Viney Limited,
Member of the BPCC Group,
Aylesbury, Bucks

IN MEMORY OF
The Most Reverend and Right Honourable
LANCELOT BLACKBURNE
(1658–1743)
Archbishop of York
and buccaneer

BOOK
THE FIRST

CHAPTER
THE FIRST

t began in the old and golden days of England, in a
time when all the hedgerows were green and the
roads dusty, when hawthorn and wild roses
bloomed, when big-bellied landlords brewed rich
October ale at a penny a pint for rakish high-booted cavaliers
with jingling spurs and long rapiers, when squires ate roast
beef and belched and damned the Dutch over their claret
while their faithful hounds slumbered on the rushes by the
hearth, when summers were long and warm and drowsy, with
honeysuckle and hollyhocks by cottage walls, when winter
nights were clear and sharp with frost-rimmed moons shining
on the silent snow, and Claud Duval and Swift Nick Nevison
lurked in the bosky thickets, teeth gleaming beneath their
masks as they heard the rumble of coaches bearing paunchy
well-lined nabobs and bright-eyed ladies with powdered hair
who would gladly tread a measure by the wayside with the
gallant tobyman, and bestow a kiss to save their husbands'
guineas; an England where good King Charles lounged
amiably on his throne, and scandalised Mr Pepys (or was it
Mr Evelyn?) by climbing walls to ogle Pretty Nell; where
gallants roistered and diced away their fathers' fortunes;
where beaming yokels in spotless smocks made hay in the
sunshine and ate bread and cheese and quaffed foaming
tankards fit to do G. K. Chesterton's heart good; where
threadbare pedlars with sharp eyes and long noses shared

11

their morning bacon with weary travellers in dew-pearled woods and discoursed endlessly of 'Hudibras' and the glories of nature; where burly earringed smugglers brought their stealthy sloops into midnight coves, and stowed their hard-run cargoes of Hollands and Brussels and fragrant Virginia in clammy caverns; where the poachers of Lincolnshire lifted hares and pheasants by the bushel and buffeted gamekeepers and jumped o'er everywhere . . .

An England, in short, where justices were stout and gouty, peasants bluff and sturdy and content (but ready to turn out for Monmouth at a moment's notice), merchant-fathers close and anxious, daughters sweet and winsome, good wives rosy and capable with bunches of keys and receipts for plum cordials, Puritans smug and sour and sanctimonious, fine ladies beautiful and husky-voiced and slightly wanton, foreigners suave and devious and given to using musky perfume, serving wenches red-haired and roguish-eyed with forty-inch busts, gentleman-adventurers proud and lithe and austere and indistinguishable from Basil Rathbone, and younger sons all eager and clean-limbed and longing for those far horizons beyond which lay fame and fortune and love and high adventure.

That was England, then; long before interfering social historians and such carles had spoiled it by discovering that its sanitation was primitive and its social services non-existent, that London's atmosphere was so poisonous as to be un-breathable by all but the strongest lungs, that King Charles's courtiers probably didn't change their underwear above once a fortnight, that the cities stank fit to wake the dead and the countryside was largely either wilderness or rural slum, that religious bigotry, dental decay, political corruption, fleas, cruelty, poverty, disease, injustice, public hangings, mal-nutrition, and bear-baiting were rife, and there was hardly an economist or environmentalist or town planner or sociologist or anything progressive worth a damn. (There wasn't even a London School of Economics, which is remarkable when you consider that Locke and Hobbes were loose about the place).

Happily, the stout justices and wenches and gallants and peasants and fine ladies – and even elegant Charles himself, who was nobody's fool – never realised how backward and insanitary and generally awful they might look to the cold and all-too-selective eye of modern research, and if they had, it is doubtful if they would have felt any pang of guilt or shame, happy conscienceless rabble that they were. Indeed, his majesty would most likely have raised a politely sceptical eyebrow, the justices scowled resentfully, and the wenches, gallants, and peasants, being vulgar, gone into hoots of derisive mirth.

So, out of deference and gratitude to them all, and because history is very much what you want it to be, anyway, this story begins in that other, happier England of fancy rooted in truth, where dates and places and the chronology of events and people may shift a little here and there in the mirror of imagination, and yet not be thought false on that account. For it's just a tale, and as Mark Twain pointed out, whether it happened or did not happen, it could have happened. And as all story-tellers know, whether they work with spoken words in crofts, or quills in Abbotsford, or cameras in Hollywood, it should have happened.

Thus:

It was on a day when, for example, King Charles was pleasantly tired after a ten-mile walk and was guiltily wondering whether he ought to preside at a meeting of his Royal Society, or take Frances Stuart to a very funny, dirty play whose jokes she would be too pure-minded to understand;

when Barbara Castlemaine was surveying her magnificence in the mirror, regretting (slightly) the havoc wrought by last night's indulgence, and scheming how to foil her gorgeous rival, the Duchess of Portsmouth;

when, in far Jamaica, fat and yellow-faced old Henry

13

Morgan was blowing impatiently into the whistle on the handle of his empty tankard for a refill, and wistfully reminiscing with the boys about flashing-eyed Spanish dames and treasure-stuffed churches of Panama and Portobello;

when Mr Evelyn was noting in his diary that the Duke of York's dog always hid in the safest corner of the ship during sea-battles, and Mr Pepys was recording in *his* diary that on the previous night he had urinated in the fireplace because he couldn't be bothered going out to the usual offices (and anyone checking these entries will find they are years apart, which gives some idea of the kind of story this is);

when Kirk's mercenaries were tramping sweatily across the hot sands of the High Barbaree, licking parched lips at the thought of sparkling springs, or dusky Arab beauties in the *suk* of Tangier, or the day when their discharges would come through;

when a dear old tinker was dying of the cold, poor and humble and unnoticed by the great world, with the sound of choiring angels in his ears and no notion that one day he would be remembered as the greatest writer of plain English that ever was;

when the sound of the Dutchmen's guns was still a fearsome memory along Thames-side, and Louis XIV was dreaming grandiose dreams and summoning his barber for his twice-weekly shave . . .

All these things were happening on the day when the story begins, but they don't really matter, and have been set down for period flavour. The real principals in our melodrama were waiting in the wings, entirely unaware of each other or of the parts they were to play. They don't actually come on just yet, but since they are the stars we should take a preliminary look at them.

First:

Captain Benjamin Avery, of the King's Navy, fresh from distinguished service against the Sallee Rovers, in his decent lodging at Greenwich, making a careful toilet, brushing his

14

teeth, combing his hair, adjusting his plain but spotless neckcloth, shooting his cuffs just so, and bidding a polite but aloof good morning to the adoring serving-maid as she brings in his breakfast of cereal, two boiled eggs, toast and coffee, and scurries out with a breathless, fluttering curtsey. Captain Avery straightens his coat and decides as he contemplates his splendid reflection that preferment and promotion must soon be the lot of such a brilliant and deserving young officer.

If you'd been there you would have seen his point, and the adoring maid's. Captain Avery was everything that a hero of historical romance should be; he was all of Mr Sabatini's supermen rolled into one, and he knew it. The sight of him was enough to make ordinary men feel that they were wearing odd socks, and women to go weak at the knees. Not that his dress was magnificent; it was sober, neat, and even plain, but as worn by Captain Avery it put mere finery to shame. Nor did he carry himself with ostentation, but with that natural dignity, nay austerity, coupled with discretion and modesty, which come of innate breeding. His finely-chiselled features bespoke both the man of action and the philosopher, their youthful lines tempered by a maturity beyond his years; there was beneath his composed exterior a hint of steely power, etc., etc. You get the picture.

For the record, this wonder boy was six feet two, with shoulders like a navvy and the waist of a ballerina; his legs were long and shapely, his hips narrow, and he moved like a classy welterweight coming out at the first bell. His face was straight off the B.O.P. cover, with its broad unclouded brow, long fair hair framing his smooth-shaven cheeks; his nose was classic, his mouth firm but not hard, his eyes clear dark grey and wide-set, his jaw strong and slightly cleft, and his teeth would have sent Kirk Douglas scuttling shamefaced to his dentist. His expression was at once noble, alert and intelligent, deferential yet commanding . . . sorry, we're off again.

In short, Captain Avery was the young Errol Flynn, only more so, with a dash of Power and Redford thrown in; the answer to a maiden's prayer, and between ourselves, rather a pain in the neck. For besides being gorgeous, he had a starred First from Oxford, could do the hundred in evens, played the guitar to admiration, helped old women across the street, kept his finger-nails clean, said his prayers, read Virgil and Aristophanes for fun, and generally made the Admirable Crichton look like an illiterate slob. However, he is vital if you are to get the customers in; more of him anon.

Secondly, and a sad come-down it is if you're a purist, meet Colonel Tom Blood, cashiered, bought out, and all too obviously our Anti-Hero, in *his* lodgings, a seedy attic in Blackfriars, with a leaky ceiling and the paper peeling off the walls in damp strips. He has five pence in his pocket, his linen is foul, his boots are cracked, he hasn't shaved, there's nothing for breakfast but the stale heel of a loaf and pump water, and his railing harridan of a landlady has just shrieked abusively up the stairs to remind him that he is six weeks behind with the rent. But Colonel Blood is Irish and an optimist, and lies on his unmade bed with his hands behind his head, whistling and planning how to elope with a rich cit's wife once he has brought the silly bag to the boil and she has assembled her valuables. He'd need a razor from somewhere, to be sure, and a clean shirt, but these – like poverty, hunger, and a shocking reputation – were trifles to a resourceful lad who had once come within an ace of stealing the Crown Jewels.

One should not be put off by the bad press given to Blood by that prejudiced old prude, Mr Evelyn, who once had dinner with him at Mr Treasurer's, and kept a tight grip on his wallet during the meal, by the sound of it. 'That impudent bold fellow', he wrote of the gallant Colonel, 'had not only a daring, but villainous unmerciful look, a false countenance, but very well spoken and dangerously insinuating'. Not quite fair to a dashing rascal who, if not classically handsome, was decidedly attractive in a Clark Gable-ish way, with his sleepy dark eyes, ready smile, and easy Irish charm. Tall, strong and well-made, perhaps not as slim as he would have liked, but trim and fast on his feet for all that; an affable, deceptively easygoing gentleman and quite a favourite with the less discriminating ladies who were beguiled by his trim moustache and lively conversation. A tricky, dangerous villain, though, when he had to be, which was deplorably often, for of all the Colonel's many and curious talents, finding trouble was the first.

So there they were, the two of them, miles and poles apart, and hardly a thing in common except youth and vigour and blissful ignorance of the fate that was being determined for them four thousand sea-miles away . . .

For now the scene shifts abruptly, to grim Fort St Bartlemy, lonely outpost of England in the far Caribbean, where at the watergate of the great rockbound castle, bronzed and bare-backed seamen sweated in the humid tropic night as they carried massive iron-studded chests up from the boats at the sea-steps, and along the arched, stone-flagged tunnel to the strong room deep in the heart of that impregnable place. Guttering torches lit the scene as the sailors grunted and heaved and chewed quids of plug tobacco and spat and swore rich sea-oaths as they laboured, for every tarry-handed mother's son of them had learned his trade in the Jeffrey Farnol School of Historical Dialect, and could growl 'Belike' and 'Look'ee' and 'Ha – cheerly messmates all!' in that authentic Mummerset growl which would one day keep Robert Newton in gainful employment. So with hearty heave-ho-ing and avasting they worked, under the stern blue eye of their grizzled commander, a weather-beaten salt of suitably bluff appearance with a blue coat and brass-mounted telescope, who may well have been called Hawkins or Bransome, but not conceivably Vavasour d'Umfraville.

"Aaargh!" cried the burly captain, twice for emphasis. "Aaargh! Easy, handsomely, I say, wi' they chests, rot 'ee! 'Tis ten thousand pound you'm carryin', ye lubbers!" This was his normal habit of speech, since anything else would have been incomprehensible to his crew. "A pesky parlous cargo it be, an' all, an' glad am I to be rid on't, burn me for a backstay else."

"Not as glad as my garrison will be to see it," replied the fort commandant, a stout and sunburned soldier who was equally perfect casting in his buff coat, large belly, and plumed hat. "Three years without pay is a long time in such lonely fortalice as this." He hesitated, and ventured to add: "Damme for a lizard else."

"For a what?" inquired the captain, rolling an eye.

"A lizard," said the commandant defensively. "You know."

"Aaargh!" said the captain thoughtfully. "A lizard, eh? Humph! Us seamen don't use to swear by no crawlin' land-lubberly varmints, us don't. Handspikes an' marlin-spikes an' sich sailorly things be good enough fer we, by the powers, choke me wi' a rammer else. Howbeit," he went on, "I be mortal glad to see the last o' these damned dollars; a thousand leagues from old England be a long way wi' such a lading, through pirate waters an' all, d'ye see, rot me for a Portingale pimp if it bain't." And he dashed the sweat from his brow with a horny hand. "Aye, split an' sink me, a risky v'yage, look'ee, a passage right perilous, an' happy I am 'tis done wi', an' they doubloons snug i' the cellar at last, scuttle me for a—"

"How about some supper?" said the commandant quickly.

"Vittles, sez you!" cried the captain, rolling both eyes. "Why, then vittles it is, sez I, wi' all my heart, aye, an' a flagon o' ale, devil a doubt, or Spanish vino, sa-ha! to wet our whistles, an' damn all, wi' a curse. Scupper me wi' a hand-spike," he added triumphantly, "else."

The commandant having conceded game set and match, they rolled off to supper, while the toiling seamen heaved and beliked and spat as they trundled the last of the precious chests into the strongroom, and the great door clanged to and was locked with a ponderous key. Thereafter they repaired to mess with the garrison, while in the commandant's chambers the officers supped off pepper-pot and flying-fish broiled, with many a tankard, and the sea captain amazed his hosts with the richness of his discourse. Sentries stood outside the strongroom, but the long stone tunnel to the watergate lay deserted, and from the sea-steps outside the fitful light of the torches shone on empty water to the little harbour entrance. Above on the battlements other sentries lolled – those dispensable sentries of fiction who doze at their posts in their ill-fitting uniforms, mere cannon-fodder to be knocked on the head or smothered by agile assailants, or at best wake up too late to fire a warning shot and yell "Turn out the . . . ugh!" If the commandant had lined the walls of that lonely fortress with his entire force, instead of boozing and stuffing and throwing his wig aside in the carouse, all might have been well, but of course he didn't. They never do.

So within Fort St Bartlemy was all cheery complacency and unbuttoning, and without the tropic moon shone on that familiar scene . . . the grim silhouette of the castle, the torch-lit peace of the watergate, the wind sighing gently through the palm trees, the soft surf lapping the silver sand. All was tranquil, the moon's wake throwing its golden shaft across the rum-dark sea, the scent of bougainvillea and pimento on the breeze, and one might have imagined the soft strains of 'Spanish Ladies' on the lulling air, fading gradually away . . .

. . . to be replaced by another music, the almost imperceptible beat of something far out on the dark water, the chuckle of foam under a bow, the faint creak of cordage and timber, the soft whisper of a command, and the rising ghostly cadence of a wild sea-march as a great dark shadow came gliding, gliding out of the night. For an instant the moonlight touched the pale loom of canvas furled, then it was gone, and the dozing sentries never heard the soft plunge of oars, or caught the phosphorescent glitter of ruffled water, or the grating of long-boat bows on shingle, the splash of bare feet and sea-boots in the surf, the glint of steel, the clatter of gear instantly hushed, or the shadowy passage of silent figures slipping through the palm-groves. No, the sentries were dreaming of distant Devon or half-caste wenches or beer or whatever sleepy sentries dream about, and by the time one of them glanced seaward it was too late, as usual, because the Menace was there, unseen, crouched in disciplined quiet beneath the very castle wall on the narrow path that skirted round to the open, inviting, torch-lit watergate and its deserted steps, where only a few convenient boats rocked unguarded at their moorings.

Wolfish bearded faces in the shadows, earrings, head scarves, hairy drawers, dirty shirts open to the waist, bad breath, great buckled belts, cutlasses, knives and pistols gripped in gnarled and sweaty hands, and at their head, all in snowy white from breeches to head-kerchief, big as a house-side and nimble as a cat, Calico Jack Rackham, none other, cautiously edging his brutally handsome, square-chinned face round a corner of the watergate, grinning at the sight of the torch-lit empty tunnel, turning to his followers, motioning them to be ready for the assault, whispering his final orders. First among equals was Calico Jack, by reason of being literate and smart and able to navigate and do all things shipshape and Bristol fashion, look'ee, as his admiring associates often agreed. Also he was strong enough to break a penny between his fingers, which helps, and having served a turn in the Navy, he was reckoned dependable. In our day he would have been a paratroop sergeant, or a shop steward, or a moderate Labour M.P. He was a pirate because it offered a profitable field for his talents, and he was saving for his old age.

First behind him came Firebeard, six feet both ways, barrel-chested, with hands like earth-moving equipment, and so covered in the fuzz that gave him his nickname that he looked like a burst mattress with piggy eyes glinting out of it.

He was enormous and roaring and ranting and wild and so thick he had forgotten his real name; he had been dropped on his head at an early age and never looked back. Nowadays he might have been an all-in wrestler or a Hollywood stuntman or an eccentric peer – or, indeed, all three. His idea of living was to hit people with anything handy, grab any valuables in sight, and blue the lot on wenches and drink. He was a pirate for these reasons, and also because he enjoyed bellowing those hearty songs which John Masefield would write in course of time. His eventual claim to fame would be as the model and inspiration of Edward Teach, who would copyright the habit in which Firebeard was at that very minute indulging, of tying lighted fire-crackers in his beard to terrify the enemy. He always did this before action, fumbling and cursing as the matches burned his huge clumsy fingers, while his comrades coughed and fanned the air.

"He's at it again!" they muttered severally. "Gor, what a kick-up!" "Thou lubberly guts, wilt set thy hair afire – fo!" "Turn it up, for God's sake!" "They reek offends, thou smouldering ape – 'tis nauseous to rob i' thy company!"

This last contribution came from Bilbo; tall, lean, rakish Bilbo, pretending to elegance in his tawdry finery of embroidered coat, plumed castor, soiled lace ruffles, and fine Cordovan boots with red-lacquered heels. (Actually, they pinched him excruciatingly, having been taken from the corpse of a small grandee whom Bilbo had skewered at Campeche, but Bilbo knew they were the height of fashion, and hobbled grimly in them through skirmishes and boarding-parties innumerable.) He was a sad case, Bilbo, really, although he looked anything but. A Wapping guttersnipe, he yearned for gentility, having observed something of it as a bare-foot stable lad in a great household, and later as a page-boy – after his lithe young figure and raffish good looks had caught the jaded eye of his master's wife. His amorous energies had led to similar posts in the houses of susceptible ladies of fashion, and some of the airs of the beau monde had stuck to him, along with the jewellery pilfered from the dressing-tables of his exhausted paramours. Among sea-scum he passed as a gentleman, having picked up a few tricks of speech from Congreve and Vanbrugh to supplement his gaudy wardrobe. He sneered and minced in sinister fashion, and made play with a rather grubby Mechlin kerchief, and wore a cut-price gem in his steenkirk. But don't underrate Bilbo – he might be a social pretender whose feet were killing him, but he had won his captaincy in the Coast Brotherhood by cunning, courage, and fighting ability. He wasn't called Bilbo for nothing – the long black rapier on his hip was reckoned the deadliest from St Kitts to Coromandel, with stoccata and imbroccata and punta rinversa, sa-ha! and he had a nice showy trick of spinning up finger-rings and impaling them on his flourished blade, like the Duke of Monmouth. Not easy. Nowadays Bilbo would have been a lion-tamer or an advertising executive. He hoped to make enough from piracy to buy an estate and title; for the moment he sneered at Firebeard's efforts to get his crackers going, and took a pinch of snuff from the box proffered by Goliath, his faithful dwarf.

"A barbarous affectation," he lisped. "Thou vulgar big birk."

"At least I don't have a bloody goblin in tow," growled Firebeard, and Goliath, who was all of two feet tall and had a wooden leg, hopped and gibbered in rage. Suddenly the fire-crackers took light, and Firebeard chortled while the air turned blue.

"All ready?" whispered Calico Jack, and a fierce chorus of "Aye, aye, cap'n, we'm ready for sart'n" answered him, with the odd "Belike" and "Look'ee" as an afterthought from the more eager spirits. And as they crouched for the assault, up from the rear came the fourth leader of that desperate enterprise, cat-footed and stately, and those hairy ruffians fell back, eyeing her askance with lustful respect as she stalked by, hips swaying, with a trace of Pierre Cardin lingering on the sultry air as she passed.

Six gorgeous feet she was, from the heels of her tight-fitting Italian thigh boots (from Gucci, undoubtedly) to the curling plume of her picture hat, breeched and shirted in crimson silk that clung to her like a skin, lithe and sleek and dangerous as a panther – Sheba, the black pirate queen, looking like something out of Marvel Comic with her lovely vicious face and voluptuous shape, her dark eyes flashing against her ebony skin, smouldering silently as she un-sheathed her dainty rapier with its Cartier hilt, and posed with the contemptuous grace of a burlesque star, indifferent to the ecstatic sighs and groans of her besotted followers. She had that sort of effect on men – it was notorious that when, in boarding a galleon, her shirt had been ripped off by an enemy pike, her entire crew had had to go on bromide for a fortnight. She never walked, she prowled, exuding menace and sex-appeal at every step, but none was so hardy as to presume on her femininity, for Sheba was as cruel and deadly as she was beautiful, and her scorn for men was proverbial. (True, in the focsle they breathed rumours of sizzling orgies in her secret fortress on Octopus Rock, with prisoners who were afterwards done diabolically to death, but that's focsle gossip all over.) Born a Barbados slave, she had clawed her way to power in the Coast fraternity by a piratical genius and ruthless ferocity that had made her the toast of women's liberationists all along the Main. Her fellow sea-wolves respected her, had astonishing fantasies about her, and went in terror of her, and she despised them all with a curl of her shapely lip and a lift of her perfect Egyptian nose and a low-lidded glare from her smoky slanting eyes, fingering her one long silver earring the while. Only to Rackham did she show the respect due an equal, and the big man treated her as a brother. Three centuries later Sheba would have been on the cover of Vogue, or leading a soul group; she was a pirate because she hated the world for enslaving her, and took a sadistic pleasure in killing – men, for choice, but women given half a chance, and quite small animals.

All round, they were a happy little gang of eccentric cut-throats who crouched in the shadows under Fort St Bartlemy's massy walls that balmy tropic night, waiting for the word from Rackham – and then they were storming up the passage, yelling bloody murder, while sleepy sentries above fired futile warning shots and ran about with their muskets at the high port. By then the pirates were slicing up the guards at the strong room, forcing the door, bursting open the first chest in a cascade of gold coin, into which Firebeard, exploding all over the place, threw himself bawling:

"It's the dollars! A bloody fortune! Har-har! Calico! Sheba! Bilbo! We'm rich!" He always shouted this on taking a prize, whatever its value, while his fire-crackers set his hair ablaze and those nearest choked and spluttered. A tiny Welsh pirate crouched by the open chest, eagerly counting the coins: "One, two, three . . ." until someone yanked him aside.

Up in the commandant's room they were exclaiming and belching and grabbing up their wigs and over-turning chairs, and shouting useful things like: "Pirates!" and "The pay-chests!" and "Sound the alarm!" and "Goose me wi' a handspike, we'm beset!" and by the time they tumbled downstairs all hell was breaking loose. The pirates were bearing out the treasure-chests under Rackham's directions, while Bilbo, firing his pistols with an elegant air and tossing them to his dwarf for reloading, was commanding the covering party who were at grips with the belated redcoats. It was desperate work, what with shots banging in the enclosed space, and powder-smoke everywhere, and pirates cursing as they were wounded, and redcoats falling down obligingly when they were shot, and Bilbo fleering and shooting, and Black Sheba leaping like a leopard, skewering with deadly daintiness, and Firebeard bashing and bawling. The commandant rallied his men with cries of "Blister me!" and blundered bravely ahead, crossing swords with Sheba over a couple of fallen bodies. He thrust clumsily at her chest . . . and paused, shaken, as he realised that his target, instead of being a conventional masculine torso, was more like something painted by an enthusiastic Rubens, and bouncing most distractingly to boot.

"Sink me, it's a woman!" he concluded loudly. "Strike me speechless!" he added, which was prophetic, for:

"With pleasure!" hissed Sheba, and glided in like a dancer, perfect teeth bared in an unholy smile, and the commandant tripped and fell flat on his back. A high heel pinned him as she flicked aside his hat with her rapier point, whispering "Doff, dog – doff to a lady!" and the last thing the commandant knew was that black face mocking down at him and a tearing pain in his throat.

The soldiers fell back, appalled, and as the last of the chests was borne down the passage Rackham roared his followers back and away. They retreated, firing, down the great stone tunnel, while Sheba, the blood-lust on her, slashed and stabbed and laughed, with Firebeard beside her swinging his cutlass roaring "Take that, ye lousy lobster! Kill 'em! Tear 'em! Kill the honest men!" and Bilbo carefully shot an officer in the shoulder, and turned to supervise the stowage of the chests in the waiting long-boats. Shepherding his men, Rackham looked back along the shambles of the tunnel, to see Sheba alone, fronting the disheartened soldiery, flourishing her rapier and screaming:

"Come on, you King's men! Fight! Is one woman too many for you, you mangy cowards? Fight – that's what they pay you your shilling a day for!"

And it's not enough, either, was the universal thought among the military as they faced that black and crimson fighting fury; but the wounded officer tugged at a lever in the wall, and above Sheba's head, through a slit in the stone, a great portcullis gate came swishing down. Too late Rackham cried a warning, too late she saw and sprang back; the great steel frame fell to divide the corridor from wall to wall, and although Sheba snaked beneath it to the seaward side, it pinned her ankle cruelly to the floor, and she lay trapped and helpless, her face contorted in agony, her rapier clanging on the flags. The pirates, with appropriate oaths, ran back to help; Firebeard strained his mighty thews in a vain effort to raise the portcullis, roaring "Heave, ye maggots!" and getting back the usual excuses, like "'Tain't no manner o' use we heavin', cap'n, look'ee, she'm caught, like, an' us can't shift the bugger no-how!"

Meanwhile the soldiers, encouraged by the fact that there was now a stout steel gate between them and the pirates, surged foward, shooting; one even rushed up and tried to bayonet the fallen Sheba through the bars. But Bilbo snapped an order, the dwarf Goliath sprang to the bars like a monkey, through them went his wooden leg, and out of it shot a steel blade to drink the soldier's heart's blood. (Full of tricks, those pirates were.) But Sheba, writhing on the flags, was fast as ever, and as the others banged away overhead, Rackham knelt beside her.

"It's no use, camarado! We can't shift it! D'ye want to go quick, girl?" For garrison reinforcements were crowding down the tunnel, and Rackham looked to the priming of his pistol.

"Leave me!" gasped Sheba. "Each takes his chance . . . law of the Brotherhood!"

Firebeard, of course, was having none of that; he was a proper pirate, after all.

"We'll fight it out, by the powers!" he bellowed. "I don't leave no mess-mate in the lurch, by cock, burn damn and blast me if I do!" And he beat his fists on his chest.

"Balls!" cried Bilbo, forgetting his affectations in the heat of the moment. "She's right! If we linger, we are undone! Anyway, we've got the loot! Shove off!" No nonsense about Bilbo; he strode to the sea-steps, and the long-boats surged into the night, heavy with the booty. Several pirates dragged Firebeard into the last boat, heedless of his bawling: "We can't leave her! Let's cut off her leg!," and for a brief moment, with the last pirates on the steps keeping the soldiers at a distance with their pistol fire, Rackham was left alone by the pinned and helpless woman.

"Go, Calico! Quickly!" she gasped, and the big man stared down at her with tears in his eyes, and stooped to kiss her brow.

"I'll be back for you, camarado! Wherever they take you – we'll get you out!"

And then he was gone, springing down the steps to the last boat, and it shoved off into the darkness, with the pirates singing "Fifteen men on the Dead Man's Chest," which is not actually a very good song to row to; consequently they caught crabs all over the place, and wallowed in a welter of gold coins and bilge-water and rum, with the boats bucketing about. The redcoats on the battlements should have picked them off easily, but as everyone knows, in such circumstances redcoats never hit anything, but pop off their blanks in a most desultory fashion.

But while the pirates eventually regained their ship, the soldiers in the tunnel were bearing down triumphantly on the slim crimson figure pinned beneath the portcullis; Sheba cast one agonised glance after her departing comrades, choked on tears of pain, gnashed out a truly disgusting oath at her enemies, and then lapsed gracefully into a swoon. The wounded officer, clutching his shoulder, ordered the portcullis raised, and kicked the insensible figure cruelly in its shapely ribs, snarling: "We've got this heathen slut, at any rate! Gad, but we'll make her pay for this . . ."

Which is a suitably dramatic moment to bring this first chapter to a close, with the powder-smoke a-reek in our nostrils, our principals introduced, and Delectable Dusky Villainy in the clutches of the law. What will the brutal beastly soldiery do to Black Sheba? Will they . . . ? What of Rackham's promise to save her? Does Bilbo even care? And what has all this got to do with the handsome Captain Avery and the rascally Colonel Blood? We shall e'en see in Chapter the Second.

CHAPTER
THE SECOND

In fact, while Sheba was languishing decoratively in her chains in the grim dungeon of Fort St Bartlemy, having beaten off the advances of her leering jailers till her arms ached, and her pirate shipmates were falling about in drunken celebration singing 'Mouths were made for tankards and for sucking at the bung,' while their ship headed erratically towards Tortuga with the loot, Captain Avery was bowing gracefully – not too little, not too much, but just right – on the threshold of Mr Pepys's office at the Admiralty. And Mr Pepys, hurriedly adjusting the wig he had laid by, and guiltily shoving his Diary under some papers, could have done without him. For one thing, Pepys had been looking forward to neglecting the victualling estimates in favour of sneaking in a few fresh entries – he was itching to record the details about his fine new broadcloth coat, and the red-head who he was sure had winked in his direction at Drury Lane, and the curds and small beer he had had for breakfast, and his wife's all-night card parties. But there it was in his appointment book: "Capn Everie, at 10 of the clock," so he sighed and composed himself to receive his visitor.

Another reason for the Secretary's discontent was that he was meeting Captain Avery for the first time, and suffering the common reaction to such masculine perfection. Nobody, decided Mr Pepys resentfully, had any business to go around looking like that; it made you feel positively sub-human. But there he was, like some naval tailor's fashion model, announcing himself the Secretary's humble obedient in a smooth, well-modulated tone that proclaimed him anything but; to Mr Pepys's paranoid imagination he conveyed the impression that he had many more important things on hand – probably conferring with Dr Newton or Lord Clarendon – but that he was graciously prepared to give the Admiralty ten minutes provided they got on with it. Right, thought the normally amiable Pepys grimly, we'll cut this one down to size. To which end he looked at his visitor severely over his spectacles and inquired:

"Captain Avery, are you an honest man?"

It didn't work, of course. Far from being taken aback, Avery raised one brow a millimetre and replied, in a tone of gently amused tolerance:

"I am a gentleman, sir."

Mr Pepys almost said "So's the King, and look at him," but fortunately refrained. Covering his chagrin by fiddling with the rigging of a ship's model – his cosy little office was full of them, and globes and charts and waggoners and maps – he went on as amiably as he could:

"I ask, sir, because when I requested their lordships to find me a young officer for a desperate and confidential business, they told me that of all men, Captain Avery was the most capable, expert, brave, discreet, and intelligent gentleman in his majesty's service."

He paused, and gave up fiddling with the model's mainsail, which was in a hopeless tangle. Avery said nothing, but took a deferential pace forward, twitched a thread, and the mainsail rose smoothly into place.

"Indeed, sir?" said he politely, and Mr Pepys ground his teeth.

"But they omitted to tell me whether you picked pockets," he blurted out.

Captain Avery regarded him with maddening compo-

30

sure. "Is that the service you require, sir?" he wondered, and Mr Pepys took a grip on himself.

"No," he said tartly. "It isn't. I merely impress on you, captain, that I have a pocket that must not . . . be picked. See here."

He touched a spring in the panelling, which slid back to reveal a cavity from which Mr Pepys took a box of polished oak, perhaps a foot square. Lifting the lid, he brought out an object covered in black velvet cloth, and set it on the desk. Then abruptly he pulled the cloth aside – and if that doesn't rattle the cocky little bastard, he thought, nothing will. For what he exposed was an object so dazzling that Mr Pepys, who had seen it before, still found himself catching his breath in wonder.

It was a crown. Its dull radiance bespoke pure gold, but the circlet itself was so encrusted with tiny jewels that the metal beneath was all but hidden. Yet these stones, priceless though they were, seemed dim by comparison with the six great gems which shone in the six gold crosses fixed at equal intervals round the circlet. Each as large as a pigeon's egg, they glowed in their golden settings – the rich crimson of a ruby, the eery green of an emerald, the brilliant blue of a sapphire, the milky white of an opal, the frosty brilliance of a diamond, and the ebony sheen of a black pearl. Blinking in awed silence at them, Mr Pepys felt his ill-temper vanish like summer dew, and he was gratified to see that the Captain's eyes had opened a trifle and that his breathing checked for a brief instant.

"A pretty bauble, is it not?" said Pepys. "A million – if ye can imagine such a sum – would not buy it."

"I hope," said Captain Avery reverently, "that you have stout locks to your doors."

"Stout enough to serve," said Pepys lightly, and stole another glance at his visitor. "Could I trust you, captain, with this treasure?"

Captain Avery looked from the crown to the Secretary,

31

regarding him gravely for a moment. "Yes, sir," he said, "but I had rather you did not."

So the paragon was human after all. Mollified, Mr Pepys smiled, covered the crown, and waved his visitor to a chair. "Do you know," he wondered, "of an island called Madagascar?"

"The great isle of Africa," said the Captain confidently, "lying betwixt the twelfth and twenty-fifth south latitudes, six hundred leagues bearing east-nor'-east from the cape. Of unknown extent, peopled by savage aborigines practising abominable rites, yet are its birds, fishes, animals and vegetation even stranger than its human inhabitants, being like to none other on the globe of Earth. Fable doth impute to it," he went on, "such strange creatures as the *roc*, the great bird of the Eastern story-tellers, and Sir John Mandeville peopled it with his marvellous imaginings. I have not," concluded Captain Avery modestly, "been there myself."

"But ye're sure ye've heard of it?" said Pepys sarcastically. "Well, God be thanked for that. Know then, sir, that this crown is for the king of that strange land, a mad, barbarous fellow who, in his vanity, hath sent the choicest gems o' price in his treasury to our London goldsmiths, that they might therefrom fashion a diadem befitting his savage majesty his proud estate. These sambos," reflected Mr Pepys, "do love to deck themselves more than do civil princes. Howbeit, there it is – now it must be returned to him. Safely. That, captain, is why y'are here."

He sat back in impressive silence – it would have been more impressive but his belly chose that moment to rumble from a deep growl to a high bubbling treble. Mr Pepys writhed and damned curds and beer, but Captain Avery seemed not to have noticed. He wouldn't, the good-mannered sod, thought Mr Pepys savagely. Ten seconds passed, and Avery nodded and stood up.

"I understand, sir," he said briskly. "You may leave all to me. One stout naval brig under my command – I shall choose officers and crew myself – should answer the purpose . . . with a sufficient escort, of course. Two sloops should serve, so they are well found and manned. I think," he added, "I had best attend to that. But let me see . . . six weeks to the Cape . . . two months . . . at Christmas, with God's help," he announced, "I shall be here to inform you that the business has been happily concluded."

I can't believe you'll need God's help, and if you do, he'd better not shirk, eh, thought Mr Pepys. He wondered had he ever seen the like of this coxcomb's assurance; it seemed a pity to deflate it, almost.

"My dear captain," he shook his head, "things are not ordered in such broadside fashion. Consider: the existence of this bauble is known. Goldsmiths have tongues, and if a King's ship were to prepare for Indian waters, at a time when ships are ill to spare, and no good reason could be given – why, all the world would guess, and you and your cargo would be a target for every sea-thief between here and Malabar." He popped the crown back into its box, locked it, and extracted the key. "No, here must be stealth and secrecy; only you and I and Admiral Lord Rooke, who goes shortly to command the East Indies Squadron, must know of the crown's passage forth of England. So you shall bear it alone, and guard it with your life, for its safe delivery imports o'er all. You have not visited Madagascar, but out of your vasty fund of knowledge –" Mr Pepys beamed over his spectacles as he put the boot gently in "– you know how vital is the friendship of its ruler to our Indian trade. With his good will, we may set up stations in Madagascar, to shield our sea-lanes and harry the Utopian pirates who swarm on its northern capes. And his good will depends on . . ." he tapped the box with the key ". . . this."

If Captain Avery was disappointed, he did not show it. He inclined his handsome head, and if a voice can shrug, his did as he said: "As you please, sir. Shall I take the box now?"

"Hold on a minute," snapped Mr Pepys, who had been

getting ready to enjoy overruling a protest. Could nothing shake this boy's outrageous composure? (Of course not; this boy's the Hero.) "There's a receipt to sign," he muttered lamely. "In triplicate."

But there wasn't, not right away, because Mr Pepys had mislaid it, and his temper was not improved at having to scrabble through his mess of papers while Avery stood by with an impassive patience which the Secretary, his wig slipping askew and his glasses misting up, found positively crucifying. He stood, breathing heavily, as Avery finally signed the three documents, in a flawless copper-plate, and took the box. Never mind, thought Pepys, we'll see you taken down a peg in a minute, or I'll eat this ruddy wig.

"Come with me," he said, and led the way from his office down a long passage where sentries clicked to attention and clerks hurried busily between the departments. Captain Avery paced leisurely along, while Mr Pepys's fat little legs went nineteen to the angry dozen, until they came out through a door into a sunlit garden, where ladies and gentlemen took their ease in the pleasant August morning, walking and flirting and playing pell-mell and generally looking like a pastoral scene by Canaletto, and Mr Pepys peered about short-sightedly until his glance lighted on two tall gentlemen strolling arm in arm along one of the walks. He gave a grunt of satisfaction, shot Captain Avery a look, and bustled in their direction.

The King and the Duke of York were taking their ease together, and the court was keeping its distance because it realised that his grace had just returned from Scotland and was undoubtedly filling in his majesty on matters of great pitch and policy. And indeed the younger royal brother was talking with animation, while the famous swarthy man two yards high, his spaniels round his feet, his beribboned cane in his hand, plumed hat and curled wig on head, and all magnificent in dark blue velvet, was listening with what appeared to be interested attention.

" 'Twas at the short fourteenth," the Duke was saying. "Need I tell thee what 'tis like? A hint of slice and you're dead. I laid my pitch pin-high, and damme if Paterson didn't miss the putt!"

"Codso!" exclaimed King Charles.

"By great good fortune, we halved the next two," went on the Duke, "for I tell thee, brother, had I not held firm, all had not served. Paterson shanked and hooked, and I was sore put to it."

"D'ye tell me?" marvelled his majesty, stifling a yawn.

"At the seventeenth," resumed the Duke remorselessly, "all was to do, for Rockingham drove like Jehu, and Paterson's second was sorrily astray. I marked it not, but took my brassie – ye mind, Charles, the brassie that Grandfather James had of the steward at Blackheath? – and struck me such a shot over the sheds as would ha' done thy heart good to see. Ten score yards," he murmured beatifically, "into the wind, and ran me down 'twixt the pits to the edge o' the green. Rockingham cried, 'The bugger!' and my good Paterson 'Amen!' "

"Gad's wounds!" murmured the King absently, his eyes straying to where a Junoesque redhead was swaying provocatively along on the arm of an elderly nobleman.

"Then Paterson," said the Duke darkly, "put his chip into a bunker. What think ye, brother, did I do?"

"Ten stone if she's an ounce," mused the King, "and forty-five to boot, so they tell me. Forgive me, James – you were saying?"

"I holed out from the sand," said the Duke triumphantly, and following his brother's glance he added curtly: "Danby's new pullet, a great quilt of a woman. He likes 'em big and bouncy."

"Don't we all?" sighed the King.

"At the eighteenth . . ." the Duke was beginning, but realised he had lost even the King's pretence of listening. "I see," he said coolly, "that I weary your majesty. I crave your majesty's pardon. It is very well. I shall remove, and take me –"

"Jamie, Jamie," said the King tolerantly. "Ye beat the gentlemen of England two up, and had Paterson not hindered, t'would ha' been eight and seven. I know," he added mildly, "because ye told us last night at supper, till poor Nell dozed in her chair, and again at breakfast." He laughed and clapped his glowering brother on the back. "Dear lad, ye play golf for Scotland indifferent well, but ye could bore for her in every court of Europe."

"Right!" snapped the Duke, furiously pale, and breathing through his haughty nostrils. " 'Tis very well! That did it! *I* bore for Scotland! When I consider," he went on bitterly, "how often I've been dragged up that bloody oak tree after Worcester –" But he was prevented from further lésé majesté by the arrival of Mr Pepys, with Captain Avery in tow. The King hailed the Secretary pleasantly, and took stock of our hero while Pepys made the introductions.

"Captain Avery," said his majesty genially, and held out his hand, over which the young captain bowed with becoming grace. "I'm glad to see ye, sir." As always, he plainly meant it, and Mr Pepys looked to see Captain Avery fall under the spell of the famous Stuart charm; after all, everyone did. But Captain Avery merely stood up straight, respectful and composed, and it occurred to the Secretary that if a stranger from Muscovy had been shown the three – the two tall and undeniably handsome royal brothers, and the King's captain – he might have been puzzled to know who had the most commanding personality and aristocratic air. This kid's gunpowder, Pepys decided.

"Captain Avery," he went on, "is the officer to be employed on the Indian business your majesty doth wot of."

"Ah, yes," said the Merry Monarch with polite interest, wondering what that business might be; wasn't old Rooke going out to deal with the pirates . . . something like that? He played for time by reproving the tiny spaniels playing round

36

his ankles. "Mind, Bucephalus, where you put your great feet. Their lordships, captain," he went on, lying courteously, "have given me golden reports of you. Now tell me how old are you, and what service ye have seen."

"Your majesty," said Captain Avery respectfully, "is gracious. I am twenty-two years old, and have had the honour to serve your majesty these five years. Lately I commanded one of your majesty's warships, and have fought 'gainst the Dutch, the French, the Spaniards, and the corsairs of Barbary, having the good fortune to take ten prizes and two fortresses, as well," he added dismissively, "as three wounds. I am a bachelor of arts of Oxford, where I made some study of Mathematicks, Physicks, and the other Natural Sciences, tho' less than I could have wished. If my service permits, I hope to repair that and take my Master's Degree in time. Other than that," he concluded, "there is little to tell."

Mr Pepys was watching the royal pair to see how they received this catalogue, and was gratified to see the Duke blink; his majesty, more experienced, made a nice recovery.

"Physicks, eh?" he said. "Have you perchance, captain, studied Master Newton's *De Analysi*, of which there is much learned talk?"

Try that on for size, thought Mr Pepys triumphantly; trust old Charley to return serve. He looked to see Captain Avery confess ignorance at last, and indeed the captain was frowning, his handsome face turned to the King's.

"The method of fluxions," he said gravely. "Indeed, sire, I have considered it briefly, but with indifferent profit on such short acquaintance. What is your majesty's opinion of the calculus?"

Bloody hell, thought Pepys, and his majesty may have been similarly moved, since he had listened to Newton's explanation in a fog, and had just been name-dropping. "Ah, well," he said, improvising gamely, "there is much to be said for it; aye, indeed, and will be. But tell me, captain, what shall you make of these Indies pirates?"

Captain Avery looked surprised. "If such should come in my way," he said, "I shall hope to do your majesty's service upon them."

"To be sure, to be sure," said the King hurriedly. He was beginning to find such simple self-assurance daunting, especially from one who was two inches taller than he was. He wasn't used to either phenomenon, and like Mr Pepys, was beginning to suspect that Captain Avery was too much of a good thing. But he mustn't be hard on the lad; maybe it was just another case of meeting-royalty nerves.

"Well, well, captain," he said heartily, "we wish you a prosperous voyage. Is there aught ye need?" he added almost hopefully.

"You majesty is kind," said Avery, "but I have my sword and your majesty's trust. I need no more." And he bowed with deferential calm, leaving the King as disconcerted as it was possible for that sophisticated gentleman to be.

"No," said the King, rather wistfully, "I don't suppose you do. Aye, well." He looked about helplessly, and became aware that his spaniels were busily chewing the rosettes on his shoes. "Stop it, you little bastards," he said irritably.

"If your majesty pleases," said Avery, and glancing at the dogs he gently snapped his fingers. As one spaniel they stopped chewing, and hid behind the King's legs. The captain transferred his gaze from them to the astonished monarch, and bowed for the last time. "Your majesty, your grace, Mr Pepys," he said, and backing gracefully away, turned and strode off across the lawn. They watched him go in a stunned silence, until his majesty murmured, almost in awe: "Well, God help the Indies pirates!" and sighed. And then their wonder changed to interest, for as Captain Avery reached the gravel walk, there swayed into his path the opulent red-haired beauty whom his majesty had remarked earlier on the arm of Lord Danby. She had, in fact, been eyeing the captain hungrily for the past five minutes, and thinking, wow! there's a boy who needs an experience, and I'm going to be it.

38

Subtle in all the amorous arts, she now undulated towards him, shooting him a smouldering glance from shadowed eyes, pouting seductively, and drawing a flimsy lace kerchief from her heaving bosom. She dropped it artlessly in the captain's path, and he stopped, glanced at it, and at the heavily-breathing lady.

The King, the Duke of York, and Mr Pepys waited entranced; the lady sighed and fluttered her eye-lids; Captain Avery, his face impassive, glanced round, observed a serving-man, snapped his fingers, and indicated the fallen kerchief. The servant shot forward to retrieve it, Captain Avery indicated the lady, gave her the briefest of bows, and strode majestically on, leaving Beauty fuming in frustration and Royalty looking at each other in astonishment.

"That fellow," said the King in wonder, "is just a walking mass of virtue and genius. Rot me," he added, "if he isn't. Well, thank God he's going to the Indies, for if he stayed here he'd make us feel mightily inferior."

"What's a fluxion?" asked the Duke of York, but if the King answered, Mr Pepys did not hear it; he had become suddenly conscious that he was chewing the end of his wig.

As it chanced, Captain Avery's departure was less speedy than his majesty had supposed. He was to travel out with Admiral Lord Rooke, the new commander of the East Indies Squadron, but his lordship had the misfortune to trip over a chamberpot at a wayside inn while travelling up to Town, and broke his ankle. So while the veteran salt convalesced, roaring at the doctors and being reproved by his domineering daughter (who suspected, quite rightly, that he had been tight), Captain Avery kicked his perfectly-shod heels in London for over a month. This entailed returning his precious cargo to the Admiralty for the moment, and since Pepys had lost the receipts, there was wrath and bad language, not lessened by Captain Avery's maddening forbearance. At last, however, all was ready; word came that Lord Rooke was on his way, Avery collected the Madagascar crown again, and on that very day, two interesting events occurred in the great city . . .

Deep in a noisome hold in Newgate Prison, Black Sheba was pacing the slimy floor like a great cat, her fetters jangling as she strode. She was in a passion, and no wonder. We left her resisting the advances of horrid jailers at Fort St Bartlemy, remember; it might have gone ill with her womanhood there, for the garrison had remarked her beauty, and hung around outside her cell muttering and slavering: "Ar, a choice black pullet it be, a plumptious piece for lovesome sport an' ravishment, mates, har-har!", but fortunately the senior surviving officer at the fort was a fairy, and wasn't having any of that sort of thing. Scenting publicity for himself in the capture of the notorious pirate virago, he had sent her home by fast frigate, and she had lain like a great black beast in the foul lazarette, eyes gleaming in the dark, fed on slops, her fine silk attire reduced to rags – she was in a sorry state of unkemptitude by the time they brought her ashore in the Pool, and thence she was haled to Newgate, where they made a show of her, with fashionable society flocking to see the savage sea queen caged at last. Fine ladies smirked and gloated, and their gentlemen stared and thought "Cor!" while Sheba watched them from behind her bars with red sparks glowing in her amber eyes, and dreamed of them suffering torments indescribable.

They looked for a grand spectacle at her trial, and she gave it them, fighting like a spitfire all the way to the dock, raking her warders' faces with her nails, so that they had to chain her to the bar. She spat at the spectators, snarled threats at the jurors, and even screamed filthy abuse at Jeffreys himself. And he, like Lord Foppington, remarked in an aside to his fellow-judges that he would not have missed such a trial for the salvation of mankind. But when he came to pass sentence on her, for piracy, murthers, robberies, slaughters, arson, putting in fear, and operating without a Board of

Trade certificate, there was amaze, for he put aside the black cap and said, in that famous dry whisper:

"Richly though ye ha' merited death a thousand times over, yet for that ye are a woman – as indeed is plain for all to see, heh-heh! (laughter and whistles) – and for that his majesty's plantations are in need of labour, it is the merciful sentence of this court that ye be transported to the East Indies, and there sold in bondage for the rest of your natural life . . ." (sensation in court, cries of "Fix!" "Boo!" "It's a cut-up!" "We want to see her swing!" and "Good old Jeff!".)

It was rumoured that the King himself had intervened, having seen her in Newgate and done a quick double-take before observing that they couldn't hang a female who looked like *that*, it would be criminal, etc., etc. But as she heard the sentence Black Sheba screamed with rage, and clashed her fetters at the bar.

"Damn your mercy!" she snarled. "I've been a slave! I'd rather die, you foul shrivelled bastard, you!"

At which Jeffreys, with commendable restraint, had hurled himself frothing about the bench, bawling at her:

"Why, so ye shall, ye vile black bitch – so ye shall, in God's good time! And I trust they'll have lashed every inch of hide off your foul carcase first, thou wanton, smelly, perverse slut, thou! Take her down, take her out, take her anywheres so she be away!" And he had thrown his wig at her in his passion, calling her beldame, whore, slattern, harlot and jigaboo, but since Sheba had given him back cuckold, honky, pimp, snake, and faggot, the spectators decided it was a draw, and ought to be replayed. Sheba was dragged back to her cell, and there she was, pacing and snarling, waiting to be haled off to East Indian bondage, while . . .

Colonel Blood reluctantly tore his eyes away from the cleavage of the buxom serving-wench who was hanging admiringly over the back of his chair, considered his cards, and glanced, sighing, at the fat, ugly, gloating, richly-dressed gull who sat across the table in the taproom of The Prospect of Whitby. Blood was looking slightly better than when we last saw him, having shaved, found a clean shirt, and apparently spent his last five pence on a shampoo and set. He had also acquired a lace jabot, an embroidered red coat with a sword worn modishly through the pocket, and a pair of steel-rimmed spectacles. (Spectacles? What have we here?)

"Come on, come on, sir!" cried the fat man. "Ya' play, damme!"

Blood sighed again and played the king of spades; the fat man played the queen and gleefully nudged his crony, another podgy vulgarian. They eyed the pile of guineas on the table; money for jam, they were thinking.

"Ya' last card, sir! Hey?" cried Fatso. "What, sir? Come, sir! Eh, sir?"

"Just the seven o' clubs," said Blood innocently, and faced what is usually the duddest card you can hold at picquet. The fat man and his friend gaped, and swore, and the fat man dashed down his useless king of diamonds. Blood raked in the cash almost apologetically, removed his spectacles and tucked them in his sleeve, rose, kissing the serving-wench lightly on the cheek, and flipped a guinea down her ample frontage.

"Blast me vitals!" cried the fat chap. "How – how, sir, did ye guess I'd sloughed the ace o' clubs? What? Hey?"

"Irish instinct, me old joy," said Blood, winking at the wench. "My mother was frightened by a knave of hearts."

"The fiend's own luck!" groaned the fat man.

"Devil a bit," said Blood. "All my luck's reserved for love, eh, sweetheart?" And he squeezed the wench again, bade his opponents an affable good day, and sauntered upstairs whistling 'Come lasses and lads', jingling his winnings. There he turned into a bedroom, where a dark and languid lady, slightly past her prime, extended a plump hand to him from the froth of lace which surrounded her as she reclined among the pillows, purring amorously.

"Dah-ling!" she breathed, and Blood gallantly slipped on to the bed, kissing ardently up her arm to her buxom shoulders and bosom, at which she reproved him coyly, and then began to eat his ear, murmuring hungrily: "I vow ye've been away from me so long, I thought ye had forgot your dear little pigeon," and she tried to drag him under the sheets.

"A mere half-hour, ye fascinating houri," said Blood, and poured his winnings into a purse before her eyes. "A trifle of pin money I've been earning, me heart's darling – forty guineas against our travelling expenses to Gretna."

At this the lady cried out fondly: "Why, thou foolish dear fellow, where was the need? Have I not ample funds . . . and there is all my jewellery." And she fingered her necklace and stroked his cheek, all of which the Colonel bore with equanimity.

"Only a vandal," he murmured, nuzzling the necklace and the soft skin beneath it, "could bear to see it removed from its rightful place – tho' faith, it's dim by comparison with such a lovely setting."

He would have been less poetically carefree if he could have seen the serving-wench at that moment, discovering the spectacles which had slipped from his sleeve during his last departing fondle, to hook themselves in her apron-string. She squeaked with surprise, exclaimed: "Ow, look, the gennelman's left 'is glasses!", giggled, and clapped them on her pert nose for the entertainment of the customers. "Caw, look at me!" she exclaimed, peering affectedly, and then her eyes fell on the cards scattered on the table, and she gasped in genuine dismay.

"Ow!" she cried. "Caw, bleedin' 'ell! Ow, me! Lookathat! Ow, the rotten cheat!"

For through the spectacles she could see that on the backs of the cards their identities were clearly marked, and even she, dumb trull that she was, knew that this was irregular. The defeated gamesters gaped, and seized the glasses from her, and peered through them, and observed their cunningly-tinted glass, and with one accord cried: "Burn my bowels! Bubbled, by God! Where is the knave, the sharp, the cut-purse!" and were on the point of making for the stairs, to wreak vengeance, when a stentorian voice thundered at the tap-room door:

"Landlord! Hither to me! Have you a rakehell black Irishman in your house, hey? A rascal that calls himself Colonel Blood?"

"Colonel Blood, sir?" spluttered the fat man. "My word, sir, the villain has just made off with my forty guineas!"

"Damn your guineas, sir!" roared the newcomer, who was huge and masterful and magnificently dressed. "The villain has just made off with my wife!"

Since no one kept their voices down in Restoration England, it followed that every word of this exchange was audible upstairs. The languid lady, suddenly distraught, shot bolt upright with a violence which pitched Blood on to the floor, clutched her bosom, and cried "My husband!", followed by a shriek of dismay as she realised that her erstwhile lover, hoisting his breeches with one hand and grabbing his purse with the other, already had one leg over the sill. She stretched out an arm in dramatic entreaty and shrilled: "False heart, will you desert me now? Oh, stay!"

"Just slipping out for a breath of air, my sweet," said Blood reassuringly, and vanished, blowing a kiss, for he liked to observe the polite niceties.

"What shall I do?" cried the lady, wringing her hands like anything, and Blood, who would deny no one advice if it might be helpful, poked his head back in to suggest: "Tell him ye walked in your sleep," before dropping to the street.

Now, in any romance of fiction, he would have slipped nimbly up a side-street and hid, grinning rakishly, in a doorway, while the pursuit rushed futilely by. But since this is a highly realistic, moral tale, it has to be recorded that he fell slap on to a pile of empty beer-crates, and was thrashing about cursing when the outraged husband and his burly minions (all outraged husbands in those days engaged burly minions, from some Restoration equivalent of Central Casting) emerged to seize him wrist and ankle. And they tore off his fine coat (which was the husband's anyway, having been provided for Blood by his doting leman) and beat the living daylights out of him with stout canes, to the great satisfaction of the cheated gamesters, and the vicarious excitement of the deserted lady, who watched, biting her lips, from her bedroom window. Indeed, she became so emotional that when her lord, after a final cut at the hapless Colonel, strode into the inn, up the stairs, and confronted her with a lowering scowl and a "So-ho, madam!" she flung herself sobbing at his feet, begging forgiveness and pleading, in piteous tones, her youthful folly – she was forty-seven, to be exact, but her contrition was such a change from her customary wilfulness, and she looked so fetching in her dishevelled negligee, that he forgave her on the spot, and taking a leaf out of Marlborough's book, pleasured her (once) in his boots, and they lived happy ever after, or so we may assume.

A comfortable and loving note on which to end our second chapter. But sterner matters await us. Avery, his hair brushed and his heart pure, is about to set off on his perilous mission to Madagascar – will his path cross that of Black Sheba when they ship her to the Indies? And what o' Blood, caught in the acts of abduction, seduction, marking his cards, and causing malicious damage to beer crates? He is right in it . . .

CHAPTER
THE THIRD

n the taproom, whither they had dragged him battered and bruised as he was, Colonel Blood fetched his breath while the gamesters reviled him, the wench giggled, one burly minion brushed the stolen coat, and another snarled: "Bide you there, ye muckrake, whiles Oi fetch a constable. 'Tis the Roundhouse for 'ee, aye, an' the gallows therearter, damn 'ee!"

This seemed a reasonable forecast to Blood, who promptly swooned lower on his bench, gasping 'Water! Water!', at which they reviled him harder than ever, but relaxed their guard, with the result that one minion was suddenly rolling on the floor, clutching his groin and making statements, the other had the fine coat wrenched from his grasp (the Colonel, a realist, knew that you can't get far in your shirt-sleeves) and an iron fist smashed against his jaw, and before the wench could even squeal or the gamesters swear, foxy Tom was off and running.

Naturally, they pursued, minions, gamesters, landlord, bystanders, and other interested parties – including, eventually, the outraged husband, once he had recovered from his unexpectedly joyous reunion and hurried downstairs. And nip and double as Blood might, his beaten limbs (not improved, of course, by late nights, booze, women, and too much smoking the day before the match) would inevitably have let him down had his headlong flight not carried him suddenly out on to a long cobbled wharf thronged with porters, hawkers, fishwives, seamen, loiterers, and all the motley of the waterfront. In an instant the Colonel was lost in the shifting human tide, which bore him along while he got his breath back, straightened his coat, and regretted that he had no hat to complete the appearance of a genteel saunterer slumming.

A great ship was making ready for sea, and Blood paused by her gangplank to look round for signs of pursuit. All clear behind, and he was about to stroll on when he saw, dead ahead, the breathless figures of the fat gamester and one of the burly minions moving questingly through the crowds in his general direction. The Colonel wheeled smartly about – only to see emerging, from the alley down which he had run, a constable, the other minion, and in the rear the cuckolded husband, buttoning his weskit askew and inquiring thunderously about a black-avised rascal in a red coat. As heads turned and the two sets of pursuers continued to converge at random, Colonel Blood looked desperately for a bolt-hole. The gangway was before him, and as two seamen staggered on to it under the weight of a furled tarpaulin, he hesitated no longer, but used them as a shield to slip swiftly on to the ship's crowded deck. One quick look back showed him the outraged husband and the fat gamester hailing each other over the heads of the mob; Blood pushed hurriedly past a couple of bare-footed seamen, rounded a pile of casks, and came face to face with a bawling red face in a brass-buttoned coat and cocked hat.

"Sink an' be damned!" it roared. "An' how in thunder do I know where the swab o' a surgeon should sling his hammock? 'A can sleep i' the scuppers; 'a'll be drunk enough not to notice! How now, sir?" it demanded of Blood. "What make ye here? We're putting to sea, or damme! No, we're not – not while them tarts an' trollops are fouling my ship!" And he rolled furiously past Blood, a bosun at his heels, bawling the odds at the waterfront slatterns who were keeping his men from their work forward; at his instructions the bosun passed among them with a rope's end, belabouring them towards the gangplank, while all around the seamen hurriedly pulled ropes and battened hatches and shouted through cupped hands and spat resoundingly – doing all those things needful, d'ye see, to get a ship under weigh.

"Avast there! Get in the forrard plank!" yelled the red-faced man. "Yarely, an' be damned, wi' a pox on't!" Plainly he was another Farnol graduate, one of that barnacle-crusted band whose natural ancestor is the bosun in 'The Tempest' – the one who is responsible for the greatest stage-direction Shakespeare ever wrote: 'Enter mariners, wet.' He rolled about the place, roaring and belaying, and then his eye fell on Blood again, and he bellowed – but with a certain respect for one well-dressed: "Now then, you, sir, blast me bollocks an' by y'r leave! What, sir? What make ye, master? It's go ashore or go to Calicut, or hoist me for a lubber, what?" And his gesture invited the Colonel to the gangplank – at the foot of which the fat gamester was plainly visible, craning his neck as he surveyed the crowded wharf. Colonel Blood had his choice, and took it.

"But, captain," said he, with desperate nonchalance, keeping under cover of the casks, "Calicut is where I wish to go. News came this morning . . . my rich uncle's dead o' the flux or the gout or the fever or somewhat. Shocking sudden, and the plantation going to the devil. I had your direction . . . and where the devil my man Jenkin is with the dunnage, God knows. Ye can give me passage, I dare swear?"

"What, sir? Carry ye to Calicut, rot me? Why, sir, now, sir!" The captain rubbed grizzled chin wi' horny paw and considered the appellant – rich lace, good coat, rakehelly genteel, dressed in a hurry . . . but then, he'd admitted as much. "Why, y'r worship, it might be," he conceded. "A four-month passage, let's see – I could make room at a pinch, for . . . forty guineas, now?"

Above the ship's noise a distant voice could be heard

complaining: ". . . and the dam' gallows-bait had my guineas, too!" Colonel Blood did not hesitate, but pulled the purse from his pocket and tossed it over negligently to the captain. "A bagatelle," said he, and the roaring skipper promptly knuckled his hat, and beamed, crying "Thank'ee, y'r honour, I'll see ye have a comf'table berth, y'r honour, crisp me liver if I don't! Yardley's the name, sir; Cap'n Yardley. Steward! Hell's bells an' hailstones, will ye lay aft, steward, damn 'ee?"

The Colonel was too old a hand to regret his lost cash; it had been necessary. The question now was whether to kiss it good-bye and steal ashore later, or to avail himself of this unexpected magic carpet away from London – a place which might be uncomfortably hot for him. India? He had never been there, and had no great desire to go . . . on the other hand, he was one who had always lived where he'd hung his castor – why not? He'd have four months' board and lodging in the meantime. As he considered, he lurked, and presently saw his baffled pursuers take themselves off; the resolve was forming in his mind . . . he'd quite enjoy a sea-trip, and the Indies, by all accounts, offered a fruitful field to men of his talents. He allowed himself to be shown his berth, shed his too-conspicuous coat, and sallied forth on deck again to view the orderly bustle of the ship as the final preliminaries to sailing went ahead right handily, with cheery yo-ho and bronzed backs bending to haul, pipes twittering, captain bawling, men hasting aloft, capstan turning, and that sort of thing, with salty baritones roaring:

> *Where is the trader o' Stepney Town?*
> *Clap it on, slap it on,*
> *How the hell should I know?*

And up the gangplank, striding tall, came a superbly handsome young man in a naval coat and hat, his buttons glinting keenly at his surroundings; he bore a polished oak box under one arm, and his sea-chest was wheeled behind by an awestruck urchin whom he rewarded with a groat, a kindly word, and a pat on the head. The urchin went off swearing foully at the size of his tip, but the skipper was all over the newcomer, crying welcome aboard, Cap'n Avery, look'ee, here's j'y, or rattle me else! The young man nodded amiably, but looked down his classic nose when the beaming skipper presented him to his fellow-passenger.

"Blood?" he said, bowing perfunctorily. "I seem to have heard the name," and his tone didn't imply that it had been in connection with the last Honours List; plainly he was not enchanted with the Colonel (trust Avery to spot a wrong 'un every time). "You are a soldier, sir?"

"Oh, here and there," said Blood easily. "You're a sailor?"

"I am a naval officer," said Avery coldly.

"Ah," said Blood wisely, and wondered: "Don't they sail?", at which Avery's cuffs stiffened sharply as he favoured the Colonel with that steely glance employed by Heroes on mutinous troops, rioting peasants, and impudent rakehelly villains, who respectively quail, cower, or gnash their teeth when exposed to it. Colonel Blood met it with an amiable smile, and the two of them detested each other from that instant.

A coach came rumbling along the cobbles, and Captain Yardley swore picturesquely, excused himself to Avery, and stumped off bawling: "Admiral's a-comin', damme! Ho, bosun, blister me bum, lay up here, d'ye see? Hands on deck!" And as the coach stopped by the gangplank, a massive-limbed figure with an order on his silk coat and a ruffled castor on his head, stepped ponderously down from it – Admiral Lord Rooke, with a face like a ham, brilliant grey eyes, grizzled head, weatherbeaten feet, tarred elbows, and all that befits a sea-dog of seniority and sound bottom. He was just what an admiral ought to be: tough, kindly, experienced, and worshipped by the salts of the Navy, who referred to him endearingly as Old Pissquick, in memory of the time he extinguished a lighted fuse accidentally at the intaking of Portobello, or the outflanking of Mariegalante, no matter which. He bellowed a command in a voice which had blown look-outs from their crows'-nests e'er now, and a lackey leaped from the box and quivered in his livery.

"You're not English, are ye, fellow?" growled the Admiral.

"No, sair, pliz, je suis un Frog," smarmed the lackey.

"Just the thing!" cried the Admiral. "On thy knees, rat!" And as the lackey knelt on all fours in the mud, providing a step, a dainty foot emerged from the coach, shod with a trim spiked heel, and cased in white silk, and planted itself in the small of his back. A second dainty foot followed it, with a flurry of lace petticoat which revealed a modish velvet garter buckled with brilliants below a shapely knee, and there stood the Admiral's daughter, Lady Vanity, her tiny gloved hand holding a parasol, waiting to be helped down.

"Lower away!" bawled the Admiral, kicking the lackey's behind, and the lackey subsided obsequiously into the mud, allowing Lady Vanity to step down to the cobbles, over which forehead-knuckling salts had laid a red carpet. Examine Lady Vanity for a moment.

She was, of course, a blonde whose hair shone in sun-kissed golden ringlets on either side of a roses-and-cream complexion which she knew to be dazzling. Her eyes were sparkling blue, her nose haughtily tip-tilted, her little chin imperious, her lips a cupid's bow whose perfection was no way impaired by its provoking pout; practically everything about Lady Vanity pouted, including her shapely figure, which would have done credit to the Queen of the Runway. She was not tall, but her carriage was that of a fashion model who has been to a Swiss finishing school and knows she has the equipment to stop a battalion of Rugby League players in their tracks with the flick of a false eyelash. She was dressed by Yves St Laurent, in pleated white silk, and her jewellery alone had cost her doting father all his last cruise's prize money. Lady Vanity was a living doll; even the plump little negress who was her maid was pretty enough to be Miss Leeward Islands.

Captain Avery and Colonel Blood stood together by the rail, drinking her in – one in respectful worship, the other with thoughts of black silk bedclothes and overhead mirrors.

"Will ye look at that, now?" invited the Colonel in an enchanted whisper. "Maybe there's compensations to a life at sea, after all. I hope to God the old feller isn't her husband . . . not that it matters."

Avery's eyes blazed frostily at this lewd effrontery. This fellow's foul tongue, he decided, must be curbed, and speedily.

Lady Vanity was surveying the ship. "Are we expected to sail to India in *that*?" she cried petulantly.

"Seen worse," growled the Admiral, and kicked the lackey again for luck.

"No doubt *you* have, father," said Lady Vanity chillingly. "But *I* did not run away to sea as a cabin-boy at the age of twelve."

"Ye're still that cabin-boy's daughter, m'dear," chuckled the Admiral, bluff as anything, "even if they call me 'me lord' nowadays."

He handed her aboard, and there were big introductions at the gangway, with Captain Yardley blistering and damning and apologising with great geniality, milording and miladying and bowing as far as his guts would let him as he indicated Avery, whom the Admiral hailed with delight.

"Why, young Ben! Good to see ye, lad!" He waved a great paw. "M'dear, this is Captain Avery, that fought wi' me against the dam' Dutchmen – m'daughter, Lady Vanity . . ."

Their eyes met, the brilliant maidenly blue and the clear heroic grey, and although the lady's glance remained serene, and the young captain's steady, atomic explosions took place in the interior of each. Captain Avery felt a qualm for the first time in his life; his knees may not have trembled, but they thought about it, and a great gust of holy passion surged up from his pelvis and thundered against his clavicle. Lady Vanity, normally careless of masculine adoration which she took for granted, suddenly felt as though 'her silken stays were contracting and forcing a flight of doves up through her breast to her perfect throat, where they elbowed each other in fluttering confusion. As he took her hand and bent over it, murmuring 'Servant, ma'am,' his mind was saying, 'Nay, not servant, worshipping slave – and master and protector, all these and more!' And Vanity, whispering 'Sir,' was thinking 'Oh, dreamboat!' and feeling thoroughly ashamed of all the fan letters she had written in the fifth form to Prince Rupert (who had just sent a cyclostyled autographed picture, anyway). So they met, and as he raised his eyes to hers, and she for once shielded those haughty orbs 'neath fluttering lashes, their unspoken love was sealed like Bostik; beside them, Dante and Beatrice were nothing but a ted and a scrubber at a palais hop.

She never even noticed Blood, who was giving her his pursed, wistful leer. Her attention was all for Avery as she murmured softly: "We shall be companions on the voyage, sir. You shall tell me all about the ropes and anchors and keel-haulings and things," and he replied "I shall be even more enchanted than I am now," with such a look of fervent adoration that she dropped her reticule. Blood picked it up, and she never even looked at him as she said, "Thank you my man," and passed on while Rooke drew Avery aside.

"Ye have it safe?" he asked, rolling an eye at the box containing the Madagascar crown, and Avery assured him that he had, and would bestow it secretly in his cabin. "Aye!" rasped the Admiral, in what he imagined was a conspiratorial whisper. "In y'r cabin! Secretly, that's the word! But mum!"

Possibly they heard him as far away as Chelsea, for he had a carrying voice; at any rate, Blood did, and made a note that the box which Captain Avery carried so carefully might be fraught with interest.

But his speculations were now rudely interrupted, by Captain Yardley thundering: "Make haste, then, bring her aboard, d'ye see, wi' a curse!" and the passengers of the *Twelve Apostles* turned to see who this might be. A barred cart had drawn up on the quay, and from it two sentries with muskets were manhandling Black Sheba, her wrists and ankles loosely secured by lengths of chain. Blood stared with interest, for the fetters made up most of her attire, her fine red breeches surviving only as a pair of frayed shorts, and her shirt little better than a rag. Her silver earring had gone into the pocket of her first jailer, and her hair was bound tightly behind her head, giving her face the appearance of a polished ebony mask from some Egyptian tomb. That, and her height, and the fact that she was struggling like fury with the sentries, made her a sufficiently striking spectacle to turn every head on quay and ship.

The officer in charge grabbed her wrist-chain and hauled her forward so violently that she stumbled and fell, whereon he shouted "Get up, you slut!" and kicked her brutally, in approved romantic redcoat style. Which was a mistake, for she got up faster than he bargained for, blazing with rage and fetters whirling; the chain caught the officer across the face before the sentries hauled her back, writhing, and the officer dabbed blood from his cheek and swore most foully.

"Thou black vermin!" he shouted. "Ha! Wouldst thou, eh? Shalt learn the price of raising hand to thy betters, thou snarling slattern, thou! Sergeant, hoist me her up and we'll ha' the cat to her!"

The redcoats having come provided for such contingencies, as they always did in those days, in a trice Sheba was spreadeagled against the cart, her wrists lashed to it with cords, and the sergeant, a burly, grinning brute with bad teeth who hadn't shaved (or washed either, probably), strode forward and tore away her shirt before flourishing the long cat-o'-nine-tails in a hand whose finger-nails would not have borne inspection. The spectators stared, and dainty Lady Vanity clutched at the Admiral's arm in maidenly distress.

"Nay, father – stop them! They mustn't!" Her sweet soprano was tremulous wi' entreaty. "Not in public! Can't they lambast her behind a building or somewhere?"

The sergeant spat a brutal stream of tobacco juice on Sheba's bare back, saw her flinch, roared wi' sadistic glee, and struck with all his might. Sheba choked a scream into a gasp as the tails tore at her skin, the officer gloated "Nice one, fellow!", and the sergeant was winding up for another stroke – when the cat was plucked from his grasp and he spun round to face a reproachful Colonel Blood, who had vaulted nimbly from rail to wharf, and was shaking his head as he tossed the cat into the dock.

"Wait till ye're married afore ye do that sort o' thing, son," he reproved the sergeant. "Ye're too young altogether."

The officer surged forward, raging. "Who the devil art thou to mar our discipline and condign punishment?"

"Me?" said the Colonel innocently. "I'm a Tyburn hooligan, the kind that breaks up executions and gets spectator sports a bad name." He beamed on the officer. "But I can see you're a man of taste, and ye wouldn't want to spoil anything as pretty as this, now, would ye?" And he ran an appreciative hand over Sheba's shuddering bare shoulder.

"Avoid, upstart!" hooted the officer, and Blood frowned.

"Och, don't be so hasty – sure it's a teeny scrape she gave ye, an' her just a slip of a girl! Use a little Christian charity," coaxed the Colonel, "ye bloodthirsty bastard. Abate thy spite, an' think on gentle things – apple pie, an' Christmas, an' little lambs a-gambol, an' your own dear old hag of a mother –"

"Damn thee, thou damned thing, thou!" shrieked the officer, fairly demented. "You'll answer for this –"

"Then so shall I!" rang out a crisp, clear, well-modulated, upper-class, R.A.D.A.-trained baritone, and down the gangplank strode Avery, all clean-limbed virtue. Sheba twisted her head to look, and forgot the smart of her back in a surge of relief (if ever you're tied to a cart and they're going to give you the business, an approaching Avery is just what you need).

"You're a disgrace to your commission," he chilled the officer, "creating a scene like this with ladies present. Stand aside, sir!" And the officer stood. Avery strode to the cart, and where you or I would have stopped foolishly, wishing we'd brought a knife, he simply reached up and snapped Sheba's bonds with two quick twists of his powerful fingers. Sheba regarded him with wonder, and as she turned from the cart he gulped and blushed, hastily averted his eyes, whipped a convenient cloak from the cart, and dropped it over her shoulders.

"Off you go now!" he told her sharply. "Mustn't catch cold. Aboard with you, and slip into something comfortable."

Sheba, stricken into an awe quite foreign to her, was suffering precisely the shock which Lady Vanity had sustained a few moments earlier – it was the sort of thing impressionable teen-agers used to feel when they saw Valentino or Paul Newman for the first time: that brave new world reaction of Miranda's. She fumbled the cloak round her like one in a dream, and moved unsteadily towards the plank, staring back at the Apollo-like figure of her rescuer, who was withering the sullen officer with a final glance. As Sheba reached the plank, there was Blood, all casual charm, waiting to pat her wrist.

"Don't thank me, darlin' – it was nothin'." He smiled beguilingly at her, and she came out of her Avery-induced trance just long enough to spit in his eye, before re-focusing on the splendid captain as he followed her aboard. So intent was she that she tripped on her ankle-chain and hit the deck with a blistering oath which caused the nearest seamen to press their knuckles to their teeth and stop their ears.

Lady Vanity, looking down in disdain from the poop-ladder, was heard to remark: "Fie! what a disgusting creature!" and Sheba, sprawled on the deck like Cat Woman, glared up at her with diabolic venom.

"You should pray, my lady," said she in a sand-papered hiss, "that you never find out how disgusting I can be!"

"How now, baggage o' midnight – wilt bandy, ha?" Captain Yardley dragged her to her feet. "An' wi' lady o' rank, look'ee, aye, an' prime quality, as far above 'ee as truck be above keelson!" He frowned, considering – yes, the truck *was* above the keelson, he was pretty sure. He thrust her roughly towards the hatchway. "Stint thy hoydenish clack or we'll ha' thee in the branks – you there, down wi' her an' clap her in bilboes, wi' a wannion!"

He turned apologetically to usher his quality passengers to the poop, where they thrilled to the spectacle of the *Twelve Apostles* being warped from her moorings. Men threw ropes about, and dropped tardy wenches over the side, sails were unfurled and bumboatmen fell in the water, articles of all descriptions were clewed up, the crowd on the dock sang the seventeenth-century version of 'Auld Lang Syne', the stench of bilge mingled evocatively with the rotting refuse of the river, the jolly sailormen swung their pigtails and strained at the capstan bars wi' heave and ho, Captain Yardley was quietly seasick in a corner, and only Blood spared a last glance (a leer, actually) for Black Sheba as she was hustled below. But even he missed her sudden start as a huge brute of a seaman yanked cruelly at her fetters with a coarse guffaw of: "Har-har, me fine lady – allow me to show ye yer quarters – a right dainty chamber, sink me!" He was a great bearded ruffian, all shaggy with red hair from crown to breast, and he quickly bundled Sheba out of sight. Blood sighed, and wondered where they would put her; maybe in some quiet corner where she'd be glad of a little company . . . provided she wasn't guarded by daunting thugs like that red-haired gorilla. Big, tough rascal he looked. Come to that, these sailors were a pretty muscular lot; Blood's eye dwelt for a moment on another seaman lingering by the hatchway, a clean-shaven heavyweight in spotless white calico who looked as though he could comfortably have taken three straight falls from Odd-job. Of course, the Colonel mused, sailors probably had to be large and fit in order to cope with squalls and doldrums and other nautical hazards; it stood to reason.

He dismissed them from his mind, and set to studying how to cut in on Avery, who was explaining to a fascinated Vanity that the sharp end of the ship was at the front, and if you consulted the compass you could point the vessel the way you wanted to go; she was astonished at his expertise. Admiral Rooke observed them fondly, and Captain Yardley, having dosed himself liberally with Kwells and Alka-seltzer, stumped his deck and berated the topmen who were clinging to the futtock-shrouds in lubberly fashion.

Thus, wi' her strange human cargo, did the stout ship *Twelve Apostles* set out on her fateful journey to the far-off Indies, gliding down the Thames through a forest of lesser shipping which gave way, d'ye see, before her stately passage. Tall and proud she stood down for the open sea, dipping her peak to their Lordships' flag at Greenwich, dropping the pilot off the Medway, bumping into the pier at Southend, and running down a shrimp-boat off Clacton. Old salts viewed her admiringly as she passed, and wished her a prosperous voyage with ale-mugs raised in half-stoned salutation, none guessing what strange destiny awaited her 'neath tropic stars beyond the ocean rim . . .

Night found her in the Downs, pursuing her steady course beneath all plain (and decorated) sail, her crew and passengers a-slumber as she bore southwards. Did I say all? Nay, there were those that waked – the man at the wheel, more or less, and the look-out aloft, although he was surreptitiously reading a dirty book, possibly *Moll Flanders*, by shielded candle-light in the crow's-nest. And others there were who as yet were sleepless – what thoughts, think you, reader, crowded their minds as they pondered the unknown future? How the hell should we know, says you. Then I'll tell 'ee, says I, and ye may lay to that.

There is Captain Avery, strong chin in firm hand, his keen grey eyes veiled for once in thought as he dreams of . . . flag rank? Naval glory? The Madagascar crown and his perilous mission? Or is he envisioning a perfect roses-and-cream complexion framed by gold ringlets, dreamy blue eyes, a small soft hand brushing against his own, a sweet musical voice inquiring: "What are scuppers?" Of course he is, the susceptible big jerk. Vanity, Vanity, all is Vanity, as far as he's concerned.

And Vanity, her petal-like cheek resting on her lace pillow, is drowsing fondly over the memory of that marvellous profile, that vibrant baritone, that strong arm that supported her up the poop ladder. Mm-mm, if only he has ten thousand a year . . .

Blood, too, has his thoughts as he lies in his berth. That big spade bint is a bit of all right, he reflects; of course, so is Blondie, if a little upstage. Still, four months is a long time . . . suppose he was shipwrecked with both of them? A happy dilemma, and the cad falls asleep with a blissful smile on his raffish countenance.

And they weren't the only ones astir on the *Twelve Apostles* as she cruised gently south in the velvet night.

Far below the waterline, in the nethermost bowels of the ship, in the foul reeking orlop where rats scurried beady-eyed in the dark, and the bilges slopped around wi' foetid plash – there, in a far corner, a light guttered palely, casting the shadows of three figures. Black Sheba, fettered by slim ankles to a bulkhead, reclined her shapeliness on matted straw, eyes agleam like eager anthracite, and with her the red-bearded gorilla and the tall fellow in white – you know who they are, but how did they get here? Listen . . .

". . . all the way to England, camarado, dogging the King's ship that brought you, till we sighted Portland, when we dropped ashore, while Bilbo lay off, d'ye see? When we had word o' where ye was bound, we shipped aboard as focsle-jacks, and –" here he winked a shrewd Calico Jack wink "– with a score or so stout lads as we can count on, look'ee. Bilbo's been tipped the word, and lays course south for a rendezvous agreed wi' Akbar the Damned an' Happy Dan Pew . . ."

"– an' when the time comes, a right merry meeting we'll ha' on't, rack, rat, an' rend me for a sea-slug else!" chortled Firebeard. "Har-har! These misbegotten King's pimps don't dream what a flock o' lovin' lambs they's got aboard – an' when Bilbo and the lads lays alongside – why, good day an' good-bye to 'em, honest men! Then, little Sheba darlin'," gibbered the hairy scoundrel, "ye can pay 'em for this sal-oobrious accommodation, an' this jewellery they've give ye!" And he jingled her fetters gleefully.

"Oh, friends!" Sheba, the proud, fearless sea-queen who gutted Spaniards before breakfast, and had been known to roast cathedralfuls of nuns just for laughs, choked back a sob of pure feminine emotion. A tear welled on her dusky cheek, and Firebeard wiped it tenderly away with the tail of his shirt, blushing coyly to the eyelids, the only part of him visible through his tangle of hair. "Dear comrades," continued Sheba, "I know not what to say . . . shall we barbecue 'em first and keelhaul them after? Or flog and carbonado them, and then disembowel and flay them by inches? Could we, perchance, do all six, and woold and dismember them later on? Oh, I know these are mere womanly fancies," she went on, with a catch in her voice, "but it's been so long! And if it's the last thing I do –" she clenched her fists till her chains rattled, and ground her pearly teeth "– I'm going to fix that stuck-up little blonde bitch in the St Laurent outfit with the puffed sleeves and those pleated seams going round above the hips and gathered in under the little bows along the back so that it fits snug at the waist and looks as though it's creaseless material and probably costs a bloody fortune to have altered supposing you can get a woman to do it. She won't," Sheba added venomously, "have much use for it by the time I'm through with her –"

"There, there," said Firebeard soothingly, patting her manacled ankle with his great paw, "she han't got near such nice legs as you, I'll lay, an' I bet she sunburns somethin' rotten – ha, Calico?"

"Patience, camarado," said Rackham. "There's long sea-miles to go afore we call our reckonin' – so mum, an' leave all to us."

As they were going, Sheba suddenly checked them. "Calico, wait. When they were going to flog me today . . ." she looked askance, and her voice was over-casual ". . . who was yon that loosed me?"

"Which one?" asked Firebeard. "The cocky black Irisher or the mealy swab wi' the long legs?"

"The Englishman," said Sheba coldly, "thou untutored bladder."

"Name o' Avery," said Rackham. "Captain in Charlie boy's navy. Why?"

"Oh . . . nothing," said Black Sheba, and stretched herself like some great black cat on her straw, her eyes stoking up 'neath lazily-lowered lids, a strange enigmatic quiver agitating her sensuously-parted toes . . .

A Canberra cruise this isn't, but who can tell what lies ahead as the Twelve Apostles *skids round the corner of the Kentish coast, her passengers all unaware of the mischief brewing below decks? What dark purpose does Sheba harbour Avery-wise? What will come of his infatuation with the lovely Lady Vanity? Is her dress of creaseless material, and could it conceivably be altered to fit a corsair virago six inches taller? What dark schemes revolve in the fertile mind of Colonel Blood? How would you like to be chained up in an orlop? Read on . . .*

CHAPTER
THE FOURTH

he *Twelve Apostles* followed the course charted by movie art directors since time immemorial, in which the image of a tiny galleon is seen gliding gently across an Olde Worlde map with whales spouting bottom right – down from the Channel, across Biscay (where everyone would be ghastly sick and heaving, but you don't see that bit), round the top left-hand bump of Africa, and down into tropic waters, at which point the map dissolves into a long shot of the actual galleon cruising briskly across a sunlit sea. Then we get a quick shot of life on board – first the captain with a telescope on the quarter-deck, just to let you know that everything's under control, possibly a long shot of filling sails in case you've forgotten how the ship is actually propelled, and lastly to the matter in hand, whatever it may be. Right.

In this case we see Captain Yardley and Admiral Rooke looking down indulgently on a specially-holystoned part of the main deck, where Lady Vanity, clad in biscuit-coloured muslin, is playing shuffleboard with Captain Avery, trilling merrily when she wins, and pouting prettily when she loses. She doesn't often pout, because Avery is the shuffleboard champion of the Royal Navy, and his keen eye and sinewy wrist enable him to leave his rings just that bit short every time, or nudge Vanity's shots into the centre of the target. (After all, he's besotted with the girl, and knows that his wooing won't prosper if he whitewashes her 12-0 every time.)

And as they play, the jovial Firebeard galumphs about retrieving the rings and crying "Rare shot, milady!" and "Bravely thrown, cap'n!" and "Bloody hard lines, ma'am!" and bobbing and grinning and knuckling his forehead and generally grovelling like anything. For he and Rackham have shipped aboard under the names of Knatchbull-Carshalton and Wentworth respectively (Bilbo's suggestions, naturally), and have been at pains to impress their superiors with their trustworthy, seamanlike, forelock-tugging qualities. With the result that Captain Yardley has remarked to Admiral Rooke on the rare good fort'n, by cock, of getting two such prime hands, and Rackham has won such golden opinions by his resolution and intelligence that he has been appointed quartermaster, with responsibility for steering in the night watches. (Significant, eh?) Firebeard isn't much good at navigation (let's face it, when he watches the sunrise he has to spin a coin to decide whether he's looking east or not), but he is something of a mascot because he organises dice-horse-racing and deck quoits and sweeps on the ship's mileage for Vanity's amusement, and is the caller for Bingo in the evenings, crying "Eyes down, look in, clickety-click, legs eleven, Kelly's plonk, blind sixty" and the like, to the hilarity of all. Vanity thinks he is a perfect pet, and calls him (wait for it) Master Nittywhiskers, and generally treats him like a tame retriever, and no one ever notices the occasional mad piggy glint in the eyes of the grinning, fawning sycophant.

Not even Blood, with his villain's nose for villainy. For he had other things to think about. To start with, he found himself sent to Coventry in the first week, after Avery suddenly remembered where he'd heard the Colonel's name before, and the Admiral, Yardley, and Vanity were thunderstruck to discover that their fellow-passenger was the notorious ruffian who had recently scandalised London by his attempt to glom the Crown Jewels, for which daring exploit he had unaccountably been pardoned by King Charles and

64

set at liberty. (Fact, and no one has solved the mystery to this day.) However, after that it was the cold shoulder all round for our Tom, the gentlemen turning sharply on their heels and Lady Vanity elevating her exquisite little retroussé nose and daintily fanning the air if he came within ten feet of her. The Colonel endured philosophically his exclusion from after-dinner whist and 'I spy', and having to eat in his cabin alone, and not having anyone tell him the right time. His isolation enabled him to ponder two matters which were intriguing him – one being the mysterious oak box which Avery kept hidden in his cabin (the Colonel having watched its bestowal from a convenient skylight on the first day of the voyage), and the other being how to arrange an undisturbed visit to the orlop to teach Sheba postman's knock. Being a patient man, he set himself to wait, ignoring the slights of Cabin Society, and fingering his clarkie moustache with a slow smile as he leaned nonchalantly against the rail.

His double opportunity came on a balmy tropic night as they sailed smoothly down towards the Cape over a limpid azure sea beneath a moon so golden that it almost dripped in the purple sky. Stars twinkled, scented breezes blew, in the great cabin the Admiral and Yardley, stuffed to surfeit and drowsy with port, hiccoughed and reminisced, and in the seclusion of the stern gallery Captain Avery and Lady Vanity clung in an ecstatic embrace, munching each other's lips and only occasionally coming up for air.

(Avery? Necking? Has our idol got feet of smouldering clay? By no means. Left to himself, he would have worshipped his blonde divinity from afar, or rather from close quarters, but never laying a glove on her; he didn't have all his Scout badges for nothing. His love was chaste and holy, and he had never so much as held hands at the church social. But Vanity soon took care of that. Delicately nurtured at a finishing school where panty-raids by ardent young males were commonplace, and where she and her schoolmates had been wont to classify Society bucks as N.S.A.V., N.S.I.S.C., and N.S.A.* respectively, she had quickly realised that this dream-man was such a spiritual Galahad that he would need tuition in how to get physical. Her course of instruction took about eleven seconds, consisting of a glance at the moon, a gentle sigh, a hand on his arm, her eyes wide and uplifted to his, a parting of her moist lips, and before the hypnotised Avery knew what he was doing he was glued to her like the Magdeburg hemispheres, finally parting after three solid minutes of osculation with the sound of a drain unblocking. After that first memorable kiss, which he quickly convinced himself was not only a perfectly seemly, but courteous thing to do – for this adorable girl deserved every treat she could get – it was plain sailing; Vanity could relax contentedly and let him make the running – all good clean fun, mind you, for she was a proper and toward young lady who permitted no undue familiarities, which she guessed Avery wouldn't know how to make, anyway.)

So they smooched away blissfully and decorously, as lovers will, until Vanity decided that she had now got this superman softened up sufficiently to start moulding him to her imperious will – a necessary preliminary to the marriage which she had determined would follow eventually, when she felt like it. From this point the lovers were observed by Colonel Blood, out for a twilight prowl, and cheerfully eavesdropping from the stern rail above their heads, the swine. This is what he heard:

VANITY (panting): Easy, boy, easy! Golly, you don't know your own strength! Is my hair a mess?

AVERY: Nay, sweet goddess, 'tis immaculate as thy perfect self. (With an indulgent male chauvinist smile.) I fear me y'are well named Lady Vanity.

VANITY (checking make-up in mirror): Too right. I'm gorgeous, proud, and insufferably spoiled. Very properly. Now, what's all this rot about getting off at Madagascar, and leaving me to be bored witless all the way to Calicut?

* Not safe at Vauxhall, Not safe in sedan chairs, Not safe anywhere.

AVERY (sighing): Alas, dearest, I have my duty.

VANITY: Indeed? I can see we shall have to get your priorities straight. One, duty is what other people do. Two, if ever you find yourself faced with a choice between duty and me, I shall whistle – once. Three, if you're to be Sir Benjamin before your twenty-fifth birthday, and we're to be Earl and Countess before you're thirty – for I won't settle for less, and flag rank for you into the bargain –

AVERY: Angel, I shall win these trifles and lay them at your feet!

VANITY: Trifles, quotha! You win whatever you like, Tyrone, and I'll manage the essentials. For know that I am an Admiral's daughter, a Very Important Lady with immense influence – the King has spoken politely to me –

AVERY (frowning): Has he, though?

VANITY: – and before I'm through you're going to have a seat in the Cabinet. Don't fret, I can keep Charlie at a distance, and arrange your preferment, advancement, and finances perfectly satisfactorily. Ah, 'twill be very bliss, you and I together, our future golden –

AVERY (friendly but firm): I still have to get off at Madagascar.

VANITY: Forget it – I shall speak to Father –

AVERY: Dear heart, even he is powerless. 'Tis royal command.

VANITY: Straight up? Oh, blast! Then let us make the most of what little time is left to us for the moment. Hold me, my darling . . . renew our fleeting rapture . . .

AVERY (ardently): Yum-yum!

VANITY (slightly muffled): Mind my beauty patch . . .

By this time Blood had given up in disgust, not untinged with envy, and judging that Avery would be occupied for some time, descended stealthily to the young captain's cabin and began operations on the oak box with great patience and a bent nail. (No end to the fellow's criminal versatility.) Presently he had the lid up and was squatting reverently muttering 'Bejazus!' as he contemplated the gleaming glory of the crown. So this was the precious secret – and it was going to Madagascar! Fat chance. For about five seconds he gloated greedily, and then, being a highly practical scoundrel, relocked the box and went on deck, where he lurked chin in hand – and he wasn't considering his next contribution to Dr Barnardo's, either. How to acquire this wondrous bauble – it must be thought upon. In the meantime, with the crew all asleep and the Quality either swilling port or snogging, it occurred to the Colonel that he knew an excellent way of celebrating his splendid discovery. Watching all that boy-and-girl stuff on the stern gallery had reawakened the beast in him, rakehell that he was . . .

Captain Avery, having bidden the delectable Vanity good-night with a last fond grapple at her cabin door, had thereafter repaired rather unsteadily to his quarters for a cold bath. He had been hopelessly in love for several weeks now, but actually petting with beautiful blondes was something else – so *that* was what Ovid and Count Orsino and the poet Herrick got all worked up about, he reflected breathlessly. Well, he could see what they meant. Wow! And she loved him, and melted in his arms, and her kisses were like perfumed darts from Cupid's bow . . . but enough was enough – well, no, it wasn't, but in the meantime he was Captain Benjamin Avery, after all, with responsibilities and duties and things, and it was time to climb off Cloud Nine for the moment. He would take a brisk walk round the deck before retiring, and this slightly dizzy feeling would go away.

So he dressed rapidly, and going quietly on deck, was just in time to see a stealthy figure descending the main hatchway. It looked like that awful scoundrel Blood . . . in a moment the lover was transformed into the cool, alert man of action as the captain, narrow-eyed and treading softly, followed to see what mischief the fellow might be up to when all decent folk were in their pits for the night.

It did not occur to the Captain that there was anything

demeaning about snooping after his fellow-passenger in this fashion. After all, Blood was widely known to be as bent as a boat-hook and, as head prefect at Uppingham Avery had been accustomed to trailing nocturnal bounds-breakers and confiscating their illicit cherry brandy and copies of *Playeboye*. So now, his magnificent shapely ears pricked, he crept down the companion after the softly sneaking Colonel; past the focsle where the crew snored and the atmosphere was thick enough to sell as coal briquettes, past the main cargo deck, into the hold, and then through dark narrow ways among the piled-up gear, where rats squeaked and scuttled, and only the occasional horn lantern guttered i' the gloom. Once the Captain paused, when his foot got jammed in a bucket, and then he was hurrying ahead towards a distant gleam of light, whence came the sound of voices, one tense with fury, the other soft and sinisterly mocking . . .

"Get away from me!" Black Sheba, crouched against the orlop bulkhead, clutched her rag of shirt across her breasts with one hand and swung the slack of her fetters with the other. "Another step and I'll lay your face open!"

"Now, stab me if I understand you," Blood was saying, and Avery could picture the sinister smile on his lips. "What's the matter with me? I'm good-looking, young, charming, clean, amiable, and I shaved this morning. Bigod, ye don't know what a lucky girl ye are; all I want is to help you pass the time pleasant-like –"

"Some day I'll pass the time with you," snarled Sheba, her bazoom heaving like anything, "and you'll beg to be let die!"

"Ah, come off it," said Blood, eyeing the fetters warily. "It's going to happen to you in Calicut anyway. You'll be sold off, every delectable pound of ye, to some greasy old hog of a planter, and *he* won't take no for an answer. Whereas with me, it'll not only be a rewarding experience, I'll even engage to buy you myself – if I can raise the money . . ."

The artful stinker had been edging closer, and as Sheba

let fly with her chains he ducked nimbly underneath, and with a caddish chuckle tackled her low and pinned her on the straw, smiling mockingly into her blazing eyes. She struggled vainly while he got himself comfy.

"Now, then," he said, "what I propose is one little kiss, and if ye don't like it, then on my honour I'll leave you be. Tom Blood doesn't stay where he's not wanted. But I can't believe a fine strapping lass like you won't think better of it . . ."

And the bounder's lips were descending on hers when steely fingers closed on his shoulder, and he was dragged up to meet Avery's eyes glittering wrathfully, and Avery's voice ringing in icy scorn:

"Muckrake! Stinker! Jerk!"

And he hit the Colonel a big one, splat! which sent the startled amorist hurtling headlong across the orlop, and serve him right. Avery, fists clenched, towered over him in manly indignation, while Black Sheba crouched on her straw, wide-eyed. The Colonel presently sat up and nursed his jaw reflectively.

"Some days are like this," he sighed. "Ye just can't please anybody. A man goes about trying to promote a little happiness, but . . ." He shrugged and came to his feet, smiling to conceal his anxiety about his bridgework. "That's a fair wallop ye have in that hand, Captain. Is it as ready when it's holding steel?"

"Get out," snapped the Captain, in refrigerated contempt.

"So soon?" wondered the Colonel amiably. "We could have a three-handed game of brag . . . no?" He winked regretfully at Sheba. "Sorry, sweetheart, ye'll just have to contain your passion for another time. If you're staying, captain, and she starts fiddling with those chains – duck."

And with insolent aplomb the hardened scoundrel tipped them a salute and went off, whistling. Avery waited till his footsteps died away, and then glanced at the swarthy Juno crouched at his feet.

"Did he hurt you?"

Sheba shook her head, and slithered up sinuously to lean against the bulkhead while Avery looked about her cramped prison. What a filthy hole, he was thinking, even for a wild female blackamoor; why, his gundogs, Buster and Doodles, had better kennels at home. And Sheba, her smoky eyes devouring him, was thinking: what a profile, what class, what style! Even the way he tramped accidentally on her water-dish, and wrinkled his Grecian nostrils in distaste, sent gusts of passion surging up from her ankles. And now those wonderful grey eyes were turned on her as he asked, in his best orderly officer manner: "Any complaints?"

Any complaints! The words seemed to turn her shapely knees to buttermilk, but all she could do was shake her head again dumbly, at which he nodded in a way which clutched at her heart. As he turned away she found speech, huskily: "Captain Avery?" He paused inquiringly, and the gentle lift of his moulded eyebrows hit her like a battering-ram.

"I have not been able to thank you," she breathed, "for saving me from the whip, the day we sailed. Why did you?"

He frowned. "Didn't like it. Not British. Cruel."

Sheba considered him. "Cruelty can have its uses," she husked, gnawing her lip and smouldering a bit, but Avery didn't notice.

"Anyway," he said, fair-mindedly, "that blighter Blood was the first to help you. Just shows, he can't be all cad."

Sheba's lovely lips writhed in a sneer. "He had his reason, as you saw just now. Were I old and withered, instead of . . ." Here she let actions speak louder than words by doing a gentle bump and grind, ". . . they could ha' flogged me to mincemeat and he'd not have lifted a finger, he." And she called Blood a horrid name.

Avery pursed a doubtful lip – after all, Blood did hold the King's commission, and that sort of talk from a person of her class struck him as subversive. But before he could chill her with a mild reproof, Sheba had glided forward as far as her ankle-chain would allow, and repeated in that hot sandalwood voice:

"I have still not been able to . . . thank you, captain." And she made a little helpless gesture with her fetters which would have won her a contract at Minsky's. "These chains . . ."

"What about 'em?" said Avery innocently, and stepped closer to look. The great sap couldn't see what was coming; he was all off balance as two slim dusky hands were raised to caress his cheeks, two amber-flecked eyes gazed into his, and two crimson lips were pressed fiercely against his mouth – you wondered for a split second if she was going to strangle him, didn't you? Not Sheba. She was giving that sudden embrace all she had, which was plenty, since she had had lots of practice. Whereas Avery, apart from his brief session with Vanity earlier on, was a total novice. Consequently, the effect on him was electric. For a moment he was petrified, and then jungle drums began to throb in his ears, ritual fires blazed up, fogs of musky incense swirled through his senses, erotic cymbals clashed, and he found himself inexplicably thinking of silk cushions and Turkish Delight, of all things. He drew back in some confusion, disengaged her hands, and automatically adjusted his neckcloth.

"That," he said, slightly hoarse, "was not necessary."

"That," panted Sheba, her eyes like open furnace doors, "is what you think."

What an odd woman, thought Avery. Barbarian, of course, just expressing thanks in her primitive fashion. Rather touching, and indeed not unpleasant, in a peculiarly disturbing way – just for a moment, there, he'd felt a sort of dizzy, hypnotic attraction . . . in fact, he still did, even at a range of four feet. Extraordinary . . . yet how curious that he who had never been kissed before this evening, should be embraced by two women within an hour. Vanity would be vastly amused when he told her . . . or then again, perhaps she wouldn't. The dear child might not understand that the touch of her sweet lips was utterly different – pure, exquisite, holy bliss, quite unlike this savage creature's crude display of gratitude . . . yes . . . very different . . .

Now that he looked at her, this black female was quite striking, if not altogether seemly in appearance. Very tall girl – and how oddly she was regarding him, with that intense stare while she licked her lips and growled deep in her throat. Captain Avery swallowed; he was feeling that dizziness again. Very close down here; he needed a breath of air. Abruptly he turned about and left the orlop.

Black Sheba stared after him hungrily, her eyes heaving and her chest smouldering (just by way of a change). Then she relaxed, a feral, enigmatic smile playing about her chiselled lips as she reclined on her bed of straw. Playing hard to get, eh, she thought . . . but not for much longer, you gorgeous Greek god, you. Any minute now, buster, any minute.

Meanwhile the object of her unholy passion was leaning against a bulkhead some way from the orlop, muttering 'Phew!' and shaking his head to clear it, when he became aware that Colonel Blood was sitting with folded arms on a nearby cask, head cocked and a dirty look in his eye.

"Now what," wondered the Colonel, nodding towards the orlop entrance, "have you got that I haven't?"

Avery straightened. "Decency, perhaps?" he replied frostily, and his gesture invited the Colonel to precede him up the companion. Blood rose lazily.

"Faith, is that what ye call it?" he reflected as they went up. "Well, ye didn't take much advantage of it. Ye'll regret it, in your old age, see if you don't."

"My only regret," said Avery, "is that necessity compels me to consort aboard this ship with such lewd scoundrel as you."

"You can mend that as soon as you like," said Blood. "Or

does your courage stop short at hitting from behind?"

Avery was before him in a flash, all icy contempt. "When we touch dry land at the Cape, sir, I shall accommodate you face to face, with what weapons you choose."

Blood looked him up and down (and until you've seen Blood's eye travelling north and south you don't know what provocative insolence is.) "The number of times," he drawled, "that some coxcomb has said to me that he'll meet me next week, or next month, or the first Shrove Tuesday in leap year – and when the time comes, damme if I haven't had the ground all to meself. I see that ye're another lad . . . of promise." And he turned on his heel at his cabin door.

Crimson mantled the flawless cheekbones of our Hero, and his jaw set like frozen yogurt. He spun the Colonel round with steely fingers. "That taunt becomes you, coward," he grated. "Well you know 'tis impossible we should meet aboard ship. Affairs of honour are not settled so –"

"Why not?" grinned Blood. "There's a stern gallery yonder where none should hear us – faith, it's familiar ground to you and your paramour – the blonde one, not the darkie –"

Schooled in imperturbability though he was, it took Avery all his time to suppress a yowl of fury. His eye flamed, and the colour drained from his face to his ankles. "With you on the instant!" he snapped, and strode into his cabin for his rapier.

Now what, you ask, is crafty Thomas up to? It cannot be that he is intent on repaying the merited buffet bestowed on him by Avery for getting fresh with Captive Africa. No way; Blood is used to chaps taking swings at him. Nay, he is needling Avery in furtherance of some dark design, to wit – if they cross swords on the stern gallery secretly, and Blood can give Avery the mortal stuck-in and heave his corpse into the main, he can then snaffle the Madagascar crown. And next morning, when investigation takes place, who is to point a finger at T.B.? Poor Avery, he must have fallen overboard in

74

the night; too bad – that will be the official version, and if Tom can't keep the crown safely secreted until they reach the Cape, he isn't the man he thinks he is. Thus did the cunning rascal reason as he repaired to the stern gallery with his own rapier, to find his stalwart antagonist awaiting him wi' un-bated tuck.

They faced each other on the narrow gallery in the moonlight, the ship's bright wake creaming beneath them. "When you fall," said Avery sternly, "I may be hard put to it to explain why we met thus irregularly, but it sorts not with mine honour to let you live who have sullied a fair lady's good name with –"

"Save it, son," said Blood coolly. "Any explaining will be in good hands – mine. You can kiss it goodbye." He was grinning and snaking his blade in and out á la Rathbone, and Avery drew himself up, very academic as you might expect, and slid a foot forward into the attack, his eyes like chips of solid helium.

Well, you've seen it before – glittering blades rasping, feet slithering, close-ups of Blood's grinning teeth and rumpled curls, and Avery's icy composure as he breathes brilliantly through his nostrils. Gosh, he was good – so was Blood, of course, but bouncing about with cits' plump wives and drinking mulled canary at 4 a.m. had sapped his vigour and slowed him down just that little bit. Avery, by contrast, was trained to a hair and pure of heart, so it was inevitable that after one of those engagements in which the blades whirl too quickly for the eye to follow, Blood should spring back with a curse, a livid cut across his left forearm, and gore dripping on the planks.

"Lucky bastard!" was all he said, and sprang again to the attack, but with his fertile brain ticking over at speed. This boy was hell on wheels, all right, he was thinking, but he was Olympic gold medal material, no more – wide open to such unorthodox stunts as a good kick in the crotch, for example. Yet how should that profit Blood now? Even if he killed

Avery, he had taken a wound and there was blood on the deck – even dimwits like Rooke and Yardley would be bound to connect these facts with the young Captain's disappearance. So . . . the crown in Avery's cabin must wait for another day. In the meantime, how to emerge from the present hoo-ha with his life – and, if possible, lull Avery's enmity for the nonce, perhaps even win something of his regard? A tall order, but meat and drink to our Irish mountebank.

So he bore in with all the considerable science at his command, recklessly expending his energy while Avery broke ground with close-playing wrist (whatever that is) and perfect control, husbanding his strength, as prudent heroes always do, until his opponent's fury should have spent itself, which it inevitably does. Blood, lashing away like a carpet-beater gone berserk, bore him back by main force until they were in that well-known close shot, chest to chest, both heaving away like crazy, the baddy fleering and sneering sweatily, the goody keen-eyed and straining manfully, at which psychological moment Blood asked casually:

"Tell me captain – when I've fed ye to the fish, what becomes o' that precious bauble in your cabin?"

Since he was almost on his knees with exhaustion, the words came out in a sort of ruined wheeze, but they earned full marks for effect. For a split second Avery's icy composure faltered; to be honest, he gave a passable imitation of a gaffed salmon, and in a trice the crafty Irishman had stamped on his toe, disarmed him by seizure, and whipped his point against Avery's Adam's apple. And there they stood, Avery aghast and biting his lip with vexation, Blood panting asthmatically and trying to hold his sword steady. At last, having regained his wind, he lowered his point and stepped back, looking for somewhere to lean on.

"Ye know," he remarked, "you're a mighty pretty swordsman, but ye're not fit to be let out alone, so you're not. An old dodge like that – letting your opponent talk ye into a tangle. Faith, it's as well I'm not the rogue ye think me, or it's dead meat ye'd be by this. And where would your bonny jewelled crown be going then, eh? Not to Madagascar, sonny."

Avery, hero though he was, looked (and probably felt) as though he'd been jumped on by the Wigan front row. "The Madagascar crown?" he gasped. "What know ye on't?"

"Everything," fibbed Blood smoothly. "What d'ye think I'm here for?"

"You mean – y'are an agent of Master Pepyseses?" stammered the Captain, his eyes like bewildered gimlets. "But . . . but he told me none knew of the mission save he and I, his majesty, and my Lord Rooke!"

"That's the civil service mentality for you," sighed Blood sympathetically. "Never tell you a damned thing." He improvised boldly. "I've been privy from the first. They thought the job was too important for just one man."

Just one man! The words were a karate chop across the windpipe of Avery's self-esteem. "I could have done it standing on my head!" he snapped.

"So we've noticed," said Blood drily, but the Captain wasn't listening. His nostrils flared delicately with mistrust.

"And you'd have me believe they sent *you* to guard *me*?" he cried. "Nay, 'tis thing impossible! Y'are a notorious foul villain of rank repute and noisome infamy, steeped i' knavery and treason, a seasoned rascally cutpurse profligate who tried to nick the Crown Jewels, a foresworn skunk, crud, creep, and renegade –"

"All right, all right!" Blood interrupted warmly. "Can you think of a better cover?" he asked knowingly.

"You mean," whispered Avery incredulously, "that you're *not* really a notorious foul villain of ill repute –"

"Rank repute."

"– rank repute and noisome infamy, steeped i' –"

"If I was, you wouldn't be standing here running off at the

mouth, remember?" snapped Blood. "Some of us," he went on virtuously, "don't mind being given a bad name if it enables us to serve his majesty the better. We don't insist on going poncing about like Sir Walter Raleigh. We are content to wear," he added bitterly, "dishonour's mask in honour's cause." Here, that's not bad, he thought; a nifty to remember.

"But if you're not a seasoned rascally cutpurse profligate," demanded Avery, "what were you climbing all over that poor defenceless black female for?"

"Your benefit," said Blood, and got all austere. "I have observed you, sir, and methinks you spend overmuch time in dalliance wi' my Lady Vanity, to the neglect of your duty. Nay, belt up till I ha' done. Marking this, I provoked you – the black trull means no more to me than a squashed grape; such carnal employs engage not my senses, I thank God – to test me your metal, to recall you to your duty, and to inform you –" and here he laid a hand on Avery's astonished shoulder, "– that in whate'er perils may lie ahead, y'are not alone." Rugged nobility was just oozing out of him.

"Stone me!" was not an expression that Captain Avery ever used, but it was a near thing. For what Blood had told him was flawlessly logical when weighed in an ice-cool brain – he *must* be a Pepys muscleman, or he'd have used his momentary advantage – a cad's trick, incidentally, stamping on a chap's toes – to kill Avery and trouser the crown. And it was just like those old sneaks at the Admiralty to stick a second man on the job, without telling a fellow. Blinking cheek, thought Avery, and quite unnecessary – and then a flush of shame mantled his fair young brow as he remembered how he'd been canoodling with Lady Vanity and never thinking twice about his precious charge. He let out an anguished woof.

"And I was found wanting!" His face was pale as a mortified parrot's. "You are right, sir – a fine guardian, I, spooning and duelling to indulge my base appetites!" He ground his flawless molars in remorse, while Blood patted his arm reassuringly.

"We all make mistakes, lad," he crooned. "Bedad, on me own first mission, charged wi' letters o' rare import to the Grand Sophy – ye won't believe this – didn't I get so engrossed in 'Paradise Lost' that I missed the last caravan to Aleppo . . . or was it to Damascus . . . no, t'was there I slew the four Spanish agents, was't not? No matter. Anyway, I nearly blew the whole deal." He made a deprecating gesture, and blood from his wounded arm splashed on Avery's snowy shirt. The Captain yipped with contrition.

"And I wounded you!"

"Pish!" said Blood. "A flea-bite." For which you'll pay, my smart-assed friend, he thought grimly, while yet smiling so winningly that Avery gulped with emotion. How could he ever have mistrusted this honest, sturdy gentleman?

"Colonel Blood," said he, frank and manly, "I ha' done you great wrong. You're all right. One of the lads. My eyes are opened." He proved this by giving Blood his steady First XI glance, and clasping his hand. "What more's to be said, save that I –" he shrugged modestly, "– yes, even I, shall sleep sounder o' nights knowing that in you I have a loyal and steadfast . . . ah . . . assistant."

You do that, son, thought Blood, and arm in arm they repaired to the slumbering passenger quarters 'neath the poop, where all was still save for the sweet murmurous breathing from Admiral Rooke's berth, and the thunderous snorting from Lady Vanity's. (Eh?) There they bade each other a comradely good-night, and sought their respective cabins, Avery thinking, what a worthy fellow, and Blood thinking, what an amazing birk.

Hand it to Blood, he's slicker than wet paint. What next impudent villainy does he intend? And Avery, that honest lad – are his dreams refreshed by pure, blissful visions of Lady Vanity, or do strange phantasms of our

Ebony Hebe disturb his repose? Does Vanity really snore? Who's minding the ship? Let's lay aloft, says you, and we'll ascertain.

CHAPTER
THE FIFTH

ilence . . . as the *Twelve Apostles* glides on over the dark green sea bounded by distant banks of thin sea-mist. The moon is down, the sky a dark arch overhead, eastward there is still no shimmer of dawn. Upstairs the ship is deserted, save for the yawning lubber propped against the wheel, and the look-out in the crow's-nest who has finished *Moll Flanders* and is frowning over the crossword in the *South Sea Waggoner*. One across, 'What ships usually sail on', three letters. Rum? Bog? He peeps down to see what the *Twelve Apostles* is floating on at the moment. Water? Too many letters. He sighs; another bloody anagram, probably . . . what kind of nut thinks these things up?

Below, the crew packed tight in their focsle hammocks have really got their heads down; even the rats and weevils are flat out. Aft, in the First Class, everyone is lapping it up except Captain Yardley, who pores over a chart in his great cabin, scratching grizzled pate and muttering 'Belike an' bedamned' as he plots his u-turn round the bottom of Africa. Vanity, beautifully made up even in slumber, sighs gently as the distant tinkle of eight bells is faintly heard. Of course she doesn't snore! It was Rooke all the time, sprawled in his cot across the passage, his stentorian rumblings bulging the ship's timbers and causing his dentures to rattle in their glass. Avery, in his cabin, is kipping away like an advertisement for

Dunlopillo, eyes gently closed, hair neatly arranged, mouth perfectly shut and breathing through his nose. A smile plays about his mobile lips: he is dreaming of Vanity darning his socks in a rose-bowered summer-house, you'll be glad to know. Over the way Blood grunts and mutters in his sleep, one hand on the hilt of a dagger 'neath 's pillow – if you've a conscience like his you keep your hardware handy. And deep in the foetid orlop Sheba writhes restlessly on her straw, her fetters clanking dismally.

Everybody bedded down, right? All serene? You know better.

As the last bell sounded, ending the middle watch, a stalwart figure in neatly-pressed white calico took over the wheel, and a massive untidy heap crouched by the side-rail clawing his red hair out of his eyes the better to scan the distant sea. Seeing nothing, he started striking matches, instinctively setting his beard on fire and having to put his head in a bucket of water to douse the blaze. But the brief conflagration had served its purpose; far off in the sea-mist a pale light blinked, and as he coughed and spluttered and threw away clumps of burned hair, Firebeard was able to cackle triumphantly:

"'Ere they be, Calico! Good dogs! Brave boys! They'm dead on time, wi' a curse, say I, an' that! Unless," he added doubtfully, "it's some bloody fool as we don't know on, playin' about wi' lights unauthorised an' wanton! Eh?" Rage suffused his unwashed features. "I'll tear him, I'll kill him, I'll cast anchor in him!" he was starting to rave, until a curt word from Rackham sent him lumbering below, where he blundered about among the hammocks whispering: "We have lift-off! Rise an' shine! Rogues on deck, honest men stay where ye are! Get your cold feet on the warm floor! Up and at 'em!"

In a trice his accomplices among the crew had piled out, pulling on their socks, hunting for their combs and tooth-brushes, adjusting their eye-patches, and scampering silently up the companion, while the honest sailors turned over drowsily muttering: "Shut that bloody door! Is that you up again, Agnes?" and the like, before resuming their unsuspecting slumbers. Up on deck the little knot of rascals received Rackham's urgent whispered orders, and scuttled away to seize the arms chest and guard the hatchways, the tardier spirits among them goofing off and tying knots in the rigging to make it look as though they were working. Firebeard blundered up last, to report "All villains roused an' ready, by the powers, d'ye see, Calico camarado, aarrgh like!" and Rackham despatched him to the mast-head to deal with the look-out. Firebeard panted busily upwards, taking several wrong turnings along yardarms and getting his leg stuck through futtock-shrouds, lubbers'-holes, and possibly even clew-lines, before he arrived at the crow's-nest to hear from within fevered mutters of "Pot? Tea? Gin? It's another flaming misprint, that's what is is!" Firebeard sandbagged the look-out smartly, snarling "Take that, ye bleedin' intellectual!" and hastened down again to join Calico Jack who, grimly smiling, was at the rail watching Black Bilbo keep their rendezvous.

Out of the mist they came just as the first glimmer of sun topped the eastern horizon – three fell shapes o' doom and dread, surging in on the hapless merchantman. First, the rakish corsair galley of Akbar the Damned, its great steel beak aglitter, the green banner of Islam aloft, its oars thrashing the water as the drivers flogged the naked slave-rowers and rounded up those who had nipped aft for a quiet smoke. Its deck crammed with swarthy, bearded rovers of Algiers and Tripoli, flashing their teeth, brandishing their scimitars and getting their spiked helmets caught in the rigging, the galley was a fearsome sight to Christian eyes, and hardly less disturbing to Buddhists or even atheists. And naught more fearsome than the dark, hawk-faced, hairy-chested figure of Akbar himself, lounging on his stern-castle in gold lamé pyjama trousers, his forked beard a-quiver as he munched rahat lakoum proffered by nubile dancing-girls, his fierce eyes glinting wildly as he practised cutting their gauzy veils in two with his razor-edged Damascus blade.

Secondly came that gaily-decked galleon of evil repute, the *Grenouille Frénétique*, or *Frantic Frog*, flagship of Happy Dan Pew, French filibuster, gallant, bon vivant and gourmet, who was given to dancing rigadoons and other foreign capers as his vessel sailed into action. Clouds of aftershave wafted about his ship, whose velvet sails were fringed with silk tassels in frightful taste, its crew of Continental sea-scum lining the rails crying "Remember Dien Bien Phu!" and "Vive le weekend!" as their graceful craft seemed to can-can over the billows with élan and espièglerie.

[In fact, Happy Dan Pew wasn't French at all. His real name was Trevor O'Grady from St Helens, but he had been hit on the head by a board-duster while reading a pirate story during a French lesson, and his mind had become unhinged. From that moment he suffered from the delusion that he was a Breton buccaneer, but since he spoke no French beyond Collins' Primer, his crew had a confusing time of it.]

Third and last came Black Bilbo's ghastly sable barque, the *Laughing Sandbag* – he was last on account o' he bein' barnacled, d'ye see? Or, in the rather coarse expression of the time, his bottom was foul. Consequently Bilbo was in a rare passion, stalking the poop, inhaling snuff and pistolling mutineers with murderous abandon. He couldn't bear being second to Happy Dan, who had pipped him for Best-dressed Cut-throat o' the Year.

As his fellow-rascals brought their ships in against the ill-fated *Twelve Apostles*, Calico Jack snapped to his small band of villains, "Down and take 'em, bullies!" and with glad cries of 'Geronimo!' 'Carnival!' and 'After you!' they raced below to overpower anyone who happened to be around – crewmen who were still in the focsle ringing for their coffee, or had gone to the bathroom, or were doing their early morning press-ups. Having disposed of these, the pirates stormed howling to the stern of the ship, recklessly disregarding the 'First Class Passengers Only' notices, and bursting into the cabins without knocking. Thus:

Captain Yardley stared at his chart, in which a thrown knife was quivering beside his pencil point; ere he could so much as cry out a despairing "Belike!" pirates were jumping all over him, binding and gagging him, untying his shoe-laces, giving him a hot-foot, and playing with his set-square and compasses. His discomfiture was complete.

Admiral Rooke awoke to find an apple being stuck in his open mouth, and Firebeard's shaggy countenance leering down at him yelling: "Breakfast in bed, milord, har-har? Nay, then 'ee'll make a rare boar's head, wi' a curse! Haul him aloft, give him the message, do him the dirty, wi' a wannion, by the powers, har-har!" And as the unfortunate Admiral was secured, gasping and choking, Firebeard began to break up the furniture.

What of our two bright boys? Blood, seasoned in alarms, was rolling out of bed, sword in hand, even as the first pirates came ramping in yelling: "Surprise, surprise!" He blinded one with hair-powder, kicked a second in the stomach, crossed swords with a third, and then, having weighed up the odds, dropped his weapon and raised his hands, automatically reciting: "I'll-come-quietly-officer-but-devil-a-cheep-ye'll-get-out-o'-me-till-I've-talked-to-a-lawyer." Thus tamely did the rascal chuck up the sponge.

Not so across the passage, where a flashing-eyed Avery was holding crowds of desperadoes at bay with his whirling blade, jumping on tables, swinging from chandeliers, throwing chairs at their shins, knocking over candlesticks, and swathing his attackers in torn-down curtains. It couldn't last, of course; it never does. They bore him down, cursing foully (them, not him, he never cursed), and he struggled vainly in their brutal grasp, his hair becomingly rumpled, his shirt slightly torn, and the teeniest trickle of blood on his determined chin. But his eyes gleamed undaunted; by Jove, they'd better watch him.

Down i' the foetid orlop an exultant Sheba was being unchained by the little Welsh pirate, who had also brought her a fresh wardrobe so that she can be properly attired for the big confrontation scene on deck, which comes in a minute. She hurled aside her loathed fetters, gnashing with delight, and the little Welshman modestly looked away as she donned her scarlet silk breeches and shirt, buckled her diamanté rapier at her hip, drew on her long Gucci boots, exclaimed at the state of her coiffure, clapped on her plumed picture hat, dabbed a touch of Arpège behind her ear, and then spent ten minutes selecting one long earring and applying her lipstick. Finally, with a curt "Tidy up!" to the little Taffy, she strode lithely up the companion, pausing briefly at the full-length mirror in the gun-crews' recreation room, to adjust her hat fractionally and turn her voluptuous shape this way and that, wondering if she had lost weight during her captivity. A pound? Pound and a half? Mmh, maybe not . . . still . . .

She was brooding about this when she stepped into the cabin passage, to meet a bawling Firebeard, who had bagged Rooke's coat and wig, thrown on any old how, and was kicking in doors just for laughs. He swung her up in his hairy arms, yelling:

"She's all ours! Ho-Ho! We'm masters o' the ship, look'ee, and Bilbo an' t'others be layin' alongside, shiver me timbers! Har-har! Tear 'em up, bully boys! Sick 'em, pups!"

"Put me down, you walking tank of pigswill," hissed Sheba, "and if you've got spots on my new outfit I'll carbonado you! And get that drunken rabble on deck!" She pointed imperiously at Firebeard's mob who were looting and rampaging and writing graffiti on the walls and knocking the tops off bottles. They cowered before her flashing eyes, knuckling their foreheads and belching guiltily, and Sheba scorched them with a look before pirouetting neatly to the last unopened cabin door. She flung it wide, and –

Lady Vanity sat bolt upright in bed in a froth of lace, gold ringlets, and confusion, blue eyes wide, ruby lips parted, eye-lashes fluttering like net curtains in a high wind. She was distraught, astonished, and envious all in one at the brilliant spectacle of Sheba swaggering in, a hateful smile on her proud lips, one fist poised on a shapely hip as she gloatingly pondered the petrified English rose. What an absolutely stunning colour combination, thought Vanity – lipstick not *quite* the right shade, though, but what else could one expect? . . . and then she saw the monstrous Firebeard rolling and goggling in the doorway, and squealed with indignation.

"How dare you come in here without permission? Leave at once, you inferior persons! Underlings! Peasants! Savages!"

"Savage! That's me!" howled Firebeard gleefully, drumming his chest with his fists. "I'll show ye savage, me little honey-flower! Har-har!" And he rushed lustfully towards Vanity, great mottled hands outstretched, but Sheba, whose hips were not just for decoration, body-checked him elegantly as he galloped past, and he went flying in a tangle of shattered furniture and lay there roaring. Sheba stalked past him to a table where fruit and sweetmeats o' Peru were temptingly piled, and crammed handfuls into her mouth, for prison rations had left her with that between-meals feeling, and she wanted to restore that pound-and-a-half without delay. Vanity shrieked with outrage.

"Put that down this instant! Oh! How dare you, you insolent black wench! Those are my personal goodies! Put them –"

And she scrambled out of bed indignantly, only to be met by a well-aimed squashy fruit, and staggered back, tripping and falling into the embrace of Firebeard, who crowed with unholy joy, pinning her arms and pawing and nuzzling lasciviously. "Wriggle away, me plump little dove!" he chortled.

"Split me, but ye'll coo soft enough presently!" And it might easily have been X-certificate stuff then and there (always assuming that Firebeard, not overbright at best and in a confused state after his fall, had been able to remember what to do next), had not Black Sheba, gulping a final avocado and wiping the juice on Vanity's costly coverlet, kicked him sharply in the groin.

"Drop it, thou whoreson randy old badger! She's not for thee – yet. Take her on deck!" And she turned her attention to Vanity's dressing-table knick-knacks while Firebeard, muttering "Coo-o-o!" and holding himself painfully, hauled his struggling captive to her feet as she beat dainty fists on his matted chest.

"Let me go! Ah, unhand me thy vile clutches, reeking knave! Oh, the indignity! That this should happen to me, Deb of the Year and daughter of an Admiral! Eek! My jewels – put them down, thief!"

This last was addressed to Sheba, who was proddling with her rapier in Vanity's jewel-box, sneering at the merchandise but privately thinking that these Society bitches did all right on Daddy's allowance. With one vicious sweep of her blade she sent box and all in a glittering cascade across the room, and stalking menacingly over to Vanity, thrust her dusky face to within an inch of that pale peach-blossom complexion.

"*Your* jewels, sister? Pah!" Sheba's voice was like oiled gravel. "You have no jewels, tender little lady – no perfumes o' price, no fine garments, no dainty kickshaws and furbelows – none!" Her sword swept Vanity's scent-flasks away in splinters, and slashed great rents in those hanging dresses which Sheba had decided were too short in the sleeve anyway. "And soon," the sepia nemesis chuckled evilly, "shalt have no body, neither . . . and no soul! I see you use Helena Rubinstein's pasteurised special," she added, "but I'll find a home for that, since you won't be needing it. Take her away!"

For the first time Vanity's intrepid spirit quailed. "Not the Helena Rubinstein!" she quavered. "You can't get it these days . . . ah, of your pity, dark and sinister woman, not that! The line's been discontinued . . ."

"Don't I know it?" growled Sheba, scooping up the precious pots. "Haven't I scoured every boutique in Tortuga? Away with her, Firebeard!"

As Vanity, wailing piteously, was dragged out, and Sheba was sizing up a suede number by Balmain which might just do if it was let down a smidgin, the other passengers were likewise being rudely hustled aloft. Blood, an old hand at being apprehended and frog-marched, was murmuring: "Right, all right, fellows, I know the way," as they thrust him up the companion; Avery, tight-lipped and pinioned, came face to face with Rooke, who was still in his night-shirt, leering pirates grasping his elbows. The Admiral was in fine voice, though, damning them for pirate scum and promising to see them quartered and sun-dried; he cheesed it momentarily to inquire of Avery in a hoarse whisper: "Is *it* safe?", and Avery, inwardly cursing this indiscretion, nodded imperceptibly. Not imperceptibly enough, however, for a silky voice cut menacingly in:

"Is *what* safe?"

And there, on the ladder just above them, was the fearsome figure of Black Bilbo, who had come aboard and made straight for the quality's cabins in the hope of finding some Sea Island steenkirks or spray-on talc. He lounged wolfishly, hand on hilt, taking snuff delicately from the case proffered by Goliath the dwarf.

"Now, gentles," quo' he softly, his dark eyes gliding from one to t'other, "what precious item, what thing o' price, is this – that is 'safe', ha?" They remaining silent, Bilbo nodded, making play with a soiled lace kerchief from which, to his annoyance, he realised he had forgotten to remove the laundry tag. "So, so," he hissed, clipping Goliath over the ear for luck, "we shall discover anon. Keep me this bellowing bullock below –" he kicked Rooke savagely "– and hale the fighting cock on deck."

The scene which met Avery's eyes may be old stuff to you if you saw 'The Black Swan', but it was new to him – a helpless merchantman in the talons of the hawks of the sea. Chaps in hairy drawers and coloured hankies staggering about, draped in loot, letting off pistols, getting beastly drunk, singing 'Blow the man down', throwing bottles around, and manhandling hapless prisoners. Firebeard had thrust Vanity sprawling on the deck in her scanty night-rail, to the accompaniment of wolf-whistles and cries of "Hubba-hubba!"; she scrambled up, trying to look haughty, which isn't easy when there's nothing between you and the goggle-eyed rabble except a wisp of brushed nylon and a few ribbons. "Shake it, blondie!" they chorused, and Avery clenched his teeth in fury.

Looking down from the quarter-deck was the stalwart figure of Calico Jack, the barbaric splendour of Akbar, and the slender finery of Happy Dan, who viewed the scene through his quizzing-glasses and exclaimed Froggishly.

"What is what is this what? I am aboard. I look about myself. Zut alors donc! What a doll, that! What talent! Ah, ma chérie, mon coeur est toujours à toi! How about it, hein?" He minced and bowed and fluttered his fingers at Vanity, while Akbar's eyes glowed with strange fires, and Rackham threw up a hand to silence the motley mob swarming beneath – bearded white faces, coal-black Nubians, slant-eyed Chinese devils, swarthy Asiatics, squat and evil Malays – the usual lot on pirate ships in those days. Now among them glided Black Sheba, her glance dwelling darkly on the bound figure of Avery ere she took her place, lounging on a convenient capstan.

"Camarados, brothers!" cried Rackham. "We ha' ta'en this fine ship, and released our dear comrade and fellow-skipper Sheba from durance shameful and doom o' hellish slavery! (Cries of 'Hear, hear!', applause, breaking of bot-

90

tles, and an attempt by the little Welsh pirate to lead a chorus of 'We'll keep a welcome in the valleys'.) And we ha' ta'en also captives o' rank and quality – a Lord Admiral, no less –" Yells of hatred and blowing of raspberries, with Firebeard bawling: "Hang him up! Rip his guts out! He's an honest man – I hate him!" He rolled on the deck in a frenzy of rage, and the pirates cheered amain. Bilbo sauntered forward, sporting his shabby finery, his tight boots squeaking painfully.

"All in good time, lambkin," quotha. "But, by y'r leave, Brother Rackham, I ha' matter to impart to the company. (Cries of 'Order, order!' 'Chair, chair!'.) I learn that there is some precious 'thing' aboard this vessel, and that this –" he flicked a tiny poniard from his sleeve so that it quivered in the mast by Avery's ear; a shocking show-off, Bilbo was "– fortunate fellow is privy to its whereabouts. Shall we inquire, ha?"

"Aye, aye!" roared the pirates. "Go on, ask him; it can't do any harm."

"Well, bully?" said Bilbo silkily. "What is't, and where, eh? Discourse, friend, and discover. Don't be shy."

This was the chance that Avery had been waiting for. Jumping on tables, pinking adversaries, was all right in its way, but this is the kind of moment he is in the book for, really. His handsome head came up, his contemptuous glance swept from sinister Bilbo to frowning Rackham to swarthy Akbar to epicene Happy Dan, to the ring of hideous snarling ruffians, dwelt softly for an instant on Vanity, beauteously pale, got contemptuous again, and finally settled back on Bilbo with unfaltering disdain. Avery's lip curled, and his perfectly-modulated voice might have been addressing a careless servant as he spoke with the calm good-breeding of his kind.

"Up yours," he said crisply. He had no idea what it meant, but he had heard it hurled at the Moors by an officer refusing to surrender one of the Tangier bastions, and had rather liked the sound of it. Brief, punchy, and definite.

The pirates went bananas at his defiance. They howled round him, hurling vile threats and making lurid suggestions for his interrogation. A heated debate broke out, the nub being to decide which torture would best satisfy the twin requirements of getting the information and providing an interesting spectacle. Happy Dan Pew's proposal was finally carried, and a bucket of offal was hurled over the side to attract sharks, while Avery was lowered by one leg from the ship's rail until his head was just above the water racing past the ship's side.

This is a rotten position to be in, and it taxed even Avery's powers to keep up a dignified appearance. He preserved a poker-faced nonchalance, of course, but this was wasted since no one could see it. The spray lashed through his hair, the salt water stung his eyes, and the rope round his ankle burned like fire; up on deck Vanity was swooning on the planks, and the callous villains holding the rope were saying grace. A yell of delight greeted the sight of two hideous dorsal fins cutting the water towards the ship's side, at which point they lowered Avery so that his head and shoulders were immersed.

Our hero was now perturbed. Not on his own account – this, he told himself, as his keen eyes pierced the green murk and detected the great dark shapes homing in on him, was what he was paid three shillings a day for – nay, his concern was all for the fair and graceful figure which he had seen collapsing becomingly when they gave him the old heave-ho. What should become of her, when the sharks had retired burping gently to look for the sweet trolley, and all that remained of him was a sock and a buckled shoe? He must get out of this somehow, for her sake . . . and Captain Avery's eyes narrowed underwater, his lips parted in that grim fighting smile as he observed the horrible monsters rolling neatly to get under him and come zooming up, their enormous jaws parting to reveal serried rows of glittering fangs.

That gave him an idea – he would bite the brutes; it was the last thing they would expect . . .

But even as he prepared to meet them, tooth to tooth, he felt himself suddenly whirled upwards, into the fresh air, just as the first shark leaped and snapped its great jaws close enough to clip his hair. He banged painfully against the ship's side, and then he was hauled brutally over the rail and dropped on the deck, opening his eyes to find a pair of Gucci boots bestriding him, and hear Black Sheba's voice scorching the pirates who yet clamoured for his blood.

"Unthinking dolts! He'll never talk! I know his kind!" And she flashed him a glance in which he seemed to read yearning admiration behind the feral glare of the amber eyes. "But he'll sing like a canary if you threaten his friends!" she added spitefully, and Avery groaned inwardly as the ruffians roared approval and seized on the swooning Vanity with cries of "Now you'm talking! Heave the doxy over! Har-har, here be plumptious titbit for the sharks, wi' a curse, an' that!"

"Belay that!" snapped Sheba, and drawled cruelly: "We'll find a better use for her mealy milksopishness, damn her! No . . . that one!" And she flung out a hand towards Colonel Blood.

You may have wondered what the Colonel was doing during all this excitement. Looking inconspicuous, that's what, and wondering how he could pass himself off as one of the pirate gang. Even now he tried to look puzzled, glancing over his shoulder to see whom Sheba meant, but it was no go. They whipped the rope round his ankle, bundled him protesting on to the rail, and were about to launch him when he found his breath and wits together.

"What's the hurry, now?" he wondered. "Let's talk it over, boys . . . don't do something ye'll regret."

Firebeard, gripping the Colonel's shoulders, hesitated, growling and rolling his eyes. "What was it you were asking, now?" inquired the Colonel, and Avery, in sudden alarm, cried from the deck: "No! Blood, you cannot! You must not!"

"Och, be reasonable," said the Colonel, slightly exasperated. "D'ye expect me to be a fish's dinner for the sake of your bloody crown?"

Since the answer to that was 'Yes', but it isn't the sort of thing that any self-respecting hero can say, Avery was silent, but the glare he shot at Blood would have curdled minestrone. His first instinct had been right – why, the blighter *was* a blighter, after all; when any decent chap would have been spitting in their eyes with a dauntless smile, he was actually perspiring shiftily and demanding:

"If I tell ye, will ye spare our lives?"

The pirates growled, disappointed of their sport. There were cries of "Yes!" "No!" and "Toss for it, best out of three!", and then Rackham came shouldering through the press to confront the desperate Colonel.

"Speak," said he bluntly, "and the sharks can go hungry."

It wasn't total reassurance, exactly, but when you're perched on a ship's rail with Firebeard giving you the benefit of his halitosis and the jumbo-sized piranhas waiting underneath, it's worth stretching a point. "Under the bunk in his cabin," gasped Blood, nodding at Avery, and as the Captain's furious gaze took on a disgust so icy that it almost froze the sea-water in his hair, Blood added philosophically: "Ye see, Captain, where I come from there are no heroes' graves – just holes in the ground for fools."

You may imagine the indignant rage that boiled through Avery's manly thorax at this caddish cynicism, but it was nothing to the shame and anguish he felt when the Madagascar crown was exposed in all its brilliant effulgence on the deck, and the pirates, after a moment's stunned silence, stood around exclaiming "Hot tamales!" and "Jackpot!" and "You won't pick up one o' those at Woolies!" while their leaders regarded the unbelievable glittering prize with racing thoughts. For each realised that this was the Big Time, with a vengeance – to Akbar, grinding his molars and tugging his forked beard, it was the bankroll that should buy him his way to supremacy in Barbary, perhaps even to the throne of the Sublime Porte itself; to Bilbo, as he clenched his soiled kerchief in nervous fingers, it was that estate in Bucks, a seat in the Lords, and – oh, rapture! – membership of the Army and Navy Club; to Rackham, slightly pale under his tan, it was a fortune invested in Building Societies with enough over to start a modest pub; to Happy Dan Pew it was a villa at Antibes, his own permanent private suite at the Negresco, and a custom-built coach with tortoiseshell panels rolling him along the Croisette while starlets from the Comédie Française vied for his attention; to Black Sheba it was her own private desert island plantation where all the enemies and oppressors of her past should labour in misery and torment while she lived it up in Balenciaga creations (this was her fondest dream, and with a start she realised that it now included Captain Avery, in powdered wig and buckled shoes, taking her in to dinner and exchanging glances of adoration with her from the other end of their sumptuous table). To Firebeard, the sixth of those desperate commanders, it conjured up visions of unlimited booze, wrecked taverns, senseless constables, and shattered fruit machines – and the wherewithal to impress that snooty barmaid at the Bucket of Blood in Tortuga, the blonde one with the big knockers.

And then the fight started. With one accord the pirates flung themselves on the marvellous trophy, clawing and biting to be at it, and if Rackham had not kept his head and hurled them back with boot and fist, aided by Bilbo's flashing rapier and Firebeard's enormous strength, things might have degenerated into anarchy. Back the captains drove them, a snarling, loot-crazed mob, and Rackham set the great gleaming crown on the capstan and demanded of the captives what it might be.

Avery, of course, preserved a glacial silence, but Blood, at one growl from Firebeard, sang like a bird.

" 'Tis the crown for the new king of Madagascar. He was to deliver it –" this with a nod to Avery "– and if ye've any sense you'll offer it for a ransom to the British Government rather than try to flog it on the open market. I'd be willing to act as go-between myself, for a consideration," he went on smoothly. "After all, I've got contacts and that sort o' thing –"

But the pirate mob would have none of this. "Shares! Shares!" they roared. "Fair does among mates! Divvy out, we're all on the coupon!" and Rackham raised his hands to still the clamour.

"Brothers, hear me! We share, according to articles, but 'tis plain we cannot divide this great treasure among all at once. Now, there are six captains here, and six great crosses on this crown – so let each captain take one and be responsible for selling it and sharing among his followers. Agreed?"

The pirates whooped approval, and Avery watched in horror, writhing helpless in his bonds, as his precious charge was laid on the deck and a huge Chinese, wielding a massive axe, chopped it with six mighty strokes into as many glittering pieces, while the gleeful buccaneers chanted:

"One! Two! Three! . . ." at each blow. Then, as Firebeard turned his back, the Chinese held up each cross in turn, and according to age-old custom Rackham cried out: "Who shall have this?" and Firebeard named the captains in any order that occurred to him, beginning with Sheba and ending with himself. So each captain received a cross, and their crews crowded round, wolf-eyed, to handle the pretty baubles and gloat on the prospect of their own shares.

Avery watched the scene appalled; it occurred to him that the recapture and eventual safe delivery of the crown – which had never been far from his active mind – was now going to be rather complicated. However, he would come to that; in the meantime, could he gnaw through his bonds, or cut them on a bit of the broken bottles which the pirates were strewing carelessly all over the place, seize the half-fainting Vanity in one arm and a sword in the other, fight his way aft, release the captured loyal seamen, and turn the tables on the villains? It seemed the obvious course – yes, and then they could hang the treacherous Blood, and no doubt a dab of Airfix would put the crown to rights, and Admiral Rooke would probably recommend him for a decoration, and Vanity would be wide-eyed and weak-kneed with gratitude, and the whole affair wouldn't do his promotion chances any damage, either. Yes, he was thinking along the right lines – but before he could put his plan into operation the pirates, having gloated their fill and finished off all the drink, forestalled him by remembering that there were prisoners to play with. With cries of "Let's sort out the helpless captives!" "Aye, aye, let's fall to merry torturin' an' that!" and "Who's for a gang-bang wi' the Admiral's daughter?" they advanced on the hapless trio.

Naturally, they concentrated on Vanity, who shrank back in terror from the bearded leering faces and lecherous paws while Avery struggled like a madman in his bonds, but before their sweaty hands could tear away her shortie nightdress and confront the censor with all sorts of problems, Black Sheba had slipped lissomely between, one hand outflung to restrain them, the other on her rapier hilt.

"Hold!" cried she, and before the command in those fiery amber eyes, the hardened ruffians paused. As Goliath the dwarf, with a chortle of "Bags I first!", made a grab at Vanity's thigh, Sheba kicked his wooden leg from under him and sent him sprawling on the deck. "Calico, I claim disposal o' this woman!"

At this there was hubbub and amaze, in which you may well be sharing. What is this? Has womanly pity touched the agate heart of the ruthless corsair queen? Is she moved by finer feelings to shield Vanity from shame and ravishment? Perchance has some memory from her own dark past – as when she was the star attraction of 'Strip, Strip, Hooray!' at the Port-o'-Spain Rotary stag night, and the patrons rushed the stage at the torrid climax of her bubble dance before she could escape to the wings – stirred her compassion for the defenceless English maid? Don't you believe it. Baser motives far were at work in Sheba's evil heart. She had remarked the distraught looks of anguish and concern that Avery had been shooting in Vanity's direction, and had thought: aha, so he's got the hots for Miss Cheltenham of 1670, has he? Right, we'll fix her wagon. And reasoning that the satisfaction of seeing her rival ravished by the crews of three pirate ships would be better foregone in the interests of getting the insipid pullet out of the way permanently, thus leaving Sheba a clear field with Avery, the sepia Medusa had hatched a diabolic plan.

She fronted the frustrated pirates imperiously, while the tremulous Vanity clutched her flimsy nylon about her and wished she'd gone in for sensible long flannelette.

"Back, blind besotted curs!" snarled Sheba. "You can't all have her – why, 'tis pampered, puling ninny would die o' the vapours wi' the first of you! But –" and her eyes narrowed in a cruel smile "– all can share in the price if we sell her!" She jerked Vanity brutally to her feet and held her in a steely grasp while she stroked a dark finger across the girl's soft cheek. "Think what the rich rajahs and fat degenerates will pay for such a plump white pigeon in the slave-marts of Basra or Goa! You know how they go for Bluebell Girls – she'll fetch enough to buy each of you a real wench, not some flabby reserve for the Upper Fifth tennis team. Let Akbar take her and sell her on behalf of us all!"

Prolonged applause greeted this monstrous proposal, and Sheba turned with a triumphant sneer to run mocking fingers through the ringlets of the horror-stricken prisoner.

"Try that on your clavichord, duchess!" she hissed spitefully. "Golden Vanity – pah! We'll see how you enjoy your slavery!"

If aught had been required to cement Avery's adoration for the Admiral's beauteous daughter (and frankly, not much was), it would have been her response to Sheba's gloating taunt. Her face pale but proud, her bosom heaving with hauteur in a manner which caused some of the pirates to wonder whether selling her was such a bright idea after all, Lady Vanity countered with a swift one-two. "Among slaves I shall still be a lady," she cried proudly. "Among ladies you will always be a slave!" Even the callous ruffians could not forbear to chant their approval of her dauntless spirit. "One in a row, boo-boom!" they cried, while Sheba sprang clawing to avenge the insult. But Akbar, with a hellish laugh, had already swung Vanity's struggling form up on his shoulder, and bore her swiftly to his galley while Avery went ape, alternately cursing his captors and demanding that they sell him in Vanity's place. They pointed out, reasonably enough, that he was down-market stuff by comparison.

"An' anyways, we got a better use for you, cully, an' ye may lay to that!" bawled Firebeard. "What say we keelhaul him, mates? It's ages since we had a good keel-haulin' –"

But again Sheba barred the way. "Avast there, blubber-guts!" She paced slowly to Avery, thoughtfully plucking her nether lip 'twixt shapely fingers. "This King's captain is too good a man to lose – 'tis lad o' rare mettle has earned the right to join us as a free companion, if he so chooses. That – or slow death," she added, with a look of smouldering ardour at Avery that would have melted treacle. At which the pirates nudged each other and stifled discreet coughs, glancing innocently at the mast-heads and whistling airily. Happy Dan Pew sniggered and grimaced froggishly.

"Great round basins behind the house of Monsieur and Madame Desgranges!" exclaimed he, all roguish-like. "One addresses to oneself the question: what companionship does La Belle Noire have in mind for our prisoner so stalwart and gallant, hein? Is it to make the promenade au bicyclette in search of cabbages, jewels, small pebbles, and stained-glass windows? Not on votre vie, if you ask me!" And he minced and chuckled lewdly, while Rackham frowned 'neath knitted brows and glanced from Sheba to Avery.

"Well, bully, what say ye? Wilt join us on th'account, ha?"

Avery was on the point of replying coldly that he would rather be shot from a cannon, but it occurred to him that there was no point in putting ideas into people's heads, so he maintained a contemptuous silence. Not so Blood, who clamoured to join, inquiring eagerly about pension rights, sickness benefits, and overtime. They shushed him impatiently, crowding round Avery with menace in their looks, while Sheba gnawed her lip in anxiety and tensed herself to spit the first man who laid a finger on him. It was one of those explosive moments when eyeball rolls at eyeball and wills clash in ponderous confrontation and no one has much idea what the hell is going to happen next because they've forgotten what the question was in the first place. Rackham, that canny leader of men, read the situation in one shrewd glance, and moved to defuse it.

"Right," quo' he, "break it up. We'll give him a few hours to think it over. Not fair to rush the chap. Put 'em both in irons – and then let's get sail on this rust-bucket afore she grows barnacles! About it, ye dogs! Firebeard, man the larboard scuppers! Bilbo, have thy villains lay aft the focsle! Sheba, your mascara's running! Happy Dan, write out the verb être six times before lunch, and the rest of you for heaven's sake join in the chorus!"

These sailorly words acted on the fractious pirates like magic. In a trice they had hustled Avery and Blood below decks, swept up the broken glass, clewed up everything in sight, and repaired to the Merino Lounge for before-lunch cocktails while they discussed the exciting events of the day so far. Only Black Sheba brooded sombrely on her high stool at the bar, and many there were who remarked how she was moodily squeezing that pink pimento stuff out of her martini olives, and wondered what this might portend.

> *Well, it's all happening, and no mistake. Our principals are right in it. Will Avery join the pirates? (Don't be daft, of course he won't.) But what then? Will Sheba's unholy passion for him provide the twenty-four hour all-round body protection that every young executive needs? Will the insurance company pay up on the Madagascar crown? Will Lady Vanity's purchaser be able to get her a work permit? It's all very worrying.*

CHAPTER
THE SIXTH

It was really rotten down i' the foetid, stinking, dim-lit orlop, where timbers creaked and rats scuttled, etc. Blood and Avery had been fettered wrist and ankle to facing bulkheads, which was uncomfortable enough, but to make matters worse the cleaners hadn't been in, the straw hadn't been made up, or the scuppers hoovered, or the bilges refilled, and there wasn't any Kleenex left. To cap it all, the pirates had taken over the ship's intercom, and instead of the normal hymns and rousing sea shanties, the muzak now consisted entirely of dirty drinking songs illegally taped from Radio Tortuga. Avery bore it all in stoic silence, the chaotic mess of his tortured thoughts concealed 'neath a cold, imperturbable mask, but Blood griped incessantly; it was just like these swindling foreign tour operators, he said, to grab your money and then forget you existed; he should have read the small print when he came aboard, and so on, and so on, until even Avery's icy control snapped in one bitter denunciation of his fellow-captive.

"Hear ye, fellow," said he, and each acidic word was like a blade rasping from its sheath, "wouldst be better employed making peace with thy beastly soul, for mark me, when this hand o' mine is free again, its first task will be to wring the putrid life out of thy mangy carcase –"

"What the hell are you going on about?" demanded Blood. "Is it my fault we're stuck down here?"

Avery's eyes flamed like 1000-watt icebergs. "Base renegade, fink, and traitor —"

"Traitor?" exclaimed Blood. "Me? Oh, for God's sake, ye haven't got your galligaskins in a twist over the measly crown, have ye? As if that mattered — they'd ha' found it sooner or later, and if you'd had your way we'd have been nothing but a couple of shark's belches by now. Which," he added unhappily, "is what we're liable to be anyway, unless you can sweetheart that big spade wench into a happier frame of mind."

"D'you think I care a jot for that — or even for the crown?" Avery's voiced quivered like a trampoline with noble indignation. "Aye, though shame, ruin, and disgrace may be my merited portion, forasmuch as I have goofed up my mission and let the side down — what can I think on but my dear Lady Vanity?"

"Well, if it's any consolation, go ahead," said Blood. "Although what I always say is, there's a time to fantasize about blondes and a time to think about getting the hell out of the mess we're in, and I'd advise the latter —"

"I didn't mean think on her in that way, ye carnal muckrake," snapped Avery, his teeth clenched. "Have you no conception of what her fate will be, in the clutches of yon Moorish hellspite? Of what —" and his voice grew all roopy with apprehension "— it may already have been? You know what such heathen do with Christian women captives. You've read the colour supplements?"

"Oh, aye," said Blood carelessly, "'Au pair milkmaids trapped in harem hell', and 'I was a sex-crazed sultan's plaything'." He shrugged callously. "When all's said, it's just what happens to any married woman on her honeymoon. I daresay she'll be well looked after . . . three square meals a day, and that . . ."

At this point they were interrupted by the little Welsh pirate who, in his capacity as shop steward of the local branch of the Amalgamated Brotherhood of Piratical Operatives and Filibusters and Allied Trades, was eager to see Avery enrolled in that powerful offshoot of the Coast Brethen. His overtures our intrepid captain received with a befitting silent scorn which the suspicious Taffy immediately misinterpreted.

"Them other bastards been gettin' at you, isn't it?" he demanded. "Them from the CBI (Co-operative Buccaneers International) an' NUPE (Nautical Union of Piratical Employees), eh? You don't want no truck wi' them, boyo – the CBI's just a neo-fascist gang of boss's blacklegs what'd sell their bourgeois souls for so-called alleged professional status an' a couple of expense-account noshes at the Nombre Dios Hilton. Don't think, comrades," he went on with fine vehemence, "that we don't know what goes on – back-handers from colonial governors and free week-ends at Defoeland and the Gallows Beach Country Club in return for alleged so-called productivity deals negotiated in direct and flagrant disregard of democratic decisions taken at focsle-floor level an' ratified in congress by card vote. Oh, we know! We may just be ordinary workin' cut-throats, but we're not bloody stupid, look you!" He was really going now, full of pithead passion. "An' the other lot's just a long-haired bunch o' Trotskyite hippies an' so-called alleged students engaged in subversive activities which our union execattive 'as condemned as totally counter-productive at this moment in time an' diametrically opposed an' prejudicial to the basic interests of true loyal grass-roots piratical workers. You got no idea – at the intakin' o' Panama we couldn't get near the Dons' barricades for this unwashed rent-a-mob with their banners: 'Red Rory Must be Reinstated' an' 'Young Socialist Filibusters say No to Inquisition Brutality'. Bleedin' troublemakers – an' half o' them on drugs an' all. Now, brother, if you was to enroll wi' our shop . . ."

And such was the magnetic power of this little enthusiast's oratory that Avery and Blood dropped off peacefully in their shackles and slept soundly while he discoursed,

104

all unaware that up on deck big things were happening . . .

The pirates were putting Admiral Rooke and the honest men over the side in small boats, to the accompaniment of the gloating jeers and taunts with which they were wont to revile castaways on such occasions: "Captain Rackham and his crew bid you God speed on your journey to the nearest port of call, which is about a thousand leagues off roughly in that direction. We would draw your attention to the safety leaflets pinned to the thwarts, and to the life-jackets under your seats. The emergency exits are located all round the gunwales. For your comfort and safety we advise you to row like hell and keep clear of cannibal-infested islands. Smokers please occupy the seats on the port side . . ." It was like the knell of doom to those unfortunates as they huddled in their frail craft, clutching their pathetic bundles containing toothbrushes, clean underwear, packed lunches, and Customs forms; Admiral Rooke, his face grey with fatigue and anxiety, shuddered as he gazed down on them as they fought for possession of head-sets. How could he hope to bring this sorry band safe across the trackless waste of sun-scorched tropical ocean on half a pound of yams and a pannikin of water a day, and not so much as a sea-sick pill among them? But he braced himself like the stout old salt he was, and with his foot on the ladder he flung a last defiance at the sneering scoundrels who crowded the rail in the hope of seeing him slip and do a belly-flop into the water.

"Thou vile pirate out of hell," growled he to Rackham. "If I have to swim home, yea, through seas o' blood, yet shall I live to see thee swing and rot at Execution Dock. Aye, every foul mother's son of you – and that includes daughters, too", he added, turning his enflamed eye on Sheba, who lounged, lissom as a great scarlet cat, on the rail, swinging a booted leg and idly tossing up and down in her gloved palm the jewelled cross which was her share of the Madagascar crown. The Admiral's ruddy cheek blenched at sight of it, and his dentures rattled in dismay.

"What ha' ye there?" gasped he, wi' staring eye.

"Recognise it?" mocked Sheba. " 'Tis from the gewgaw o' price with which your gallant Captain Avery was entrusted. Aye, stare away, dotard – your fine captain was not so brave and loyal after all." And she bared pearly teeth in railing laugh which curdled with dread the Admiral's circulatory system. "He betrayed it to us – along wi' your daughter's honour – as the price of his life."

"My daughter?" exclaimed Lord Rooke. He'd known there was something he'd meant to ask about, but what with one thing and another it had slipped his mind. "What, hell-cat? What o' my daughter? What hast done wi' her? My child, my sweet Vanity – where is she?"

"Think it over on the long voyage home," chuckled Sheba spitefully. "It'll help to pass the time." And with her foot she spurned the Admiral from his hold into the boat, and minced off, well pleased with herself.

So while the boats pulled away, with the pirates crowing "Bon voyage!" "Drop us a card from Antananarivo!" and "Give my regards to Broadway!" Sheba slipped the precious cross into her pocket; her exchange with Rooke had been another step in her diabolic plan to enwrap our hero in her unholy toils, and now she was ready to apply the final touch. Pausing only to freshen her lipstick and dab a touch of Prince Matchabelli behind each ear, she made her way down into the bowels of the ship.

Thus it was that Avery and Blood, snoozing peacefully in their fetters – although the little Welshman had long since departed in a huff – were awakened by the intercom playing a sultry version of 'Big Spender' with throbbing bongo accompaniment, and Avery opened his eyes to find Sheba regarding him with hot, smoky orbs, one hand poised on her hip and the other holding a pannikin of water.

"Thirsty?" she breathed huskily, but though his parched lips yearned for the proffered snifter, pride forbade that he should accept it from this evil virago. He averted his head in a marked manner.

"The time has come," continued Sheba in her soul-singer contralto, "for you to choose. Speak – will ye be one of us, a free companion, a liberated spirit o' joy and youth, a hellfire roaring boy owing service to none and duty to naught but your own sweet will, roving as ye list, seeking as ye choose, taking whatsoever ye wish . . . and, believe me, junior," she added throatily, swaying closer to give him the full benefit of the Matchabelli and drooping her eyelids in wanton invitation, "I mean whatsoever . . . Will ye take all this," she crooned, "or . . . ?" She left it unfinished, her dusky face within an inch of his, lips parted as she awaited his answer with dilated pupils.

"Not a chance," said Avery crisply. "I think your proposal is perfectly beastly, and if you had the slightest notion of good taste you wouldn't make it. I can't call you a cad, because you obviously aren't, but whatever the female equivalent is, you are it. Your behaviour to Lady Vanity – an innocent young lady who had done you no harm – puts you quite beyond the pale, and the same goes for your frightful brotherhood. I wish you a very good afternoon."

"Can I say a word?" said Blood from the opposite wall. "I'd just like ye to know, miss, that I don't associate meself with—"

"Hold your tongue!" snarled Sheba, but her eyes never left Avery's face. "Oh, fool and ingrate, what else is left to you? Death – why, even in England they'd hang you – the man who betrayed his mission. That's what they'll believe! Rooke believes it already! You can never return – never!"

"I don't believe you for a minute," said Avery icily, his finely-chiselled nostrils flapping in scorn. "And even if I did, it wouldn't make the slightest difference. It would merely add a minor task – that of clearing my good name – to the programme I intend to accomplish as soon as I have won my freedom from this pestilent ship. That is – one, to rescue Lady Vanity; two, to recover all six pieces of the Madagascar crown, stick it together, and see it safely delivered; and three, to arrest you and your associates and turn you over to the authorities. And that, dusky beldame, is that." And he surveyed her with calm disdain; if he had had a hand free he might have politely stifled a yawn; as it was, he curled his lip just a trifle, and almost burped.

Sheba felt her knees turn to water. What a man was this, to scorn her in the face of death, and talk as though his escape and vengeance were a mere matter of course! She couldn't let this one off the hook, she just couldn't. And he couldn't be insensible to her allure – no male between fourteen and ninety ever had been, and she wasn't intending to let this one get into the Guinness Book of Records as the first. She heaved her bosom with a passion that almost did Avery an injury, and seized his face in her hands.

"You big gorgeous dope!" she hissed fiercely. "Don't you understand? It's either join us or pop your clogs! I offer you not only life, but love! Don't you know what that means? Bliss and ecstasy beyond all imagining – wealth, power, infamy, the seas your empire, the world beneath your foot, and me in a leopard-skin track suit! Why, think of the seasons that ye may see, when ye shall sing and swear, drink and delight, sack cities and slaughter men as your cake-makers do flies, revel in the spoil o' nations, have monarchs and governors suing at your knee – and I, ever at your side, to transport you, delight you, attend your every whim, and always, always, love you!" She panted hungrily at him, and Blood made little whimpering noises and jangled his fetters in frustration as he watched and listened. "You shall rule this Brotherhood," Sheba murmured, "another Morgan, another Drake, another Douglas Fairbanks – yet greater than all these, a king of the world – and I, your queen and slave!"

And just to make sure he got the idea, she kissed him

volcanically, giving it her best shot, and not coming up for air until she felt sure that he must be thoroughly anaesthetised. Then she withdrew, her eyes hopeful behind fluttering lids.

"You've been eating onions," said Avery calmly. "I think I shall have that drink of water after all."

His disinterest was unmistakeable. In fact, he had found her embrace almost as disturbing as the first time, but now he knew her for the fiend she was, and by concentrating his thoughts on cricket, chamber music, and dill pickles, had again succeeded in remaining immune to her sensual charms. It had been a near thing, but the cold baths he had taken every day since childhood had paid off in the end.

Sheba was thunderstruck. It couldn't be true – she, the unchallenged sex symbol of the Caribbean and Indian Ocean, who had been offered (and rejected) the loot of an entire plate fleet to pose for the centrefold of *Mariners Only*, whose likeness adorned every locker-door 'twixt Portobello and the Philippines – she, given the brush by this . . . this . . . this . . . nay, even in her mortification she could not regard him as other than the ultimate dream dragon, rot him. But it was passing strange . . . could it be that he was bent? Nay, for he had shown the most ardent interest in that pink and white cream-puff Rooke – and on the thought the fierce sea-queen yowled with jealous rage, for here was the explanation of his coldness. She gnashed her perfect teeth in fury, and quivered in such frenzy of hate that her blouse creaked under the strain.

"Right!" she grated venomously. "Shalt find what it means to spurn me, rash youth! Of all the crust! Oh, but ye shall rue this day, thou insensible pillock! Sheba does not offer twice!"

And with that she turned on her heel, strode to the door, and there turned for a last gnash at the adored object.

"Er, miss," said Blood hopefully, "if ye've a moment, I'd just like to say that I've been listening most carefully to what you were saying to that unnatural an' ungrateful birk of an

Englishman, yonder, and if ye'd consider me as a substitute, why, I'd be more than happy to—"

"One more peep out of you," said Sheba balefully, "and I shall have you lightly garnished with breadcrumbs and brought to a crispy golden brown in a moderate oven. After which we'll feed you to yourself, and you'll eat up every scrap. You read me, Paddy?" Her basilisk glance strayed from the thoughtfully-frowning Irishman to Avery, lingered on him with a last, passionate yearn, and then froze to cruel implacability. "Ye both go to the Dead Man's Chest in the morning," she concluded, and stalked out, leaving them to ponder on that enigmatic threat. The Dead Man's Chest, eh? It didn't sound good – but then, as Blood gloomily reflected, it probably wasn't meant to.

You are probably as mystified as they were. After all, no one who has ever read *Treasure Island* is quite sure whether the Dead Man's Chest was a seaman's portmanteau or the torso of a corpse (which in the context seems unlikely). In fact, the Dead Man's Chest is an extremely small island, little more than a sandbank i' the limpid tropic ocean, and it was thither that Avery and Blood were taken next day, to be done to doom in fashion curious and lingering. For the pirates of those days were nothing if not spectacular in fatal invention; where you or I, if we wanted to dispose of an enemy, would simply blip him over the head or butter the stairs, the Coast Brethren got up to dodges you would hardly believe, like leaving tarantula eggs to hatch out in his tea cosy, or suspending him face down over the dreaded *maguay* plant, which has a nasty sharp point and grows two feet overnight (eek!), or chaining him in an underground cellar with the tide coming in which slowly raises a burning candle inch by inch until it smoulders through a rope from which dangles a glittering blade which falls to break a phial containing acid which eats through the lock of a boxful of black mambas. (The incoming tide will probably drown the brutes, but it's the thought that counts.)

Anyway, the pirates had devised an absolutely beezer way of giving people the business on Dead Man's Chest, as witness the crooked, weather-beaten crosses with which the long sandspit was sprinkled, each marking the grave of some unfortunate who had perished there. While their ships rode the gentle swell offshore, the pirate captains lounged around the spit, watching as Blood and Avery were prepared for their demise. All was peaceful save for the lapping of the creamy surf, the cry of seabirds overhead, the squeaking of Bilbo's boots, and the excited chatter of Happy Dan Pew rehearsing his homework: "Ah, we find ourselves au bord de la mer. What jolly! Regardez la plage magnifique, ou Marcel et Denise jouent souvent, avec les buckets and spades, les donkey-rides, et le ice-cream! Où sont les jolies mam'selles en bikinis formidable, hubba-hubba . . . ?" and so on, what time Black Sheba prowled hard by, hand on hilt, her troubled gaze straying ever and anon to Avery, seeking some last sign that e'en at th'eleventh hour he would weaken and sign on the dotted line. Why, oh why, hadn't she *worn* her leopard-skin track suit for that last interview in the orlop, instead of just talking about it? That would have reduced him to steaming clay in her hands. Too late now; he might have been made of stone as, calm and resolute, he awaited his fate.

He and Blood had been brought face to face, each with his left hand bound tightly behind his back. In the free right hand of each a rapier was now placed, hand and hilt being swathed in a tight bandage so that in no way could either drop his weapon. Finally, to each right wrist was secured a hawk-bell, which tinkled musically at the slightest movement. Avery underwent all this with well-bred indifference, but Blood raised the roof with protests and Irish wheedles. All to no avail; the pirates simply grinned and ignored him. And now came Rackham, grim o' visage, a massive figure in his spotless white.

"This be Dead Man's Chest, look'ee, where two may

come but only one goes hence," said he. "If ye want life, a' must fight for it, t'other against each."

"Suppose we won't fight?" asked Blood brightly.

"Why, then, bully, we bury you alive, right delicate," purred Black Bilbo, as he made dainty play wi' lace kerchief. "Does it like thee better – to stifle, ha, to suffocate i' shifting, slithering, choking sand, head down wi' feet a-waggle, most comical to see? If so—"

"All right, you've made your point," said Blood hastily, and Avery curled contemptuous lip. "You'll fight, renegade," quo' he, "and die better death than thou deservest, on decent steel."

"Attaboy!" croaked Firebeard, and leered at Blood. "He don't like you, matey. Vindictive, he is."

"We leave a boat, a puncheon o' water, and a loaded pistol for the survivor – if there is one, and he can get loose," said Rackham. "Goliath – put the hoods on 'em!"

And before our boys knew well what portended, tarred sacks had been slipped over their head and made fast about their necks, so that they stood in musty darkness, armed but helpless, while the pirates fell about with cruel delight at their predicament.

"You can't see, but you can hear the bells," said Rackham. "And remember – no hitting on the break, no talking in the clinches, no butting, and may the more meritorious contestant emerge victorious!"

Rough hands seized the two, as with raucous cries of "Roundabout, roundabout, roundabout mouse, up a bit, up a bit, in a wee house!" the pirates spun them to and fro and then released them to stagger blindly about the spit, their bells jingling. Almost simultaneously they pulled up, and stood listening for the sound of each other's bell; Avery's tinkled softly, and Blood immediately lunged, but since he was fifteen feet away and facing in the other direction, no business ensued. Then Avery made a sudden slash at empty air, and Blood, catching the jingle, rushed in his direction, but tripped and plunged headlong in the soft sand. Avery spun round and fell in his turn, and as they both scrambled up, by chance their blades met with rasp and slither, and they both lashed out at random, in opposite directions, thrashing about in the sand.

The pirates loved it, bawling with laughter and holding on to each other at the antics of their hapless prey. Even Black Sheba, concerned as she was for Avery, could not repress a smile as he came academically on guard, extended himself in a perfect lunge, and fell slap into the surf. Blood meanwhile was stumbling around, blaspheming horribly and tripping over one of the grave crosses. The callous ruffians egged them on and laid bets, but presently their sport was marred, for a sudden gust of wind ruffled the water, and there was general alarm as it was seen that the sea was getting up, while black clouds darkened the sky overhead. In a trice the pirates were into their boats and rowing for their ships, Sheba casting one last regretful glance where her dream man was sloshing about in the shallows, demanding in muffled tones that Blood should stand and fight like a man. Since Blood was twenty yards away, trying to use his hopelessly-swathed rapier hand to get his hood off, and having no luck, Avery was wasting his breath; it never occurred to our hero to try to remove his own hood, of course; that would have been cheating. Besides, the pirates had done their work too well.

Eventually they started prowling the spit in search of each other again, with mixed results. It was grim work, though – just put a bag over your head and try it. It's hot and stuffy, and the rustle of the material fills your ears, you can't see a thing, and somewhere close by a malevolent stinker is flailing about with three feet of razor-sharp steel. Not nice. And when you do hear his bells jingle, you haven't the foggiest notion where the sound is coming from. Twice they actually blundered into each other, and flailed away at random, without result; then Blood took to crawling on his stomach, the skunk, jabbing fiercely in the hope of hitting Avery in the ankle. But this proved most uncomfortable, so he gave it up, and thereby precipitated the crisis of their deadly blind man's buff.

"I'm just about sick of this!" he said, and added several horrid oaths. Muffled though they were, they came to Avery's finely-tuned ears, and he froze where he stood, waiting to catch the sound of the Irishman's next movement. Sure enough, there was the soft rustle as Blood climbed painfully to his feet, hoarse breathing somewhere to Avery's left, and more naughty words – swear away, rakehell, thought our Ben, t'will be your undoing. Very cautiously he turned, trying not to jingle, but as he slowly raised his hand for a desperate blind lunge the bell tinked softly, and Blood let out a yelp of panic and thrust out any old where. By sheer fluke his point ripped into Avery's hood, the Captain fell back blinded by the sudden light as the canvas was rent before his eyes, Blood's steel drove past within an inch of his face, and then Avery had sprung away, jerking his head to free it from the torn canvas.

Behind him Blood was whirling about, lashing in all directions with futile bellows of "I can see you! Stop trying to hide, it won't do you a bit of good!" and finally losing his balance yet again. Avery waited until his opponent's frenzy had subsided, and then said quietly:

"Blood . . . it is I who can see you. I can kill you when I please."

Blood leaped like a nervous ferret, away from his voice, and stood panting, his bagged head a-twitch this way and that. "Pull the other one," he said at last. "That's a right sneaky public-school gambit, that is. Ye want me to believe you, an' beg for mercy, and give my position away. Well, it won't work, me bucko, for devil a word will I say, and ye can go jump in the ocean with your dirty, underhand—"

Avery slapped him hard across the bottom with the flat of his blade, and Blood yelped and sat down.

"Now d'you believe me?" said Avery. "That's my point,

at your throat." And he touched Blood lightly beneath the Adam's apple. The Irishman started, and then he seemed to go limp as he sat in the sand.

"What d'ye want me to do then – congratulate you?" he said wearily. "Go on – get it over with." He sighed heavily. "So it ends here. Aye, well; if I've lived dirty I can die clean. Make it quick."

Well, he wouldn't fool you or me, but the crafty rascal knew that in Avery he was dealing with Simon Pureheart, and that there wasn't a dog's chance that the other would take advantage of him, especially if he sounded game and penitent simultaneously. And sure enough, Avery was impressed. Cad though Blood might be, he was evidently prepared to take his medicine like a man; the chiselled visage of our hero quivered slightly, and softened like toasting marshmallow. He could no more have smitten his helpless foe than he could have wiped his nose on his sleeve; it just wasn't in him. He sighed in his turn, and did the decent thing – he cut Blood's left hand free, and a moment later the Colonel was tearing off his hood and regarding Avery with an uneasy, wolfish grin. For Avery, with his left arm still bound, would be hopelessly unbalanced if Blood chose to renew the combat. But before the Colonel could make up his mind, the Captain had turned to him a back on which confidence and imperturbability, and just a hint of disdain, were writ large.

"And now," said Avery coolly, "you may release me in turn."

"May I now?" said Blood, and his grin became wicked. "Ye're mighty trusting. What's to stop me running you through for the soft-hearted fool ye are?"

"Don't talk rot," said Avery briskly. "I am the hero, and my survival is essential. You don't suppose that you can stab me in the back on page 115, surely? The ludicrous notion!" And he laughed lightly.

"Couldn't I, though?" said Blood, with sinister softness, and for a moment Avery's blood ran cold. "Oh, it would be unconventional, I grant you – but it would be interesting, and by God, haven't ye been asking for it, just? I'm not so sure," he went on, laying his point gently in the small of Avery's back, "that your survival's all that necessary."

"And who else, pray, is capable of rescuing Lady Vanity and bringing those pirate villains to condign punishment?" inquired Avery impatiently. "Come, sir, make haste."

"Well, I might make a stab at rescuing the delectable lady meself, now," mused the rascally Colonel. "She'd be grateful, devil a doubt, and so would her old Dad – and he's a warm man, they say. I might find meself a cosy little billet—"

"Lady Vanity wouldn't look at you," snapped Avery. "For one thing, you're a bounder, and for another – you lack attraction. Your hair is receding, and I happen to know that she considers you pathetically old."

"Old?" squawked Blood. "I'm twenty-nine, damn your skin! Well, thirty . . . three. Anyway, I don't bloody well have to rescue the choosy little bitch—"

"You wouldn't know how. And I advise you to refer to her with respect."

"– she can rot in some randy rajah's harem for all I care. I'll do all right on my own!"

"Without me to rescue you from your present predicament?" Avery's shoulders were a picture of contempt, and the back of his neck radiated amused scorn. "You don't know where you are; I do. You can't sail a small boat across shark-infested, trackless seas; I can. You aren't fighting fit, disciplined, intrepid, and (decently) resourceful; I am. Now get on with cutting me loose – I'm getting pins and needles."

It was gall and wormwood to that knavish soul, and Blood cursed quite a bit, but of course he had to give in in the end. For one thing, he wasn't *really* rotter enough to stab a helpless man – like Captain Hook, he had his own warped ideas of good form, and he realised that it would be the height of poor taste. Also, he had considerable doubts about his ability even to row a small boat, let alone navigate it. So, with the best grace he could muster, he cut Avery free, and once they had got the bandages off their respective sword-hands, Avery reviewed the situation. Far off, on the horizon, the pirate ships were disappearing under the stormy sky; they might be, he remarked regretfully, beyond immediate pursuit.

"And they can stay that way for Mrs Blood's favourite child!" snapped the Colonel. "We're well rid o' them. That Sheba!" And he shuddered at the thought.

"But they're not rid of me," said Avery quietly, and Blood read in the intrepid set of his chin, the hard calm of his clear grey eyes, the stern purpose of his clear brow, the resolute tension of his knees, and the implacable poise of his armpits, a grim determination which was awesome. "Those knaves have filched away mine honour quite. So much is clear from the words of that diabolical black female – Rooke thinks I turned stool-pigeon over the Madagascar crown, and that I betrayed his daughter, don't ask me how. I must clear my name, and that means rescuing Lady Vanity ere shame and horror befall her, and getting back every piece of that sambo's tiara. To that end, I, Benjamin Avery, R.N., hereby dedicate myself. I'm going after those scoundrels single-handed, and by George they won't know what's hit them." And he strode down to the small boat on the shore.

Blood cried out in alarm. "You're barmy! You're going to go solo after the whole Coast Brotherhood? Hold on, son; listen to your uncle." And he laid a restraining hand on Avery's impassioned wrist. "Look, we've got the boat – an' you being a dab hand, we can get to some fairly civilised port. Right? Well, I hate to remind you, but Lady Vanity's probably up to her pretty ears in shame and horror already, and anyway you don't know where they've sent her. Basra, Goa, who knows? As for the crown, what are insurance companies for? Dammit, it's in six bits – you can't hope to find 'em all, let alone recover them! I mean, try asking that bloody

Firebeard! Or that supercharged Eartha Kitt! Jayzus! Now, let's you and me just take it easy –"

"Faugh!" cried Avery. "These are the counsels of a poltroon!"

"Dam' right they are," agreed Blood warmly. "And I'll tell ye something else – they work."

"Stand aside, sir," said Avery grimly, and started rummaging through the boat. His seaman's eye assured him that she was seaworthy, and that, as Rackham had said, she contained a keg of water and a loaded pistol. Little enough, but sufficient for such as our intrepid captain. But what was this? – under the stern seat, a small box, which on being opened proved to contain a compass, Baedekers for the Barbary Coast, Indies, and Spanish Main, Good Food Guide, tooth-brush, nail scissors, ship's biscuit, great store o' boucanned beef, flask of Pimm's No 1, bandages and iodine, credit cards, and a bar of Sunlight soap. Pinned to them was a note in a sultry, smouldering hand, and Avery's eyes narrowed as he read:

Oh Blind, Oh Foolish, Oh Beloved,
      I hope you are keeping well, and that the weather continues fine. I write these lines – and enclose them wi' store o' necessities for your voyage – in the confident hope that you will easily master the creature Blood (whose death, as I trust, was slow and painful, tho' not as choicely anguished as I would ha' contrived, given the leisure), and that your valour, god-like intelligence, and other super-duper qualities will bring ye to a safe haven wi' all despatch. Give up all hope of succouring that finishing-school milksop Vanity; she is beyond all aid, and lost to you forever, and good riddance. 'Tis my belief she pads her bra, but no more o' that; she is kaput, so forget it.
      My heart and body yearn for thee, thou gorgeous beast, but I will not sue nor plead. My dark star tells me

we shall meet again, 'on another island, farther on', as we o' the Brotherhood do say, and when that time comes, thou shalt be Sheba's, and she thine. Oh, pray it may be soon, soon, soon! You haunt my dreams, my skin prickles at thy imagined touch, my lips thirst for thee, I'm off my food, and if this goes on much longer I'll look an Absolute Wreck! Oh, fly to me, barracuda baby, that I may rain kisses on thee as I do on this insensate paper!

     Yours sincerely,
     Sheba the She-Wolf
     x x x

"Well, how d'ye like that, the vindictive hussy!" said Blood, who had been kibitzing. " 'Creature Blood', forsooth, and what did I ever do that she wants me took off painful-like?"

"I could almost pity her," mused Avery, his marble brow clouded. "Poor, deluded savage, it may be that she is more misguided than evil – after all, who knows what her environment was like . . . under-privileged, wrong side of the tracks, no school lunches, parents divorced I shouldn't wonder. She may have had a cross nanny." His perfectly-sculpted lips tightened. "But her conduct to my darling Vanity – ha! that I can never forgive her, never!"

"Well, she's done all right by you," remarked Blood, eyeing the box of goodies. "God knows why, after the way ye spurned her in the orlop, an' her climbin' all over you. Tell me," he went on curiously, "don't ye find her just the littlest teeny-weeny bit attractive? I mean, she's a human cobra, we all agree, but – physically, now? Doesn't she get through to you at all?"

Avery looked mildly surprised. "She may be comely enough, in a darkish way, I suppose. I had not marked it. She has a certain . . . how shall I put it? . . . a certain . . ."

"Baaahhhrrrooomph?" suggested Blood.

". . . a certain bodily presence, I was about to say." Avery shrugged. "And, as you say, she seemed eager to attract my notice. But then, all women do, I cannot think why." He frowned, and crumpled the note, which Blood automatically trousered. "But it shall naught avail her. She goes into the slammer with the others, and to such retribution thereafter as her crimes deserve. Right – help me launch the boat."

"Thou artn't still intent on thy rash design?" cried Blood in alarm. "All that codswallop about going after Murder Inc. single-handed, I mean – ye've thought better on't?"

"I have said, and I shall do," replied Avery coldly. "But fear not for thine own precious skin, fellow – I crave not thy company, and if so be a convenient port lies in my way as I pursue these foul knaves, I shall happily be rid o' thee. Or you can stay here and wave your vest at passing ships." And he busied himself about the boat.

"You're bananas!" roared Blood. "Not the full shilling! Harpic! Ye great English goon, you haven't a prayer. You can't take on that mob . . ." And for some reason, in a slightly lame voice, he added: ". . . alone."

Avery glanced at him, and Blood leaned on the thwart, head down, and heaved a great sigh. Then he looked up, as at a wilful child, and shook his head, with that sorry crooked Irish grin of his, and while he looked there seemed to be borne to them on the wind the soft strains of that stirring wild sea-march that you know of old, which signals the moment when the rogue, old in craft and knavery, says farewell against his better judgment to selfish sense and cynical reason, and casts his lot for the nonce with Honour and Gallant Enterprise – not from conviction, but because his bold, contrary spirit cannot resist the call of venture and romance, for what is life without them? So with the music growing in his ears, Colonel Blood shook his head again, as one who marvels at his own folly.

"Aye, me," he sighed. "Look you, now – ye're a likely

lad, Ben Avery, and a canny man of your hands, I'll give ye that, but damme, ye just haven't got the kind of sin and experience for the dirty work that lies ahead of you. What you need is the help and guidance of some bloody rascal who knows the wickedness of the world and who'll see ye safe through it, more or less – not out of the goodness of his black heart, because he hasn't any, and he'll play ye false now and then, devil a doubt, but just for the hell of it – and a share of the profits, if any. Well . . . what d'ye say?"

He stood waiting, while Avery regarded him steadily – not with any softening of those finely-chiselled features, not with a hint of a smile, but after a moment he nodded, and if you had seen him you would have liked him better than at any time so far. Whatever doubts he may have felt, he concealed them, and in that moment there was nothing priggish about Captain Avery.

"Help me shove her off," was all he said, and they ran the little boat down over the shingle and into the surf. And then they were standing out to sea, with the music a-thunder in a rousing crescendo, their tiny craft riding the salt waves in the sunlight, spray lashing bracingly all over the place, Avery bursting full of high endeavour, and Blood beginning to wish he hadn't come.

Thus they set out on their desperate journey together (as you always knew they would), but of what befell them thereon is, as Mr Farnol would say, yet to tell. For . . .

Here endeth Book the First of
THE PYRATES

And there's no lack of good stuff on the slate for Book the Second, with our Beauteous Heroine to be rescued from her Unspeakable Fate (and if it's the first time she's faced it, you can bet it won't be the last), our Stalwart Hero's good name to be cleared, Villainy to be pursued wi' stern resolve and given its lumps, and six bits of crown to be recovered, where'er they are. Mayhap our Dauntless Duo will have to seek them in hair-raising exploits in all sorts of bizarre locales – Sheba's hideous Gothic castle on Octopus Rock with its infamous watercress dungeon, Rackham's shark-surrounded island lair (wi' that fatal and voluptuous adventuress Anne Bonney, whee-whew!), the steamy dens o' Madagascar, lost jungle cities where ethnic minorities practise their weird rites, the dank torture-chambers o' the hellish Inquisition (wi' a curse!), and so on. The options are wide open – cannibals, mad castaways, suave and evil Dons, poisoned darts, flashing-eyed señoritas, crashing cannonades, oodles of treasure, wild native princesses in feathers and fruit hats, dungeons, escapes, betrayals, rescues, and any amount o' swordplay (sa-ha!), boozing, singing, loving, good fellowship, an' be damned.

But the moon is up, the stars are bright, the tide's on the turn, the snail's on the thorn, and Book the Second awaits. We shall bring ye to the Treasure House o' the World, and (as a famous real-life pirate once said) blame yourselves if ye go away empty-handed.

BOOK
THE SECOND

CHAPTER
THE SEVENTH

Lovely boating weather,
Bilge on the tropic breeze,
Swing, swing together
With your fetters between your knees.
Let's hear it for Akbar!
His galliot never leaks,
We'll all swing together,
And swear by the best of sheikhs!

he dismal wailing of the lash-scarred slaves toiling at the oars of Akbar the Damned's infernal galley drifted down the night breeze, broken only by the crack of the overseers' whips and the occasional gasping cry of 'Well rowed, Balliol!' and 'Roll on the outboard motor!' from the parched throats of the rowers. It carried but faintly to the shell-like ears of Lady Vanity, as she sat in the great stern cabin, proud but palpitating, submitting to the ministrations of the eunuch hair-dresser who was preparing her – ah, well she knew it! – for the loathsome embraces of Akbar himself. He was upstairs somewhere, splashing on the Brut, oiling his beard, and humming "I can't give you anything but love, baby" in the *lingua franca* of the Barbary Coast, what time he gnashed his magnificent teeth in anticipation of the treat in store. (From which you will be relieved to gather that nothing untoward has happened yet,

125

but a glance at our heroine will inform you that it won't be long now; Akbar's hand-maidens haven't dressed her in those see-through harem trousers and gauzy bra for a walk in the park.)

So little wonder that Vanity shuddered as the eunuch fussed with comb and rollers. "Oo, I don't know what butcher last had his hands on this lot, love," he piped despairingly, "but he must have cut it with a knife and fork! It would make you sick – I daren't *think* what the boss'll say, and him that particular when he ravishes Christian maidens! He'll go mad. Hang on while I get me setting lotion . . ."

With a moan of fear Vanity started up, her ivory fingers (now alluringly a-glitter with barbaric jewels) flying to her parted ruby lips as she caught sight of herself in the full-length mirror. She stared, at once terrified and fascinated by the perfection of her own milk-white beauty, so ill-concealed by the flimsy Oriental finery. What man could resist her, she reflected hopelessly, least of all that great, swarthy, magnificently-muscled, flashing-eyed predator with his amazing hairy chest and superb shoulders and sexy forked beard . . . ? For a moment her blue eyes misted as she considered her shapeliness, turning this way and that as she pushed back her golden tresses, pouting and undulating in an absent-minded way as she murmured: 'Fry's Turkish Deli-ight . . .' ere the hideous reality of her plight returned, and she sank to her silken couch like filleted bream. Oh, why had not Nature made her thin and knock-kneed and spotty? If only she had bloated herself with chocs and milk-shakes like the other girls! But then Captain Avery, her wonderful, God-like lover, would scarcely have remarked her, let alone vowed his undying passion . . .

"Ah, wretched me!" she repined through pearl-like tears. "That peerless beauty which captured my true love's boyish senses undoes me quite, for now it must enflame the feral passion of that randy bedouin in the spiked hat! Oh, Ben, dear heart, haste to me, and for pity's sake get the lead out of your pants, or 'twill be too late . . ."

Did that virgin prayer float down the sea-wind to her lover? Probably not, and he wouldn't have heard it anyway, not half a mile off, and with Blood whingeing at him in the dark. But he was there, just the same, his keen eyes like silicon chips as they scanned the murk ahead. News picked up from a passing betel-juice tanker, and the tell-tale jetsam of used date-packets thrown overboard by the corsairs, had put him on Akbar's track; all day had he piloted his frail craft in the wake of that sinister hull barely seen on the horizon, and now that night had fallen, and the galley's pace had slowed, with the corsairs doling out their meagre measures of Horlicks to the wretched slaves, Long Ben Avery was racing in, wi' helm a-weather and molars gritted, determined to snatch his beloved from the clutches of Shameful Captivity or die i' the attempt.

"And ye know which it'll be, don't you?" protested Blood for the umpteenth time. "Hast lost thy marbles quite? We don't stand a prayer – devil admire me, man, there must be six hundred angry wogs on that galley if there's one, and we but poor two! Look, let's get sensible, and do it diplomatic like – notes to governments and U.N. resolutions and things –"

"Cheese it, Colonel," was Avery's crisp rejoinder. "Thy clack untimely stirs my just contempt. Look rather to the powder keg and fuse, for therein lies our chief hope to surprise these infidels and effect my dear one's enlargement."

"And a bum idea if ever I heard one," snapped Blood, rummaging in the gloom for the keg which Avery indicated. "All right, ye say ye've done it before – but not, let me point out, with an Irish engineer striking the matches. Which end of the fuse do I light?"

"Hist! What see ye yonder, i' the loom o' night?" cried Avery, and flung out a pointing finger in a gesture supremely dramatic, barking his knuckles painfully.

"That's our mast," said Blood caustically.

"Beyond, I mean! See there!" hissed Avery, sucking his fingers, and sure enough, through the darkling gloom shone the light from a great stern window, where the galley glided slowly ahead of them. Zoom quickly in and through the window, and we find Lady Vanity backed against the panelling, pale but peerless, trying to cover herself up with cushions, what time the swarthy Akbar, feasting hot eyes upon her, locked the door and advanced licking his chops, his Christian Dior gold medal bobbing passionately on his gleaming naked chest.

"Shalt bring a fair price from some lucky man in Basra," he growled, leering. "But first thou'rt Akbar's, aye –"

"Another step and I call the conductor!" cried Lady Vanity proudly. "Get lost, thou foulness! I want the British Ambassador –"

"Fix not thy hopes on him," snarled Akbar. "He doesn't go for blondes." And with cat-like speed he pounced, sweeping her into his embrace, his hot breath causing her golden locks to stream backwards from her ivory brow. "Aye, flutter thy soft pinions as thou wilt, little dove," he crooned hatefully. " 'Twill make for better sport." And chuckling cruelly, he rained burning kisses on lips, nose, chin, throat . . .

It's a matter of split seconds now, but the Marines have arrived, all unsuspected, making fast their boat 'neath the galley stern, jamming the powder keg under the rudder, Blood swearing and clicking his lighter at the fuse, Avery swinging up the chains like a startled marmoset, rapier clenched 'twixt flawless teeth, the light of battle in his eye and the taste of Brasso in his mouth. An instant he paused under the sill, while Blood panted up behind him.

"Wait – I've got a better idea!" hissed the Colonel. "Why don't we buy her? You know, make 'em an offer—"

A scream of mortal anguish rent the night like a steam whistle, the cry of a lost soul in the very abyss of agony and despair. Vanity had given Akbar the knee in a vital spot, and the proud scourge o' the seas was rolling on the carpet, clutching himself and gasping for the trainer. Then, with a cry of "Remember the Alamo!" Avery had surged through the window, rapier a-whirl, found he was in the wrong cabin, apologised blushing, and darted through a communicating door to the main saloon where the action was. All of which had given Akbar nice time to hobble painfully to his feet, select a convenient scimitar, wince with a ruptured oath as he straightened up, shoot a reproachful glance at Vanity, bawl for the guards, and cross blades with Avery as the latter bounded in roaring: "It's cutlasses now, men!"

Blood, following more cautiously, paused to blink appreciatively at the wide-eyed Vanity, slipped a protective arm round her waist, and got his face slapped for familiarity. He would have protested, but at that moment the powder keg exploded under the rudder, blowing half the bottom off the galley, and causing some confusion. Akbar and Avery were fencing away like crazy, jumping on the furniture, exchanging defiant remarks like: "Your sands are run, Muslim beast!" and "You've come to Nottingham Castle once too often!" (no, sorry, wrong period, but you get the idea). To and fro they stamped and slashed, Akbar gnashing desperately, for his constitution, undermined by dancing girls and rahat lakoum, to say nothing of the crunching low tackle from Vanity, was no match for the finely-tuned agility and perfect timing of his clean-living opponent. Furthermore, Akbar's curved scimitar, while ideal for thrusting round corners in a crafty, Oriental way, was ill-suited 'gainst the straight and trusty British blade (from Toledo, actually). While his minions pounded on the locked door, shouting: "Was there something, oh Falcon of Islam?" and "Last call for second sitting," Akbar fell back, sweat pouring down his face and chest and playing havoc with his carefully-applied deodorant. Avery, his blade the usual ubiquitous whirling menace, pressed his advantage, his ears beautifully poised on either side of features which were a superbly-sculpted mask of virtuous determination, and flung an order over his shoulder, not bothering to see where it landed: "Look to the lady, ho!"

Blood, who was trying to convince an indignant Vanity that there was no impropriety in giving her a fireman's lift, paused to view the lightning play of his companion's blade.

"That's it, boy!" cried he approvingly. "Take no nonsense from him, Ben; you lay on. And now, mistress, if ye'll kindly—"

"Take your clodhopping paws off me!" snapped Vanity, who had no intention of being rescued by a supporting player. "Help him, can't you? See, he is sore beset!" For Akbar, heartened by the fact that his corsairs were now beating down the door, had made a last furious effort. His gold lamé jeans stretched to the limit, his scimitar hissing in a glittering arc, he hurled himself on Avery; a shriek from Vanity, a slither and clash of blades whirling like egg-whisks, and our healthy Anglo-Saxon caught the scimitar on his forte, extended himself in a beautifully academic lunge, and sent his point through the corsair's sweaty, reeking, hairy chest. Akbar's face contorted appropriately, the scimitar fell from his nerveless hand, his forked beard quivered in its death agony, and with a strangled cry of "God, that hurt!" the great sea-wolf o' Barbary sank lifeless to the floor and began to mess up the parquet.

Vanity cried "Eek!", Blood said smugly, "See, what did I tell you?", and Avery, wiping his ensanguined blade with a sternly compassionate tissue, pronounced the swordsman's traditional valediction on his fallen adversary.

"Well, Brian, what can I say except that without good losers we wouldn't have worthy winnners, would we? I didn't know our friend on the floor all that well, but he certainly contributed to the extremely sporting contest we've had here tonight, heathen muckrake though some might call him, but this isn't the time for recriminations, is it? He did his best,

130

and I had what luck was going, I suppose, although I honestly felt I was fitter and better-trained than he was, which I owe to my old school and all the people who had confidence in me. I suppose that's about all, really, except to say I'm just sorry we can't have a re-match . . ."

His manly oration was interrupted by half the cabin floor falling in, with a raging inferno of smoke and flame surging up from the doomed vessel. Pausing only to abstract Akbar's piece of the Madagascar crown from the in-tray on the ormolu-encrusted desk, Avery sprang to the window, where Blood was supporting the swooning Vanity.

"Why d'ye tarry, man?" cried Avery. "Into the boat, for our lives!"

"What boat?" snarled Blood savagely. "You and your powder-kegs! 'We'll disable the pagan villains,' sez you. Pity it didn't occur to you that in blowing their stern off we might just blister the paint on our own little Skylark. 'Tis sunk in burning shards, wi' a wannion, and we trapped like mice on fiery hulk as shall presently founder—"

"Dash it!" said Avery, his noble brow momentarily furrowed, the ruffles on his shirt quivering with anxious excitement. His keen glance raked the water, where amidst the fiery wreckage the corsair crew were taking to the lifeboats, clutching their suitcases and six-packs of sherbet, calling on Allah and gesticulating wildly, tearing their hair, falling in the water, and doing all those things which well-trained extras do on abandoning ship. For Avery, it was money for old rope to wait until one boat drifted beneath the stern, drop into it with athletic grace, disperse the occupants overboard with a few straight lefts and karate chops, volley a crisp order to Blood, catch the falling Vanity with one hand while holding the tiller with the other, set a course, unfurl the lateen sail, tramp on the fingers of various fellaheen clutching at the gunwales, and gaze back fearlessly at the burning hulk behind them while Blood, who had fallen in the water and dragged himself aboard sodden and spluttering, laid hold of the oars and pulled for dear life. Thus, with Vanity disposed gracefully in the stern-sheets, and our hero soothing her marble brow with a sock dipped in sea-water, his calm voice calling "In – out, in – out," to the labouring Blood, the little boat glided smoothly beyond the glow of the doomed vessel and into the shielding tropic night, while the despairing cries of the shipwrecked corsairs faded behind them . . . "Bismillah, I knew that curry was off!" "It's a Zionist plot, mark my words." "Peace, brothers, what is written is written; it is kismet." "Kismet, my foot! I don't care if it's Chu Chin Chow, I'm shipping with P. and O. next time . . ."

Later, 'neath waning tropic moon, with balmy zephyrs stirring Vanity's golden tresses and whistling through her gauzy trousers as she lay in the embrace of Avery's muscular right arm, while his muscular left one managed the tiller, and he furled the sail with his foot, our lovers discoursed fondly on this wise:

AVERY: So, one villain down, five to go. As go they shall—

VANITY: Not tonight, thanks. I'm pooped. Incidentally, what kept you? Writhing i' the hated embrace o' swarthy ravisher, I thought you'd never show up.

AVERY: Nay, sweeting, we came wi' all despatch. But now all's well – see, I've copped back Akbar's chunk of the crown, which is what really matters, since 'tis first step to clear my good name, fulfil my mission, and regain th'esteem of my superiors.

VANITY (with a slight edge): Dah-ling, I seem to remember talking to you about priorities before. I mean, aren't you just a teeny bit pleased that I've been saved from a rather indelicate fate? He wasn't exactly a male model, you know.

AVERY: Nay, fond heart, how could I be other? Without thee, all is naught. I just meant that until I've mopped up these rotters, recovered the whole crown, and squared myself with your old man . . . well, how should I aspire to thy beauteous hand, if mine honour and credit were still leaking at the seams?

VANITY: That's more like it. Convince me by forgetting my hand for the moment, and concentrating on these my soft, parted lips.

AVERY: Oh, bliss! (Embracing her with enthusiasm)

BLOOD: Anyone care to take a spell at the oars?

AVERY: (ecstatically): Mmm-nymm – mmhh . . .

VANITY: (slightly muffled): Oh-h, rapture . . .

BLOOD: Ah, the hell with it, what's the use?

Anon, when the adoring duo had kissed their sweet fill, and Vanity was restoring her make-up, what time Blood opened a tin of corned beef and sulkily set out plates, Avery outlined his plan of campaign.

"As I judge from the stars, we are precisely seven and three-quarter leagues east-nor'-east of Libertatia, on the coast of Madagascar . . ."

"Well, I hope there's a decent hairdresser, but I'll bet their dress-shops are the pits," pouted Vanity, twitching at her scanty finery. "And I can't go home like this. Look at me!"

"Any time," leered Blood, buttering biscuits.

"Another fresh crack like that," snapped Avery, "and you can start swimming. Nay, fondest love," he continued to Vanity, "we touch not at Libertatia, which is notorious nest of vile pirates and related sea-scum. For that matter," he added, "I don't suppose they've got a hairdresser worth a hoot, and for raiment 'twould be strictly off-the-peg at the ship's chandlers. It behoves us to slip by and set course for the Cape, there to set thee ashore to await arrival of thy father and those with him who were cast adrift; 'tis there they'll make their landfall. I shan't come ashore myself, under cloud o' shame and suspicion as I am, but I shall rejoin thee straight as soon as I have destroyed the Coast Brethren and collared the crown. Right? Good. Have some bully and biscuits."

But haughty Vanity tossed her golden head. "And I'm to hang about in some dismal two-star flea-pit, probably without air conditioning and heated swimming pool? Not likely. Besides, who shall say where Daddy has got to by now, cast clueless on the cruel deep? Let's face it, he may be an Admiral, but he couldn't navigate across the bath – the old boy's past it; it may be ages before he blows in."

"But, angel mine," protested Avery, "I can't take you with me, can I? Not into dire peril o' bloody battle and fell mayhem, when you could be snug as a bug at the Cape – the inn probably has a suite with a balcony – and I won't be gone long." Gently he folded her in his arms, her head nestled on his romantically open shirtfront, and gave a confident, ringing laugh which reassured and deafened her simultaneously. "Why, what's to do, when all's said? A mere five stark villains and their few hundred followers to hunt down o'er the trackless waste of ocean, sort them out, collect the loot . . . two weeks' work, perhaps? . . . say three, or a month at most, and I shall be hasting back triumphant to thy side. And a sweet little side it is," he added fondly, giving her bare midriff a chaste and reverent stroke which brought a blush to her maiden cheek and sent goose-pimples rocketing round her shapely frame. What could she do but sigh and submit to his masterful persuasion, and allow him to feed her morsels of corned beef on biscuit. Blood watched them jealously over his dinner; all this Errol-and-Olivia canoodling gave him the pip, and he could guess who was going to get stuck with the washing-up, too. Moodily he listened while Avery outlined his programme.

"I shall deal first with that hellspite Sheba," quoth the captain, and his brows were knit like stern cardigans, "since, woman though she be, yet I judge her most dangerous, cruel, and fertile of evil invention among them all—"

"She's the cutest, too," remarked Blood, taking an artless swig of Oxo. "Black but comely. Yowser!"

Avery wrinkled his perfect nostrils. "You spoke, sir?"

"Oh, I was just after thinking aloud," said Blood maliciously, "that in starting wi' the Ebony Nemesis ye're on a

134

good thing, since wi' her ye may prevail with gentle rather than warlike arts – why, such is her loving regard for you that she may even prove willing ally 'stead of enemy—"

"Babble," said Avery curtly. "Likewise tripe. As I was saying, my adored one, having dealt with the pirate virago I shall next put the mockers on Black Bilbo—"

"Hold it," said Vanity, and Blood noted with satisfaction the faint frown clouding her lovely visage. "What was that crack about her loving regard for you?"

"Pish! I mean, tchah! Sorry about that," said Avery. He waved a dismissive hand. "Nay, 'tis but that the misguided trull conceived a spark of gratitude for that I stopped them lambasting her wi' cat-o'-nine-tails. Ye remember, lamb-kin . . ."

"I certainly do," said Vanity coolly. "I also remember that having boned my cosmetics and made free o' my ward-robe, she couldn't get me off the ship fast enough. So-ho!" Frost formed on her velvety lids as she regarded the captain with eyes like blue pickles. "Strange, too, that when she tipped Daddy and the other loyal hearts over the side, she kept you on the shelf. I wonder why?"

Avery shrugged modestly. "Why, for that wi' my manly address, dauntless bearing, double First, and proved fighting quality, she and her fellows would ha' had me join their company. After all, you don't pick up bargains like me every day. But I am no renegade," he concluded proudly. "I cast the base offer back in their teeth."

"It's a fact," said Blood unctuously. "Indeed, ma'am, he was proof 'gainst all her wanton arts and wiles – aye, though she cast herself panting on him like one distraught wi' passion, and babbled o' love-nests and leopard-skin track suits, yet he spurned her . . . sort of . . ."

Vanity was too much the high-bred English lady to emit more than a "wowf!" in which dismay and jealous fury were nicely blended, but her feminine instinct reached for the rolling-pin. Avery, frowning at Blood, didn't notice.

"Give it a rest," quo' he irritably. "I regarded her not. A poor demented creature—"

"A poor demented 38-24-36!" cried Vanity hotly, and the tumult of her bosom threatened to capsize the boat. "So! The ebony wanton has been pitching her curves at you, has she? That does it. If you think you're going to dump me at the Cape while you go prancing after that sable sexpot, you can think again. I'm coming with you, junior, and you can stick that in your binnacle and steer it!"

"But, love-light, what is this?" Avery was astonished. "I pursue her but to mete out merited chastisement—"

"And don't think she wouldn't love that!" scoffed Vanity.

"But she is nothing to me," protested the captain. "I disdain her quite. Her sleek voluptuousness, her steamy sensuality, her hot advances, the way she swings dem hips . . ." He paused, his pure and serene features wearing a dreamy, puzzled look, and came back to earth with a start. "Where was I? Oh, yes, these fleshly allurements, howsoever they may beguile the lewder sort, are so much cold custard to me, honest. Nay, dear ducks," he continued in fond reproach, "hast no faith, no loving trust, in this thy devoted Ben—."

"Loving trust, phooey, you big idiot!" cried Vanity. "What avails it against sultry bimbos in leopard-skin (or out of it, which she would be with one quick wriggle). That is Competition in big neon lights, and whiles I doubt not thy intended constancy, yet I do know thee for a man, and you're all alike, and it's worse in your case because you're so noble and innocent it hurts. She could twist you round her little black pinkie and you wouldn't even know it was happening!"

So now ensued a pretty lovers' tiff, Avery all virtuous bewilderment, and Vanity (being female) torn between a desire to fling her arms round him and an urge to belt him with some solid object, while Blood watched sardonically the mischief he had wrought, and hogged the tinned pears and chocolate ripple which completed their simple repast. In her vexation Vanity stamped her dainty foot, forgetting that harem costume doesn't include shoes, and got a splinter in her toe, whereon followed rich hockey-field oaths, with cries of concern from her lover, followed by Savlon and plaster and kissing it better. Which soothed her slightly, but not enough to alter her concrete resolve to stick like glue to her betrothed through whatever perils and temptations (chiefly the latter) might lie ahead.

And because Avery was so besotted with her that he could deny her nothing (and suspected he would just get a thick ear if he tried), he at length agreed to take her along at least part of the way, and proposed a compromise which, while it was later to become commonplace among romantic heroes with surplus heroines on their hands in pirate waters, was revolutionary in his day: he would bestow her on an uninhabited island paradise safely away from the action, yet close enough that he might nip back between engagements and see her at weekends.

"I know the very spot," he assured her. "The Pleasant Isle of Aves – no doubt you learned the poem at school? A very Eden, where once I wooded and watered whilst serving 'gainst the cursed Dons. There, in grotto secure, shall I build thee a two-storey bower all set about wi' fragrant blossoms and stored with jungle delicacies, the booming surf and gentle breezes to lull thy slumbers, mosquito cream by the bucket and only two minutes from the beach. What says my angel?" And I can get on toughing up the Coast Brotherhood without interference, he thought privately.

It sounded so like a travel brochure that while Vanity pouted instinctively, she decided that this was just the old boot. Four weeks on a desert island with her dream man would have him eating out of her hand, and even if he had to commute to his pirate-hunting between times, he'd hardly be away long enough to get involved with designing pirate queens. And later she would be able to flog her castaway experiences to Master Defoe, which would be useful pin money, and splendid publicity if he could work it into the *Spectator*, assuming Addison had got it under way by then. Perhaps Lely could be persuaded to paint her in a grass skirt.

"All right," she agreed, "we'll give it a whirl. But only for four weeks, mind, because I don't suppose I'll be able to get a woman in to clean, and Daddy's bound to bump into land somewhere eventually, and the old buffer will go hairless if I'm nowhere to be found . . ."

So the two lovers planned and murmured lovingly in the sternsheets, and presently Vanity drowsed off. Avery covered her with a boat-cloak, and having lashed the tiller, furled the gunnles, and done all things needful, d'ye see, to set the seventeenth-century equivalent of the automatic pilot, disposed himself reverently at his loved one's feet and flaked out. Which was careless, as we shall see.

For in the bows Colonel Blood lay wakeful, by reason of his dark thoughts and his vest riding up uncomfortably in the cramped conditions. He had long since regretted his sentimental decision to throw in his lot with our dauntless hero – the fight on Akbar's galley had scared him witless – and had been looking forward to going ashore at the Cape and trying his caddish luck with Vanity while Avery was away getting cut up God knew where. Now, from what he had overheard, that was out, and desert islands with regular excursions against the likes of Sheba and Firebeard were no adequate substitute. Also he was about brassed off with being left to make the meals and wring out dishcloths while our fond lovers snogged and giggled and generally treated him like Caliban. Not good enough, brooded the Colonel; time something was done about it.

Thus it haps that as the little craft runs down the night sea to appropriate soft violin music, with the loom of the Madagascar coast faintly abeam (off to one side, that is), there falls a sudden sinister chord of woodwinds to inform us that Villainy is tucking in its shirt, and is about to prowl around working fell design.

Stealthy movement in the boat, a catlike footfall, tense heavy breathing, the crash of a large body falling over a bucket, a muffled Irish yowl, rustle o' barked shin being rubbed, and then again silence, broken only by a placid sigh from the sleeping Vanity (dreaming about lolling on golden sands while Ben does high dives off a convenient rock) and a soft murmur from Avery (corned beef) followed by subdued swearing and laboured scratching of pen on paper in the dark, while gloom of night gave way to pearly radiance of dawn.

But what is this? There are now only two in the boat, and pinned to the thwart, where Avery will see it as soon as he wakes, a hastily-scrawled note, as under:

> Hello, sailor,
>
> Ye mind I warned you I might play false. Well, this is it, ould joy, and if I said it grieved me I'd be a liar, which I am, but that's naught to the matter. The fact is I am up to here, so I am, with a snooty blonde cupcake and a bomb-happy maniac who is so dangerously gung-ho it makes me faint to think on't (and I mean you, dear Ben, in case you're wondering). So I'm swimming for it, and doubt not I shall win to Libertatia, where fun and frolic rule among rascals o' my own kidney. Which reminds me, there's some corned beef left under a cloth.
>
> So fare ye well, and that ye keep your head down and have a care o' that big spade lady is the advice of one who knows, and signs himself, as thou usest him,
>
> Yr obdt servt and whileom messmate,
> Thos Blood, Colonel (cashiered).

Post-scriptum – to defray expenses, I have taken the crownly gewgaw ye won back from that fearsome wog. Good luck wi' the other five.

You might have known Blood wouldn't play fair for long, but pinching the piece of crown is a bit thick, even for him, since it puts Avery back to square one as he and Vanity head for the Isle of Aves – which may not be as pleasant as he painted it (it doesn't figure in the colour supplements, does it? Significant, hey?) And while Akbar the Damned has been written off, there remain the Frightful Five to be dealt with, as they gloat over their spoils and plan fresh mischief in the vile hells of Libertatia. Little does Blood know what he's heading into, as he swims his knavish, ungainly breast-stroke towards the Madagascar shore, with his ill-gotten swag . . .

CHAPTER
THE EIGHTH

t was high revelry and steamy debauch in the Keelhaulers' Lounge, the big back room of the Foundered Squid in the pirate hell of Libertatia. Here all that was gaudiest, bawdiest, and most abandoned in the pirate community gathered to riot nightly in the traditional fashion which you've seen scores of times: raffish ruffians staggering about with pint-pots, their hairy arms round bedizened trulls in big earrings and ragged off-the-shoulder finery; a wild gypsy wench with a tambourine dancing a fiery fandango on the table, while roaring bullies pound brawy fists in applause and discriminating diners hurriedly withdraw their plates from beneath her stamping heels; the air is blue with the fumes o' fragrant Sacerdotes tobacco, the smoke of joints, and the reek of Firebeard's whiskers; drink and doubloons are scattered broadcast, drunks litter the floor, bursts of obscene song echo 'gainst blackened rafters, and all in all it's absolute hell to stage and even worse to clean up afterwards.

In a side-room where only the thunder of celebration and pistol-shots from without, and the occasional body crashing in from the main room disturbed their discussion, the five pirate chiefs sat in council. Days have passed since we saw them abandoning Avery and Blood on the Dead Man's Chest, and in the interval they had dispersed briefly to their private haunts to rest and tidy up before reconvening at the

Foundered Squid to plot their next villainy. As Thus:

Rackham, methodical as always, had parcelled up his calicoes for the dry-cleaners, checked the share prices, paid his subscription to N.U.P.E. (see page 104), and forwarded his piece of the Madagascar crown by registered post to his faithful paramour, Anne Bonney, on their shark-infested island retreat, with instructions to hold on to it carefully until he had made up his mind between the Mosquito Coast Building Society and the Harvest o' the Seas Investment Trust (Cayman Islands) Ltd.

Bilbo, in his decaying colonial mansion, had removed his beautiful Cordovan boots with the help of Goliath the dwarf, sat wincing with his feet in cold water, worried about his falling hair and the absence of invitations to local social functions, and had his cross from the crown set in his rapier-pommel – by good fortune, it was the black pearl, which matched his sable attire, and Bilbo was rather pleased with the effect, practising lunges in front of the mirror and crying "Sa-ha!" while Goliath stamped his little wooden leg in admiration.

Firebeard, who had no home of his own and would have forgotten where it was anyway, had stormed ashore bellowing at Libertatia, reduced a couple of taverns to matchwood, been fined for committing a public nuisance (he had assured the magistrate with hideous oaths that he *thought* he was in the gents and how was he to know it was the dining-room of the Libertatia Inter-continental, them pimpish places all looked alike, anyway, by thunder), and lost his share of the crown playing dice with Happy Dan Pew, who had the advantage of being able to count.

Happy Dan, with suave French chuckles: "Un, deux, trois, and sept on the autre cube makes dix, mon pauvre baboon barbu, you lose again, eh bien, isn't it, but yes!", swept in the takings while Firebeard punched holes in the wall and demanded a recount. "Ne tanglez-vous avec Happy Dan Pew," chortled the lace-bedecked Frog, "not until vous avez learned to count, possibly a l'école de Monsieur Cladel, avec la craie, l'encre, et le tableau noir." And he minced off in an aroma of pounce and civet, down the street to deposit his own cross and Firebeard's at the establishment of Vladimir Mackintosh-Groonbaum, pawnbroker and agent extraordinary to the filibusters of the settlement (of whom more anon, and ye may lay to that).

Black Sheba, torn with longing for Avery, had looked in at the Goa slave-market, bought a couple of muscular Swedish galley-slaves on impulse, decided five minutes later that she didn't want them, and gone into a screaming passion when the market manager tactfully pointed out that they were at sale price and couldn't be exchanged. Reducing Goa to a smouldering shambles and staking out the market committee for the giant crabs had barely taken the edge off her temper, and she had retired in a sulk to her ghastly black castle, hung the Swedes up in chains with her other old things, and prowled the echoing stone corridors in a scarlet kimono with ermine trim, smouldering with desire for the English captain, before returning to Libertatia to have her hair done. (Vanity had been quite wrong, you see; there was a perfectly good unisex salon, with tinting, perming, blowwaves, the lot, and a Yoga class in the back.) Sheba had had her cross* converted into a necklace, and now as she presided at the pirate council it shone like a crystal of glittering fire on her tawny bosom, complementing the slinky white caftan number which she wore 'gainst the torpid evening heat.

She sipped a daiquiri and applied gold polish to her nails as Rackham read the minutes, reported on the state of the roof at the Filibusters' Home of Rest, noted the compensation awards to paid-up Brotherhood members wounded in recent actions, and proposed an interim dividend. All

---

* Just for the record, the crosses had been distributed as follows: Sheba – diamond; Bilbo – black pearl; Happy Dan Pew – opal, plus Firebeard's sapphire, both now at Uncle's; Rackham – ruby; Akbar – emerald, now in possession of T. Blood, renegade. Right? Fine.

passed, nem. con., whereafter they proceeded to 'other business' – i.e. deciding whom they would clobber next. (Just like any other board of directors, really.)

Various proposals were entertained. Happy Dan, with typical continental lewdness, was for establishing a chain of brothels and leisure centres with machines along the Coromandel Coast, but it was agreed that the market was saturated already. Bilbo's plan for a descent on the plate fleet was greeted with groans, since it came up at every meeting, and was regarded as a last resort; everyone knew that if successful it would just lead to a counter-productive rise in insurance premiums, anyway. Firebeard, who was usually silent at these meetings, save for animal grunts and bellows, and had been moodily breaking bits off his end of the table, suddenly startled them with a proposal.

"By the powers!" he bawled, crunching his glass 'tween grinding teeth, "let's sack, plunder, an' burn Tortuga wi' a curse! 'Tis rich wi' booty an' there's females a-plenty for lovin' sport an' hearty ravishment, sink me if there b'ain't!" He was thinking of that big blonde barmaid at the Bucket of Blood, of course. "Aye, an' a power o' moidores an' chestfuls o' gems o' price – we can rip, tear an' rend it wholesale, wi' hellish slaughter—"

"It's our own headquarters, thou pestilent guts!" cried Bilbo impatiently, and Firebeard scowled his mortification and muttered that nobody told him anything.

"Peace!" snapped Black Sheba, and in an instant there was silence as they eyed the sable beauty lounging in her chair, toying with her jewelled cross whose fiery gleam was not brighter than the fiendish light of cruelty in her amber eyes. Her smile was wicked, and her voice hissed like water in a hot frying-pan as she suddenly leaned forward voluptuously, a movement which caused Bilbo to swallow sharply, Happy Dan to drop his quizzing-glass and exclaim "Tout craquait!", and Firebeard to bite the table-leg.

"Hear me, camarados!" said the pirate queen. "These

ploys be but small potatoes, scarce worthy the mettle o' such as we. Why, consider – wi' the treasure ta'en from Fort St Bartlemy, wi' the British admiral cast adrift and his organisation in a worse state than China, wi' our vast fleet, secure havens o' Tortuga, Libertatia, and the Coast, our crews of seasoned, tarry dreadnoughts, are we not meet for an enterprise o' scope and splendour to make the world ring, and cause crowned heads to tremble at our power?" She paused, and her gaze scorched them like a microwave oven.

"Such as?" said Rackham soberly, powerful fingers tapping his square chin.

"Indeed, sweet sister," quo' sardonic Bilbo. "Such exploit we ha' long dreamed on – but what, ha? If thou hast such a biggie in mind, then discourse, black beauty; discuss and elaborate."

"Mais oui; I wait agog to hear of this caper formidable!" cried Happy Dan. "Je listen, me, and perpend, ain't it? Un coup énorme, sacred blue! Spillez, chérie, tout suite!"

"Where's China?" growled Firebeard, who had got lost further back. Black Sheba considered them 'neath sleepy lids.

"Of all the nations of earth," she murmured, "which is our strongest, greatest foe, whose humblement in the West would most enrich us and enhance our might?"

"Spain," said Bilbo promptly. "The Dons," agreed Rackham, and Happy Dan nodded vigorously. Firebeard's agreement might be assumed from the fact that he hurled his chair against the wall, tore down a curtain, and yelled: "Them onion-floggin', garlic-guzzlin', bull-fightin', incense-swingin' Dago bastards, I hate 'em, I despise 'em, I'll sink, split, tear an' cast anchor in 'em, so help me . . ." Etc., etc.

"Spain, indeed," purred Black Sheba. "Now, could we obtain mastery o'er her empire in the Americas, then should the Coast Brethren be a power indeed, like to a government – we, the outlaws, the landless, could become a country, to treat with others, show a flag, dispatch envoys, sign accords,

enter the Davis Cup, and enjoy rank as doth a nation-state."
And if ever we get *that* far, she was thinking, the first thing I'll
demand from the Brits is a free pardon, recognition as Queen
of Libertatia – and to clinch my good will they can lend me, as
fleet commander, a certain gorgeous Apollo from the Royal
Navy, assuming he got off that sandspit in one piece. (If this
sounds like pipe-dreaming on Sheba's part, remember she's
had a tough time in life and may not be entirely free of toys in
her attic.)

Her fellow captains gaped at her in amaze, and Rackham
cleared his throat. "It's one way of going legitimate," he said
tactfully, "but camarado, 'tis thing impossible. O'erthrow
Spain i' the New World? You're kidding. Certes we're
strong, and well-lined wi' gold, but you can't fight city hall!
Spain is First Division stuff—"

"– and ripe for the steel toecap!" cried Sheba, her
eyelashes snapping like whips. "Hear me, while I unfold a
plan whereby we may have the Dons of the Caribbean
Empire running around like headless chickens, and take over
their whole operation."

Awed by her flashing eyes and hot gusts of her Nina Ricci
perfume, those hardened ruffians waited for her to continue.

"According to the gossip column of the *Goa Reminder*,"
said Sheba, "the Viceroy of the Spanish Indies, a bloated and
evil reptile named Don Lardo Baluna del Lobby y Corridor,
is affianced to the choicest bloom o' the Spanish aristocracy,
Donna Meliflua Etcetera, a sweet, virginal child who was
Deb of the Year at the Escurial barbecue. I've seen her
picture, and she's a lulu, I have to admit," added Sheba
grudgingly. "Howbeit, Don Lardo being impatient for the
nuptials—"

Indignant cries interrupted her. "Disgusting!" "The dirty
old rip!" "Poor kid, it oughtn't to be allowed!", and Firebeard smashed a chandelier in his righteous wrath.

"– his child-bride sails from Cadiz for Cartagena next
month, in an argosy of richness to match its precious cargo.

146

Now, let us intercept that argosy as it nears the isthmus, snatch the plump little pigeon for whom this viceregal bladder is panting like a bellows, and we've got Don Lardo by the shorties, but good." Black Sheba's lips writhed in a hateful smile. "What ransom, think you, will he give for her? I'll tell you – the plunder o' Cartagena City will be our price, the surrender and disarming of its fleet and garrison, his own person in our hands, and then . . ." her jewelled finger stabbed the table ". . . then, we break faith, cut his throat, overrun his province, and with the loot and armaments at our disposal, sweep on to Panama, Maracaibo, Campeche, Mexico City, Acapulco Beach, the works! Spanish America will be as a ripe fruit that ye squeeze, savour, and consume at your good pleasure." The slim fingers clenched into a fist, and Sheba licked her purple lips as though she could taste the juice. "After that . . . who knows? Today Panama, tomorrow . . ."

Firebeard went berserk and started stamping through the floorboards in a frenzy of exultation, Bilbo inhaled a full box of snuff in his excitement, Happy Dan danced the Carmagnole on the table, and Rackham gnawed his lip thoughtfully. This girl needs a good long rest in quiet surroundings, he was thinking, but while he regarded her imperial fantasies as so much elephant gravy, he saw sure profit in kidnapping Donna Meliflua and squeezing Don Lardo for an enormous ransom.

"When sails the argosy and on what course?" he asked, and Sheba shook her sleek head.

" 'Tis close-kept secret, that," said she. "Outside Madrid, only Don Lardo himself is privy – so to Don Lardo we must apply."

"As how, dusky goddess?" croaked Bilbo, between thunderous sneezes, and Sheba smiled silkily and toyed with her necklace.

"Myself shall visit him – possibly in guise of Creole millionairess, or lady o' quality on her travels, or itinerant go-go dancer," she shrugged. "It boots not, so long as I get a chance to work on the lecherous creep. He'll sing to little Sheba, don't you worry."

"It's risky, camarado," said Rackham. "If so be as ye was recognised, 'twould be hideous death by torture at the hands o' th' bloody Inquisition, look'ee, wi' stakes an' nails an'—"

"– puppydogs' tails," laughed Sheba, and clapped the big man on the shoulder. "Never fear, Calico, I'll not be recognised what time I sex his secrets out o' the Spanish squirt. Unless, with luck, I get the chance to question him in more amusing fashion." And at the tigerish expression which flitted across her lovely features even Rackham felt an inward chill. Sooner you than me, Don Lardo, he thought.

Still, he insisted, she should not go alone. Bilbo should carry her to the Spanish Main in the *Laughing Sandbag*, and lurk in a secluded cove while she, with Firebeard as a personal bodyguard, ventured into Cartagena in what guise might seem best to insinuate acquaintance with Don Lardo. In the meantime Rackham and Happy Dan would await Akbar (little they dreamed that Avery had turned the great corsair's toes up permanently), and follow with all their force to Tortuga, there to organise the pirate fleet, make do and mend, and catch up on their correspondence while they awaited word from Sheba of the argosy's date of sailing.

So it was that on the dawn tide, her crew hastily rounded up from the Foundered Squid, the dockside hells and kennels, and the Libertatia Corporation Library, the sinister shape of the *Laughing Sandbag* weighed anchor and glided out of harbour through the pearly mist, with sailorly cries of "Yo-ho!" and "Luff a-lee!" and "All visitors ashore by the port gangway, hurry along, please!" She near as a toucher ran down an exhausted figure dog-paddling towards shore in a manner which suggested that if it had been possible to swim on hands and knees he would have been doing it. From the poop the unfeeling Firebeard threw rocks at him with brutal cries of "Har-har!", never guessing who the swimmer was (we know, though), and the keener intelligences which might

148

have detected him were both busy downstairs, Sheba going through her wardrobe to decide which outfit would most inflame Don Lardo, and Bilbo, with his cabin door locked, trying on a new hair-piece bespoken from a mail-order firm under plain wrapper, while the dwarf Goliath stood by with scissors, adhesive, and helpful remarks.

You will remember a few pages back we referred to the pawnbroking establishment of Vladimir Mackintosh-Groonbaum, where Happy Dan Pew had deposited his own piece of the Madagascar crown as well as Firebeard's. This action had not been dictated by ordinary prudence; as has been noted, Happy Dan's destiny was entirely controlled by his obsession with Collins' French Primer, and he carried in what passed for his mind a vivid picture of les voleurs who lived dans la forêt, and who, Happy Dan was positive, were always lurking behind the next bush waiting to hi-jack him; he had been much struck by Mr H. M. Brock's lively illustration of them, brandishing their swords and pistols, and whenever valuables came into his possession (which, in his profession, they frequently did) nothing would do but he must get them smartly under lock and key before les voleurs of his board-duster-disturbed imagination could get their hands on them. (Really, Happy Dan was a pretty sad case, and it was only his lifelong quest for La Jeune Fille avec la Grande Bouche, with whose picture (again by Brock) he had fallen passionately in love, that kept him going. Show him a Junoesque brunette and his eager greeting would be "Petite pomme?", only to have his hopes dashed when she failed to respond with "Petite poire".)

So into Vladimir Mackintosh-Groonbaum's safe had gone the two precious crosses – and it would be well to remark here, in case anyone thinks we are making racist jokes, that the pawnbroker's name was a fictitious one. Born Walter Puddefoot, he had decided on taking up his career that you'd better sound like what you are, and that a new handle would be appropriate. Hence the happy blend of Caledonian-Semitic, with a touch of old Mother Russia thrown in for good measure, and a cockney accent to boot. The rest of the legend on his shop-sign, "By Appointment Turf Accountant to Oliver Cromwell", was pure affectation; he never had been really.

But a smart man was Vladimir, and when on opening up shop next morning he received as his first customer a bedraggled individual with water leaking from his boots, seaweed in his hair, the airs of a gentleman, and an Irish accent, he was intrigued; when this apparition offered for sale a gorgeous emerald set in a gold cross which bore evidence of having been hacked loose from some larger object of vertu (and which Vladimir recognised in a fraction of a millisecond as being fellow to the two crosses already in his possession) he was deeply interested and a mite alarmed. He fingered unshaven pudgy jowel, screwed up piggy eyes, wiped bulbous nose, and played for time:

"Paste, o' course – an' yer can see where the brass is showin' through on the settin'," he wheezed throatily as he weighed the glittering marvel in his hand. "But not bad for a himmitation . . . yerss . . . say a fiver? Or stretch a point an' I'll make it guineas."

Now it was not without qualms that Blood had so recklessly exposed his treasure for sale at the first hock-shop he had encountered on emerging dripping from the sea, but he was rendered desperate – if you'd swum fifteen miles and had Firebeard hurling rocks at you, you'd have been anxious to cash it in yourself. But he'd been in pawnshops before, and knew the drill.

"Try again, Izzy," said he. "Sure, 'tis a genuine emerald o' vasty price, given to me by me old mother, Lady Bridget O'Hagan of Merrion Square just round from the art galleries, and worth twenty thousand if it's worth a penny." (In fact it was worth five times that, but Blood was no expert, and hungry into the bargain.) "I'll take ten thou', an' if ye don't like it I'll be biddin' you good day an' be damned to you."

"My boy!" exclaimed Vladimir, aghast. "My boy, be reasonable. I got eleven kids an' a mortgage! Let's see, nah . . ." His greasy features contorted as in thought. "I can see yore a proper gent dahn on yer luck . . . so I might stretch to five thou . . . though I'd be riskin' a thumpin' loss . . ." His piggy eye flickered suspiciously at Blood and away again. "You . . . er, wouldn't 'ave any more o' these on yer, I don't suppose?"

"I would not," said Blood, suspicious in turn. "Why?"

"Just wondered, just wondered," Vladimir fluttered hastily. "It looks like it's been chopped loose offa somethin', but mebbe it's just wear an' tear. Proper careless, Lady Bridget O'Whotsit must ha' bin, if yer don't mind my sayin' so. Tell yer wot," he went on, greasily confidential, "why don't yer take these twenty guineas as an advance, pop rahnd ter the Foundered Squid – jus' mention my name – and git yerself a shave, clothes pressed, shoeshine, an' a bite o' breakfast, and I'll get this prop'ly assayed an' valued. I can see nah it ain't paste – dunno wot's 'appenin' to my eyes these days, ole age, I 'spect." And he leered pathetically. "Lovely breakfuss they do in the Squid cafeteria – 'am an' eggs, grilled flyin'-fish, turbot au gratin, 'ot coffee an' toast, mango marmalade, the lot. An' the chambermaids is a bit of orl right, an' all," he added, with a lewd wink.

Now, Blood was hungry, and life had taught him to grab what was going, so he accepted the pawnbroker's guineas and hastened round to the Foundered Squid and breakfast, leaving behind him an agitated Vladimir hastily donning coat and wig. Happy Dan Pew, in depositing the opal and sapphire crosses, had waxed descriptive, and Vladimir knew all about the Madagascar crown and its division among the pirate leaders; he knew also that, whoever Blood was, he wasn't a member of the Brotherhood, and that his possession of a cross from the crown was something that any good sneak, grass, and nark (and Vladimir was all of these) would be well advised to bring to the attention of the Brethren as quickly as possible; you didn't mess about with those babies, or conceal information, not if you valued your neck. With a cry to his lad to mind the shop, Vladimir was out and hurrying down the quay as fast as his little legs would carry him, bawling for a cock-boat to carry him out to where the *Grenouille Frénétique* rode lazily at anchor (if Blood had had his wits about him, he'd have noticed her, as well as Rackham's brig, the *Plymouth Corporation's Revenge*, but our Colonel could never tell one ship from another, anyway, and it hadn't occurred to his feckless Irish mind that the pirates who'd taken the *Twelve Apostles* were likely to be swanning around Libertatia.)

So, all unconscious of his peril, our gallant Colonel, replete wi' hot cakes, black puddings, and the advertised mango marmalade, presently repaired to the barber shop, where a pert octoroon wench in a frilly skirt installed him in a reclining chair, fluttered her eyelashes at him, covered him with hot towels, and was just murmuring in his ear about close shaves and Turkish baths when the floor seemed to give way, and Blood was precipitated, chair and all, into a noisome cellar. Here, in the foetid dark, invisible hands trussed him to the chair, his eyes were dazzled by smoky torch-glare, and the emerald cross was thrust before his face.

"Where got ye this, cully?" growled a menacing voice.

"Never saw it in my life," cried Blood instinctively, and then, his surroundings becoming vaguely visible, he was aware of swarthy, bearded faces, hankies round brows, an eyepatch or two, naked steel, leering expressions, and two figures foremost – one enormous in neatly-pressed calico, the other in Froggy frills and satin weskit. Our Colonel considered.

"Mercy me, though, now I come to look at it, 'tis surely part o' the Madagascar crown!" he exclaimed. "Well, there's a coincidence! And surely . . ." he feigned astonishment, "ye be two o' the bully Brotherhood wi' whom I was anxious to enlist? And are ye keepin' the best, then? Faith, it's glad I am to see friendly faces—"

"Save it," said Rackham, and took the Colonel's throat in iron grip. "And, look'ee, dawcock, we ha' hot coals for 'tween thy toes, knotted cords for thy brows, keen sliver o' bamboo for 'neath thy finger-nails, and jam sandwiches to bind in thy armpits – unless ye discourse right speedily. This cross was given to Akbar the Damned – now, what o' him, how hadst thou it, where is the Admiral's daughter an' th' King's man Avery, whence come ye, and how the hell did you get off the Dead Man's Chest, anyway? Ye have five seconds, starting – now!"

"Let's go upstairs and have coffee," suggested Blood. "Or, better still, the drinks are on me . . . all right, all right, I'll talk!" Which he did, succinctly and (since there was no point in lying, and the thought of jam-butties in his armpits was too much to bear) accurately, whereon his captors swore in amaze, beliked, look'eed, and invited the Powers to rend, blast an' shiver 'em. Happy Dan Pew was distraught.

"Ah, but I am disconsolate, me! Le pauvre Akbar – we were like frères, and now he is mort, hélas and purple patches, and has gone to the grande salle de classe in the sky! Ah, but that Aver-ee is gros stinkaire, 'e must 'ave fought foul, the referee was bent, it is what you call a carve-up—"

"Nay, now," quo' Rackham, tapping shaven chin in narrow-eyed thought, "this Avery is canny lad and wight o' skill an' enterprise. And he purposes our downfall, doth he? Well, now, here's food for thought – and ye say he intends to bestow the Admiral's daughter on the Pleasant Isle of Aves, eh, what time he ventures forth against us?"

"That's the place," agreed the recreant Blood, who had no shame. "I heard him, plain as ye like. Well, I'm glad ye've got Akbar's cross back, so I am . . . it's been worrying me, a valuable thing like that, and not knowing where the lost property office was—"

"The Pleasant Isle of Aves," Rackham was murmuring, and his teak-like clock softened in reminiscence. "Aye, I mind the verse . . . 'where we listened to the roar, o' breakers on the reef outside that never touched the shore . . .' How does it go after that?" He closed his eyes. ". . . 'all day we fought like bulldogs, but they broke the booms at night—' "

" 'Burst the booms at night'," corrected the little Welsh pirate, who was a know-all.

" 'Broke', blast your eyes!" shouted Rackham.

" 'Burst'," insisted the smug Taffy, and found himself swung bodily by the shirt-front up before Rackham's steely eyes.

"I say 'broke'," said Rackham softly, "so 'broke' it is, ye psalm-singin' Pontypool smart-ass, an' ye may lay to that."

"Have it your way, then," sulked the small Welshman. "But it's still 'burst'," he added sotto voce as Rackham tossed him aside and became again the resolute pirate skipper.

"We must take order instant," said the big man. "Happy Dan, ye'll lay course for Aves, straight, and pick up the doxy – she may be worth more as hostage than as slave. Then shall you join wi' Bilbo an' Sheba at Cartagena; I'll to Tortuga, t'apprise the Brotherhood that this Avery cull is on the loose and like to work us mischief – he must be bloody Captain Marvel, he must," added Rackham frowning, and his eye fell on the pinioned Blood, who was trying to look inconspicuous – difficult, when you're trussed to a barber's chair in the middle of a gang of ruffians with guttering torches.

"As for this muckrake," continued Rackham. "Shalt along wi' Happy Dan, in irons, so that if so be ye've lied to us, and Vanity wench proves to be otherwhere than Aves, he may dispose o' ye right painful an' slow, wi' Frogsome tricks and torments—"

But at this his followers cried out. "Nay, cap'n, let's grill him now, tasty-like! See, the brazier gleams white-hot, an' it'd be a shame to waste the coal! An' the knotted cords, an' all, an' bamboo slivers – why, Mike an' Peg-leg has spent half-an-hour sharpenin' 'em, an' the jam-sandwiches gettin' stale an' curly at the crusts . . ." But Rackham was adamant, and ere night had fallen the *Grenouille Frénétique* had weighed anchor for distant Aves, Happy Dan reclining on a day-bed on the poop with a yellow-backed novel while his crew chattered excitedly and hoisted the sails in lubberly Frog fashion, emotional tears streaming down their striped jerseys as the ship's orchestra played the "Marseillaise" and "Dance in the old-fashioned way," and in the perfume-drenched orlop, where even the bilge was by Chanel, Colonel Blood stirred restlessly in his chains and had a screaming visit from the ship's cook who said that prisoners who sent back their frogs'-legs and snails would get them warmed for breakfast, so there.

Hard on the heels of the Frenchman, the *Plymouth Corporation's Revenge* stood out for Tortuga, and Libertatia was left to comparative tranquillity, which pleased the sober citizens (all three of them) but caused great discontent among the rest of the population of drabs, sharps, bawds, trulls, fences, pimps, cutpurses, licensed victuallers, innkeepers, swindlers, and dentists, all of whom agreed that at this rate it would be the lousiest season on record, with bookings down all round and 'Vacancies' signs in the windows of every hell and bawdy-house. The chairman of the tourist board explained plaintively to a meeting of infuriated citizens that the cost of holiday fares to Madagascar was prohibitive, and they couldn't expect to attract union conferences while Port Royal had a better beach, at which the mob roared to the hangman to turn him off the ladder, and his tarred corpse swung in chains below high-water mark for months thereafter.

However, it was about a week after Rackham and Happy Dan Pew had sailed that a skiff put in at the Libertatia mole, and dockside idlers observed a tall, athletic figure, dressed as a boucan-hunter, his skin so bronzed that it might almost have been stained with walnut juice, his face hidden in the shadow of his broad-rimmed palm-leaf hat, step from the boat and stride up the mole with clean-limbed grace. (You think it's Avery, but it's not; it's just another tall, athletic, but perfectly genuine boucan-hunter.) However, if you look over *there*, along the crowded waterfront street, you will see our gallant captain in person, threading his way with commanding agility through the crowds of hawkers, vendors, fruit-pedlars, pedal-fruiters, and other waterside riff-raff. He pauses outside the premises of Vladimir Mackintosh-Groonbaum, and his keen, level, grey eyes scan the advertisements pinned in the window.

This must strike a discriminating reader as one beezer of a coincidence, and it is, the author's only excuse being that if Avery were to turn up in Reykjavik or Darwin, Australia, it would cause fearsome logistical problems and play absolute havoc with our plot. No, it has to be Libertatia, but you are entitled to know how and why he got there.

Simple, really. Having woken in his boat to find that Blood had absconded with Akbar's cross, our hero had lost no time about setting his jaw in lines o' firm resolve, clenching his perfectly-formed teeth, making sure that there *was* some corned beef left under the cloth, setting a course for Aves, arriving there two days later by dint of masterly seamanship, peerless navigation, dead reckoning, and rowing like blazes from time to time, handing Vanity ashore, running her up the promised two-storey bower, furnishing it and strewing its floor with fragrant herbs, stocking its larder with tropical fruits and fresh-caught fish which he salted with sailorly skill, constructed her a bathing-pool in the nearby stream, building a path to the lagoon, showing her how to load and fire a pistol, rearranging the furniture to her liking, dashing off a quick pencil-sketch of himself, autographing it 'To my adored mistress,' biting his lip in doubt, doing another sketch and autographing it 'To my adored dear one soon to be officially betrothed', sticking it over the mantel-piece, pushing back a lock of hair which had fallen over his marble brow, and remarking "Well, that'll do for the moment, I think. Like it, darling?"

Vanity had clapped her hands with girlish pleasure and cried that it was top-hole, and if he could just arrange on his return to warm the water for the bathing-pool, it would be simply perfect. Avery, for the first time in their acquaintance, had drawn in his breath ever so slightly, but had assured her fondly that it would be his first concern when he got back no later than next Friday evening. Vanity had then shyly presented him with a kerchief which she had worked up from the gauze of her harem-pants, and he had dropped on one knee, his eyes misting with nobility, pressed it to his lips, and said it should be his guerdon. She said, well, actually it was a sweat-rag, and they came jolly useful on hot days, and whenever he wiped his brow or cleaned blood off his rapier, she hoped he would think of her.

Thereafter they embraced on the edge of the golden sands, the creamy surf lapping at their ankles, the amber sun sinking beyond the turquoise ocean rim, parakeets shrilling 'midst the foliage, coconuts plumping from palms, mosquitoes buzzing in the mangrove, and the roof of the bower caving in where Avery had skimped a bit – oh, it was real Blue Lagoon stuff, and when presently he shoved off in his frail craft, his last sight of her was the slim, golden-headed figure on the headland, waving a palm-leaf in farewell, or beating off the midges, he wasn't sure which.

He laid course for Libertatia because (a) it was where Blood had been making for, and it seemed a sound move to repossess himself of Akbar's cross to start with, and (b) it was the most likely place to recruit the kind of following which reflection told him he was going to need. In the intervals of building Vanity's bower, furnishing it, strewing fragrant herbs, etc., the captain's razor-keen mind had been busy, as thus:

"If I'm going to scupper this Coast Brotherhood, t'were well to furnish myself with vessel more commodious than this rather inferior rowing-boat – something with three masts, a hundred guns, and a sizeable crew for choice. Right. But since, through fell mischance, I am the whiles without the law, and old Rooke will have reward notices in every shipping office by this time, it'll have to be a rented job, and not at a civilised port, either. Libertatia's about as uncivilised as you can get, so ho for't."

So now you see why he's pressing his aristocratic nose against Vladimir's window, studying the want ads ... "Stately Spanish galleon XKE, 1668, one owner, 50,000 leagues, authentic shot-scars, gilded coachwork, offers over two chests moidores ... Experienced buccaneer (v'yages Morgan, Montbars, L'Ollonois) willing exchange Corsair or Coromandel slaver. References, please ... LOST – Plate fleet, missing off Florida Keys since July, answers names *Santissima Trinidad*, *Concepcion*, *Maria Gloriosa*, etc., contact owner in confidence: Philip R., Escurial, Madrid, or PO Box Cartagena, reward . . ." and one real tear-jerker: "Galley-slave, slightly scarred, experienced Barbary, Adriatic, seeks new interests, anything considered." Avery shook his handsome head, went inside, and called "Shop-ho, within!"

Vladimir's reaction to this godlike visitor was much what Mr Pepys's had been: you ought to be in pictures, boy, but who'd model for the B.O.P. covers while you were away? Awe and a sense of his own wormlike unworthiness abashed the little shyster, and when Avery demanded a well-found second-hand man-o'-war crewed by two hundred seasoned desperate fellows, he assumed his most ingratiating smirk.

"Cash or cheque, sir?"

Avery hesitated. Strapped for ready, he yet scorned to mislead this honest tradesman. "Neither, master pawnbroker," he replied frankly. "I pledge mine honour to make full payment after my mission is accomplished."

"Quite, quite. Yerss . . ." Vladimir scratched dubious unshaven chin; only respect for the captain's muscular size, and some strange instinct, prevented him from giving this proposal the horse laugh it deserved. "Er . . . might I 'umbly inquire wot yer honner's mission might be – jus' for me own confidential files, like?"

"To extirpate utterly," replied Avery crisply, "and to sweep from the seas as ye might blow froth from a pint, that vile fellowship who do style themselves Brethren o' the Coast."

"I see . . ." Vladimir restrained an urge to call for four strong men and a canvas jacket. "The Coast Bruvver'ood, eh? Jus' so . . . ah . . . would yer lordship be a private gentleman, or was you representin' a firm?"

"A firm, fellow?" Disgust and disdain competed for space on Avery's mobile lips. "D'ye take me for huckster or base commercial monger, I?"

"Not fer a minnit!" cried Vladimir, fawning. "I see you was a toff first go! It's jus' that wivaht collateral an' ref'rences . . . I mean, I'd advance yer a man-o'-war meself, no sweat, if I 'ad one 'andy – but as it is, I'd 'ave ter shop arahnd, an' times being wot they are, even the Co-op is askin' cash on the nail . . . I dunno . . ." He scratched his matted locks, wondering why he should feel vaguely sympathetic to this superb loonie. "I'm afraid yore goin' to 'ave problems."

"But hang it all," expostulated Avery. "How do chaps get ships, then – chaps without . . . without oodles of oof, I mean?"

"Well . . ." Vladimir considered. "I 'ave 'eard of people pinchin' 'em." Seeing Avery stiffen indignantly, he added quickly: "I mean, tain't *reely* pinchin' if it's a foreign ship, is it? No? Oh, well . . ." He considered again. "I don't suppose you'd feel like shippin' on a King's vessel an' startin' a mutiny? No, I thort not . . . Or if I was to steer you to a rich widow wiv a merchant fleet – I mean, one look at you an' the ole bag'd fall over 'erself . . . sorry, sorry, jus' thinkin' aloud

. . . Let's see . . . difficult . . . o' course, if you was a plantation slave unjustly condemned an' toilin' under the lash an' the tropic sun, you'd be laughin' . . . jus' wait fer a pirate attack, lead a slave uprisin', save the settlement, collar a vessel, an' Bob's yer uncle. Takes time to organise, though, an' I 'spect yore in a nurry.'' Vladimir sighed, contemplated his slightly crestfallen visitor, and of a sudden his beady eyes squinted and his jaw dropped. " 'Ere!'' he exclaimed. "Ain't I seen you afore somewheres? Surely . . . that fearless bearin', eagle eye, an' perfectly-creased profile? That clean-limbed youthful grace blended wiv the air o' one born to command, them faultlessly-manicured nails—"

Avery sighed impatiently. Not again, he thought. "Naval officers,'' he said coldly, "do not give autographs. You may write to the Admiralty for a picture, enclosing postage—"

"That's it!'' cried Vladimir. "Naval orficer! Yore 'im! Yore Long Ben Avery – beg parding, Cap'n Benjamin Avery, R.N.! I seen you in the papers!'' He pawed at the rubbish on his counter and produced a crumpled broadsheet. "See, there's a woodcut in column one, but it don't do yer honner justice, if I may make so bold. Well, I never . . .''

But Avery had plucked the sheet from his hand; it was the *Daily Look'ee*, Libertatia's leading quality journal, and our hero's face set pale as drying emulsion paint as he scanned the glaring headlines:

TWELVE APOSTLES TA'EN. BLACK SHEBA RESCUED AS BROTHERHOOD SCORE AGAIN. VASTY BOOTY, ADMIRAL ADRIFT, KING'S CAP'N TURNS FINK, TRAITOR. By Our Staff Writers.

Avery's head swam, and he could not repress a ruptured squawk as he conned the lead paragraph: "Buccaneëring and official naval circles were rocked from truck to keelson last week by the dastardly defection . . ." There it was, the lying tale of his supposed betrayal . . . the loss of the crown, Vanity's abduction, the breakfast menu for the fatal day . . . but not a word of his own defiance when they fed him to the sharks. "I knowed 'e was yeller fust time I clapped deadlights on 'im," Captain Firebeard told our reporter . . . a fictitious interview with Rooke headed WHAT HAVE THEY DONE WITH MY BABY, PLEADS PANIC DAD; an advertisement for a forthcoming series entitled MY CAPTIVITY CAPERS WITH KING CHARLIE: BLACK SHEBA TELLS ALL; a lurid account of the fate awaiting Vanity in the slave-mart, and a letter protesting at the import of 'whitey tarts' into Muslim seraglios and demanding a quota, signed 'Disgusted Concubine, Baghdad'.

"It's inna populars, an' all." Vladimir was holding up a tattered tabloid with the enormous banner: **ROOKED!**, and a front-page opinion column headed 'Har-har!'

"There was a full frontal o' that Sheba in the Startrull spot on Page 3," sighed Vladimir. "Cor! But some bleeder tore it aht," he added bitterly. His little eyes peered at the captain shrewdly. "But this stuff abaht you turnin' traitor – it's a load o' cobblers, innit, yer honner?"

"Cobblers, sirrah?" Avery shrugged as he dropped the broadsheet. "The public appetite ever did prefer decked gaudy falsehood to plain sober truth."

"I thort as much!" Vladimir slapped the broadsheet wi' sweaty palm. "Talk abaht proper gander – these ruddy rags are worse'n *Pravda*! I knew it must be bleedin' lies abaht you betrayin' this Madagascar crahn thing! Course it is – you wouldn't stoop ter nuffink like that – not you!" His porcine peepers shone with fawning reverence. "Not Death-ter-the-Dutch Avery, voted Most Promisin' 'Ero o' the Year, winner o' the 'Ornblower Award fer Dago-bashin' – oh, yes sir, I bin follerin' yore career fer years!"

Avery was touched by the greaseball's admiration. "Alas, my insanitary friend, thy good opinion shall not mend my credit."

"It wouldn't need to, would it – not if you cleaned up this perishin' Bruvver'ood? That's wot yore goin' ter do, innit?" Suddenly the eager note in Vladimir's voice changed to pure

Camay; his jowels bristled cunningly. "No problem ter you, cap'n – you'd do it standin' on yer 'ead. Cor, the Admiralty wouldn't 'arf be chuff, never mind the King o' Spain! Never mind credit, there'd be big rewards for you, I dessay, honners an' gravy an'—"

"Tush! Bagatelles o' no import," flicked Avery. "My present need is ship and crew, to smite these villains and recover the Madagascar crown."

"That's right!" cried Vladimir, eyes agleam with the light of pure cupidity as startling visions of profit revolved in his unkempt head. The moment he had realised who Avery was, something had told him that Opportunity was not merely knocking, it was battering the door down. For here, in the shape of this splendid specimen, was a Winner if ever Vladimir had seen one. True, the Coast Brethren were a profitable connection, as well as being a bunch with whom it was perilous to monkey – but where would the Brethren be when this human dynamo had finished with them? Up the creek, down the stank, that was where. And Avery – he'd be on top of the heap. So . . .

"That's right," repeated Vladimir, licking blubbery lips. "And when you get this crahn back –" he omitted to mention that three of its crosses were in his safe at that minute "– you'll collect a power o' prize money on it, ter say nuthin' of all the other ill-got loot the Bruvver'ood 'as stowed away . . . I mean, the gov'ment would 'ave to give you a percentage – but I'm keeping you standin' my boy – honnered sir, that is. Pray be seated, an' tell me somefink – 'ave you got an agent?"

Avery smiled in puzzlement, and the oily knave explained.

"Yer know, like a manager – someone ter take care o' the office work an' busines details, fer a modest commision. You 'aven't? Oh, but you'd need one, you reely would. See – if yore goin' arter these pirate bleeders, off yer own 'ook, you'd 'ave ter do it by sorta turnin' pirate yerself, wouldn'tcher

162

– very respectable pirate, o' course, sort o' privateer, like."

"You may be right," conceded Avery. "What then?"

"My boy," crooned Vladimir earnestly, " 'ave you any notion wot it costs? I mean, the over'eads on a pirate ship is chronic! There's the mortgage, an' interest, an' victuallin', and pahder an' shot, an' ship's tackle, an' you 'aven't even got ter the bloody crew yet!"

"I thought they were on piece work?" said Avery.

"An' wot abaht third party cover, an' their stamps, an' sickness benefit? You oughta see what them perishers get fer the loss of a leg, frinstance, yer wouldn't believe it!" Vladimir waved grimy paws. "All them hopalongs on the waterfront like Long John Silver, *somebody's* payin' fer that, y'know! It'd break yer 'eart. One broadside, off goes the pin, 'I'm sore stricken, cap'n,' and next you know the bugger's runnin' a pub on the insurance! You gotta 'ave corporate fundin', I'll tell yer that!"

Avery was sore amazed; he'd had no idea.

"Then there's bribes fer port officials, an' the licence fees is cripplin' – I could name you well-established filibusters who've 'ad to take 'arf their ships off the water, never mind the runnin' costs. An' o' course, if yer get a strike – that's it an' wrap up! It was strikes knackered Sharp an' Kidd, yer know. Even 'Enry Bleedin' Morgan, arfway back from Panama wiv a ruddy fortune, an' the idle bastards sat dahn on 'im. Straight up! If 'e 'adn't bin a ex-shop steward 'isself (an' Welsh at that) 'e'd never ha' got back to Chagres! Oh, it's a business, I tell yer!"

"This is outrageous!" Avery, a practical man who had supposed it was a simple matter of yo-ho-ho and lay on, my hearties, was appalled. "Why isn't something done about it?"

"Well, that's where agents come in," quo' crafty Vladimir. "Take the Bruvver'ood – they got more managers an' accountants than flamin' gunners, they 'ave. You want ter see their publicity budget, an' all – well, Esquemelin' don't come cheap, does 'e? Cost yer a governor's ransome afore 'e sets pen ter parchment. But money's the least of it; it's the paperwork – you can't cope wi' that an' expect to be shootin' away spars an' layin' alongside and blowin' Dons to 'ell at the same time, can yer? But wiv a good agent, nah – a class man 'oo wouldn't arsk more'n 90 per cent, an' well worth it – why, yer can concentrate on the essentials, can't yer?"

Avery had a sudden inspiration. Listening to this honest fellow, it had come to him, and while he was accustomed to being dazzled by his own genius, he had to admit that this time he'd excelled himself. He glanced down at the vulpine, greasy face leering up innocently at him, what time Vladimir washed his grubby paws in air, and smiled to think how this simple shopkeeper had unwittingly pointed the way.

"Master Mackintosh-Groonbaum," said he, "it is in mind to appoint thee my agent. Ninety percent, you said?"

Vladimir's ratlike eyes opened wide, he gaped, and caught at the table for support. "Ooh, sir!" he quavered. "Ooh, I never! Yer mean – *me*? But . . . well, I'm all took aback!" He gazed at the smiling captain with shark-like devotion. "Sir, I am most deeply honnered, no kid! Nah, I wonder if I 'ave sich a thing as a contract anywheres? 'Ere, jus' you glance through these back numbers o' *Playwench* while I go an' see . . ."

It's a moot point whether Vladimir is listed as an accredited agent in the Filibusters' Yearbook, *but although Avery little dreams it, the pawnbroker's possession of three of the crosses could halve our hero's work for him – if Vladimir is to be trusted. (Ha!) And other perils and horrors lie ahead – there's Vanity stuck on Aves, defenceless, wi' Happy Dan and his cutthroats closing in, and Black Sheba and Bilbo prepar-*

ing to work their hellish design against Don Lardo (who cares?) and sweet Donna Meliflua (that's something else). Hurry, Avery, hurry . . .

CHAPTER
THE NINTH

I t was towards dusk of a balmy tropic Friday when the cursed hellship *Frantic Frog* came gliding out of the setting sun, her tasselled sails limp in the sultry evening air, and dropped anchor with a colossal splash and a shriek from one member of her crew who hadn't let go in time, on the edge of the Isle of Aves lagoon. In the drawing-room of her bower Lady Vanity heard the distant clank of the chain, and with a muttered "About time, too!" flung aside her year-old copy of *Vogue* (for Avery had omitted naught for her comfort), and moved with graceful yet petulant stride to the bamboo window. Yes, there was a ship at anchor, and this would be him, hours late, and the corned beef omelette and paw-paw mousse which she had so lovingly and inexpertly prepared would be respectively flatter than old beer and curdled in its cowrie shell. Well, he could ruddy well eat them, anyway, coming home at this hour when he'd *promised* to be punctual, and if he thought that the fact that he'd obviously captured one of the pirates was any excuse, he could think again. It was jolly sickening, and her all glamoured up to welcome him in the red bikini which she had woven painstakingly during the week from jungle blossoms, all for his delight, rot his boots.

Across the water a boat was pulling towards shore, and Vanity's pouting lips parted in sudden surprise. She couldn't make out the rowers, but they were undoubtedly singing

"Mademoiselle from Armentières," and her beloved would never have permitted such continental levity, surely? A sudden shiver of apprehension flapped the hibiscus blossom behind her shapely right ear and her blue eyes widened in alarm as she stared at the distant forepeak of the anchored ship. Could that be a black flag, a skull and crossbones surmounted by a capering frog with a frilly tricolour undergarment in its paw and the dread legend "Vive le sport!" underneath? Vanity drew in a sharp breath, and with it inhaled a distant drift of hair-oil. That did it – Avery wasn't even *late*, the selfish rotter hadn't arrived at all, and instead she was at the mercy of beastly foreigners, including almost certainly that ghastly person who had ogled her in her shortie nightdress aboard the *Twelve Apostles*.

Sure enough, as the boat grounded she could hear them singing "Milor'", and a hatefully-remembered voice was exclaiming: "So, we return ourselves from the lifeboat trip avec plaisir. Maman likes not the sea, and rests sur le pont, hélas! Has Papa purchased to himself the tickets? Mais non, le douanier has trouvé Papa's packet of smuggled heroin and called les flatties. We mount for to seek places in the paddy-wagon. Ah, mais que c'est drôle . . ."

By this time Trembling Beauty was leafing frantically through the instruction leaflet which Avery had left her in case of emergencies. Her slender fingers flew through the pages . . . in case o' Fyre . . . burst pypes . . . Headde-hunters . . . dizzy spells . . . how to pickle Yams . . . ah, here it was:

An there come Knaves to ye Isle, Lewd Fellowes bent on Myschief, seek not concealment, lest they rootle Ye oute, so should Ye be undone. But rather Attire thyself right smartly as a Barbaric Native Female or Hottentot, the which ye may do by stayning thy Flesh and Hair wi' juice of Galoopa nuts boyl'd, therewith shall Ye be darken'd. Then, venturing Boldly forth, if any stay or

question Thee, answer only 'Me Aloma, me good girl,'
that hearing the which they may take thee for a Savage,
and be Satisfyed, and so pass by. (But in no case answer
'Me Tondelayo, me bad girl,' lest Shame and Ill-usage
befall Thee.)

Galoopa nuts . . . in a trice she had them simmering on
the hob, watching the dark liquid bubble as the distant tread
of booted feet crunched across the shingle. Happy Dan Pew's
voice was upraised in altercation with an imaginary hotel
manager who had refused him entrance to the salle à manger
because it was after dix heures moins le quart, while his
raucous followers were now singing 'Auprès de ma Blonde,''
which to the terrified Vanity sounded horribly prophetic. In
haste she plunged her golden tresses into the stew, but before
she could proceed to staining her skin there fell a thunderous
crash of pistol-butts on the front door, followed by:

"Knock-knock. 'oo ees thaire? Absinthe. Absinthe 'oo?
Absinthe makes the 'eart grow fondaire!" The French filibusters fell about in childish glee and began to kick the door in,
and with a sob of panic Vanity, now a rather damp brunette,
fled through the back door to the concealment of the jungle.

She crouched, towelling her hair and peering through
the fronds at the hideous havoc being wreaked on her
little bower by the brutish invaders. With disgusted oaths
they sampled her corned-beef omelette, with rude cries of
"Quelle horreur!" they flung her paw-paw mousse into the
bin, with lustful whistles they tore the corset ads from *Vogue*,
and finally, having reduced themselves to staggering confusion with reckless draughts of the galoopa juice which they
supposed to be some choice native drink, they built a fire on
the beach and had a sing-song. Vanity trembled and covered
her ears; what sub-human wretches were these, and what
must be her fate when they found her? Even with her thought
there arose a cry of "Cherchez la femme!", and urged on by
Happy Dan Pew, who advised them to look under the buffet,

les fauteuils, le tabouret, les coussins, et le tapis de table (he was in his 'Familiar-things-in-the-living-room' stage by now), they began to advance on the jungle, horrible bearded figures in culottes and buckled shoes and floppy hats, brandishing torches and cutlasses, and shouting:

"Yoo-hoo, belle fille d'Admiral! Nous vous cherchons, ready or not! Un, deux, trois – allons! Vive la blonde bombshell Anglaise!"

Swiftly arranging her coal-black hair in an elegant bouffant, Vanity strove to remember her instructions. She must sally out boldly and pass herself off as a native wench, but would her jungle-blossom bikini pass muster as authentic savage costume? Well, whatever the locals wore, it wouldn't be twin-set and pearls . . . if only she had a basket of breadfruit to go over her arm, and a bone through her nose . . . Drawing herself proudly erect, the pearl of English womanhood took a deep breath, hastily replaced her bikini top, murmured: "Chin-chin-chingo, Cheltenham, ra-ra-ra!," walked through the bushes, and out on to the beach.

There wasn't a pirate in sight. They were all plunging blindly through the jungle, crying 'Hélas!' and getting their wellingtons full of water, falling over branches, blundering into thickets, and squealing when crawly things slipped down their collars; the only figure in the fire-glow was a tattered specimen swinging by his thumbs from an improvised gallows, humming "Galway Bay" and giving an occasional anguished groan. Vanity peered at him doubtfully, cleared her throat, and said hopefully: "Me, Aloma, me good girl."

"Are ye hell-as-like!" snapped the hanging figure.

"Colonel Blood!" exclaimed Vanity, her hand flying to her parted lips. "Ah, what shall this portend, and what are you doing up there?"

"What the devil does it look like?" was the sarcastic reply. "If I can chin meself a hundred times on this bar, the pirates have promised to let me go. Ye brainless biddy!" he added violently, "I'm strung up here because I'm a prisoner, and like to be carbonadoed by these hellions, and you come primin' along as if ye were in the last three o' Miss World and ask damfool questions! Cut me down afore me thumbs come loose, can't you?"

"Why, art well served for a turncoat!" cried haughty Vanity, and set him swinging with an indignant push. "Who beetled off and left us in the boat, you rotter? Of all the sneaky tricks – aye, and whipped my dear one's piece o' the Madagascar crown, and gutsed all the tinned pears, and I am *not* primping along like Miss World, I am disguised as a jungle maiden, so there!"

"Ye wouldn't fool an infant!" cried Blood. "And what the divil have ye done to your hair?"

"Galoopa juice," said Vanity. "Like it?"

"Not bad", gasped Blood, writhing. "Mind, it doesn't suit ye as well as blonde, wi' your milkmaid complexion—"

"And blue eyes, of course. But you're quite right, it's the flesh-tint that's really important."

"That's a fact," whimpered the Colonel, "although given a touch . . . oh, Jayzus, me poor t'umbs . . . a touch o' the sun—"

'We-ell, perhaps . . . but only a smidgin, and lashings of Ambre Solaire, or I'll look like a beetroot."

"To be sure, just a light tan, an' the new hair colour'd tone is a fair treat. Prithee," groaned the pendant rascal, "get a knife an' cut me down, or I am like to croak untimely."

"Well," said Vanity severely, "it would serve you jolly well right if I didn't, because you've behaved like an absolute beast, but . . . Dost truly think I would show to advantage i' the Miss World competition its finals? True, this costume is but sorry makeshift—"

"Ye could win wearin' dungarees and wi' a paper bag over your head!" babbled Blood, dangling in anguish. "A knife, acushla, quick as ye can!"

"All right. Hang about," said Vanity, a trifle tactlessly, and discovering a convenient snickersnee among the pirates' litter, she had just sawed through his bonds and brought him to the sand in a complaining heap, when uproar broke out on the jungle edge. Vanity turned in dismay, Blood scurried on all fours to the concealment of a couple of rum-casks, and out on to the beach swarmed a gesticulating mob of pirates. Fed up with blundering around, they had turned back, and now they swooped on their hapless prey with triumphant whoops of "C'est her, là! Elle était içi tous les temps! Ah, méchante blondie! Come to Papa!" Rough hands seized her, bearded faces leered, eyepatches flapped, waves of garlic made her senses swim, and hoots of derision greeted her pathetic plea that she was Aloma and a good girl.

"Do not attempt to pull our eyes over your sweater!" bawled a burly Breton. "You are no hula-hula girl, although it's not a bad idea, by example! See, mon capitaine, here is la bébé fantastique, Milady Vanity Rooke, en bikini formidable et une perruque noire, tres kinky, n'est-ce pas?"

Through the raffish throng minced Happy Dan Pew, brave in galloons and flounces, one ring-bedecked hand on hilt o' rapier, the other raising quizzing-glass to view the supple body writhing in the cruel grasp of his followers. He lamped the shapely form, the proud loveliness of feature, the glossy blackness of the bouffant coiffure, and above all, the crimson perfection of the cupid's bow lips. A moment he gaped, gulped like a throttled ferret, dropped his quizzing-glass, staggered, and clutched his brow.

"Nom d'un Meerschaum, what is this?" he cried distraught. "Par la grande règle de Monsieur Cladel le professeur – it is she! Her! Elle! Le hairdo brunette, les lips rouge, les curves extraordinaire – tous les works as depicted by Monsieur H.M. Brock!" He glared in frenzy at his crew. "Ce n'est pas Milady Vanity, bombheads – c'est ma grande amour, la femme j'ai been cherching ever since la classe 2B Moderne! Ah, chérie, j'ai trouvé'd vous at last!" He fell to his knees and rained passionate kisses on Vanity's toes, panting out his adoration: "Ce petit cochon went to market, ce petit cochon stayed 'ome, ce petit cochon avait roastbif . . . je suis, tu es, il est, elle est – ah, how elle she est!"

Hands clasped in entreaty he gazed rapturously up at her. "Parlez-vous français, doll? Then parlez-moi, ma belle – ma Jeune Fille Avec La Grande Bouche!" The words trembled fearfully on his ashen lips. "Petite . . . pomme?"

Convinced that he had at long last gone Harpic beyond redemption, his buccaneers stared at each other in embarrassment. Vanity was at a loss: why should a dark dye-job have rendered her an object of worship to this grotesque French fruit-cake? Petite pomme? Something stirred in her powder-puff brain . . . a memory of schooldays, guzzling marshmallows and reading Angela Brazil in the back row during French – yes, a lesson about some snooty-looking piece who did facial exercises before the mirror and chuntered on about fruit. What was it again . . . another catch-phrase; she hesitated, nervously viewing the love-smitten head-banger nuzzling her insteps.

"Petite poire?" she ventured, and promptly wished she hadn't, for with an ecstatic yell of "Chaud chien!" Happy Dan bounded to his feet, swept her into his embrace, rained burning kisses on her upturned face, flung her half-swooning over his shoulder, and bore her forthwith aboard his vessel – or rather, he didn't quite, because emotion and Vanity's well-nourished charms brought him exhausted to his knees before he'd got halfway down the beach, and they both had to be carried aboard by his grumbling crew, Vanity unconscious with terror and Happy Dan burbling dementedly about bridal cabins and honeymoon cruises. Whereafter the Frantic Frog stood out o' the Aves lagoon, cleaving the purple swell, with Vanity once again in the amorous clutches of a pitiless sea-wolf (and a doolaly one, at that), and no hope o' succour, unless . . . unless . . .

Toiling in the vessel's wake, and just catching hold of her rudder before she moved into overdrive, came the Forgotten Man – for in all the excitement the lubberly matelots had overlooked their prisoner (who had been hiding behind the rum-casks with his ears flapping). Faced with the choice of rotting on a desert island, or hitching a ride, the Colonel had reluctantly chosen the latter, and now he drags himself blasphemously from the water, sucks his thumbs with little whimpers, and finally disappears, appropriately rat-like, through a dark hawsehole.

But while all these portentous events are breaking loose on Aves, what of our hero Ben? We last saw him in Vladimir's shop, blushing hotly as he goggled through *Playwench*, while the conniving little crook prepared the contract under which he agreed to kit out our captain for his anti-Brotherhood campaign, in return for a 90 per cent cut (whew!) of all prize-money, loot, rewards, and kindred lettuce which might accrue. From which you will deduce that Avery, his Mathematical Tripos notwithstanding, was no whizz at the fine print (as what respectable hero is?), and that Vladimir's spiritual home was Pico Boulevard, with private lines to the Valley and Culver City. Hovering like an unwashed guardian angel as Avery inscribed his copperplate signature, the happy shyster gloated silently at the prospect of jyenormous profits; like Lady Vanity, he foresaw a golden future with his waggon hitched to Avery's shooting star, and lost no time in fulfilling his own side of the contract, sort of.

Which is how we now find Avery at sea, hundreds o' leagues to loo'ard, and if a frown mantles his features as he scans the horizon, it's because he's had it up to here these past few days. For one thing, the first-rate man-o'-war procured by Vladimir looked suspiciously to our hero's trained nautical eye like a converted coal-barge, and the two hundred prime seamen were either from the Libertatia Remand Centre (Vladimir had an understanding with the authorities), or had had to be dragged bodily from the Y.M.C.A. by the press-gang. Whereof came black mischief within the first day's sailing, when the rum-vending machine broke down and bloody mutiny erupted, which Avery had had to quell in person, and skinned his knuckles. Worse still, the vessel leaked abominably, and our hero had spent hours swimming alongside in heavy seas, labouring wi' plugs, oakum, buckets o' tar, and scotch tape, d'ye see, while the crew baled and pumped sulkily and hung around in groups discussing industrial action. Since then they'd weathered a couple of hurricanes, beaten off a Sallee Rover, lost their mizzen top-mast (Avery had conducted a thorough investigation, but no one seemed to know where it had got to), run aground on dreaded Cape Banana, by the powers, warped and garbled their way clear, revictualled at Port Fortnum, flogged the carpenter (for a quite decent price, actually), marooned a chronically intoxicated bosun on a sandpit with a loaded pistol and a latrine bucket, and after all these misadventures had finally beaten their way west to a point roughly *there* on the chart, or a little to the left.

And all this because Avery, who had hoped to run down his quarry in African waters, had learned to his chagrin what we knew ages ago; that the pirates were off to the Caribbean. It was all in the "Kidd Stuff" column of the *Daily Look'ee* – Bilbo and Sheba listed as stateroom passengers on the *Laughing Sandbag*, with Firebeard travelling scupper-class; Rackham bound for Tortuga in the *Plymouth Corporation's Revenge*, and the *Frantic Frog* headed for the Spanish Main "via Aves." Those last two words had struck Avery as a remarkable coincidence, and reminded him that Vanity was expecting him back on Friday. Well, since he must lose no time pursuing his enemies, Friday was out, but he had prevailed on Vladimir to have her picked up and conveyed to the Cape – a promise which his rascally agent (who believed that the fewer dumb blondes Avery had to distract him from pirate-hunting, the better) conveniently forgot, with what dire consequences we know. Unconscious of Vladimir's knavish neglect, Avery had sailed west with a tranquil mind, assuaging his love-sick yearning for the Admiral's daughter by writing her daily love-letters which he dropped overboard in bottles, telling himself it was the thought that counted.

But our gallant hero's chief concern as he paced the rotting poop of the *Rocketing Spitfire* (the name which Vladimir had caused to be painted hurriedly over the legend "West Hartlepool Dredging and Maintenance Company") was whether this decomposing hulk would be adequate to deal with the entire buccaneer fleet when he reached Tortuga – assuming it stayed afloat that long; he didn't care for the way the ship's rats had taken to building their nests in the lifeboats. And the crew were undoubtedly restless; here they came again, surging across the deck bawling "Avery out! Avery out!" firing pistols and hurling knives; a marlin-spike whizzed past the captain's head and thudded into the mast, and he sighed irritably as he drove them back for the umpteenth time wi' flashing rapier and ringing command.

"Down, sea-scum! Down, I say! To your kennels! Stop it, you rotters!" He disarmed one mutineer, pinked a second, kicked a third carefully *above* the belt, and kayoed a fourth with a perfect straight left. "It's action you want, is it, my bullies?"

"Action, nothing!" roared a bearded ruffian lunging with a boarding-pike. "We want to go home!"

"Home, is it?" Athletically poised on the ladder, flicking back lace from immaculate cuff, Avery smiled proudly down on the snarling faces and glittering blades. "Travelling in style, three-course dinners, pockets stuffed wi' loot – is that what you want, eh?"

It gave the scoundrels pause, plucking whiskers, rolling eyes, and spitting doubtfully. "Aye," growled the boarding-pike expert at last, "that'd be favourite. I'd 'ave to consult the membership, like, but in principal, it sounds a'right." A suspicious growl from the crew confirmed him; they'd been here before. "Can you guarantee these proposals'll be implemented across the board?" they chorused.

Avery's reply was a gay (gay cheerful, not gay peculiar)

laugh, and a whirling gesture of his rapier to point abeam.

"Right on!" cried he gallantly. "There she is – fame, fortune, riches, dollars, all the grub you can eat, and a safe passage home . . . eventually!" As one man they turned, and there it was, sure enough – a magnificent Spanish galleon, the sun gleaming on the gold paint of her beak and sterncastle, and on the brazen muzzles of the tiers of cannon thrusting from her ports, towering sails in white pyramids of canvas, and the red and gold flag of Spain fluttering from her staff. She surged across the cobalt water, a veritable queen of the seas, and Avery's voice rang out again:

"Fear not, my hearties – she's one of theirs! A proud and vaunting Don, so there's nothing unethical about giving her the business! Yon be symbol o' King Philip's tyranny! I warrant there's not a man aboard her who is C of E, or drinks honest ale, or can speak good English, even! Furthermore, they're insufferably conceited and have far more money than is good for them. Ho, trumpeter – sound to quarters! Huzza!"

An echoing roar from two hundred lusty British throats answered his stirring call to battle.

"Are you kidding? Attack *that*? They'll murder us! Nay, cap'n, we'm outgunned, outnumbered, out of our ever-loving minds if we venture broadsides wi' such as yon! 'Tis stark madness, belike an' look'ee!" Bawling, they clamoured round the intrepid figure erect on the ladder, and his lip curled and his fierce glance exploded on them in scornful sparks.

"Ha! What? Are ye British seamen, or crawling curs?"

"British curs!" they roared. "So forget it!"

But Avery was their master. With one lightning spring he was at the binnacle, a pistol plucked from his belt, and his jaw jutted with a determination little short of reckless.

"One more step!" he shouted. "Just one – or even a dirty look – and I blow the compass to pieces, and you'll never find your way home! Why, you illiterate rabble, you don't even know where you are, or which is north, or anything!" They checked their rush, muttering, some crying that north was over there, beyond the sharp end, others shouting no, no, you had to point the hour hand of your watch at the sun and divide by two-fifths. Avery smiled grimly at their confusion.

"Choose, ye lubbers! It's sail round in circles till ye rot – or death to the Dons, honour, glory, and money in the bank!"

His dauntless bearing had its effect. With yells of panic they flung themselves to the gun-tackles, hurled up the ports, rummaged in corners for powder and shot, ran up the colours, thrust the helm hard over, let fly the sheets, and with defiant screams of anxiety bore down on the startled Spaniard. Aboard the galleon was sudden bustle and shouting of words ending in "-o," donning of morions and blaring of trumpets, flapping of sails and strutting around the poop by proud figures in backs-and-breasts of polished steel with little forked beards and haughty faces, while across the azure sea the pride of the West Hartlepool coastal trade came racket- ing in like gang-busters, swarthy bearded faces peering through the ports, teeth chattering, closing their eyes, fumb- ling for their matches, and wishing they'd joined the army, belike. Poised on the rail, rapier in hand, head flung back, sleeves rolled up, flies securely buttoned, and the light of battle in his eye, Avery measured the narrowing distance to the enemy.

This is what we came in for. This is the moment, as the great sea-castles run to meet each other, when the trumpets sound and Erich Wolfgang Korngold's music thunders to a crescendo that culminates in crashing broadsides, billowing smoke, spurts of flame, shots smashing into timber hulls, masts toppling, tangles of cord and canvas hurtling all over the place, smoke-blackened faces glaring, voices screaming, decks shuddering – and perhaps in some more sober moment we might spare a grateful thought for the nameless scoun- drels who, for the basest of motives no doubt, broke the power of Spain in the western oceans in just such actions, and all unwittingly made the world a better place to live in, before they went to their unhonoured account, leaving behind as their own memorial only the doughnut (which they invented) and a pantomime figure with a patch over its eye, a scarf round its beetling brows, and a parrot on its shoulder.

But for the moment it's all romantic blood-and-thunder as the *Rocketing Spitfire*, its sides torn with shot, the water pouring into its hold, its masts gone, its powder spent, its focsle furniture damaged beyond repair, and even the rats huddled forlornly in a corner squeaking in unison something that sounds like "We'll meet again . . .", crashes wi' rending timbers into the Spaniard's stern. Locked together in the battle-smoke, the two ships swing together, and this is where Avery earns his money, as with a yell of: "Follow me, men, and remember it's a foreign ship, so behave as you would at home!" he launches himself rapier-first into the mob of moustachioed grandees on the quarter-deck. For a moment he is alone, with his crew shouting "Good riddance!" and trying frantically to cast off, but as they realise that the *Rocketing Spitfire* is finally giving up the ghost and sinking beneath their feet, they opt for the only solid surface in sight, and pour in a yelling wave over the galleon's bulwarks.

Well, that's it. Never in romantic fiction has a horde of buccaneers, roaring "Belike!" and "Aaarrgh!" and "Where's the purser's office, Jack?" stormed the decks of a galleon with any result but one, and the Dons knew it perfectly well. They thrust and parried haughtily for a minute or two, crying "Caramba!" and subsiding with blood on their ruffles, while their inferiors did a bit of pushing and shoving on the main deck before scuttling away in search of safety, life-jackets, and white flags. But once Avery, fencing athletically with that eager fighting smile dazzling the opposition, had skewered a couple of hapless extras, engaged the Spanish captain, disarmed him with a masterly lunge and flick, presented his point courteously at the crestfallen Dago's throat,

178

accepted his gasping surrender with a bow, and slashed the halliard which brought the red-and-gold banner flopping to the deck – well, after that there was nothing for the Spaniards to do but throw down their weapons, draw themselves up proudly, mutter the Spanish equivalent of "Sod this for a game of soldiers," and call it a day.

With a wave of his hand to his exultant followers, and an indulgent, "All right, men, settle down now, and smoke if you want to," Avery turned to the stricken commander, and explained in fluent Castilian that they needed his ship, that complaints could be forwarded to the Admiralty, Whitehall, SW1, and he would be obliged for the keys to the main cabin and officers' washroom. He then invited them to step over the side, with such aplomb that they did so before it was realised that no lifeboats had been launched, and some confusion followed before this was remedied and the disconsolate Dons had been rescued and placed in inflatable dinghies, with wet wigs and Sodden Finery.

Some of the wilder elements in Avery's crew took advantage of this disorder to run out a plank forrard and coax some of the prisoners off the end of it, but Avery soon put a stop to that. He summoned the boarding-pike gorilla and addressed him sternly.

"Belay that, Mr Bellamy!" he thundered. (The gorilla's name was in fact Hector Smallpiece, but Avery knew what a buccaneer mate ought to be called, even if Hector's parents didn't.) "Get that plank in at once before it's damaged, and never let it happen again! Plank-walking is a Victorian fiction, and I won't have it aboard my ship, d'you understand? Right – they can have ten minutes debauch, and then I want the entire crew formed up for inspection, kerchiefs straight, earrings polished, cutlasses clean, bright, and slightly oiled – oh, and put out that blaze forrard and straighten that mainmast, it's all crooked."

"Aye, aye, cap'n!" bawled the beaming hooligan. "Wi' a will, an' yarely, an' bedamned, an' that! What, lads? A rouse

179

for Long Ben Avery, wi' a curse!" At which the triumphant buccaneers roared their acclaim, and threw up their sweaty nightcaps, toasting their lucky commander in the Perrier water which their piratical instinct had already discovered in the galley stores.

"Make 'em go easy on that stuff, Bellamy," said Avery curtly. "It causes flatulence and it's foreign, so heaven knows where it's been. And now I mind me, this vessel shall be known henceforth no longer as the *Santa Cascara*, but as—" He paused, and a tremor of emotion quivered his larynx, causing Bellamy to ponder slyly, 'allo-'allo, "– as the *Golden Vanity*, so have it inscribed on bow and stern immediately."

With that he left them to tidy up and throw overboard all the litter of the battle, including any Spaniards who had got left behind, which they did while abusing the Perrier incontinently and bawling ribald songs. Avery went below to the luxurious compartments of the Spanish commander. Cleansing his rapier fondly with Vanity's sweat-rag, which he dropped in the laundry chute, he sighed deeply at the blue-eyed vision conjured up by that mundane act, blew a kiss to the empty air, and feeling renewed and rededicated, breezed into the great stern cabin.

A gasp of female agitation greeted him, and he stopped amazed at the sight of two women crouched against the bulkhead. One was black, and built along the lines of Hattie McDaniel; the other – well, suffice to say that even though his thoughts were full of Lady Vanity, the sight of her stopped Avery, brrdoing! as though he had walked into an oncoming bus. How to describe those magical dark eyes, the glossy black tresses, the crimson parted lips, creamy skin, sweeping lashes, and girlish perfection of figure encased in a white lace gown, all blending into a mixture of virginal sweetness and gypsy wildcat – call her a sort of Audrey Hepburn with Sophia Loren overtones and you're not far out. Wild fear blazed in her eyes as she regarded Avery.

"Stop!" she shrilled, and a slender stiletto gleamed in her

tiny hand, poised over her snowy bosom. "Anothair step an' I weel keel myself!"

"I do beg your pardon," said Avery politely. "I had no idea the cabin was occupied. If you'll excuse me." And he was preparing to withdraw when she shrilled again.

"Stop! Another step an' I weel keel —" she hesitated, grabbed Hattie by the hair, and flourished the poniard at her throat "– *her*!"

Avery frowned. "There seems to be some misunderstanding. I am Captain Benjamin Avery, of the Royal Navy. I don't think I have the privilege of your acquaintance, Miss . . . ?"

"I am the mos' nobble, serene, an' 'igh-class Donna Meliflua Etcetera, daughter of Don Miguel Alonzo Bonanza Verandah Etcetera, Knight of Sant Iago de Compostella, Grandee of España!" flamed the flashing-eyed beauty. "Lay a defiling feenger on my person, or even raise your eyes een my direction, an' you weel answer to my 'ateful an' loathsome betrothed, Don Lardo Baluna del Lobby y Corridor, Viceroy of the Eendeez!"

"How do you do?" said Avery, and Donna Meliflua's wondrous eyes widened. "You meen . . . you are not goeeng to – how you say een Eengleesh? – to raveesh us, helpless weemen that we are?"

"I must apologise for my intrusion," continued Avery, affecting not to hear her, "and for any inconvenience caused to your ladyship by the recent disturbance—"

"Wee are nott to bee ray-ped, or soobjected to shayme, or solded as-a slayvess?" Donna Meliflua's astonishment was such that she let go of her black maid, and Hattie gave one last squawk and fainted in a massive heap. "But . . . I nott unnerstan! Yoo are endemonised heretical Eengleesh pirate, an' I yam beyooteefool Spaneesh laydee – and I yam only seexteen!" she added indignantly. "How ees poseeble you don' wan' molest-a me?"

"I assure you, marm," Avery was beginning, when a

bearded face appeared at the open stern window, flourishing a paint brush. " 'Ow many enns in Vanity?" it asked.

"One," snapped Avery. "Idiot."

"Ta," said the face, and disappeared.

Donna Meliflua placed one snowy hand on her lissom hip and put her head on one side. " 'Oo eez thees . . . Vanitee?"

Avery went faintly pink. "A lady of my acquaintance," he explained stiffly, and Donna Meliflua placed a dainty pinkie between her flawless teeth and smiled.

"A-a-ah . . . now I unnerstand – shee ees your belov-ed!" She frowned. "Yet shee cannot bee more beeyooteefool nor mee! So I steel theenk it ver' strange you don' wan' to—"

"If I may say so, marm," said Avery, shocked, "such froward talk ill becomes lady o' your years and quality, especially one who is, as ye inform me, betrothed to the Viceroy o' the Indies. Howbeit," he added, and could not refrain from bestowing a brotherly smile on this gorgeous if eccentric young poppet, "ye need fear naught. That we should have taken your ship, I regret, but be assured that my first essay shall be to lay course for Cartagena and deliver you safely to your betrothed in two shakes of a duck's rudder, as we sailors—"

A shriek as of escaping steam interrupted him. Donna Meliflua's splendid eyes blazed like bonfires, her fists clenched, her bosom heaved, her proud head tossed, and her tiny foot stamped. My God, thought Avery, she's not going to do the Mexican Hat Dance—

"I 'ate 'eem!" she spat. " 'Ee eez gross peeg, what I shall nevaire marry, nevaire, nevaire, nevaire! Not for a meelion Papas an' Mamas! So thaire! I yam told 'e eez old, thees Don Lardo, an' a blubbery bladdaire of bull-droppeengs! I shall die before I submeet my virgin sweetness to 'eez deezgusting embraces!" And to Avery's concern she hurled herself on the sofa and began to feed short-arm jabs to the cushions. Then she wrenched off a shoe and broke a mirror with it, kicked

Hattie McDaniel's prostrate form, and set about the cabin upholstery with her stiletto, sobbing hysterically.

"Ah," said Avery. "Well, I'll just send the steward down with some tea, shall I, and perhaps your ladyship will condescend to honour me with your company at dinner? Seven-thirty for eight, quite informal, no need for long gloves. My respects, marm." He withdrew amidst a crashing of crockery and screams in Spanish schoolgirl slang which he was rather glad he didn't understand.

But it was a very different Donna Meliflua who presented herself on the stern gallery that evening, where Avery had made free of the Spanish captain's snowy napery, choice crystal, and EPNS o' Toledo for her entertainment. As the *Santa Cascara* glided o'er the ultramarine surface o' the Carib sea for distant Cartagena on the Main, while the crew were all forrard watching the in-voyage puppet show, and only dusky stewards hovered round the table, and the ship's steel band waited concealed behind a canvas screen, the imperious Spanish half-pint emerged from her cabin all demure delicacy in gown o' scarlet satin, diamonds of price twinkling 'neath her mantilla, a fan of black lace concealing her face south of those coyly downcast eyes.

Avery seated her with all solicitude – but don't for a moment think that he was going to all this bother with any improper intentions. Certainly not; he was simply behaving as an English gentleman should, and if you imagine that his pash for the absent Vanity was in any way abated by the presence of the luscious Spaniard, you don't know our Ben. Solid worth, that's what he is. Indeed, as he helps her to the hors d'oeuvres, and watches her set about the sardines and scotch eggs with Latin daintiness, his regard is positively patronising. I mean she's just a child, jolly pretty, no doubt, but probably not much past the teddy-bear stage, and not in Vanity's street.

He set himself to put her at ease, answering her occasional shy murmurs with descriptions of his naval career, with a few digressions about trigonometry, cricket, and his dogs Buster and Doodles, and she listened wide-eyed, interest colouring the creamy texture of her skin, her satin lips parted in admiration, her slender fingers drooping in wonder, and her white shoulders gleaming with attention. Presently, when the waiters had cleared away, they took their coffee and petits fours standing side by side at the stern rail, while the phosphorescent wake of the ship creamed beneath them, the balmy air mingled with Donna Meliflua's haunting perfume, and the hidden steel band played a soft samba arrangement of "What Shall We Do With The Drunken Sailor?"

And now, having won her girlish confidence, Avery tactfully turned the talk to their destination, and her impending union with Don Lardo.

"You see, dear Meliflua, I'm sure your Mummy and Daddy know best," he told her, "and he's probably quite a nice chap, for a Dag – I mean, for a Viceroy. You don't get that kind of job unless you're a sound man, you know. Anyway, when we get close to Cartagena, it may be slightly tricky, since I, as enemy o' thy country – though sure friend to thy sweet self, if you'll pardon the familiarity – must ashore in secret, to see how I may best convey thee to him without creating a diplomatic incident. Don't want to embarrass him, I mean, or get myself arrested, for that matter—"

He paused, his sailorly ears detecting the sound of splashing close at hand, and to his distress saw that great tears were plopping into her cleavage. Pity seized him, and he seized her (just by the hand, and in fond concern). She raised her lovely face towards him, her lips trembling like red plastic cushions, and breathed a scented sigh what time another pearly drop rolled from her perfect lid.

"Oh, Capeetan Ben!" she murmured, and he thought, what a dashed nice thing to call him. "You are so kind to poor leetle Meliflua – an' yet so crooel! If you only knew what a vile dog's deenaire ees thees Don Lardo . . . an' I yam but a tender maid. But . . ." she heaved another sigh which knocked her coffee cup off the rail, ". . . what mus' be, mus' be . . . I suppose . . . ah, but how I envee your Vanitee, who may marry as her heart chooses!"

At mention of that magic name Avery raised his eyes to where it had been painted on the stern overhead. There it was: *Glodden Vattiny*. Oh, well, he thought, you can't win them all, and turned again to regard the sweet resignation of the lovely flyweight at his side. Gosh, what a ripping little sport she was, taking it on the chin this way, and what a cad Don Lardo must be to constrain her, and she such a decent pippin. Why, he thought, if he were a Dago himself (perish the thought, but just suppose), he couldn't ask for a better kid sister than young Meliflua. And wouldn't his Dago pals cluster round her, just, with those gorgeous eyes and jolly attractive little mouth, and silky hair and swanlike neck and smooth shoulders and . . . and things. Awfully nice, really.

Meliflua shivered. "Oh, but I yam cheely . . . no, I like eet out 'ere . . . per'aps if you 'old your coat aroun' my shouldaires . . . ah, that ees more comft'able ; . . . thenk you." And she gave him a timid smile of sisterly gratitude, and snuggled up. "Ah, your Vanitee ees so luckee . . . eef my parents were kind, like 'ers, I might 'ave marreed Jaime, or Andrea, or Pedro, or Rodrigo, or Arturo, or Ricardo, or Alfonso, or Juan, or any of thee gang who used to play their guitars beneeth my weendow an' throw flowers an' confectionery an' love-tokens an' boxes of fruit to my balconee . . ."

"Good eggs, were they?" said Avery sympathetically.

"Not eggs, fruit, I say. But none of them," she added pathetically, laying her head on Avery's shoulder, "was thee man of my dreams." Her glowing eyes misted, and she stifled a glooping sob. "I used to pray I might meet 'eem."

"What was he like?" asked Avery, smiling indulgently.

"Ah . . . 'e was my Cid, my caballero . . . about seex-two, I theenk . . . weeth broad shouldaires, yet so sleem an'

185

elegant, what you een Eengleesh call a lovely leetle moovaire, weeth light brown 'air, an' a cheen so proud, an' eyes like . . ." She was gazing up at him intently ". . . yes, like a clear grey sky . . . oh, an' so 'andsome an' strong an' kind, an' brave, an' sexee . . ."

"My, you're what we English call well away," smiled Avery. "Ah, little Meliflua, I know not where such paragon might be found, save in fond poetical romance, but I tell thee what – if I knew a chap like that, hanged if I wouldn't introduce you, Don Lardo or no Don Lardo, because you're such a stout little fella, you deserve this dream-chap of yours, honestly, and if he comes along . . . well, just you collar him, is my advice, and I'll be the first to weigh in with a toast-rack as a wedding-pres—"

Meliflua gave an ecstatic yip and a crooning moan, and an amazed Avery found slender arms about his neck, warm lips opening moistly on his own, and a lissom form glued to his frontage. Hold on, he thought, I only said *if*, so you needn't be so grateful for a purely hypothetical promise, you dear giddy little goose. Really, she was a most impulsive child, but he mustn't appear unsympathetic . . . what awfully pleasant perfume these Spanish gels used, he'd have to ask her what it was and get some for Vanity; why should it make him think of throbbing guitars and castanets and Donna Meliflua dancing in that rather abandoned way? Pity her dream-chap didn't exist, because she'd look absolutely stunning in bridal white, with a lace veil and a red rose clenched between those tigerish little teeth . . .

Heavens, she'd fainted. At least she'd come unglued and was lying limp in his arms with her eyelids fluttering, muttering some nonsense about thunderbolts and prayers being answered. Fagged out, of course, poor kid, after a trying day, and he'd kept her up far too late. With a cheerful: "Come on, young stager. Beddy-byes," he swung her easily up in his arms, carried her to her cabin, and turned her over to Hattie McDaniel with a courteous kiss on the hand and a brotherly pat on the cheek, but she just stared at him in a trance-like sort of way; totally bushed, obviously.

Well, the sooner he delivered her to Don Lardo and she got these Mills and Boon notions about handsome cavaliers out of her girlish head, the better; one couldn't but feel sorry for the little squirt, but there it was. He took a last look round to see the masts were straight and the ship pointing the right way, and found his thoughts straying fondly to Vanity, as usual . . . dear Vanity, with her silky blue-black hair and dark appealing eyes . . . half a sec, had he got that right? Well, near enough, probably; he'd had a long day himself.

So! Likewise Hm-hmh. If Avery wasn't such a straight shooter we might wonder if the strain wasn't beginning to tell at last. Has he succumbed to the Latin charms of the gorgeous Spaniard? No, he's just confused – which is nothing to what he'll be when he discovers that Vanity has become a brunette indeed, always assuming the dye-job lasts and she ever escapes the besotted clutches of Happy Dan Pew. As for Meliflua, who can blame the impressionable chit for falling for Avery like a ton of nutty slack, especially when the alternative is the repulsive Don Lardo, whom we'll meet in a minute. If he wasn't such a snurge, one could almost feel sorry for Lardo, what with his fiancée going sour on him, and Bilbo and Sheba planning him evil despite, which is what they're doing, e'en now . . .

CHAPTER
THE TENTH

o here's the map of the Caribbean, that great blue beautiful sea bounded to west and south by Mexico and Latin America, and to north and east by the curving island chain of Cuba, Hispaniola, and the Antilles. Focus on a point where the Isthmus of Panama snakes down to join South America at what is now Colombia, and the map dissolves into a sweeping aerial night shot of huge purple hills and dark emerald jungle fringed by a strand that gleams silver under the moon. And brightest of all is the spot where old Castile has stretched out its stately hand and placed the jewel that is Cartagena, that glittering citadel of the most famous sea-coast in all romance, the Spanish Main. Churches and palaces lie white under the night sky, their glory mirrored in the dark sea at the city's feet, its lights twinkling like a carpet of fireflies through the dusk – you can almost hear Ravel's Bolero swelling to its great crescendo when those spine-tingling trumpets blare suddenly from ambush, and then the music throbs away into silence.

That was Cartagena of the old days, when Spain held and plundered the New World from California to the Amazon, while the heretic fleas of England, France, and Holland clung almost unregarded to their tiny footholds round the edges of the great sea, and none dare challenge the vast empire of His Catholic Majesty, with its great garrisons and galleons, its fortresses and harbours, its far-clung cities and mines and

188

provinces and plantations with their armies of slaves and priests and settlers and soldiers, its unlimited wealth and power and glory – none, that is, except a lawless company of bare-legged hunters, wood-cutters, renegade seamen, gentlemen, fugitives, and scoundrels; one or two of them would write books some day, and win their little fame as explorers and naturalists and historians, and one would even become Archbishop of York and roar for pipes and rum in the vestry; but mostly they were plain ruffians, and in the time when they hit and ran and harried the Spanish giant by land and sea with their tall ships and long guns, they were called by a name detested in the Escurial, disowned by nervous governments, idolised by their Protestant country-men, and patronised by history. Buccaneer.

So much for the record, and to explain why, as we look down on that tropic fairyland in the summer night, guarda costa sloops scuttle to and fro along the palm-fringed coast like water-beetles, and massive cannon peer from battle-ments above the anchorages. For no honest Spaniard knows when, out of the blue north, may come those terrible tower-ing ships, flying their Union Jacks or Jolly Rogers, and bearing crews of even more terrible men who growl in the tongues of the North and Channel seas, and lust for the blood and treasure and women of New Spain.

But on this night all was tranquillity, and the guarda costa crews snoozed sweatily at their posts, or munched tacos and tortillas and garlic sandwiches while they listened to the strains of 'Carmen Carmella' strummed on mandolins. They didn't see the great galleon which came dipping in after nightfall to anchor out beyond the roads, but if they had they might have recognised her as the *Santa Cascara* from far Cadiz (it would have been too dark to see the hideous crossed-out scrawl on her stern, which now read *Goalend Van Titty*). Nor had the guarda costas bothered to patrol beyond Isla Baru – not that they would have detected, in a gloomy mangrove-screened inlet, the rakish silhouette of that lean black cruiser known to the filibusters of Cayona as the Sac de Terre Qui Rit, or *Laughing Sandbag* to you. Aye, 'twas dread Black Bilbo on the prowl in the Dons' very backyard, d'ye see, lurking most frightsome unseen – for ye'll mind he and Sheba intended to venture incognito into Cartagena, there to learn the sailing date of the Viceroy's fiancée from Spain. Little did they guess the *Santa Cascara* had sailed several weeks ahead of time (trust the *Goa Reminder* to get it wrong), and was now at anchor only a few miles away, with Donna Meliflua reclining in her cabin, being fanned by McDaniel and tapping crimson lip what time she schemed, all innocent-eyed, how best to get her girlish hooks into the marvellous Avery. The designing hussy – and her only sixteen! Meanwhile the object of her passion is up on deck wondering how to convey her discreetly to Don Lardo – for you can't just breeze in on a Viceroy, even a Dago one, with: "Hello, Lardo old man, I'm Avery, discredited naval hero and English heretic, and I've got your intended out yonder on my ship – well, *your* ship, actually, if everyone had their own, but I had to sort of requisition her, wi' bloodsome slaughter . . ." Not good enough; bound to raise awkward questions, to say nothing of trouble with customs and quarantine. No, better scout ahead first . . .

A similar problem had faced Bilbo and Sheba earlier that day, but they'd had longer to think about it. As a result, a remarkable entourage had entered Cartagena's Baranquilla Gate at the hour of siesta, led by a stately gentleman brave in black and silver, wi' plumed castor and long beribboned cane, his modish Cordovan boots squeaking something fearful. At his heels stumped a perspiring dwarf who shaded his master with a multi-coloured golf brolly and gasped sotto voce: "Not so bleedin' fast, cap'n, a screw in me wooden leg's come adrift!" They had paused at a joiner's shop in the Plaza to have the leg rawl-plugged and let the townsfolk have a good gape at the rest of the procession, which consisted of a score of slaves staggering under matching luggage, and a sumptuous mule-litter guarded by an enormous red-bearded goon and containing a mind-boggling beauty of Dusky Hue. Clad in a leopard-skin track suit and picture hat, with diamonds dripping from her shapely wrists, she had reclined languidly, yawning while a maid silvered her toe-nails, and demanding in a bored voice of the stately gentleman when the hell they were going to get to the goddam' hotel, and if there wasn't a sunken bath she would throw up. She had paid for the dwarf's leg repair with a jewel tossed to the joiner by her maid, and the entourage had passed on.

All of which had created a sensation, reported within the hour to Don Lardo himself. The Viceroy's eyes narrowed in thought as he listened to his chamberlain's breathless account:

". . . she ees the Countess Passionata Eclaire, fabulously wealthy weedow of the Preseedent of Plantation Slaves and Human Cattle, Inc., makeeng a tour of 'er late 'usband's eestates, an' Excellencee, beleeve me, she ees the oreeginal Cherry Blossom bimbo! But *stacked*! When she moves eet ees like a boa constreector struggling to get out of a wet-suit, her eyes are smouldereeng coals of deesire, strange seens lurk in her velvet elbows —"

"Enough!" lisped Don Lardo, lowering jaundiced eyelids. "Command her to my masked ball and knees-up this evening, and if she is less than you describe . . ." he stifled a yawn ". . . I may have you impaled on stakes of burning bamboo."

"Save your matches, boss!" chortled the chamberlain. "Thees leetle number is truly tall, tanned, an' terreefeec, por Dios!"

So now we come to the grand ball and knees-up scene, where a brilliant throng of cavaliers and ladies in costly finery tread elegant measures 'neath the glittering chandeliers of Don Lardo's state apartment, to the music of Xavier Cugat and his Orchestra playing 'Rum and Coca-cola.' At the buffets, groaning with crystal and gold plate, other guests punish the choice viands and sweet wines o' Peru; among them the stately gentleman in black and silver, whom we recognise as Bilbo, is having the time of his life among the anchovy canapés and stuffed olives – for this, to Bilbo, is gracious living as he always dreamed it would be, with lackeys proffering goodies and brimming his glass, bold-eyed beauties o' quality ogling his raffish elegance through their masks, hidalgos exchanging bows with him and calling him esteemed señor – and to complete his bliss, he has discarded those damned boots for elegant diamond-buckled shoes, and his full-bottomed hairpiece is glued down with Airfix. When a ravishing Duchess murmurs huskily, "Shake me, hand-some," he whirls her into the conga line, the while his crafty eyes stray to the Viceroy's dais to see how Sheba is doing with Spain's answer to Billy Bunter.

Sheba is finding it distinctly rough. Magnificent in a silver Marie Antoinette wig, with matching mask and off-the-shoulder cat-suit in clinging lamé, the sable villainess has never been more bewitching, and the pasty-faced ape loung-ing with her on the Viceregal sofa, his piggy eyes devouring her, has whispered no fewer than four highly indecent pro-posals into her dusky ear in the past two minutes. Sheba, smiling evilly through the slits of her mask, responded in her husky murmur with counter-suggestions of such obscenity that the little greaser's corpulence quivered with delight and clouds of steam rose from his lace collar, wilting his fine suit of purple taffetas (in the worst possible taste, naturally). He humphed his obesity still closer, and in a lustful croak invited her to come upstairs and view his collection of Aztec petit-point.

"You fascinating wicked boy," purred Sheba, "how can you tease a poor girl when all the world knows you are to be married to the most beautiful lady of Spain? . . . the lucky little beast," she added, flashing splendid teeth. "I could scratch her eyes out."

"That eesn't for ages yet," panted the portly lecher. "Ah,

Passionata, my ebony dove, my cocoa bean—"

"Not for ages?" said Sheba, as he nibbled at her fingers. "Why, when does she sail from Spain?"

"Ah, that ees a state seecret," he leered, munching at her wrist. "Anyway, 'oo the 'ell cares? Let's you an' me go shake the universe, baby—"

"But if I don't know", crooned Sheba, moving her elbow out of his jaws, "how can I rearrange my schedule, so that I stay as long as possible in Cartagena with you? . . . you mad wild boar, you."

"Schedule, schmedule!" crowed the rotund amorist. "We'll talk about eet tomorrow! Ah, your shouldair tastes deevine! Come to my love-nest on the second floor, Passion-ata—"

Aztec petit-point, here I come, thought Sheba with an inward shudder; well, she'd better tip Bilbo the wink that this was going to be an overnight job. "First take me in your arms for a quick whirl round the floor, foolish Hercules," she husked, sensuously disengaging her neck from the Viceregal teeth, and with a glad cry the taffeta-clad Lothario dragged her into the dance, where they gyrated to the intoxicating rhythm of the Inquisition Twist, the latest dance craze from the old country.

But who's the splendid figure standing at gaze in the doorway of the vast apartment, elegant in long-skirted coat o' crimson camlet wi' ruby buttons, his half-cut features clean concealed – sorry, his clean-cut features half-concealed by a silken mask? The very picture of a Spanish grandee (and he's got the papers to prove it, if necessary), he holds by the hand a diminutive stripling lad, equally masked and modish, who hangs back in cheesed-off reluctance. Let's eavesdrop on their whispered converse:

GRANDEE: Thus far have I conveyed thee in disguise, wilful Meliflua, at no small risk to myself, so I think you might stand up straight and not droop in fashion unmaidenly –

STRIPLING: 'Ow can I be maidenlee in drag? An' I do not

weesh to be conveyed, me! Ah, Capeetan Ben, 'ow can you be so croo-el? Seence I met you, an' lay een your arms, an' felt your keesses on my leeps –

GRANDEE: No such thing, you kissed me, and I thought it was out of innocent gratitude.

MELIFLUA: – an' lost my girleesh 'eart, 'ow can I contemplate any othair man – least of all that jeeterbuggeeng jellee Don Lardo – look at 'eem – 'e ees vile, fat, yugghy, an' 'e queevers mos' deezgusteeng!

GRANDEE: Astaire he's not, yet kindly heart may beat 'neath exterior o' blubber and purple taffeta. Anyway, old girl, he's your parents' choice, and you can't ask fairer than that.

STRIPLING (pathetically): I can ask for thee man I love – thee 'an'some, nobble, yummy, croo-el Capeetan Ben 'oo spurns me!

GRANDEE: Oh, come off it, I don't!

STRIPLING: You do! Spurn, spurn—

GRANDEE: Oh, Meliflua, we've been through all that, and it boots not, honestly. Your juvenile passion for me, though natural, will pass like measles or acne – and be a sport, thou knowest my affections are bestowed otherwhere—

STRIPLING (gnashing): Ah, the endemonised Vanitee! You shall nevair 'ave 'er! Eef I denounce you now – cry out that 'ere ees no grandee of Spain, but an 'eretic Eengleesh pirate—

GRANDEE: I'll pretend I didn't hear that, because I know you'd never do anything so mouldy. I'm trusting you to give me time to get clear before you make yourself known to old Lardo – just wait here after I've gone, and when he's finished dancing with that tall black lady in the silver combinations, you can . . .

As he spoke, Avery glanced at the lady in question, saw her clearly for the first time, and ended his sentence with a sharp "gloing!" Where had he seen that queenly chassis before, that feline assembly of whistle-bait? One hand clutched his brow, the other dropped to rapier-hilt – and then as she swung he saw the glittering diamond cross about her neck, and with a curt "Hold it right there, half-pint!" to the astonished Meliflua, he had stepped smartly to the side of a flashing-eyed hidalga who was hanging about spare, bowed with courteous flourish, murmured invitation in fluent Castilian, and borne her in among the dancers, the better to get next to that sinuous silver shape that had driven all other considerations from his mind . . .

Sheba, grinding effortlessly to the music, was noting with interest that Don Lardo was obviously a dance freak; the panting Viceroy, wig askew and eyes agog, was jiving it up a storm, his little fat legs going like pistons. "Groove down!" he cried, as he shook revoltingly. "Let eet all hang out-a!" Sheba trucked elegantly clear of his clammy paws as she looked about for Bilbo, and found herself face to face with a cavalier in crimson whose mask seemed riveted feverishly on hers. She gasped: that chin, those magnificent shoulders, that style, those very ear-lobes that shrieked class . . .

"You!" she hissed, faltering as she twisted.

"On the contrary," said a metallic voice which turned her ankles to jelly. "You!" A steely arm which thrilled her by its very touch encircled her waist and swept her like thistledown into the crowd of dancers, Don Lardo's plaintive cry of "Where she go?" sounding in her ears; then she was frugging as in a dream with this crimson stranger, his eyes gleaming through his mask like iced tonic.

"You came after me?" Her voice trembled with wonder.

"Like Nemesis, not Cupid," was the grim retort. "So we'll have that diamond cross for starters – or shall I inform the Viceroy who is the black velvet Venus who dances masked at his ball?"

"Rash fool!" hissed Sheba over her shoulder as they freaked out back to back. "Betray me, and ye blow the whistle on yourself. Spain has a long score to settle with Captain Avery of the Navy!"

"Here is no Avery," said he, turning to peck either side of her sleek head. "None knows my face, and at need I ha' papers shall prove me Don Espresso, captain of the *Santa Cascara*. Try that on for size!"

"The *Santa Cascara*?" Sheba's head swam. "Why – 'tis the argosy shall bring Donna Meliflua from Spain – but she sails not for weeks, when we shall—"

"Aha!" Avery sank and rose again in elbow-swinging triumph. "So – your foul Brotherhood purposed evil to th'argosy and that tender lady? Too late, duchess. She has sailed, I have her, and Donna Meliflua lies under my protection."

To regain her composure, Sheba executed a torrid limbo routine, and when she came up again her voice shook with emotion. "Oh, Long Ben Avery! If this be true, y'are even better than I thought! Sworn enemy ye may count yourself – but congratulations!"

"Thanks." Avery samba'd modestly round her, but his voice was rock-hard as ever. "Naytheless, I'll have that cross – and be sure thy doom shall follow another day, at my more leisure."

He clasped her close, and they cut a torrid rug the length of the ball-room and back through the frenzied throng. Sheba, her emotions ravished not only by shock but by his presence, found herself slipping the diamond from about her neck. Strutting, she twirled it on its chain, her amber eyes fixed on Avery. "Ye swear not to discover me to the Dons for the nonce?"

"Is that wet, is that dry?" asked Avery, rattling off a quick tap routine, and as he ended in the hoofer's classic lunge the diamond cross smacked into his palm. With a grim smile he trousered it. "Wisely conceded, Black Sheba. 'Tis but the first trick in the game I play 'gainst thee and thy carrion kin. The dance was a gas, by the way – a pity your last measure shall be trod 'neath the gibbet. So, adieu."

He dropped a finger on her head, she whirled automatically – and when she looked again he was gone, leaving her limp. Cospetto, what a man! To have frustrated her Donna Meliflua caper before it was even hatched! To have traced her here – and bearded her in the Viceroy's very palace! Aye, and won back from her the Madagascar gewgaw! And how he danced – and he had chosen to bargain with her rather than turn her in! Was it possible that some tenderness for her lurked beneath that frigid public school frontage? Nay, it must be – and if not, she would yet awake it, somehow, somewhere . . . But here was Don Lardo coming to claim her; at least she didn't have to butter up the little creep any longer, now that the Meliflua kidnapping was up the spout. Sufficient for her to extract herself in safety; she must warn Bilbo, and Firebeard who lurked somewhere without, guarding the sedan chair.

"A-ha!" cried Don Lardo roguishly, "'oo ees a teasing leetle temptress? You play 'ard to get, my Passionata, but I 'ave you at last! One more cha-cha, and then I carry you to paradise on the second floor. Keep the show moveeng, Cugat!" And as the orchestra let fly again, he whirled Sheba into the dance with wild cries.

Avery, having quitted the floor, was pausing to compose his racing thoughts. If Sheba was here, could the other villains be far away? First things first – he must return to the disguised Meliflua and coax her into revealing herself to Don Lardo, while he, Avery, retired discreetly and took order. He glanced towards the great doorway, and saw to his consternation that it was entirely devoid of Melifluas, disguised or otherwise. This was what he had feared, and why he had insisted on bringing her as close to Don Lardo as possible – the tempestuous young snirp had slipped her cable rather than be delivered up to her odious fiancé! Well, he couldn't blame her, but what now? Chin in hand, his shapely calves taut in testimony to his mental tension, our young skipper mounted the marble steps to a secluded verandah giving on to the palace garden, there to plot his next move. With a sigh he decided that Meliflua was now beyond his scope; he'd discharged his responsibility by bringing her to Cartagena. As for the Brotherhood, he would keep a weather eye open, and if none of them seemed to be about, he would retire wi' all speed and secrecy to the *Santa Cascara*, lying beyond the roads, and seek them elsewhere.

A muffled yelp reached his keen ears as he paced the verandah, which was screened from the dance floor below by boskage, rammage, and plant-pots. The yelp came from an alcove a little way along, and was followed by a plaintive voice which was strangely familiar.

"Get them off, damned mannikin!" it said. "My feet burn! My bunions are like to burst! 'Twas the conga that did it – and odd's bobs, hammer and tongs, my toupee is coming unstuck! Pull, rot 'ee, thou halfling nit! Pull, I say!"

All Avery's gentlemanly instincts surfaced at these sounds betokening some cavalier in distress. He turned the corner, and there was a splendid figure in black and silver, sprawled on a marble bench while a red-faced dwarf tried to remove its shoes. For Bilbo's elegant evening footwear had turned traitor at last, and his dogs were barking in protest; Goliath was making heavy weather of de-shoeing him, and Avery, never suspecting who the masked grandee might be, stepped forward and offered to help. (Old ladies with heavy baskets, stray cats, maidens threatened by dragons, or chaps with sore feet, it was all one to Rover Scout Avery, reared in the groat-a-job tradition.) Bilbo, seeing only a blasted interfering masked exquisite in crimson, bit back a blistering oath, and answered as politely as his anguished corns allowed.

"I thank you, señor, we shall do very well! My cursed shoon, you see . . . but I would not trouble you." This in his best Spanish. "Pull, you puny little bastard!" he added to Goliath in English, and Avery started.

"You are English, sir?"

"Nay, nay!" cried Bilbo, appalled at almost giving himself away to this damned Don. "But this handless lout – my valet, you see – is an English slave, and I address him according."

"Ah," said Avery. "Permit me, then." And with two quick flicks he had removed the constricting shoes. "Pooh, gosh! I think," he added, stepping back hastily, "some cold water, embrocation, and bags o' camphor, should meet your need, sir. As to your wig—"

"There's nothing wrong with my wig!" cried Bilbo, clutching at it. "I mean, señor," he added, with an ingratiating grin, "that I would give you no further trouble. I am much indebted, sir. I am now very well . . . I would not detain you . . . your servant, sir . . ." He bowed from his seat, massaging his toes.

"I understand, señor," said Avery politely, "yet, if, as I apprehend, your wig will not stay in place—"

"It stays in place admirably, señor!" cried Bilbo adjusting it feverishly and getting it all askew. " 'Tis in perfect nick, I thank you. Pray give it no thought, I beg – and so, good evening to you, sir—"

"I was about to advise," added Avery helpfully, "that wigs adhered by gums and goos and suchlike are wont to come adrift i' the heat, and stout strings looped about the ears were better security—"

"Oh, bugger off, nosey!" shouted Bilbo, his temper exploding. "My wig is no business o' thine, split me—"

Too late he checked on the English words; too late remembered the part he was trying to play. Instinctively his hand swept to his hilt, and Avery's eyes, following it, widened at the sight of the great black pearl and golden cross glittering in the pommel. Like lightning he twitched aside Bilbo's mask, even as the buccaneer came to his unshod feet.

"Bilbo!" The captain's voice cracked like a fractured walnut, and he swept off his own mask to let the villain see what he was up against. For a split second they stared, and then the two blades leaped from their scabbards, and Goliath, with a squeal of "Don't hit me, I'm too small!" hopped behind a plant-pot even as the razorish steel grated and rang along the verandah.

Rash, you think? Precipitate on both sides? Absolutely, the pair of them going off at half-cock like that, in a place where both were imposters and liable to have to do some awkward explaining – aye, but when two such as Black Bilbo and Long Ben Avery cross swords, d'ye see, then sense and reason take wing, wi' a wannion, and naught's to matter save the bright eyes and whirling point o' th'adversary. There isn't an instant to draw breath, or spit a curse (like "Ha, villain!" or "Government ponce!"), or mess about with the furniture, for this is world title stuff, from prime to octave, high lines and low, wi' imbroccata, stoccata, alongez, and all that jazz, the two lithe figures shuffling, gliding and lunging with what looks like a bright buzz-saw flickering and clashing between them, too fast for the eye to follow.

Any bets on the outcome? Bilbo's fantastically good, and has the advantage of stockinged feet (which not only affords a better grip, but makes Avery keep his distance). Avery, on t'other hand, is a genius, as we know, and younger and fitter – but then again, Bilbo has the experience, and knows lots of tricks – but curiously enough, black scoundrel though he is, the thought of using them never crosses his mind. He's enjoying himself too much, as he feels that electric impulse that surges from body to body along the grating steel to warn him that this time he's fighting for his life, and must fence as he's never fenced before.

Along the verandah they went, their shadows fighting along the wall beside them like huge grotesque seconds (Michael Curtiz would have loved it), Avery coming within an inch of victory as his point slashed through Bilbo's coat, Bilbo countering with a whirling thrust that Avery only kept from his throat by turning the blade with his left hand. And now came uproar and feminine shrieks from the ballroom, hurrying feet as the dancers suspended their revels in alarm as the sounds of combat reached them, while through the garden little Goliath hopped as fast as his timber leg would permit, looking for Firebeard – which was a waste of time, since the big ape had got thirsty, found a side door to the palace cellar, and was now lying prone in a puddle of yellow Chartreuse, singing "One-Eyed Riley," tho' sadly off-key. Goliath, finding the sedan chair unattended, wasted five minutes tracking him down, and another five minutes in futile first aid and blasphemy over the sodden giant. Let's leave him to it, and back to the ballroom.

It was scatter and scream among the dancers as the two figures, black and crimson, fought their way down the steps from the verandah and across the tessellated floor, neither sparing a thought for his surroundings, Bilbo grinning like Rathbone and perspiring in rascally fashion, Avery grim and gorgeous and apparently dusted with talc. The orchestra searched frantically for a Max Steiner score as the blades and feet of the fencers whirled and stamped ever faster, caballeros gasped and señoritas squeaked, every eye on the flashing swords – and none wider than those behind Black Sheba's mask – save perchance those of the pale-faced modish stripling who peeped out anxiously from behind a pillar at the back (no, Meliflua hadn't absconded very far, not yet). This is the way it should be: two of our hero's female admirers watching distraught as he fights for his life. Yes, it was lip-chewing, bosom-heaving, finger-twisting time for the two of them, while the blades rang and the watching crowd gave vent to courtly Castilian exclamations like "Five to two the crimson!" and "Show us your muscles!" and "Who told you two bums you could fence?", and none applauded more vociferously than the portly Viceroy, which puzzled Sheba, for surely he should have been calling the cops to stop this brawling in his personal ballroom? Something fishy here, thought the pirate queen, but even as some instinct prompted her to flee, Don Lardo's podgy paw seized her wrist, and he

201

was leering at her vindictively, piggy triumph in his chewed-toffee eyes.

"Goeeng somewhaire, baby? But eet's jus' getteeng to thee exciteeng beet, eh? Stay, my Passionata – or should I say, come back, Leetle Sheba?"

Rumbled, thought Sheba, and with a desperate warning cry of "Bing avast, Bilbo!" she sank her teeth in Don Lardo's arm. He tasted rotten, like a very old Portuguese hot-water-bottle, and his yowl brought scarlet-clad guards who had Sheba pinioned in no time. But Bilbo, hearing her cry (which is cant for 'Run for it!'), acted like quicksilver. Deftly turning an Avery lunge, he bolted at speed for the nearest exit, only to find a dozen guards, rapiers drawn, in his path. With a cry of "West Ham for the Cup!" Bilbo launched himself at them like a tiger, pinking a couple before they grappled him, fell with exultant cries on his stockinged feet, and tickled him into submission before dragging him helpless to where Don Lardo was rubbing his fat paws and gloating over the captive Sheba.

"So!" he cackled. "W'at 'ave we 'ere? Thee famous Capeetan Beelbo an' thee delectable Capeetan Sheba of thee Coast Brother'ood, hey? Fools! Deed you theenk to go unrecognised – Donna Passionata Eclaire an' 'er cavalier escort?" He snapped his fat fingers, jeering. "I knew you from thee first, Eengleesh pirate scum! I lured you 'ere, an' played cat an' mouse weeth you, because I'm smart, me, an' now you are een my powair—"

"Are you trying to steal my thunder again, worm?" lisped an icily musical voice, and a deadly hush fell as the gay throng, with squeaks of apprehension, gave way bowing and scraping before the most terrifying creature Avery had ever seen in his life. Through the parting courtiers he advanced, a huge and utterly repulsive figure, all the worse for being dressed in the height of fashion, scarlet satin from unspeakable head to misshapen foot. Fatter and even more yellow than Don Lardo, his face would have made Guy the Gorilla look like Mr Universe. It was all there – flabby jowls, bulging lips, squashed beak of a nose, and pale, red-rimmed gooseberry eyes which seemed to gleam with a crazy light; he even had yellow, fang-like dentures which slipped out from time to time, to be retrieved and replaced by one of the swarm of lackeys who followed him, bearing a great red throne. He lurched forward, leaning his enormous gaudy bulk on a scarlet cane, and his free hand played with a live black widow spider, raising and lowering it on its thread like a hairy-legged yo-yo. A right charmer, in fact, looming monstrously over the scene, glaring at the hapless Don Lardo, who cringed and dropped to his knees as the liquidly musical voice issued again from those blubbery lips.

"As I recall," lisped the newcomer, " 'twas *I* who recognised the descriptions of these pirate vermin, and instructed *you* to impersonate me for their benefit, to find out their criminal designs. Right, Enchillada?"

"Sure, boss! Mercy, boss!" babbled the purple-taffeta fatso, and shrieked as the scarlet ogre swung the black widow menacingly in his direction. "Not the spider, boss, please –"

"What makes you think my spider would go near you, you detestable excrescence?" lisped the other, pale eyes fiendishly a-glitter. "No . . . if you displease me, by letting our little charade go to your head – *you* lured them here, indeed! – I shall have you impaled on burning bamboo after all, and listen to you sizzling in your own fat." He lowered his great bulk onto the throne, and the dreadful eyes rolled at the prisoners. Suddenly the deadly sibilant voice rose to a scream. "Why aren't they grovelling? I want to see them crawl!"

Enchillada scrambled quaking to his feet. "On your knees, 'ereteec peegs!" he squealed. "Abase yourselves before 'Ees Excellencee Don Lardo Baluna del Lobby y Corridor, Viceroy of the Eendeez!" And Sheba and Bilbo were thrust prostrate before the throne.

Well, here's a turn-up – and if it's a surprise to you, picture the astonishment of our principals, especially the disguised Meliflua peeping horror-struck from behind her pillar at the back. This nightmare creature was the real Viceroy, the man she was to marry? Her senses performed a terrified sidestroke. Why, this was a Grade A tarantula, and obviously barmy to boot – the fat little chamberlain, who'd been posing as Don Lardo, was almost attractive by comparison. A greasy, lustful little podge, admittedly, but sane at least, and she could always have shut her eyes and thought of Aragon . . . But this hideous fruitcake! Oh, parents dear, she moaned, how *could* you?

Sheba, crouched at the tyrant's feet, was reaching the same conclusion. No melting sundae herself, she felt a nameless dread as the real Don Lardo's mad, evil eyes slithered over her; cruelties and vices undreamed of lurked in their empty depths, and she shuddered as he reached down a huge hairy hand to fondle her shoulder.

" 'Tis a most exquisite jungle bunny," hissed the Viceroy. "No wonder you slobbered over her, Enchillada – but you shan't have her, oh no! I shall enjoy her exclusively – and afterwards have her racked to pieces. Unless," he added with a hideous chuckle, "I decide to combine the two operations . . . what better accompaniment to love-making than her screams of agony and snapping bones?" He laughed crazily, and the courtiers squirmed uneasily and muttered that it was a great idea, and why hadn't they thought of it? The Viceroy's staring eyes raked them, and stopped suddenly at Captain Avery, who was still standing sword in hand where Bilbo had left him. "Who's he?" cried Don Lardo, glaring at Enchilla-da. "I don't know him! Is he another endemonised foreigner? Why isn't *he* grovelling, por Dios?"

Now, you or I would have been frozen witless, but not our Ben. With courtly grace he sheathed his rapier, made a leg, shot his cuffs, composed his eyebrows with urbanity, and strode gracefully forward, tripping only slightly over the prostrate Bilbo. With a flourish he drew a document from his breast pocket.

"Permit me, Excellency," said he, and the fluency of his Spanish would have done credit to a coffee commercial. "I am Don Espresso Banana, commander of His Catholic Majesty's ship *Santa Cascara*, which lies presently beyond the roads. My credentials."

Cries of astonishment rose from the crowd as Enchillada, at a nod from Don Lardo, took the document and scanned it.

"These are luncheon vouchers from the Escurial cafeteria," he cried in bewilderment.

"What?" bawled Don Lardo, goggling.

Avery frowned in vexation. "My mistake," he said, and pulled papers from another pocket. Enchillada took them.

"Why, Excellencee!" he yipped. "Eet's a fact! Thees ees eendecd Don Espresso, an' 'e breengs your Excellencee's nobble an' raveesheeng child-bride, Donna Meliflua, from Spain! But, señor", he added, as the crowd gasped at this sensational news, "we deedn't expect you for weekses!"

Avery made a gesture of elegant deprecation. "What would you? The lady was so eager that we sailed ahead of time". He bowed tactfully to Don Lardo. "Who could blame her?"

"But of course!" Don Lardo grinned wolfishly, shuddered with delight, and gave Enchillada a brutal belt over the ear. "Wasn't it obvious, animal? She couldn't wait, the avid little cupcake! They never can! Caramba, but I've got the message for the birds, me!" Sycophantic cries of agreement came from the courtiers, while the lackeys replaced Don Lardo's gnashers, which had fallen out again in his excitement. "But where is she, then, the fortunate chiquita?" he demanded eagerly, and Donna Meliflua gave a stifled moan of terror and shrank behind her pillar.

Avery sighed. "Alas, excellency, she is a trifle fatigued from the voyage, and begs your indulgence that she remain aboard tonight. I was hasting to announce our arrival when I

205

recognised this desperado," he boldly indicated Bilbo, "and engaged him immediately, as duty demanded. Pray accept him," he bowed over the prostrate buccaneer, "with my compliments."

By jove, he can think on his feet, can Avery. He had been ready, as we know, to deliver the reluctant Meliflua to her betrothed, but now that he's seen Don Lardo in close-up, he's realised that it just isn't on. This ghastly gargoyle, playing with his beastly tarantula and looking like Boris Karloff after an unsuccesful face-lift, simply won't do. A bounder without taste, and not the full hod of bricks, either; certainly not a fit mate for a sweet señorita, whatever Mummy and Daddy may think. No, Avery has decided that he'll have to find her again and get her out of this monster's clutches somehow, but for the moment he must stall for time and hope that his borrowed clothes and Castilian accent continue to pass muster – which they would have done, but for one thing. Bilbo, held face down before the Viceroy's throne, and keenly conscious of his position, was shot if he was going to let Avery get away with this. He writhed in his captors' grip, and prepared to bawl denunciation.

"Od's blood!" he shouted. "Thou King's pimp, d'ye think we'll go down the drain without taking you with us? I'll learn you to cross swords wi' me and make personal remarks about my wig! Shalt share our fate! Hear me, Dagoes! This Don Espresso is—"

"Mum, Bilbo!" cried Sheba. "Shut your scuttle!" And as much from amaze as in obedience to the Brotherhood code, Bilbo cheesed it, while Don Lardo went ape.

"They're talking!" he frothed, clenching his enormous fists and rolling his goosegog eyes in frenzy. "They're not grovelling in abject silence! It's unbelievable! Why doesn't someone tear out their tongues, or sew up their lips with red-hot needles, or tell them to shut up? I can't stand it! Take them hence! Chain them in dungeon dank and deep! Notify the Inquisition! Take their names, ranks, and numbers!" He flung his enormous scarlet body about on his throne, ghastly features suffused, dabbing at his emerging dentures wi' flimsy kerchief (a sure sign this, in any seventeeth-century villain, of approaching apoplexy), and at Enchillada's urgent chivvying the two pirates were dragged hastily out, Black Sheba darting Avery a smouldering glance in which entreaty, warning, concern, passion, perplexity, and come-hither were admirably blended. The gross Don Lardo, who had squashed his spider in his rage, was fanned into tranquillity by his attendants, who replaced his teeth and gave him a new black widow, which he yo-yoed breathlessly.

"God, I knew it was going to be one of those days!" he hissed breathlessly. "Where was I?" His pale, empty eyes blinked redly at Avery. "Ah, yes . . . Don Espresso. So my little bride wishes to rest – no doubt she is apprehensive about meeting my own standard of perfection." He leered horribly, beckoning Avery with a finger like a hairy cucumber. "Tell me, as hombre to hombre, is she as worthy of my bed as her portrait promises?"

Dashed bad form, as well as being one of those tricky have-you-stopped-beating-your-wife questions, thought Avery. He answered guardedly, lest he provoke this nutcase to frenzy, whether of jealousy or enthusiasm. "'Tis not for me to say, gracious excellency," quo' he smoothly. "Yet did I remark rather the lady's beauty of character and perfection of nature, her delicacy and taste—"

"You mean she enjoyed the floggings and keelhaulings on your voyage?" cried Don Lardo, his ghastly map alight with hellish animation. "Oh, goody! A consort after my own heart!" He yo-yoed the black widow up and down, licking his dreadful lips. "I think," he lisped, "that I shall give her an auto-da-fé as a wedding present. Ah, the crisp fragrance of relapsos burning at the stake – she will adore it! I can't wait to meet her!"

Little Enchillada, nodding greasily at his master's elbow, murmured: "Then you won't be needing that chocolate cookie Sheba, weel you, Excellencee? Don' worry, I'll arrange to have her disposed of—"

"One more peep out of you," lisped Don Lardo icily, "and it'll be burning bamboo time, remember? Which reminds me, in the morning I shall preside at the interrogation of the rogue Bilbo – he shall tell me where lies his ship, and any other snippets of information about his pirate brethren that we can wring from him. Thereafter, what's left of him can be turned over to the Inquisition. The black tomato," he went on with a mad cackle, "shall afford me amorous sport before she goes the same way. Then a quick shave and shampoo, and I'll be all set to receive Donna Meliflua when you, Don Espresso –" his mad pale eyes glinted in Avery's direction – "bring her ashore tomorrow night. Until then, you remain here as my guest – see to it, Enchillada, and the rest of you: On with the dance!"

He waved a huge scarlet arm, and as he was borne out on his throne, yo-yoing his spider and laughing crazily, the band struck up "Viva España," the courtiers abandoned themselves again to the heady Latin measure, or crowded round the buffets for a quick blast (Don Lardo's appearances invariably sent the alcohol consumption rocketing), Enchillada handed back the luncheon vouchers which Avery had presented by mistake, our hero nonchalantly retrieved Black Bilbo's fallen rapier from the guards (that's two bits of the Madagascar crown he's got now), Donna Meliflua continued to hide behind her pillar, Sheba and Bilbo were chained up by their brutal jailers in the loathsome gloom o' dungeons far beneath the palace, and in the wine-cellar Goliath the dwarf gave up his attempts at artificial respiration on the sozzled Firebeard, and feeling like a drink himself, mooched among the casks of Amontillado and Fiesta Burgundy in the hope of finding a bottle of Bass. There wasn't any. "Guzzling Dago gits," observed Goliath moodily, and with a sigh, got stuck into the yellow Chartreuse.

Just another typical night at the Viceregal palace, Cartagena, and it isn't over yet. Avery's got problems. Will his disguise be pierced? Can he rescue Donna Meliflua before tomorrow night? Will his guest room be away from traffic noise and the laundry chute? Why doesn't the loony monster Don Lardo consult a decent dentist? It's all very distracting, and liable to play havoc with the schedule of our hero's campaign against the Brotherhood; at this rate it'll be weeks before he gets back to Vanity who, he fondly supposes, has been picked up from Aves by Vladimir Mackintosh-Groonbaum. We know better – or do we? Where is Vanity by this time, for it's thirty-seven long sea-pages since we last saw her helpless in the grasp of the love-sick Happy Dan Pew. Whither has he borne her, and what's the score, and how is Blood doing, an' that, wi' a curse, eh? Just a minute while we scour the oceans for a sight o' that vessel of ill-omen, the Frantic Frog . . .

CHAPTER
THE ELEVENTH

ne of the great things about pirate ships in the good old days was that they were purpose-built – not for cargoes of crude oil or containers or package tourists, but for knavery and conspiracy and swashbuckling and, in a word, Romance. There had to be a stateroom spacious enough for the likes of Tyrone and George Sanders to fight their climactic duel (well, try and stage that sort of barney in some four-by-two cabin on G Deck with twin bunks and a corner wash-basin and see how far you get). And there had to be smaller cabins with stout oaken doors and heavy brass locks, for kidnapped heiresses and hapless señoritas to cower behind, while drunken Dons or people like Firebeard smashed the panels in. There had to be doorways high enough for stalwart heroes to stride through masterfully without catching their heads a shattering crash just as they were about to say: "So, proud Isabella, we meet again," or "Ha-ha, Gomez, our reckoning is due!" as the case might be. Then there had to be foetid compartments deep i' the bowels o' the vessel for plotting bloody mutiny, d'ye see, secret nooks for hiding treasure-maps or jewels o' price, rat-filled orlops for confining prisoners, pitch-black holds for knife-fights with gigantic Negroes, and a great network of secret passages for stowaways, assistant heroes, and various eccentrics to lurk in, and for dreadful nameless Things to pop out during the middle watch and knife the man at the wheel.

Without these basic amenities a pirate ship simply was not complete, for it was an unwritten law of the period that no one, especially the captain, should be aware exactly who was on board, or where, or why, at any given time. Consequently, when Colonel Blood scrambled unseen aboard the *Frantic Frog* off Aves, he had no difficulty in lying low; in fact, he had a hell of a job avoiding the other stowaways who were hiding out beneath its decks and behind its bulkheads – a couple of wandering madmen with white beards and ragged trousers who whimpered round the focsle heads at night, a rather vague scholar surrounded by pet mice and the works of Proust in a forward lazarette, two Huguenot refugees under the floor in the crow's-nest, an absconding Italian contessa shacked up with her stable-boy in the cable tier, and three large families of Pakistanis en route for Bradford.

Indeed, it took Blood several days' burrowing and stumbling around in the dark before he found an untenanted priest's hole near the rudder; once he'd heaved out a couple of skeletons and discovered the secret passage to the galley store-room where victuals could be stolen night and morning (except Sundays, early closing), he was beginning to get the hang of things, and by peering through spy-holes, listening at scuttles, and prowling warily, he soon learned something of what was afoot in the regular, above-decks part of the ship, where the pirates were.

It wasn't reassuring: the *Frantic Frog* appeared to be sailing full speed towards Cartagena on the Main, there to rendezvous in secret with Bilbo and Black Sheba who, Blood gathered, were contemplating some frightful devilry to do with the Spanish Viceroy and his bride-to-be; Rackham was assembling other buccaneer vessels at Tortuga, and they were going to devastate Latin America, by the sound of it. Not that Blood gave two hoots about that; his one concern was how he was going to slide out to safety, preferably in territory not infested either by pirates or Spaniards. (Difficult, on the Main in those days.) Anyway, since they seemed to be entirely surrounded by Atlantic at the moment, there was nothing for our Tom to do but keep his head down and enjoy the bilge-water which sloshed around in his hiding-place.

But being Blood, of course, he couldn't keep still. He prowled around the secret places of the *Frantic Frog*, from one peep-hole to another, getting occasional glimpses of focsle laundry, Frenchmen's knees, the backs of furniture, and some quite interesting bits of plank. But nothing of great moment until one day, snooping in a hitherto-unexplored passage towards the stern, he found two spy-holes close together high in the bulkhead, guessed that they were the cut-out eyes of some portrait hanging in a cabin, and clambered up on a rickety packing-case for a dekko. Sure enough, he was looking into a richly-furnished cabin with ormolu-encrusted chairs, buhl tables, tasselled curtains, Impressionist doilies, fin-de-siecle dart-boards, a beribboned guitar with the sheet music of "L'amour est bleu," and all the fixings one would expect in a French marine stateroom of the period, including . . . the Colonel gave a startled gasp as into his view came a trim foot and ankle, a well-turned calf, and finally a smooth white thigh whose owner was adjusting a suspender on the top of an elaborately-clocked stocking. Almost dislocating his neck in an effort to squint, wicked Tom lost his precarious foothold, and with a despairing cry went head-first through the painting and crashed full-length on the cabin floor in a cloud of dust and lumps of canvas, to the accompaniment of feminine squeaks.

"As I suspected, there's death-watch beetle all through the panelling, and it'll cost a mint to put right," he was improvising hastily, and then—

"You!" cried Vanity, shrinking back, all corset and fripperies. "Why, thou arrant peeper and transom-lurker! Wouldst spy on my deshabille, wastrel? Out, I say, thou rakehelly—"

"Keep your voice down!" hissed Blood, "I'm a stow-away!" And having assured himself that they were alone, he quickly brought her up to date, while Vanity got behind the couch, eyeing him mistrustfully.

"So ye see, we're after bein' companions in distress," he concluded with his manliest smile, which sent Vanity skipping back even farther. "But what o' the mad Frog Pew? Last I saw he was ravin' about you bein' the light o' his life, on account o' your turnin' brunette. Has he . . . ah . . ." he coughed delicately, eyeing her peekaboo undress, ". . . that is . . . have you an' he . . . ye know . . . ?"

"Certainly not!" snapped Vanity indignantly. "Know that he hath used me wi' all respect – nay, it ran close on reverence, the which," she admitted, frowning, "I am at a loss to understand, for while I know well that I have the message for the chaps, yet are they wont to get physical rather than spiritual, and Captain Pew's passion has thus far been that of a worshipper towards a deity – mind you, it takes all sorts; there was a gardener at our school who used to steal my gymshoes—"

"Ye mean he hasn't touched you?" Blood was incredulous. "But look at the way you're dressed—"

"*Stop* looking!" cried Vanity. "Thou muckrake! These are but the garments he provided for me, before he had his nervous breakdown – it's true, I tell you," she added, moving a chair between them. "The day after we sailed from Aves, he vowed undying devotion at my feet, calling me little apple and little pear, and swearing to wed me as soon as he had mastered the irregular verbs at the end of Book Two—"

"Thou kidd'st! Is he clean cocoa, then?"

"You better believe it, for of a sudden he clutched his brow, pale-faced, and staggered, crying: 'Croire! Joindre! Offrir! Pouvoir!' and fell down in a fit. His crew put him to bed, where he lies and babbles o' the imperfect indicative of 'connaître' and crying sore for his Beauteous Beloved wi' the Big Mouth, whatever that may mean . . ."

"Wait!" Blood snapped his fingers. "It's comin' back to me. Did ye do French at school? Well, then, d'ye not recall the lesson about the wench whose mouth was too big, an' the doctor bade her say 'petite pomme, petite pomme,' over an' over, so should her trap diminish, but she, bein' flighty piece an' misrememberin' what fruit he had specified, repeated 'petite poire, petite poire,' so that her gob got bigger than ever? I mind me there was a picture of her in our school-book, a well-curved and oomphish brunette, an' 'tis my guess this lunatic Pew did fall in love wi' it, an' seein' thee wi' thy hair stained wi' galoopa juice, supposeth thou art she! See? So keep up the dye-job an' you're safe enough, for—"

"Safe?" shrilled Vanity. "Safe, i' the clutches of a buccaneering hophead who devours me wi' wild eyes, and drools of honeymoons in Bermuda? Anyway, my mouth is *not* too big, sure 'tis small and dainty rosebud!" And she turned to regard it indignantly in the mirror.

"He probably wasn't lookin' at your mouth," observed Blood drily, edging closer. "No wonder, the way you traipse around in shortie night-rails, gauzy pants, floral bikinis, an' frilly corsets – I can't think when I last saw ye wi' your clothes on, thank God," he added, taking a playful pat, but Vanity hadn't played mixed lacrosse for nothing, and as the Colonel hopped and swore with a hacked shin and a finger-jabbed eye, she grabbed up a heavy brass candlestick and stood on guard.

"What was that for?" cried Blood. "A mere brotherly gesture of affection, to comfort thee—"

"Try it again," threatened Vanity, "and I scream for help, then shall we see how Happy Dan's crew do serve the molester o' their captain's intended."

"Ye've got me all wrong," protested Blood, and hastily revised his strategy, the crafty knave. "I mean only thy service, for consider that once Happy Dan hath recovered from his irregular verbs, thou'rt right in it, gorgeous child. Aye, unless ye want to end up as Mistress Pew, legal or not,

214

ye must rely on honest Tom Blood to pluck you from this pickle, and he's the boy to do it, so he is."

"Ha! In a pig's ear, I'll warrant!"

"In a nutshell, rather. Dear Vanity, this cursed ship is bound for Cartagena on the Main, there to join wi' Black Sheba, Bilbo, an' t'other o' the damned Coast Brethren in fell design 'gainst the Spanish Viceroy. If you want to find yourself playin' tig wi' that lot, I don't," said the Colonel earnestly, "an' since we're only a few days' sail from Cartagena I suggest ye let me devise our evasion forthwith." He drummed up his most winning, crinkly smile. "Come, lady – is it a truce?"

Vanity weighed the candlestick suspiciously. "Shalt keep thy paws to thyself? No playing footsie, even?"

"Perish the thought," promised Blood, crossing his fingers unseen. Not until we're safely out of this lot, he reflected lecherously, the rotter.

"Pax, skinch, and keys? Honest Injun?"

"On me ould mother's grave. Ye'll be as safe wi' me as wi' your precious Ben Avery, wherever the hell he's got to."

At this mention of her lost love Vanity was so moved that the candlestick fell from her nerveless fingers, her eyes misted, and a great shuddering sigh convulsed her bosom. Blood gave a sharp moan and bit his lip.

"Please don't do that," he pleaded. "Not in that corset."

Touched by his restraint – and not a little flattered, the minx – Vanity composed herself and recounted how she had been awaiting Avery on the Isle of Aves when Happy Dan abducted her. "Though how he knew of my whereabouts is more than I can guess," said she frowning, while rascal Tom shook his head innocently, "nor why my darling Ben was late in coming for me. I fear he may have met with some mischance . . . ."

"Miss Chance," murmured Blood absently. "Or Miss Barbados."

Vanity stiffened. "What was that crack?"

"What? Nothing!" Blood started elaborately. "It just slipped out . . . thinkin' aloud . . . forget it . . ."

Vanity went pink, white, and several more becoming intermediate shades. "Creep!" cried she. "D'ye imply that my dreamboat is gallivanting after yon beldame Sheba? 'Tis foul lie, told out of jealous spite by treacherous marplot, thou! Ha! I mind how you tried to sow dissension 'twixt us in the boat! Just because his perfection makes you look like something left out for the bin-men, you seek to sully him in mine eyes! Typical!" Her perfect lips whiffled and her corset creaked with contempt. "And about what I'd expect from a cad who tried to cop the Crown Jewels, betrayed my love's mission, snuck off with a piece of the Madagascar crown, and e'en now invaded my toilet and made passes! Why, what a caitiff stinkard art thou, and where," she demanded, as Blood (the sly skunk) turned away meekly and started to climb through the shattered picture towards the secret passage, "d'you think you're going?"

"Back into the woodwork," said Blood humbly. "Since I am not wanted, and have by thoughtless inadvertence given offence to your ladyship, I'll e'en hie me back among my friends the rats and cockroaches. I beg your ladyship's pardon." He sighed heavily. "Fare ye well," said he, in a quivery voice, and as he began to clamber through the wrecked painting the artful villain sneaked a scrap of paper from his pocket and let it flutter to the floor.

"Take your litter with you", said Vanity coldly, and picked up the paper to thrust it at him with disdain, when she noted the dread signature: "Sheba the She-Wolf" and the row of kisses writ as crosses. Her beauteous orbs bugged, and in an instant she had conned the note and yowled with rage and dismay.

"*I* . . . pad my *bra*?" she shrilled. "What infamy is this? Who . . . to whom . . . what . . . yikes! Whence had ye this vile libel?"

Now you'll have guessed that this paper was the letter

which Sheba had written to Avery, and which the Colonel had purloined unnoticed on Dead Man's Chest (see page 000). Ripe stuff, in which the pirate queen had poured out her passion. Blood, half-way through the wall, feigned vexation and made a feeble snatch at the letter, a pretty piece of acting marred by his accidentally rending his breeches painfully on a splinter. Vanity goggled distraught at the letter.

"Did that saucy sable slut write this to Captain Avery?" she gnashed.

"No, she wrote it to Louis the XIVth!" snarled Blood, his composure disturbed by splinters in his rear. "Of course she wrote it to Avery! Ah, what have I said?" He smote his forehead in pretended remorse. "Ochone, I would ha' spared ye this, but . . . aye, she wrote it to him. Why not? She's a woman, an' he's God's gift. D'ye wonder she dotes on him? Didn't he save her from a flogging, an' show her tender regard—"

"So did you!" cried Vanity wildly, white to the gills.

"But I'm a caitiff stinkard," said Blood, all martyred. "Everyone knows that. Not like Wonder Boy". He gave a wounded shrug. "Mind you, I didn't go drooling after her first chance I got, having lulled an' abandoned my trusting betrothed on a desert island to be scooped up by Happy Dan Pew. Nay, I didn't vow eternal love to the purest, sweetest saint that ever curved a corset, while engaging in secret correspondence with a virago who says that you pad your bra – a malicious an' laughable lie, incidentally, from where I'm standing". He shook his head with a brave, sad smile. "Such are not the ways of Colonel Blood."

Vanity stared from him to the letter in stunned dismay, like the class idiot called on to solve a quadratic equation.

"My senses swim!" she faltered. "Oh, can he be false indeed? What am I to believe?" She sank limply to the couch, and a great tear sploshed on the crumpled letter. "See, this abandoned cow writes to my personal fiancé as 'beloved' and 'barracuda baby' and I know not what . . . would she do this if he had spurned her, as he pretended? Ooooh, if he's two-timing me, the rat! Nay, but 'tis not on! He is an English gentleman, and she an alien tramp whose very colour must repel!"

"Some people go for black jelly beans," observed Blood cryptically, and as Vanity clutched her temples the oily rogue climbed swiftly down into the cabin again and took up a strategic kneeling position by the couch. "Ah, sweet Vanity, to see thee thus ill-used!" he murmured, and although the amount of silken leg on view cried out for a juicy pinch he schooled himself to imprint a chaste kiss on her little toe. No fires broke out, so he essayed a reverent smooch on her instep.

"Don't do that!" moaned Vanity, distracted, "it reminds me of Happy Dan Pew." She clasped her brow and seemed to become aware of him all of a sudden. "What are you doing, for God's sake?"

"Worshipping", said Blood pathetically.

"Eh?" Her wits were quite disordered. "Ah, of your pity, one emotional crisis at a time! Here am I, distraught lest my lover has handed me the welly, and you nibble at my nylons!" She shook a bemused galoopa'd head. "Hold on – when you spoke a moment since of the purest saint who ever curved a corset . . . did you mean me? You?"

"Who else?" Blood looked at her like a distempered poodle.

"And . . . that your regard for me is . . . honourable? That y'are not mere groper and nuisance?" Blood nodded dumbly, and Vanity stared amazed. "Oh, pull the other one! Or rather, don't!" And she hastily swung her legs aside, while the wily ruffian shook his handsome curly head.

"Oh, Vanity acushla," quo' he. "Get a grip, take a deep breath, and consider the facts. 'Tis true I betrayed the Madagascar crown to the pirates – well knowing that if I did not, thy precious self would ha' been next on the sharks' menu. And thereafter, compare my conduct wi' a certain

218

other's. Who rushed to thy side in Akbar's cabin an' gave thee a fireman's lift, cruelly tho' you requited him – and who neglected thee in his eagerness to slaughter the wog an' grab the jewellery? Who washed the dishes in the boat, humbly preparin' bully an' tinned pears for thy delight – and who lolled i' the stern an' beguiled thee wi' fair words? Who, rather than stay on Aves (where he might ha' lapped up the goodies in safety) followed thee here aboard, an' now kneels at your feet, offering his life in your service – and who couldn't wait to get after Black Sheba an' may e'en now, for aught we know, be workin' the zipper on her tracksuit? I name no names," crooned the insidious scoundrel, "but leave it to your woman's intuition to judge what the hell I'm talkin' about."

"I can't cope," whimpered Vanity. "I'm in a state. Ah, what is a poor friendless maid to think? Gosh, I'll break that blighter's neck if, as I suspicion, he has the hots for yon dark Delilah! And you, making like Galahad – and yet ye deserted from the boat, swiped Akbar's cross, and left a note in which ye maligned me grossly and spoke of living it up in the stews o' Libertatia—"

"A mere device to cover up the suicide on which I was intent, distracted as I was at seeing you in the arms o' that smoothie Avery," protested Blood glibly. "If 'twas known I'd done away with meself, how could me ould mother have collected the insurance, an' her livin' on mouldy spuds in a turf pigsty in Galway? But a chance current bore me ashore, God be thanked, since I'm spared to serve you in your sore need, an' prove the depth of my . . . ah, dare I say it? Oh, go on, why not, unworthy though I am, an' timid an' hesitant an' misunderstood . . . aye, the depth o' my true love for thee, dear delectable Vanity."

Strong material, and if she half-swallowed it, well, de-fenceless females in need of rescuing from pirates seldom remain indifferent to Clark Gable respectfully stroking their toes and giving them the dimple. And if you wonder why the bounder was pitching such ardent woo, it was because he was looking ahead to the point where he had borne her safely back to civilisation (he was Irish and optimistic, remember), and had earned her gratitude – and possibly some warmer emotion, the scheming snake. His raffish charm might well catch her on the rebound from Avery, whom he had so cunningly discredited, and there were worse billets than being old Rooke's son-in-law with Vanity's charms as an added bonus.

So the rascal reasoned, while Vanity heaved another bewildered sigh and absently smoothed her stockings (actions which forced Blood to keep a tight hold on himself), raised her lovely tear-stained face, screwed up Sheba's note with a final jealous gnash, and regarded the kneeling Colonel with a gym-mistress tilt to her queenly chin.

"Right," she said. "Little choice have I. The galoopa juice is growing out, I'll be blonde again before you know it, and heaven knows how that screwball Pew will react when he realises I'm not Miss Bigmouth after all. Whether Captain Avery be false or no, 'tis to thee I must look for present aid – easy, boy, easy!" she cried as Blood pressed ardent lips to her extended hand, "swallowing my arm is not part of the deal. As lady o' quality and ranking society pippin I am far above thy touch, so don't get fresh, understand? But extract me from this garboil, and shalt have such reward . . ." here she shot him that cool hands-off-but-wait-and-see look which had ravished the Whitehall beaux ". . . as I may deem fitting. Cripes, what's that?"

For from an adjoining cabin came strange sounds, a voice that babbled: "Connaître, connaissant, connu – present indicative, and . . . and . . . ah, mort de ma vie . . . connaissais!" followed by an exultant scream of laughter. "I 'ave found eet! Eureka! The imperfect indicative, n'est-ce pas?" And as Blood and Vanity stood rooted, came running feet and roars of "The Captain recovers 'is marbles! 'E ees cured! Bring aft the rum, Darby, an' listen to this!"

220

"We are undone!" gasped Vanity. "Pew has mastered his irregular verbs!"

"Are ye sure?" Blood was tense. "He hasn't got to the present subjunctive yet—"

"It skills not!" cried Vanity, clasping her corset and stamping her foot impatiently. "He'll be in here any moment to claim me as his bride! We must flee! Quickly, plan our escape while I get a dress on!"

She shot behind a screen, and Blood rushed to the stern windows – there, not a mile distant, was a green jungly coastline. The Main, probably, peopled by terrors indescribable, but what the hell, if it wasn't Blackpool beach it was still their only hope. Outside the tumult grew:

"Connaissais, imperfec' indicative!" Happy Dan was chortling, amidst rapturous applause from his followers. "Et aussis, connaîtrai – the future! How's about that, hein?" His crew stamped and shouted, while Blood considered and rejected various means of escape as feverishly as Vanity, behind her screen, was running through a selection of garments. Thus by the time the Colonel had decided against swimming (too far), floating ashore in barrels (too slow) and building a raft (sure to attract attention), the fair captive had discarded mauve taffeta, flowered silk, see-through scarlet nylon (not safe, she felt, in view of Blood's propensities), and cloth of gold, and had emerged in a most becoming maroon velvet number with her hair up. Blood was peering out of the stern window, and swearing foully.

"There's no boat!" he cried. "Jayzus, trust the French! Whoever heard o' pirate ship without a small boat moored 'neath the stern an' provisioned wi' all necessities, so that fugitives can light out unseen!"

"But they're coming!" cried Vanity. "Listen!"

Sure enough, from without the cabin a great cheer had gone up: "Vive l'imperfect indicative! Dix out of dix for le capitaine, and it's his turn to clean the tableau noir!" And then the voice of Happy Dan Pew, sounding distressingly sane: "Merci, mes enfants. An' now to claim my bride, La Jeune Fille avec la Grande Bouche!"

Blood didn't hesitate. With one hand he snatched a convenient rapier from the wall, and with the other he swept Vanity almost bodily through the gaping hole in the picture and into the passage behind. An instant later and they were crouched in the dark of the secret passage, while the cabin door burst in, and Happy Dan's glad cry of "Ouvrez la porte, ma belle!" ended in a shriek of dismay. "Où est-elle? Elle n'est pas ici! Ah, but I am staggered, me! I feel not well! I should 'ave stayed on the deck avec Papa!"

"With any luck he'll have a relapse," whispered Blood, "an' we can lurk unseen an' get our breath back."

"But will they not see the great rent i' the canvas picture?" hissed Vanity, huddled against him. "Hang it, it's about three feet across!"

"Not a chance," hissed Blood. ".What wi' the shock o' your disappearance, he's probably back to Lesson One by now. I doubt if he could tell ye what 'je suis' means. They'll have eyes for naught else—"

Pat on his words came a yell from the cabin. "Mais regardez, mon capitaine! Un grand trou dans l'image sur le mur! Cette's the way elle has gone!"

"That's a nuisance," said Blood, and as hairy heads thrust through the hole to stare into the gloom of the passage, he got to his feet, carefully pushed Vanity behind him, and fell on guard. Scoundrel he might be, but when the chips were down and there was nowhere left to run, our Tom knew what to do. "I'm sorry, acushla. Fine help I've been to ye, after all. I'll hold 'em as best I can, an' when they've finished me, ye can tell 'em I was kidnappin' you; play along wi' Pew, an' take your chance when it comes."

Vanity's gasp was lost in the yells of the French pirates as they spotted the fugitive pair crouched in the gloom of the passage. They swarmed through into that narrow place, a wild-eyed Pew at their head, flourishing his épée in one hand and a lace hanky in the other.

"Ah, scélérat! Irish chien!" he cried. "Vous êtes un voleur – de la forêt, pas de doubt! What do I see but that you ravish away my love, méchant! Now we pay you back for Lansdowne Road! En garde! Don't worry, petite pomme, 'Appy Dan is 'ere to rescue vous!"

The blades clanged, and as Blood faced his crazed adversary and the horde of ruffians pressing behind him, he was conscious of Vanity's hand on his shoulder; just a moment it pressed there before it fell away, and Blood felt a strange content and lightness of heart as he parried Happy Dan's thrust and sent his point through the shoulder of a bearded lout at the French captain's elbow. Then he was retreating, parrying and riposting for all he was worth as they surged down on him three abreast, into a wider space where a convenient lantern flickered. Vanity shuddered back against the bulkhead, and Happy Dan, turning a low lunge from Blood, leaped to her side, flourishing his blade and crying:

"See, I come! Moi, 'Appy Dan! Give 'im the business, garçons!"

"Ah, nay!" cried Vanity, in the Frog's fevered grasp. "Spare him!"

"Not a chance!" roared the French pirates, closing on Blood, brandishing their cutlasses. "Regardez, Paddy, here it comes!"

"Ah, the hell wi' ye!" cried Blood. "College Mooney for ever!" And he hurled his back to the bulkhead, thrusting deep into the chest of an assailant, preparing to take their steel in his turn, and die (he reflected) in unexpectedly gallant fashion, defending Beauty from the powers of darkness. Then the timbers at his back seemed to give way, rotten boards crumbled about him, and he stumbled back and fell on a cold, half-yielding surface that clanked and slithered most strangely beneath him. His rapier, jarred from his hand, tinkled away, and with yells of amazement his attackers stopped dead, staring in disbelief at what they saw. Happy Dan, with Vanity half-swooning in his grasp, thrust through them and halted gaping at the sight which confronted him in the flickering lamplight.

Crashing through the rotten bulkhead, Colonel Blood had fallen back into a secret cell deep in the bowels of the *Frantic Frog*. He was floundering helplessly on its contents – a great shimmering, shifting heap of gold coin in which, as he staggered to his feet, he was buried above the knees.

Hidden treasure, by the powers! And about time, too, says you, and right ye are. And if its discovery has come about without the usual aids of faded maps in spidery writing and skeleton signposts pointing to "Ye Treasure Pitte", don't worry – its disposal will be bizarre enough to satisfy the most traditional taste. Let's leave Blood wallowing in it, while Vanity presses fearful knuckles to apprehensive teeth and Happy Dan's crew go into hysterics, and haste us back to Cartagena, where things ought to be hotting up nicely.

CHAPTER
THE TWELFTH

clvet night shed its peace o'er the Viceregal Palace. The great ballroom lay deserted, naught remained of Xavier Cugat and his Orchestra save a faint aroma of hair-oil and a solitary shattered maraca, pale moonlight shone through archways on empty corridors and silent stairways, continental breakfast orders hung outside bedroom doors, and even the mice were lapping it up in their nests. It can't last, though; soon no one will be getting a wink of sleep, for e'en now a fracas is breaking out in the wine-cellar, with muffled oaths and blows and excited cries in Spanish, and the unmistakable noises of people wrestling in yellow Chartreuse. Follows dread silence, and presently a thin, distant wail of agony; and now the footsteps of a female in drag running in frantic haste as a pale figure flits through the guest wing, sobbing in terror . . .

Avery awoke to sounds of scratching at his chamber door, and sprang nimbly from his pit, teeth clenched and eyes blazing – had he or had he not put out a Do Not Disturb notice, and here they were wanting to make up the room at 4 a.m! He flung open the door wrathfully, and a lithe stripling tumbled in and clung to him, gasping:

"Oh, Capeetan Ben, Capeetan Ben! All eez lost! You are lumbaired, an' we mus' flee! Queekly – thaire eez no time to lose!"

Realising almost instantly that it was not a chambermaid

225

but Meliflua, the captain drew her in, closed the door, and strove to calm her as she collapsed on the bed and panted out her tale.

Having absconded from the ballroom earlier, she had wandered the grounds in a dazed condition for some hours, until challenged by a patrol of guards. Darting into a low doorway, she had found herself in a cellar occupied by a drunken dwarf and a slumbering red-bearded giant (at which news Avery's eyes narrowed to steely slits, and he stroked his chin as he mumured: "Firebeard and Goliath – ha!"). Hiding behind a barrel, she had seen the guards lay hold of them, and from the obscenities they uttered she had judged them English. Not that the giant had put up much resistance, for—

" 'E was plastaired out of eez min', but thee dwarf 'e struggled an' called them bloddy Dagoes. Then presen'lee, that deezgusteeng Don Lardo an' the greaseball Enchillada come, een their night attire, an' they take thee two Eengleesh to the torture chamber. Thees I see through a leetle barred weendow. Thee giant they chain up, an' the midget 'e squeal an' say eef they let 'eem go 'e will tell them beeg news. So Don Lardo laff an' say, 'Let's 'ear eet, shortie', an' the dwarf 'e say 'e 'ave seen you fight weeth Capeetan Beelbo, an' you are not Don Espresso at oll, but thee faymoos Capeetan Avery, an' Eengleesh 'eretic pirate – wheech is true, as I know."

"I see," said Avery. "And did they release the dwarf?"

"No!" Donna Meliflua shuddered piteously. "They put 'eem on thee rack, an' – oh, eet was 'orreeble! They tore off 'ees laig!"

"They tore off his what?" cried Avery, aghast.

"Ees laig! 'Ees poor leetle left laig! 'E scream weeth agony w'en eet come off—"

"It's all right," said Avery soothingly. "It's made of wood. Then what?"

"Don Lardo 'e clap 'ees 'ands, an' ees teeth fall out weeth pleasure – tell me, w'y does 'e not 'ave them stock een weeth sometheeng? Ah, but then 'e say to rack the dwarf again, but the chief torturer, 'e say you cannot rack a man weeth only one leg, because 'e ees not balanced propairly, an' eet might damage the machine. I could bear no more," Meliflua concluded pathetically, "an' anyway, I mus' fly to warn you, an' now I yam 'ere, an' we mus' fly, Capeetan Ben, before Don Lardo send 'ees guards for you!"

She flung herself into his arms again, and Avery patted her shoulder while his thoughts raced. There went his night's sleep, he was thinking, and now that his cover was blown a swift retreat was probably in order, although his haughty spirit rebelled at the thought.

"Yoo weel fly, Capeetan Ben – an' tek mee weeth yoo!" Her slim arms were round his neck, and her eyes were those of a yearning koala. "I cannot stay to bee marreed to that reepulseev Don Lardo – I shall keel myself first! Pliz, pliz, tek mee weeth yoo!"

"To be sure, brave child," said our Ben, "but first I must have words with this red-bearded fellow of thine." And he buckled on his rapier, made sure his shirt-ruffles were open at the front, and smoothed his hair at the mirror.

"Wot!" Meliflua was horrified. "But 'e ees stoned, an' chained een thee 'orreed dungeon, weeth thee guards an' torture people, an' eef yoo go thair they weel keel yoo—"

"Have no fear, dear maid, but listen," said Avery crisply, "This red rascal, Firebeard by name, has an item o' price which I must e'en recoup from him. So now, you shall direct me to his dungeon, and whilst I steal thither, shalt await me at the quay where we came ashore—"

"No! Nevaire shall I bee parted from yoo, Capeetan Ben! Whair you go, I go!" And so insistent was she that Avery was melted, and kissed her in brotherly fashion, at which she fainted briefly. When she came to, it was to see our captain in the act of snapping a magnificent gold cross containing a black pearl from the hilt of a great black rapier; he placed this glittering trophy, and a similar one containing a diamond, within the tight folds of his waist-sash, and smiled on her with boyish confidence.

"Come, gallant Spanish lady," said he, "and see how Long Ben Avery struts his stuff. And fear not; a dungeon-full of Dons is a mere pipe-opener to me." He took her slim hand, and when she would have protested, stunned her to silence with a light salute on her dainty fingers.

Down the great silent stairway they stole, hand in hand, the dim lamps casting huge shadows as they passed, and they would have won unhindered to the ground floor if they hadn't met Don Lardo and his attendants coming up. The Viceroy, more hideous than ever in a scarlet dressing-gown and night-cap, with vampire bats clinging to his shoulders (black widows in the evening, vampires at night, he was very particular), was in a steaming rage; they heard him shrieking as he stamped up the stairs, and Avery drew Meliflua aside into an alcove, whence they watched in breathless silence as he passed by, Enchillada trotting fearfully beside him in a perfectly foul Buchanan tartan dressing-gown, while a file of morioned soldiers brought up the rear.

"One-legged dwarfs!" the Viceroy was snarling, and they saw his gooseberry eyes glitter palely in the half-light. "Why does it always have to happen to me? I wanted to hear his bones crack and splinter, and what do I get – plywood! Ah, but he shall roast on a spit tomorrow, wooden leg and all. By then we shall have seized the ship of this Bilbo, and our own *Santa Cascara*—"

"An' thee Eengleesh capeetan, Excellencee?" cried Enchillada. "Should we not clobbair 'eem now, while 'e sleeps?"

"Intrude your opinions again, carrion," hissed Don Lardo, "and I shall have your enormous entrails ripped from you with red-hot pincers. Have you no artistry, swine? We let him sleep, and all shall use him as Don Espresso tomorrow, while I gloat and hug myself to see him lulled – until, at my pleasure, I denounce him, and win the plaudits of all!" They heard his huge lips slobber and his teeth bounce clattering on the stair as he passed on, and Meliflua whispered tremulously in Avery's ear.

" 'Ow could I face that across thee breakfast tebble? Ah, Capeetan Ben, save me from 'eem!" Avery gave her a reassuring squeeze, and the hot-blooded young hidalga, mistaking it for affection, could not restrain an ecstatic whimper. Don Lardo checked, his great hideous face glaring round, the bats a-flutter on his massive shoulders.

"What was that?" he rasped. "An unauthorised murmur?" His mad gaze fell on Enchillada. "Gluttonous offal, have you been at the curried beans again?" His hand lashed cruelly across the chamberlain's pudgy cheek, and then he lurched upwards, mouthing horribly, and Avery drew the terrified Meliflua swiftly out and down the staircase.

Across the hall they hurried, and by many a passage the beauteous Spaniard directed Avery to where a dank flight of stone steps wound down into a torch-lit gloom where rats scuttled, nitre gleamed on the walls with their pathetic graffiti ("Up Torquemada!" "Aye, right up him!" "Morgan Rules, okay?" and "The Inquisition takes better care of you"), rusty chains dangled, and from the stygian vaults beneath came faint clank o' chain and murmuring voices. Avery, sword in hand, raised a cautionary finger to his lips and almost gave himself a nasty cut, and then, with Meliflua clinging at his shoulder, stole forward across the slippery flags towards a lighted archway, and peeped cautiously within.. . .

The Spanish jailers had spared no pains to make their prisoners comfortable for the night. Firebeard, now awake and as sentient as he ever was, had been spreadeagled on the floor, with great weights laid on his chest; his face was as red as his beard as he bore the intolerable burden that was threatening to burst his ribs. To one side, Black Sheba, her silver lamé trouser-suit sorrily besmirched and torn, was bound to a tilting platform; above her face a huge waterskin slowly but steadily dripped water, a drop at a time, on to the sodden cloth with which she had been gagged – it was nicely calculated to give her the agony of suffocation without actually drowning her.

Close by, Bilbo was confined in a devilish frame of slender metal strips like some grotesque suit of armour. From it thick wires ran to a great brazier which glowed white hot, the principle being that heat travelled along the wires to Bilbo's suit, which was gradually warming up to the point where he would be slowly grilled alive. The fourth captive, little Goliath, was hung from a strappado, his arms behind his back, his single foot supporting him – and just to add to the fun a spiked board had been placed beneath that foot. Not surprisingly, he was being vocal, but in explanation rather than complaint.

" 'Tworn't my fault, capting! If that big soak on the floor 'adn't got hisself pissed, we'd never ha' bin took! An' I didn't mean ter give away the ship's position, honnist! It just slipped aht, like – an' I'm just a little chap, capting, an' I only got one leg! Don't blame me, capting!"

"Peace, mannikin!" gasped Bilbo. " 'Tis all one now . . . we ha' come to our bad end at last . . . ah, I burn, damme! 'Tis foretaste o' hell . . . oddsooks, if I could but take one o' them with me!" And from his cage he glared at the two jailers, great bearded ruffians in leather aprons, who drank and diced and talked with their mouths full at a greasy table, and when the luck ran against them they would pelt the hapless captives cruelly with bread rolls and orange peel. One of them now rose, stretched himself, and sauntered over to leer down at Sheba as she vainly tossed her head to avoid the choking drip that fell upon her gag.

"Thirsty, chiquita?" mocked the torturer, and as the amber eyes shone hate at him he reached out to fondle her lewdly. "Ah, but you shall be dry enough when they bring you to the stake, black heretic bitch!" And with a cruel laugh he turned away to meet a fist which crashed against his jaw with shattering force and stretched him senseless on the flags.

230

His comrade was half-out of his chair as Avery whirled on him; one quick shuffle, a pile-driving left to the stomach and a right to the head, and that was Number Two taken care of.

Black Sheba felt the suffocating gag plucked from her mouth, and gasped in wonder and adoration at the splendid vision leaning over her; joy-bells rang in the ears of the dusky filibustress as she struggled for breath.

"Barracuda!" she gasped. "You came back for me!"

"Disgusting!" snapped Avery. "Our ambassador at Madrid is going to have a word or two to say about this, I can tell you! Why, 'tis against all usage o' captives! Four to a cell, too. Canst breathe, woman?"

"Aye, but my heart is like to choke me!" cried Sheba. "Ah, release me that I may embrace thee, amore mio!"

But Avery was away, kicking the spiked board from beneath Goliath's foot and slashing the ropes of the strappado with his rapier. "Donna Meliflua", he called briskly, "would you be so kind as to cast a bucket of water over that person," and he indicated the writhing Bilbo. Then he knelt beside the recumbent Firebeard and with one quick heave had thrust the weights from his body.

"Damn me deadlights if it ain't the King's popinjay!" wheezed the hirsute giant. "An' a welcome sight, by thunder, says I, split me sideways else! Why, here's j'y, an' much obleeged t'ye, wi' a curse—"

"Save it", snapped Avery, and with steely-eyed deliberation laid his sword-point at Firebeard's throat. "I come not in thy behalf, fellow, but to ask thee this: where is the cross ye filched from the Madagascar crown? Now speak, or as I'm a gentleman I'll spit you like a capon. Well?"

"Well, as you're a gentleman an' I'm a rogue, spit away an' welcome!" Firebeard's piggy eyes glared through the fuzz. " 'Tis sweeter end than the Dons'll give me, by cock! So thrust home, cully – dispatch, ha!"

Avery was snookered. Why, the great blister was right: a quick death was no threat at all, in his position – and, anyway,

Avery knew that he could never skewer a helpless man, not even such a stinker as Firebeard. He bit his flawless lip, and Bilbo, now enveloped in clouds of steam as a result of Meliflua's bucket-work, laughed weakly in his cage.

"Aye, slay away, King's man! Or – if y'are wise, make a bargain. Our liberty for the information ye seek, ha?"

"Treat with such as you – never!" Avery regarded the cloud of steam with proud scorn. "Thy lives are forfeit for thy gross crimes, and whether 'tis Spain or England visits execution on you, 'tis all one!"

"Then ye can go hang, dawcock!" roared Firebeard. "I'd sooner rot – aye, or burn at a Spanish stake – than tell ye where your precious cross is! So kill me an' be damned to you!"

Avery stood a moment irresolute, and then his eye fell on Goliath, who was sitting massaging his small wrists; he alone of the captives was free, but without his wooden leg he was more or less immobile.

"You," snapped Avery, "are but a poor minion o' the Brotherhood. To loose thee on the world again were small weight on my conscience. So, sirrah, where is Firebeard his cross? Tell me and I vow to bear thee out of this to safety."

Goliath stopped massaging to gape, and Firebeard and Bilbo gave tongue with a vengeance. "Pick on someone your own size!" they roared. "Shame! Of all the mean tricks! Why, what a feeble spirit is this Long Ben Avery, to bully a poor halfling! Boo! Who'd ha' thought it! . . ." and the like.

But Avery was implacable. "Choose, midget," he said coldly, "and that speedily. Time presses."

Goliath sweated big drops. He shot a scared glance towards Bilbo, and started violently as the supine Firebeard growled ferociously; Goliath licked his lips and cringed at Avery. "Yer promise, honnist! You'll get me away?"

Firebeard went berserk in his chains. "Maggot! Will ye truckle to this pimp, ye turncoat beetle? Rend and burn me, if I could come at ye, I'd tear your other leg off—"

" 'Appy Dan Pew's got it!" babbled Goliath. "Strite up, guv'nor! 'E won it offa ole 'Airy-Belly there at gamin', an' –"

"Loaded dice!" bawled Firebeard. "We wuz robbed! We should ha' stood in bed!"

" 'Tis very well," said Avery to Goliath. "I shall take you with me; y'are slight enough to carry till we may contrive you another leg. Donna Meliflua, we had best away."

Now, you'll have noticed that Sheba hadn't said a word during these exchanges. Sick as mud at the chilling realisation that Avery hadn't come to rescue her, she had not failed to note that the slender stripling was a young woman of outstanding oomph, albeit apparently a transvestite. Jealous fury quivered the pirate queen in her bonds, and she darted Meliflua a glance of fell malevolence.

"Aye, best away, Donna Meliflua," she sneered harshly. "Go wi' thy brave champion who abandons his countrymen to doom o' dago torture, and thinks no shame to coerce yon poor crippled gnome." She curled a lip at Avery. "And you, captain – since ye ha' forgot your precious Vanity so soon, I wish ye joy o' that skinny ninny in men's breeches!"

"Skinnee!" flared Meliflua indignantly. "At least I don' treep ovair my own lower leep!" But Avery stilled her with an upraised hand and spoke at Sheba.

"I would have ye under no misprision," said he, a slight flush suffusing his clean-cut features. "This is a distressed Spanish lady whom I shall deliver from shameful fate; she is no love o' mine, but poor abandoned innocent, so you can take your foul focsle gossip and bottle it!" But the pirates hooted with derision and made vulgar noises.

"Haw-haw! We believe you! Whoopity-whee, a likely tale, i' faith! We know! Ha, some innocent, that doth flaunt her curves in male attire! Avery's got a girl-friend, nyah-nyah-nyah!" And while Firebeard blew huge raspberries and Bilbo jeered saturnine in his cage, Sheba spat in contempt, and our Ben went beetroot with anger and scorn.

Little could they guess that while they engaged in futile

insult and denial, three flights up Don Lardo was pausing at the door of his bedchamber, frowning in sudden thought, which made his face look like granny's X-rays. He plucked at his great nether lip.

"Ha, did I misjudge thee, Enchillada?" he croaked. "For now I mind me – there were no curried beans on the buffet tonight . . ." His eyes rolled like gob-stoppers. "So . . . that strange gasp of wind I heard on the staircase . . . whence came it, if not from thee . . .?"

Back down in the dungeon Avery had gone from beetroot to off-white, his haughty gaze raking the captives.

"For shame! To bandy a lady's name in the dungeon! But why should I waste breath on you? Come, Meliflua." And he scooped Goliath under his free arm and turned away.

"Farewell, hero!" Sheba's smoky snarl followed him. "Crawl back to England and tell 'em how the Dons did your dirty work for you!"

"Aye, faith!" cried Bilbo. "He was to hunt us down, this roaring blade! Why, what a cat's-paw is he, to creep hence – aye, but he fled more nimbly before my point this night, did he not, Sheba?"

"And we did not peach on him before the Viceroy, neither." Sheba's eyes were on Avery, no longer scornful, but proud and passionate – oh, she's fairly percolating for him still, the crazy Jezebel.

"An' we give him a fair chance on Dead Man's Chest, an' all!" bellowed Firebeard. "Course, we'm just poor pirates, we – not gentlefolk like him, wi' a wannion! We don't know no better'n to stick by our mates, aye, through hell an' brimstone, scuttle me! I'll bet he got off Dead Man's Chest sneaky like, an' all!"

"Now, look here!" cried Avery. "I've had about enough of this. Firstly, you are not my mates. Secondly, Bilbo, I was miles ahead on points, and you know it. Thirdly, it's not my fault if you're in the toils o' th'Inquisition . . ."

A small hand on his arm interrupted him, and he found

Donna Meliflua regarding him with troubled eyes.

"Mus' yoo leave them, Capeetan Ben?"

"Lemme loose!" Goliath was wriggling beneath Avery's arm, kicking fiercely with his one leg. "Put me dahn! If yore goin' to scarper, I'll stay! I've changed me mind! I'll turn you free, mates, an' we'll take our chance, the four of us! Lemme go, rot yer boots!" He tried to bite the captain's arm, struggling feebly in that iron grasp, weeping and swearing something frightsome.

Then Avery looked round the dungeon again . . . well, you know what he was thinking. Only a rotter could leave them, blood-stained enemies though they were – on the other hand, if he relented, they'd probably turn on him at the drop of a plumed castor, and where would Vanity and Meliflua and his mission be then? Their parole wouldn't be worth a curse . . . and yet, Sheba *had* stocked his boat with goodies, and Bilbo was a simply topping swordsman, and Firebeard had a mental age of about three and presumably couldn't be held accountable . . . and dammit, even the dwarf was going all noble on him . . .

"Oh, all right!" he said irritably, and dropped Goliath, who promptly hopped over and drew the bolts from Bilbo's cage. At Avery's moody sign Meliflua unclamped Firebeard's shackles, and our hero himself slit Sheba's bonds with his rapier. Like a striking snake the black bombshell uncoiled from her bench, her arms flew round Avery's neck, and as her lips locked on his like electro-magnets he heard the bongo drums booming in his brain and jungle incense inflaming his senses; a strange weakness jellied his knees momentarily, and then Sheba's voice was throbbing throatily at his ear:

"Ah, mad fool! 'Twas inevitable – why must ye struggle against fate? Thou'rt Sheba's, and she thine – aye, to the end o' the seas and beyond, thou lovesome hunk! Nay, hold me, barracuda, for—"

"Don't you believe it!" Avery broke loose briskly and

slapped away her hand, which was massaging his shirt-ruffles. "I doubt not I shall repent me this weakness – but hark ye, woman, and you sea-scum," here he rounded on Bilbo and Firebeard, who were on their feet, rubbing their cramped limbs and regarding him with wolfish wariness and open-mouthed looniness respectively. "This is but truce till we be beyond reach of the cursed Dons; thereafter 'tis war betwixt us, and you'll save yourselves a ton of trouble by packing it in and throwing yourselves on the mercy of the court. For 'twill be surrender or death for you, mark me—"

"Surrender," crooned Sheba, nuzzling his ear. "Ah, 'tis all I ask – surrender in your arms, caro mio!"

"Nay, now, cully," quo' Bilbo silkily. "Here would be rank waste, rat me! For bethink you, y'are still a wanted man – aye, and will be doubly so when word gets abroad that ye ha' broken us free o' King Philip his dungeon. Aye, and hast shown thyself right apt to piracy, having taken the *Santa Cascara* like any filibuster—"

"It's a fact!" bawled Firebeard, and drummed on his chest. "Oh, a sweet stroke, burn, pink, and quarter me else! Aye, art a Brotherhood boy, Ben Avery, like it or not! So let's away, an' wi' the *Laughing Sandbag* an' this dago craft o' thine we'll raise hot hell along the Main, an' then Tortuga-ho! an' be damned, an' that!" His eye rolled on Meliflua, who was viewing with dismay and indignation Black Sheba's attentions to Avery. "Ar, an' we'll take this Spanish pullet as hostage, belike – or for some such purpose as we use wenches for, if I can mind me what it is." He tugged at his beard in perplexity, trying to remember.

"Now look here," Avery was beginning, when suddenly Meliflua screamed, a great voice in the gloom above bawled "Lights!," sirens whined, whistles blew, and the dim-lit dungeon was suddenly aflame with the gleam of torches which glittered on naked steel in the hands of armed soldiers; they crowded the stone galleries looking down on the chamber, and pressed behind the hulking figure of Don Lardo at the stairhead. His hideous face glared like a Hallowe'en mask from the shadows, his dentures clashed like castanets, and the vampires clinging to his scarlet robe squeaked and fluttered. Yes, the sneaky brute had come back to investigate the noise he had heard on the stairs, bringing the heavy mob with him, and now . . .

"So, the birds would flutter away!" he gloated. "I was right, Enchillada! I'm always right! It's terrific!" He screamed with crazy laughter, slobbering down at the little group frozen among the instruments of torture. "Down and seize them! Lash them! Bind them with chains! Lay them helpless at my feet so that I can dance on them and hear them fracture! On, on!"

Pandemonium ensued as the Spanish soldiers blundered obediently down the steps, the poor expendable slobs. You've seen them, often, lurching clumsily into the fray, ready to fall down obligingly as the big names in the cast run them through. Sure enough, the leading officer transfixed himself on Avery's point, and Sheba pounced on his fallen rapier and leaped to Avery's side. In a twinkling two more Spaniards had collapsed, covered in ketchup and crying "Aaargh!", and half a dozen others were scattered like ninepins as Firebeard, grabbing up one of the fallen jailers and using him as a club, rushed roaring to join in. Bilbo, watching his crafty chance, disarmed an opponent by seizure, and in a trice there was a pile of corpses at the stair-foot as the attackers shrank from those three whirling blades and the body which Firebeard wielded with joyous abandon. Shoulder to shoulder fought the four, while Don Lardo tore his hair in apoplectic rage, and Enchillada kilted up his Buchanan tartan dressing-gown and hid behind a pillar. Donna Meliflua screamed and shrank becomingly against the wall as the dank chamber rang with dint o' steel, for there was no lack of Spanish reserves, and no way out for our party; they were bottled, but good, as the Dons flung themselves into the fight.

Meanwhile Goliath the dwarf was using his loaf. Rightly

237

concluding that the mêlée was no place for a one-legged individual two feet in height, he had hopped to the side of the other jailer, who was coming round, and jabbing the man's own dagger at his throat, demanded to be shown the emergency exit.

"Take them alive!" shrieked Don Lardo, shredding a bat in his claw-like hands and muttering: "One for the Maiden, two for the rack, three for scorpions wriggling in a sack . . . Why don't you overwhelm them, you cowardly rabble? You're not doing it properly! Disarm them by letting them stab you, and roll away with their swords! Collapse on them, you filth!" He mowed and gibbered as his men fell over themselves before that wall of dancing steel – Avery cool and academic as always, lips pursed thoughtfully as he lunged and parried; Bilbo hurling taunts as he slid in and out in his rakish Italian style, d'ye see; Sheba shouting with cruel glee as her point gored a throat or slashed a face; Firebeard bashing away regardless of the damage he was doing to the jailer. Even so they were being forced back across the dungeon, and Spaniards were spreading out to take them in flank, when—

"This way, capting! Foller me! Quick, this way!"

Goliath was hopping and yelling in an archway across the dungeon, and as one the four turned and ran, Sheba pausing only to stab the second jailer (she never could resist an unarmed enemy). Through the arch they raced, and turned again to meet their pursuers; steel clashed as Avery and Sheba faced them in the narrow passage, there was a soggy thud as Firebeard flung his human club (now rather limp) into the press, and Bilbo snatched up Goliath and shook him eagerly.

"Whither, mannikin? What's below, ha?"

"Dahn the steps, capting – a postern to the river! Boats an' canoes an' that!" (As there always are, of course, in any properly-appointed dungeon.)

Sheba, her eye-shadow aglow with fierce excitement, buried her steel in the breast of a Spaniard, crowed with

238

delight as Avery felled a second, clung to him for one brief passionate kiss what time she enveloped a thrust and riposted into the throat of a third, and gasped exultantly:

"Ah, barracuda mine, what finer prelude to our union than this? Lust o' blood and lust o' love – both are ours!"

"Please!" exclaimed Avery, neatly disarming a fourth attacker. "Control yourself, and try not to get in the way. It's extremely dangerous."

"What is danger with you at my side?" wondered Sheba adoringly as she lunged gracefully and recovered, wiping her blade with a flourish on her collapsing victim. "See – the dogs give back before us – let us fly, camarado!" But even as they turned to follow Firebeard, who was lumbering to the steps in Bilbo's wake, a tremulous scream sounded from the dungeon.

"Ah, Capeetan Ben! Doo not leave me! See, I yam een thair cruel clutches!"

Sure enough, beyond the reluctant milling mob of Spaniards, Avery beheld Donna Meliflua struggling in the arms of Enchillada, who was assuring a goggling Don Lardo that this was a female in drag, and Spanish by the sound of it.

Bother, thought Avery, why have women no positional sense? Well, he'd just have to cut his way through to her, throw her over his shoulder, pink Don Lardo if possible, and fight his way clear again, that was all. "Back in a tick," he said rather breathlessly to Sheba. "You and Firebeard hold them in play whiles I—"

"Rash bombhead!" cried Sheba, her beautiful dusky face contorted, her lashes snapping in alarm. "She is beyond aid – and who cares, anyway? A mincing candlestick in men's weeds, and probably bent as a bottle of crisps! What is she to thee?"

"A pledge of honour," answered Avery, as with a sharp call of, "All right – mine!" he spitted a rashly-approaching Don. "Hang on, Meliflua! I'll be there, don't you worry – ulngh!"

The words died on his lips, and he had a brief vision of primroses at the river's brim. Sheba, fed up with arguing, had gestured to Firebeard, and the giant, with the ponderous delicacy of a hippo swatting a fly, had clocked our captain on the nape of the neck. Avery's knees buckled, Firebeard grabbed him by the waistband, and with Sheba's sweeping sword covering their retreat the two pirates sprang down the winding stone steps. Avery's unconscious form bumped and rattled on the rough-hewn walls as Firebeard swung him effortlessly along, and Sheba railed at the giant to mind what he was doing, for God's sake, the adored object wasn't made of wood. They raced on down the narrow spiral, and emerged well clear of the pack on a narrow jetty beside a dark, foaming torrent, where canoes bobbed at their moorings, dim-seen in the star-shine, and Bilbo and Goliath were already afloat, fumbling with the painter and chanting: "Shove off, Jack – I'm inboard!"

It was the work of a moment for Sheba to slash through the mooring of a second canoe, and order Firebeard to dispose Avery's limp form carefully in its bottom. But when the big ruffian would have clambered aboard himself, she directed him sharply to Bilbo's canoe – the she-corsair's subtle mind was already thinking ahead, and whatever might lie before them in their escape down that mysterious river, she didn't want Firebeard along playing gooseberry. This was her chance to get Avery on a slow boat to wherever, and she meant to make the most of it; furthermore, Firebeard was notorious for singing shanties in his sleep.

Thus it was that when the Spaniards emerged with gesticulations and futile cries on to the jetty, one canoe was already shooting into the mirk, and the other was wallowing after it with Firebeard sprawled across the thwarts and Bilbo yelling at him not to put his foot through the side, while Goliath crouched motionless in the bows hoping that he might be mistaken for a figurehead. The Spaniards shook their fists and fired off arquebuses, but of course they didn't come within a mile of hitting the vanishing canoes; they never do. They mooched about the jetty for a while, though, acting thwarted but secretly relieved to be rid of such frightful guests, until a young and offensively keen sergeant said hadn't they better give chase? At this there were yawns and groans of "Not again, my morion's killing me!" "Tequila break!" "No way, José," and "Get out the garlic and mandolins." All very well, shrilled the sergeant, but somebody was going to have to break the bad news to Don Lardo, and it wasn't going to be him – his words were drowned in a mad stampede for the boats, and the sergeant wondered despairingly if desertion wasn't the best way out.

He needn't have worried. The sight of blood always had a soothing effect on Don Lardo, and after the recent disturbance the dungeon looked like Dracula's dining-room. But even this, like the escaping captives, was forgotten in the tyrant's delight at discovering that the gorgeous young moppet in silk knee-breeches and ruffles who'd been left behind in the torture-chamber was his bride-to-be. True, she had fainted on being introduced, and had to be put insensible to bed, where nurses fussed about her with Ovaltine and thermometers and cologne compresses, but Don Lardo was undismayed. He gloated for a while over her pale loveliness, hardly able to believe his luck, and then lurched out, stroking his vampire bats and slavering.

"Did you see the terror and hatred in those beautiful eyes ere she swooned, Enchillada?" he croaked. "She loathes me, the little darling! Boy, what a honeymoon we're going to have!" His huge shoulders shook ecstatically and his dentures shot out broadcast. "I just hope she doesn't go mad – at least, not too quickly."

"Sure, Excellencee," cried the fat sycophant. "And she's reech, too. Meanwhile, do you weesh to have thee soldiers decimated – you know, those bums who let thee preesoners get away?"

"You're just trying to make my night," gurgled the

Viceroy jovially. "Here, have a vampire. No, Enchillada, we'll just brand the officers and flog the rest, once over lightly. As for those pirate scum – they won't get far on the notorious River of Death! And if they do, I shall hunt them down in person – yes, and their whole vile Brotherhood. That's it, Enchillada – a mighty campaign to sweep these vermin from the seas!" He cackled crazily and rubbed his hands. "Think of it – my fame will ring world-wide, the King will give me the Order of Sant Iago and take me hawking by the Guadalquivir in a mink-lined coat, people will write for my autograph, and that adorable dolly asleep upstairs . . . oh, God, I don't know when I've felt so good! Proclaim my serendipity to the people tomorrow, and in the meantime let's go and watch them cleaning up the dungeon!"

"You bet, boss!" cried Enchillada eagerly. "Jus' for laughs."

Good news and bad news, really. Our hero is off and running again, but he'll have a whale of a stiff neck, he's in Black Sheba's toils, and what o' this River o' Death bearing them into the jungle fastnesses of the Main? At least there'll be no lack of timber for Goliath's new wooden leg. Poor little Meliflua, eh? Of course, romantic reason tells us she should be all right, but in a story of this kind you never know. And that was a sinister crack Don Lardo made about wiping up the Coast Brotherhood – aye, little do our bold filibusters know what's coming to them, and in especial Happy Dan and his wild crew, bedazzled by the glitter o' new-found gold . . .

CHAPTER
THE THIRTEENTH

he reaction of anyone finding two million pounds in gold coin at the back of the garage, or in an old chest of drawers, is normally "Hell's bells, Doris, will you come and look at this!" And when they have gaped greedily, and babbled of Rolls Royces and villas at Marbella, and brewed a cup of tea to calm their excitement – then realisation dawns. Can't spend it at the shops, the stock market is too dicey . . . and aren't there laws about treasure trove, and capital gains tax, and currency restrictions, and other evil wheezes whereby greedy civil servants rob the deserving of their windfalls – to say nothing of the risk of being mugged, probably by the neighbours?

Indeed. And it was just as bad in the seventeenth century, which is why pirates, who were always acquiring heaps of the ready, invariably ended up burying the stuff in some Godforsaken spot; it was simply the only safe thing to do. Sack a city, loot a galleon, scuttle a plate-fleet – it made no odds, like it or not, the end of the day found them hacking great holes in desert islands, weeping with frustration with their socks full of sand.

Happy Dan's mob were no exception. When they saw the pile of specie into which Blood had inadvertently stumbled, and realised it must have been mislaid by some previous owner of the *Frantic Frog*, they had their customary rave and gloat ("Or! Or! Les oodles, morbleu! Nous sommes riche!

Ah, St Tropez, 'ere we come!"), but they knew it was just window-dressing, and that the stuff would eventually have to be rowed ashore in neat parcels clearly marked, and shoved underground as usual, avec un malediction.

So it is a familiar scene that meets our eyes: the blue and sun-kissed sea gently creaming a golden strand of the Main; the *Frantic Frog* riding at anchor; the raffish figures of the buccaneers delving a great pit in the sand just below high-water mark; Happy Dan Pew, now fully restored, sitting on a cask with a feather in his hat exclaiming: "Ah, les bucket-et-spades pour faisant les châteaux de plage! Où sont les souliers bains de mer de Marcel, les gym-shoes et les donkey-rides?"; Vanity all distraught in her maroon velvet between two hairy sentinels, and Blood with his hands pinioned being lowered into the pit above the treasure, and buried up to the neck. That's the picture – but we're not the only ones watching, by the powers! From the dense jungle fringing the beach, un-seen 'midst the foliage, fierce black eyes glare and sharp ears catch the distant sound of the pirates' voices, and the shrill protests of the victim.

"Haven't ye any gratitude, ye foul Frogs?" he was demanding as they shovelled in the last spadefuls and tramped it down nice and tight under his chin. "If it hadn't been for me, devil a doubloon would ye ha' seen! Pew, ye muck-rake, give me a sword an' I'll cut your dirty soul out – or better still, let's toss for it, eh? Heads ye turn me loose, tails . . ."

"Ah, oui?" said Happy Dan, interested. "Tails?"

"We can discuss that later!" cried Blood desperately. "Be a sport, man – is this fit end for an officer an' gentleman? Ye know it isn't! And it's . . . it's unnecessary! What's the point? Ye could maroon me just as easy!"

"Some fun, that, par example!" scoffed Happy Dan. "This way, fooleesh Mick, the tide approaches itself slowly, first one wave ovair your 'ead, then anothair, an' anothair, until glug-glug-glug, adieu! C'est artistic, non? An' the bones

244

of your squelette, they mark the place where the oof est enterré, parfaitement!''

The pirate crew applauded with fiendish glee, and watched as the first wave of the incoming tide broke against Blood's chin and retreated hissing over the wet sand. Then another wave, which splashed his face, and a third which broke clean over his head, leaving him spluttering. Vanity could endure no more.

"Ah, of your pity, fell and cruel men!" she cried. "Can't you shoot him, or hang him, or . . . or knock him on the head, or something—"

"Do us a favour!" roared Blood, spitting sea-water.

"Captain Pew, this is beastly!" cried Vanity, and proudly faced the foppish filibuster. "Unless you release that man immediately, you shall never have me to wife! Not that you will anyway, but that's beside the point. I shall knock off food, and grow thin and unattractive, furthermore I shall mock your rotten French pronunciation and recite 'petite poire' until my mouth meets at the back, and—"

What effect these dire threats would have had we'll never know, for at that moment an uncanny, wailing cry sounded in the depths of the jungle, and an eery silence fell over the sunlit beach, broken only by Blood's snorts and cries of 'Jayzus!' All gazed about them in wonder – and suddenly something sang in the air like a great wasp, and Happy Dan staggered back, plucking at a feathered shaft quivering in his arm and ruining his cuff. With oaths and yells the pirates sprang to their muskets, as a positive hail of arrows came winging from the trees, followed by the shrill war-whoops of lithe, half-naked brown figures breaking from ambush, feathers in their hair and faces grotesquely daubed with paint.

"Indiennes! Les sauvages rouges!" cried the startled pirates.

"Aaarrgh, je suis blessé dans le bras!" gasped Happy Dan.

"Serve you right, and I hope it hurts!" snapped Vanity.

"Whoop-whoop!" shrieked the Indians, charging home.

"Fetch a shovel, for God's sake!" roared Blood, his head awash.

Further conversation was lost in the din of battle as pirate closed with Indian; muskets banged, arrows hissed, cutlasses and spears clashed, Vanity stamped in vexation, Blood gurked and gargled, and on both sides men fell wounded and, in extreme cases, dead. Judging the combat with the eye of one who has cheered on countless boyfriends in Rugby scrums, Vanity decided that Blood would probably drown before half-time, and gallant girl that she was, heedless of the foam that threatened to damp her pumps and ruin her silk hose, she knelt and began to scoop out a hollow round his head, on the theory that the water-level would drop. It didn't.

"Give us the kiss o' life!" spluttered the Colonel.

"Really!" exclaimed Vanity, scooping away. "Don't you ever stop getting fresh?"

"Oxygen!" gasped Blood weakly. "Fill thy lungs an' breathe into me mouth, acushla, so shall I draw life-giving air from thy sweet lips!" And if I don't, he thought ardently, what a lovely way to go.

"Oh, I see," said Vanity, frowning. "A bit kinky, is it not? Still, here goes." She gulped air, locked on to the Colonel just as he submerged, and tried to imagine he was a Christmas balloon. She went under a brunette, and came out a breathless blonde, and Happy Dan, pausing in his pistol-ling, clutched his pallid brow.

"Dieu caillou les corbeaux!" he cried aghast. "Regardez sa chevelure! She 'as flipped 'er wig! What do I see, me? Un moment, ma belle brun, le next une bébé peroxide! C'est trop fort! A moi, garçons! It's all going wrong! To les bateaux!"

Seeing their leader quail, the filibusters lost no time in legging it for the boats and rowing hastily for the *Frantic Frog*, with Pew babbling weakly in the stern-sheets. The

Indians, nightmare figures in their paint and gold ornaments, were left in possession of the beach where, having cut the throats of the enemy wounded with quartz knives and danced the Hawaiian War Chant to bongo accompaniment, they gathered round the interesting spectacle of a sodden blonde in maroon velvet apparently trying to eat the head of a white man under two feet of water. Vanity, half-drowned herself, was aware of their strange guttural grunts which, although she knew it not, meant:

"Man, these honkies! Hey, Coatlputl, what this chick tryin' to do, you reckon?" "Don't look at me, Patzlqtln. Maybe she's a priestess worshippin' the Great White God from the East, but if that's him, brother, he's wet!" "How 'bout that? Think we oughta dig'm up'n take'm back to Cohaclgzln?" "Why not? He's gonna look real lousy stickin' out the beach when the tide goes back. Okay, men, dig-a-dig-dig!"

Thus it was that as the *Frantic Frog* weighed anchor, with Happy Dan sniffing smelling-salts and weeping while the crew read him 'Marcel et Denise à la Cirque' to soothe him, a weird barbaric procession was winding its way deep into the tropic jungle. Dreadful warriors with filed teeth and fiery black eyes chanted the blood-chilling song of the Great White God and the Damp Blonde Discovered Necking Under Water; their bone-whistles shrilled and their war-drums boomed in melancholy cadence as they filed down the jungle trail; the westering sun gleamed on their quartz blades, gaudy plumage, and gold bangles, and on the fair head of the lovely captive borne in a bamboo cage by stalwart savages, her nylons hung on the bars to dry. Last of all came a pathetic sight, the Great White God himself slung helpless from a pole, leaking salt water at every step. Ah, pity their plight, reader, as they are carried ever deeper into the steamy forest swamps, for their destination is the dread Lost City of Cohaclgzln, long sought by Conquistadores for its fabled wealth of gold, high-grade drinking-chocolate, and native art so revoltingly ugly that later generations of settlers would revere it as work of genius. In fact, the Cohaclgzlns were just rotten sculptors, and their unimagined ferocity stemmed directly from the frustration they suffered in their continual failures to design the wheel, which they attempted by carving enormous lumps of rock, none of which would ever roll properly, whereon they were piled up in gigantic step-pyramids which the Cohaclgzlns defiantly described as temples but which everyone knew were just industrial pollution. So this unhappy people waited bad-temperedly for a Great White God who, legend had it, would give them wheels that worked; in the meantime they put by the time in sun-worship, cannibalism, human sacrifice, and orgies on drinking-chocolate which made them sick and worse-tempered than ever.

What hideous fate awaits Vanity and Blood at the hands of these cruel and unartistic primitives? Let's find out, as the procession debouches from the jungle into a valley where step-pyramids loom skyward on every hand, their summits wreathed in mist. In the central stone-flagged plaza, a-rumble with the sound of discarded wheel-prototypes being dragged away by panting slaves, a discontented crowd of semi-clad barbarians waited as the prisoners were dragged before the stone dais on which stood Brasso, cacique of the tribe, a hawk-nosed elder with folded arms, wrapped in Imperturbable Dignity and a cloak of frog fur. His agate eyes flashed cruelly at Vanity, proudly erect in her off-the-shoulder maroon velvet, and Blood, who looked like an unsuccessful beachcomber. Brasso, with stately flowing gestures, addressed their captors in incomprehensible grunts.

"Great White God my ass!" was what they meant. "I ask you, Patzlqtln, do he have wheels? He don't. Fact, man, I ain't seen such a un-wheeled cat since Popocatepetl erupted. He looks like you dug'm up some place."

"Right on, chief!" said Patzlqtln. "We dug'm, yasser. But if you can't use'm, how 'bout the chick?"

"How the hell do I know?" cried Brasso peevishly. He drew himself up and proclaimed: "Let the Princess of the Sun decide!"

At this there was a great clashing of brazen gongs, and a solemn chanting of hidden choirs as the watching thousands prostrated themselves in the dust with moans of awe. Brasso shielded his eyes, a fanfare of horns sounded, and at the head of the temple steps behind the dais the Princess of the Sun made an entrance worthy of a Biblical epic. Preceded by maidens in gauzy skirts who swept the steps with golden fronds and sprinkled disinfectant, came a massive litter of solid gold borne by muscular myrmidons, and in it, stoned out of her tiny mind on drinking-chocolate, sat a bronzed glamazon who looked like Paramount's idea of Tiger Lily. Superbly tall and queenly, with tawny features classical enough to advertise Tabu perfume, she was resplendent in a split conga-skirt of bird-of-paradise feathers, and of gold (as Vanity noted wide-eyed) were her sandals, girdle, bra, and bangles, while precious gems glittered in her towering head-dress of plumes and tropical fruit. (Well, you didn't expect her in clogs and shawl.)

Moving in an exotic rhumba rhythm to which the Princess dazedly tried to keep time with a fan of beaten gold, the myrmidons bore her to the dais, and there she bent her sultry, slightly vacant eyes on the captives, while Brasso explained.

"The male cat's white, okay? But, Princess, the Great White God he ain't. No wheels, right? So, zilch! But with the chick, there's altern'tives. You need a hand-maiden, mani-curist, temple receptionist, jus' say the word, Princess – or we can dish her up with yams, I mean, 'n' pineapple rings at the next barbecue, jus' the way you like it. Speak, divine daughter of the Sun."

The Princess sniffed a delicate blast of chocolate dust, shuddered, placed an unsteady slender finger 'neath languid chin, and tried to focus on Vanity. Oh, man, she thought, any minute I'm gonna crash, but not in public, pleeeze dear God, or these yokels may discover I'm a runaway nun from Campeche who's exchanged one habit for another. Oh-oh-oh, steady, girl, easy does it, you're the Princess of the Sun, right? She focused at last, and her eyes narrowed cruelly as she considered Vanity. Nice threads, she thought, but I need you round the temple like a hole in the head; you're the kind who'd seduce my pusher and set me up for a bus. Blood looked cute, she thought, but he wasn't the Great White God, so what the hell? Controlling an urge to do tailspins over the valley, the Princess spoke in a vibrant contralto.

"Man . . . death . . . by . . . maguay! Ugh!" She knew how to talk like a jungle denizen, if no one else in Cohaclgzln did. "Woman . . . human . . . sacrifice . . . Ugh! Make . . . Sun . . . God . . . glad! Ugh!"

"Hot damn!" Brasso snapped his fingers in admiration. "Why didn't I think of that? Okay, cats, you heard the Princess – one maguay, one for the altar, let's move it! See, divine Princess, your people . . . oh-oh, she's gone into a trance again! Poor kid, this divinity bit is killing her!" And sure enough the Princess had collapsed with a deep groan of "Oh, God!", and lay twitching and glassy-eyed as her litter was borne up the temple steps and out of sight of the vulgar gaze. Brasso made imperious gestures, and Vanity and Blood found themselves surrounded by excited, tooth-gnashing savages who swept them away, struggling, in opposite directions.

"You say I was hit by falling masonry?" exclaimed Captain Avery, rubbing his slender but muscular neck. "Nay, 'tis passing strange, for yon dungeon seemed admirably designed and stoutly built, such as would hardly shed lumps on its occupants—"

"What does it matter?" husked Black Sheba. "We are here, alone in the depths of the jungle, thou and I . . . a man and a woman . . . here in this tropic paradise o' perfumed blooms and succulent fruits . . . alone, as in a very Garden of Love, like Adam and Eve . . ." and she slithered sinuously towards him, her hand brushing his cheek.

"Adam and the serpent were more like it!" Avery's words dropped like ice-cubes. " 'Tis my belief ye had me clobbered, that I might not rescue yon poor Spanish lady!"

"That puling twerp!" sneered Sheba. "I marked her not. Ah, barracuda mio, what can I think on but that you dared all to save me . . . again . . . and that we are free, you and I, and may fly together where we will – aye, to the world's end and beyond, in each other's arms!" She did another slither and embraced his knees, crooning contentedly.

"Oh, pack it in!" said Avery. "I enlarged thee because I'm shot if I'll leave anyone, however depraved, to the devildoms o' Spain. But know that I purpose to deliver thee to British justice as soon as I have tooled back to Cartagena and abstracted Donna Meliflua."

"Has that clock on sconce disordered thee? Tool back – with Don Lardo's soldiers already in pursuit? – for I marked the gleam o' their arms behind when our canoe foundered at dawn – and thou a-swoon, so that I must bear thee afoot in my arms (and in these heels, too), and so brought thee to this glade and nursed thee, and soothed thy brow wi' cooling water, and massaged thy poor hurt . . ." Her voice dropped to a murmur, and her fingers strayed on his arm. " 'Zounds, you've got smashing muscles, and the cutest little mole on your chest – I kissed it as you slept, all unaware . . ."

"Of all the crust!" Avery's cheek glowed like middle-cut salmon. "Have ye no shame? No, of course you haven't!" He took a big breath. "What's the use? I thank you for your . . . efforts – but now restored, I must return for Donna Meliflua—"

"Ah, cospetto!" Sheba leaped up, and raged to and fro in the remnants of her white trouser suit. "Has she bewitched thee, this Spanish punk? Fiend take her, I could rake her sheep's eyes out!" She whirled like an infuriated Lena

251

Horne. "And what o' thy darling Vanity, then – thy English milk pudding?"

"For your information," quo' Avery icily, "my fiancée awaits me in care o' my trusted agent –" that's what *he* thinks, poor sap "– and we shall be reunited and spliced as soon as I have rescued Donna Meliflua, consigned thee to the coop, and mopped up the rest of your associates. Where is Bilbo, by the way, and that other brute who doesn't shave?"

"Who can say?" murmured Sheba evilly. "Hunting thee, perchance. There's little gratitude in him, my captain, or in Firebeard . . . so why not make the most of what's in me?" She undulated towards him, hands on hips, and then, creature of impulse that she was, hurled herself on him and knocked him flat on his back, smothering him with hot kisses. "Ah, barracuda . . . come to my black castle on storm-lashed Octopus Rock," she panted. "I promise I'll get rid of my Swedes and beach boys, and love none but thee! Shalt lie soft, and feed o' dainties, and go surfing and scuba-diving and have captive commanders to wait on thee and press thee new silk cravats daily . . . or we shall cruise to the Indies and put the pleasure resorts to sack and pillage . . . casinos aflame, merchant bankers sold into slavery, the spoil o' palaces and supermarkets to drip through our fingers . . . ah, we shall rule the world together and—"

"Do you mind?" said Avery coldly. "The grass is damp and you're no fly-weight, so if you will please to remove . . ."

"I don't believe it!" Sheba ground her teeth. "Art insensate? Art immune to – love?"

"Certainly not," said Avery, brushing himself down. "Mummy loved me, and Aunt Pru, and Golightly, my nanny . . ."

Sheba gnashed and clutched her temples. "God's blood! I mean – LOVE!!!"

"I'd rather not discuss it," said Avery rising and shrugging his splendid shoulders in a way which made her feel all faint. "Now, I must determine our precise whereabouts in this trackless jungle, and then –" He stiffened suddenly, his face alight with intelligent inquiry. "Hist! What was that?"

Sheba was on her feet, every nerve a-quiver. All around was deathly still, save for the roar of the river, the scream of parakeets and chatter of monkeys in the green, the hum of insects, and the snuffle of tapirs rooting for truffles. And yet – her perfect ears quivered . . .

"Odd's guts!" she hissed. " 'Tis a human voice . . . aye, in dire torment! A far-distant, wordless scream o' agony—"

"But with an Irish accent!" breathed Avery. "We *are* in South America, aren't we?"

"Can Don Lardo's soldiery be practising on some hapless prisoner?" gasped Sheba. "Nay, or fiendish Indians trying out their poisoned darts? Whatever on't, we had best away—"

"What, and leave some poor soul (from Belfast, unless I'm mistaken) to perish by inches? Not a chance". Avery's jaw creaked with resolution. "Here, you take the sword."

"But you? Peerless master o' the rapier that ye are, 'twere best you had it –"

"You forget, I have my bare hands", said Avery calmly, and slipped into the undergrowth with an athletic smoothness that would have made Nureyev look like a shambling drunk. Sheba followed, half-dazed with worship. What a demi-god was this! If only he didn't get these Boy Scout impulses. But she'd educate him, one of these days, when she'd got him to Octopus Rock and thrown away the key . . .

Through the dense jungle they stole, Sheba marvelling at the tall Englishman's uncanny woodcraft. No twigs cracked 'neath his feet, and his sensitive fingers brushed aside creepers, rotten logs, and snakes with never a rustle; even when he fell in swamps it was with minimum splash, and lovely mover though she was, it was all that the pirate queen could do to stay hard on his heels. For what seemed like (and in fact, was) hours, they crept on, guided by the piteous Hibernian cries which sounded nearer and nearer, until, wriggling noiselessly through a cane-break, they found themselves on the edge of a clearing in which they discerned two figures, one sitting, one hanging and complaining bitterly . . .

Colonel Blood had had another shocking day, and the coming night didn't look like being much better. He was spreadeagled face down from four posts, his torso about three feet off the floor, the favoured position for those condemned to death by maguay (or Percy Thrower's Revenge, as it has been loosely called). Beneath Blood, and pointing directly at his navel, a slender, innocent-looking green shoot was growing from the soil; this was the dreaded maguay, which grows (thanks to the tropic clime, and the gro-bags with which the devilish savages are wont to tend it) at a rate of three feet per day, and since its point is wondrous strong and razor-keen, it pierces anything that gets in its way, like an Irish abdomen, for instance. It had already grown two feet while Blood watched it, bug-eyed, and he could see no way of avoiding appalling indigestion, unless he could prevail on his solitary guard.

This guard was a stranger to Blood, but if you have trod the paths of romantic fiction you'll recognise the type. He was called Solomon Shafto, and he was one of those eccentric seamen who were forever falling into the hands of the Inquisition and failing to satisfy the examiners on religious grounds. Wherefore he had endured divers torments, d'ye see, and languished i' the dungeons o' the Holy Office until he escaped, since when he had been wandering dimly in the jungle, befriending birds, eating berries, and removing thorns from the feet of Indian caciques, who had adopted him, sort of. None too bright to start with, Solomon had been intellectually reduced by his ordeals to the point where he was fit for little but political economy and rough gardening, and since courses in the former were not available in Cohaclgzln, they had put him in charge of weeds. He was old, skinny, dirt-tanned, and incredibly bright-eyed; it need hardly be added that he wore ragged skins, had white hair growing to his waist, and cackled a good deal. Blood couldn't get through to him at all.

"Prune the maguay plant, sez 'ee to me?" Solomon was exclaiming beadily, scratching his rags. "Nay, maister, us couldn't do that, not no-how. It not bein' prunin' time, sez I to 'ee. Prune in March, mulch in May, pot in August wi' a hey-hey-hey!" he chanted, and added. "An' derry-down-do, wi' a voodle-de-oy-doy, vowt!"

"Then stick a cane in the ground and train the damned thing so that it grows past me!" implored Blood. "Look, if it continues on its present course it'll get all messy and yuggh!"

"Hoop-de-doo!" exclaimed Solomon, shaking unkempt locks. "Us couldn't do *thaa-at*, maister, on account it might stunt its growth, look'ee. Aye, as 'appened to Widow Splurge's cowcumber back in Babbacombe when I wor a lad . . . aye, them were the days, wi' October apples an' crusty bread, when drippin' were on'y three-farthin's a firkin, I mind . . . aye, all stunted were the widow's cowcumber—"

"I'll be bloody well stunted if you don't help me!" cried Blood. "Look, why not cut me loose, then shall thy infernal plant suffer no whit?"

"Injuns wouldn't like it," said Solomon, dancing crazily in agitation. "Look arter 'im, Sol, sez they to me, go easy wi' the waterin'-can an' baby bio, an' when the maguay point be a-ticklin' of un's belly, do 'ee come tell us, and we'll all sit round an' enjoy the good bit. Dig-a-dag-a-phut-phut, dig-a-dag-a-phut!"

Blood groaned with despair, heaving helplessly in his bonds, watching the maguay point rise even closer – and then of a sudden a shadow fell athwart him, and a well-bred remembered voice spoke with crisp clarity:

"What are you about, sir? Explain yourself!"

"You!" exclaimed Blood, craning with difficulty. "Avery! Ben, dear lad, stout comrade, y'are in the nick o' time! Quick – knock the top off that devilish weed ere it rends me . . . oh, my God, is that the Queen o' Spades along o' ye?

Nay, keep her at a distance, an' help me, ould joy!"

Avery keenly surveyed the spread-eagled Colonel, the peering, twitching Solomon, the whole crazy set-up. He couldn't believe it. "You mean that plant is growing at a rate of knots per hour?" he cried.

" 'Tis the hellish maguay!" chuckled Sheba spitefully. "A favourite house-plant o' the savages, with which they decorate their porches. Change the bodies regular and keep at an even temperature, they last for years."

"Astonishing", murmured Avery, looking closer. "Why, such a plant presented to the Royal Society should win its donor sure election . . . mayhap a seat on the Council—"

"God gimme strength!" croaked Blood. "Cut me down first!"

"In good time, renegade." Avery was cold. "You may e'en dangle a while longer, deserter, what time ye explain your presence here, where I little looked for you."

"Who cares how he got here – we see how he shall speed hence," sneered Sheba, stroking the maguay and sticking out her tongue at the Colonel. "Here's fitting end for pestilent cur, aye, his guts shall be in sweet uproar presently. Leave him, caro mio, and let's begone!"

"Don't you dare!" bawled Blood. "Avery! If ye abandon me, you abandon your Lady Vanity in her dire peril!" He craned some more, and saw Avery for once stricken to the gills, and Sheba's eyes wide in fierce alarm. "The savages have her – it's true, ye numps! If ye don't believe me, ask the male model there!"

Avery wheeled on Solomon, who leaped nervously and pawed his rags. "Ole Sol don't mean no 'arm!" he whined. "Just a bit o' gardenin', crazy pavin', 'edges clipped, moderate terms, an' a twelve-month guarantee – ole Sol don' know nuthin' about young wimmen bein' sacrificed to the Sun God, not I!" He cringed in Avery's grasp. "You wouldn't 'ave a piece o' bread an' drippin' about ye, mate? Ar, such as ole Sol's mother made in Babbacombe all they years agone . . .

ar, rare drippin' it wor. There's some castaways," he whimpered, "as crave cheese, or rum, wi' a curse, or burned almonds, or Bellamy's pies . . . but drippin', ar, drippin' all a-sizzle, is the tack for ole Sol—"

"Do you tell me," roared Avery in controlled fury, "that some beastly pagans are about to sacrifice a woman? Speak, ancient – is she blonde, English, upper-class, and perfectly-stacked? Oh, stop belly-aching, Blood, I'm busy!"

"Did you have to use that form o' words?" winced Blood.

"Ye won't let on as I told ye?" quavered Solomon. "A'right, then – over yonder, past the pyramids, turn right, an' keep bearin' left till ye come to the plaza, ye can't miss it . . . noon kick-off, when the sun's rays strike the great altar o' Cohaclgzln—"

There was a whooshing noise and Avery was gone with a speed that left the bushes shaking, followed by a despairing wail from Blood, a cry of "Stay, barracuda, it's probably some other blonde!" from Sheba, and a prayer for dripping from Solomon Shafto. Along the jungle path stormed our hero, aware of brazen gongs booming and voices eerily chanting somewhere ahead, then of a packed throng of Indians through which he ploughed like Popeye on spinach – he marked not the great step-pyramids, the barbaric carvings, the thousands thronging the plaza, the Princess of the Sun flaked out in her golden litter on the temple steps, or the pictogram scoreboard giving the order of service. Only one thing filled his view – a shapely form in maroon velvet bound on a huge marble slab, a fair head lolling, and above it a gleaming quartz blade in the sinewy hand of a feathered and painted priest.

The sun's rays smote the marble, turning the fair head to burnished light, a huge gong clanged, the blade swept down in a glittering arc – and the executioner's wrist was clamped in a grip of steel, the blade an inch from the snowy bosom. Vanity shrieked, the executioner cried "Oooh-cor!", spectators gasped, Brasso the cacique reeled in horror at this sacrilege, disappointed punters and outraged bookies rushed forward, and the Princess of the Sun stirred, muttering sleepily: "Wha' time is it? . . . oh, Kee-rist, whorra trip . . . somebody plee-eeze fetch my head . . ."

Vanity stared up, unable to believe her eyes. Could it be? Of course it could! Those clean-cut features, the confident teeth, the grey eyes respectively ashine with mastery and tenderness, the stray lock of hair on the noble brow, the heroic shirt-ruffles barely disturbed as he flicked aside the executioner.

"Sorry I'm late, dearest," said Captain Avery.

With another flick he had burst the rawhide thongs that held her, and she was clinging to him, half-aswoon, while the Cohaclgzlns went spare. A thousand painted faces screamed hate, a thousand weapons were raised to plunge into this daring stranger who had violated their mysteries – when a faint, moaning sigh checked their mad rush, and Brasso the cacique flung his arms aloft with a shout of: "Stay! Hold the phone! The Princess speaks!"

Every eye turned towards the gold litter. Sure enough, the Princess of the Sun, blinking feebly, had come up on one elbow; she passed a limp hand over her queenly brow, stared vaguely towards the altar, made a limp but imperious sign, and subsided again, murmuring: "Oh-oh-oh-oh-brother . . ."

As one man that huge throng of thousands stopped, turned towards the stone of sacrifice, and obediently prostrated themselves, beating their palms on the ground with sonorous groans. Vanity, gripped in Avery's muscular arm, shivered in dread, her blue eyes wide as she viewed the grovelling mob.

"Ben, darling!" she quavered. "Oh, my sweet, you have saved me! Where the hell have you been? And, oh, why are they lying on the ground like that – as though in worship of us?"

Avery's glance swept fearlessly over the prone heaps

about the altar, but his brow was knit. Truth to tell, he had half-expected some protest at his cavalier interruption of the ceremony. Now his keen mind pierced the mystery.

"Not *us*, sweetheart", he replied. "After all, they were sacrificing you. Nay, I must conclude that they are worshipping – *me*." He shrugged imperceptibly. "After all, why not? Such poor heathen have probably never seen a white man before."

"They saw Colonel Blood!" said Vanity.

"That's not quite the same thing, is it?" said Avery, and his flashing eyes scanned the worshipping multitude again, and stopped at the temple steps, where Brasso was in earnest conversation with a red-skinned beauty in feathered conga-skirt and exotic accessories, reclining in a golden litter and staring in his direction with slightly glazed and rolling eyes. Their primitive grunting speech meant nothing to the captain.

"But, Princess, has he got wheels?" Brasso was insisting. "You show me, 'cos I don't see 'em. So how can he be the Great White God? Like I mean, your word is law, but . . ."

The Princess moaned softly, and focused unsteadily on the incredibly magnificent specimen who stood by the altar, all heroic disdain from chin-dimple to knee-cap. Wow! thought the Princess, her befuddled senses more aswim than ever, that's better than drinking-chocolate.

"Who . . . needs . . . wheels?" she murmured vibrantly. "Keep . . . on . . . worshipping. He . . . Great . . . White . . . God. I . . . have . . . spoken . . ."

"That's what the lady says!" sighed Brasso. "Oh, man! Okay, Daughter of the Sun, okay – but you gonna have to marry that dude, you know that, don't you? I mean, like we gotta prophecy to fulfil, so Princess baby, you better get it right, or the Sun God in his wrath is gonna bust your can, you know? You read me, Princess? . . . aw, hell, she's passed out again! Okay, Patzlqtln, get her back in the holy-of-holies . . . and somebody find the old honky Shafto and tell him to get his butt over here. This new cat may be the Great White God, but I'll bet he don't speak Cohaclgzlnian worth a damn . . ."

Thus it was that as Avery and Vanity stood in each other's arms by the altar, surrounded by prostrate adoring bodies, and wondered what this might portend, a squad of Indians descended on the clearing where Blood still hung spreadeagled, calculating miserably that the maguay had about six inches to go, and scooped up Solomon Shafto, whom they dragged to the plaza. But of Black Sheba they saw no sign . . .

Not surprisingly, since she had slithered into the tall timber at sound of their approach, and crouched there, hot-eyed and gnashing as she wondered what had befallen Avery in his impetuous folly. Well, we know — but what next, ha? What will Vanity say when she learns that her beloved is slated to take the aisle with the Princess of the Sun? Will it be any louder than Blood's comments when the maguay starts to blossom? Is a craving for bread and dripping to be compared to a main-line addiction to drinking-chocolate? Let's wait until night-fall, and then sneak closer past the deserted step-pyramids in the ghostly moonlight, until we find a convenient spot to eavesdrop . . .

CHAPTER
THE FOURTEENTH

 ohaclgzln was in a fever of excitement that tropic night. In their rude adobe houses the natives conversed in animated grunts, and for once the usual topic (what went wrong with today's wheels?) was forgotten. For had not the Great White God come at last who should provide wheels in abundance, as foretold? Had he not been led from the altar before the Princess of the Sun, and had she not risen unsteadily from her litter, tripped on her conga-skirt, smitten her forehead ritually three times with the heel of her hand while speaking mystic incantations ("Oh-God-oh-God-oh-I-gotta-quit!"), and sprinkled him with the sacred drinking-chocolate as an irrevocable sign of their impending holy nuptials? All had seen her stare at the tall stranger as in an ecstatic trance before she collapsed sighing on her litter.

All female Cohaclgzln sighed, for that matter, for the God was magnificent to behold, and charming with it; he had borne the Princess's hand to his lips, and bowed reverently when she goofed off. ("Man, we gotta find a new word for cool," the cacique Brasso had admitted.) Then the God had quieted the irate clamour of the fair woman whom, in his mysterious wisdom, he had preserved from sacrifice, and indicated that she should be taken with him to the chamber set aside for him in the temple. Thither, too, had gone Brasso with the castaway creature Shafto, and presently it was known that the God had sent for the maguay victim – and just when the plant's razor tip was scratching his sternum, too! Cohaclgzln pursed its lips and hoped this divine clemency wasn't going to become a habit . . . still, that was Gods for you, and no use beefing. Doubtless tomorrow's marriage to the Princess of the Sun would settle him down . . .

"Marriage!" A pekinese with its tail in the vacuum cleaner could not have equalled Lady Vanity for penetrative power. Lamps in the marble chamber flickered, a hideously-painted mask fell off the wall, cacique Brasso jumped three feet, Solomon Shafto dived under a sofa, and even Colonel Blood held on tight to his seat. In a fury of maroon velvet she let fly again, her eyes azure beams of rage. "Marriage? To that cocoa-bean in the fruit hat? Never! You would die first!"

Avery alone had remained unmoved, thumb on chin. "Marriage to the Princess, eh, Shafto? At dusk tomorrow? H'm!"

"H'm nothing!" decibelled Vanity. "The immortal crust!" She whirled on the uncomprehending Brasso. "Get this, barbarian – Captain Avery is affianced to me, Lady Vanity Rooke, of South Street and Torpedo Towers, Bucks, and you can tell ruddy Minnehaha that if she so much as shakes a feather at him—"

"A moment, sweet", interposed Avery. " 'Twere best say naught before this fellow, since though he has no English, yet is thy meaning perilously plain. Master Shafto, be pleased to tell the cacique that I shall present myself to her divine highness at her pleasure." His warning gesture checked Vanity's escaping steam until Brasso had got the message and departed, whereon the Captain resumed, bright-eyed and urgent.

"See now, my angel, our straits are dire and these people fickly dangerous. By humouring them with this marriage I shall gain us time – 'tis no more than their superstitious whim, and no harm done, since heathen ceremony can have no force of canon law. So, if I play along and see how things pan out—"

"Let me guess!" Vanity yowled and clenched peerless fists. "You gorgeous balloon, she's not marrying you to qualify for immigration! I saw her moon at thee wi' yearning eyes, the copper-bottomed cooze! Superstitious whim, he says! She wants to get you in the bushes and cry 'Carnival!' like all the rest of them—"

"Nay, 'tis but religious mystical union!" Avery looked shocked. "A formal matter – ha, Master Shafto?"

"Dunno, 'bout that, ding-a-dang-dee," quo' Solomon, shaking matted locks. "Heathen legend do say that when the Great White God (that's 'ee) be come to Cohaclgzln, he shall wed Princess o' the Sun (that's she), on account o' he be divinely powered to bestow wheels on the land, d'ye see? Ar . . . 'ee can make wheels, maister?"

"With much ease," said Avery. "''tis but matter of shaping wood choicely seasoned, attaching thereto spokes of ash (or such native timber as may serve), then forging rim o' metal, the which when heated is placed o'er all and, cooling, doth contract. As to the axle . . ." He caught Vanity's eye on him, and stopped with an apologetic cough, whereon Solomon resumed:

"God an' Princess be wed wi' all pomp by th'High Priest, an' there be great an' joyous feastin'." He chuckled reminiscently. "Ar, like to wedden' breckfuss when Squire Cobbold were spliced wi' young Mistress Winthrop to St Maggot's church, forty year agone – a hoydenish piece she wor, an' cuckolded he wi' the gamekeeper, heh-heh – ar, but 'twor a gran' spread, I mind, wi' pies an' pasties an' jellies o' grape an' turnip, an' the drippin' flowed like lava from a Mexican volcaney—"

"You see, fond love?" smiled Avery. "Nothing to it".

"– an' when God an' Princess be hitched, there follers the

fructifyin' o' the Daughter o' the Sun for three days an' nights—"

"I knew it!" yipped Vanity, but ere she could give vent properly, there came an unexpected interruption.

"Hold on, grandad," said Blood, frowning. "Ye say these redsticks don't know how to make wheels . . . an' whoever can show 'em, they'll accept as God?"

"How, sirrah!" Avery's brow was dark. "Wouldst horn in, ha?" But Blood waved him to silence and looked narrow-eyed on Solomon.

"How come," said he, "when you fell among these natives, ye didn't make wheels for 'em yourself? You could ha' been the Great White God, surely, an' been worshipped and lain soft o' nights wi' Long Tall Sally in the feathers? But instead y'are content all these years to live in rags, an' grub among the beans an' brussels. Now, why – eh, Slippery Sol?"

Solomon grimaced and shuffled uneasily. "Ar . . . hem . . . us can't make wheels, noways! Ar, us forgot how, see? Hoople-de-hoot!"

"Forgot?" scoffed Blood, and so patent was the cast-away's falsehood that Vanity and Avery stood arrested, watching as he plucked nervously at his rags.

"Princess didn't fancy me!" he squealed shifty-eyed. "Ar – poor ole Sol ain't a big rackety blade like t' captain 'ere! An' . . . an' I wor married a'ready, see? – on little Mall Trattle-worthy as minded Gaffer Tovey's pigs, so fiddle-de-dapple to you, an' chance it!" Seeing Blood's scornful smile, he began to gibber. "An' I didn't want no heathen dame wi' long slinky legs an' lovesome lips, be 'er belly-button never so cute! So there! An' I like gardenin' an' compost heaps an' clods wi' worms a-wriggle –" He shrieked as Blood grabbed him by the throat. "Leave us be!"

"The truth, scarecrow!" snapped the Colonel, shaking him, and suddenly Solomon seemed to shrivel, and whimpered piteously:

"Don't hurt poor Sol! Please, maister, I'll tell 'ee! Ar – I didn't want ter die, that's why! It's the truth! Ar – for arter his three days' fructifyin' wi' the Princess, these savages do dispatch the Great White God as sacrifice to the Sun – aye, by hellish disembowelment on the altar stone! An' then they serve un up for dinner, meejum-to-well-done, slutter-cum-gush! 'At minds me," he pawed pathetically at Blood's sleeve, "' 'ee wouldn't 'ave a crust an' a smidgin' o' drippiñ' for poor Sol, matey?"

There was a longish pause, in which Vanity swayed white-faced, Blood whistled noiselessly, and Avery finally cleared his throat. "I see," he said. "Well, that puts a slightly different complexion on things, of course."

"Oh, Ben!" Vanity rushed to her lover's side. "Ben, my darling, they shan't serve you up – not medium-to-well-done!"

"Nay, honeybunch." Avery scooped her soothingly against his ruffles and flashed teeth in fighting smile. "Now that I have thee again, shall I wind up 'twixt the fish and the After Eights? I trow not. At worst we shall fight our way clear – we be two stout blades, the Colonel and I, assuming," and he shot Blood a stern glance, "that the blighter's prepared to pull his weight for once. Aye, and it may be we shall have Black Sheba's aid in the pinch!"

"Hey?" Vanity snapped upright like whalebone. "What? Sheba?"

"She's out in the woods somewhere . . . I rescued her from a Spanish dungeon a couple of nights back," Avery added carelessly, "and it may be some spark o' gratitude animates yon dusky bosom—"

"Never mind yon dusky bosom!" shrilled Vanity. "What were you doing rescuing her from dungeons, when for all you knew I was twiddling my thumbs on the Isle of ruddy Aves?"

"Why, it so fell out, poppet mine. And why I think she may lend a hand now, is the way she rallied round after we'd 'scaped the Dons. Opened my eyes, I can tell you. I'd taken a crack on the roof, you see, and she carried me wounded through the jungle (in her stilettos, mind you) to a secluded glade where she nursed my hurts wi' rare skill . . . ah, but 'tis too long a tale for now, and strange enough to strain belief—"

"I'll bet! Suppose you take it from the top? I'm all ears!"

"Why, then, sweetkin, if you must . . . there was this galleon I had taken, wherein was fair young Spanish popsy, Donna Meliflua – oh, you'd like her, Vanity . . . such a brave, sweet little soul, not a day over sixteen, but what a cracking spirit!" Avery sighed grimly. "Aye, poor child, condemned by reason o' her fresh young beauty to a loveless marriage, and begged me to save her – which I jolly well will, too! Anyway . . . what's up, precious?"

For Lady Vanity had reeled back with a wordless wail into the sardonic arms of Colonel Blood, and ere Avery could inquire further, who should tool in but Brasso, accompanied by temple guards, and Solomon passed on the news that the Sun Princess required the presence of the Great White God, presumably for a wedding rehearsal and a chat with the vicar. Avery took it like a man.

"I must tread delicately," said he. "Not to worry, folks. Chins up." He bestowed a gallant smile on Vanity, who had sunk to the sofa with her head in her hands, and marched out, ready for anything. As the brazen door clanged shut, Vanity gave a great woof of numb despair, and raised bewildered blue eyes to heaven.

"What the hell have they been feeding him?" she apostrophised the ceiling. "He rescues me from hideous fate, vows me eternal love – and now I find he's been playing Galahad to some sixteen-year-old groupie in matador pants! To say nothing of barging into dungeons after that oversexed fugitive from the Hot Mikado, who seems to have carried him on her back halfway across South America, to nurse him (ha!) in a jungle glade, forsooth! And now he springs hotfoot from my side to the Queen of the Mardi Gras – nay, 'tis more than simple English maid can bear! Ah, my heart tells me he is true, yet on the face of it he carries on like some souped-up Solomon! And I don't mean him," she added, indicating the castaway, who was standing around looking squalid.

"What did I tell you?" murmured the Colonel. "Sure, an' he ought to be in some sort of home. The man's not safe."

"What am I to think?" Vanity flung up her arms, and then all the pride and passion of Cheltenham Ladies reasserted itself. "I know this much – if he goes through with marrying that man-eating rhumba dancer, I've had it with him and his godlike profile, and I hope they serve him up with duchess potatoes and an apple in his mouth!"

At which the Colonel made so bold as to pat her shoulder, what time he smiled and stroked his clarkie moustache.

The Princess of the Sun unsteadily paced her luxurious boudoir, a prey to remorse and cold turkey. Not for hours had she had a fix of drinking-chocolate, and the gremlins were getting to her; she twitched and shuddered as she swayed to and fro in her wonted conga rhythm, automatically muttering "One-and-two-and-three-*boom*!", and pausing only occasionally to glance in her mirror and scream (as who wouldn't at the reflection of a pink mongoose in a fruit hat?) Oh-h, brother, she whimpered, I wish I was back in Campeche.

But the real trouble was her conscience, dulled these many years by the insidious Cohaclgzln goof-talc. When first, as a runaway novice nun, she had strayed among the Indians and been hailed as Sun Princess on the strength of her million-dollar legs and skill in Latin-American dancing, she had become addicted to the novel chocolate dust, sniffing it, rubbing it in night and morning, dabbing it behind her ears, even having her hand-maidens (who were sworn to secrecy) shoot it at her from blowpipes; she had done everything but drink it, and the years had slipped by in a cocoa-coloured haze. Until yesterday, when she had fallen madly in love with a fair superman who might have been designed by Michelangelo and trained at Stilman's Gym, and without thought had proclaimed him Great White God and bridegroom before the Cohaclgzlns assembled.

Aflame with pure infatuation, she had determined to kick the habit, but now, as she emerged from her stoned state, returning sanity brought with it a realisation of what she had done. By claiming her mate she had condemned him to death; she would have him for three days of wild passion (she went goose-pimply at the thought) and then he would be taken from her and she would never see him again except as a nourishing fricassee. It was Catch 22. Small wonder that the proud Daughter of the Sun cried aloud and hurled her fruit headdress against the wall before subsiding in despair on her couch.

In her frenzy she had smashed quite a bit of furniture, and the noise summoned her chief attendant and confidante, a worldly little tomato who had fled the convent with her and shared her fortunes ever since. She surveyed the wreckage with a sympathetic eye, and inquired:

"Monkey on your back, sweetie? Want I should hit you?"

In broken whispers (in case anyone should overhear and realise that her official Tarzan accent was a phony) the Princess explained her dilemma. "I have doomed him, Prtzltntln! That superb man-god with his curly hair and dimples – my arms ache for him, but if ever they enfold him, he is scheduled for the chef! Ah, pity me! What am I to do?"

"Have a three-day honeymoon and forget it," counselled Prtzltntln. "Once you're back on the chocolate you'll never give him another thought."

"Ai-ee-ee!" wailed the Princess. "There is no drug powerful enough to drown the remorse I should feel! Oh, God, I could do with a blast – maybe just a teensy little one?

. . . no, no, I must be strong! Prtzltntln, I can't do it! I must forego his embraces in order to save him!"

"Get up to date, oh Daughter of Montezuma," said the practical hand-maid. "If you back-track now and say he isn't the God, they'll just stick him over the maguay anyway. And they might start asking themselves if you're the girl for the job." She patted her mistress's shoulder. "Go on, pamper yourself, honey. You can skip the main course at the feast."

The Princess hurtled upright, her lovely midriff streaked with tears. "I must get him away!" she cried wildly. "If I can't have him, at least I'll know that I set him free! Help me, sweet Prtzltntln, as you love me – how can I bust him out of here?"

"Have you been at the hash behind my back?" Prtzltntln was suspicious. "You're serious? Next thing you know, you'll be wanting to go with him!"

"And give up drinking-chocolate permanently?" cried the Princess, round-eyed. "Oh, come on!" She clutched her brow in perplexity. "There must be a way to help him fly the coop! Disguise? Laundry baskets? A garbage truck? Think, Prtzltntln, you dumb bitch, think!"

"There's the slave-traders," said Prtzltntln doubtfully. "You know, that half-caste gang who come every six months to buy our vagrants and used up priests? They'd smuggle him out, if you made it worth their while."

"The slavers?" The Princess tried to bite her lip, but missed. "Ah, what a hideous fate . . . and yet, better than going into the oven at gas-mark seven, surely. At least his death would not lie on my conscience." She closed her eyes in anguish, opened them again, and shrieked. "Where am I? Who are you, woman? Why doesn't the floor lie down? Oh, I remember . . . yes, do it, do it, Prtzltntln! Go secretly to the slavers and make a deal – tell them we'll sell them Brasso next time round – anything!"

"I'm on my way," said Prtzltntln obediently, "but I still think you're looped. Three Nights in Paradise you're passing up, remember . . . all right, I'm going! And while I'm gone, suppose you have the Great White God put in the Hall of Catzlotlbotzl, alone."

The Princess was baffled. "To what end? And why are these green beetles doing a square-dance on my coverlet?"

"We've got to get him alone so the slavers can make a clean snatch, don't we?" cried Prtzltntln impatiently. "Say it's so he can contemplate his divinity or something – and tomorrow we'll tell the peasants the Sun God couldn't wait to claim him, and drew him up to heaven in a gilded chariot drawn by . . . by . . . by green beetles, for Christ's sake! They'll buy any story if it's goofy enough. Then you'll be off the hook . . . and back on the sauce, if I know anything."

"Dear Prtzltntln, you think of everything," palpitated the Princess tearfully. "Stick me with a fix before you split, will you? The blow-pipe's on my make-up tray . . ."

So now we have Prtzltntln speeding through the darkened streets on her way towards the slavers' camp, Captain Avery answering the summons to the great shadowy Hall of Catzlotlbotzl, and out in the surrounding jungle . . . what, ha? Can that be an elegant black figure whose trouser suit needs invisible mending and a dry clean? See, it crouches in the loom of a step-pyramid, rapier in hand, eyes and finger-nails ferally agleam in the moonlight – Black Sheba is on her way to mount a one-woman rescue of Captain Avery, wheresoe'er he may be (it's astonishing what women will do for our hero, and one can only hope that whatever it is he's got, the government let him keep it).

But, hist! . . . still deeper in the jungle, on a shadowy trail, a light blinks, metal clanks softly, and there is the muffled sound of stealthy feet, as of a great disciplined multitude tripping over things in the dark and walking into trees. Surely it isn't the slave-traders? No, they're over there, in the opposite direction, swarthy ruffians listening agog round their camp-fire to the urgings of fair Prtzltntln, nodding grim assent to her proposal, sealing the bargain with an invitation to join them in rum sodas and a game of strip pontoon, which she declines, bidding them haste to do the Princess's bidding. Here they come now, half-a-dozen hairy unwashed half-breeds with hankies round their brows and slave-shackles in their back-pockets, sneaking along behind Prtzltntln, who points ahead through the gloom to the distant temple and the ajacent Hall of Catzlotlbotzl . . . the slavers give her the thumbs-up, and she slips away through the darkness to rejoin her mistress.

(What about the armed multitude, then? Easy does it; we shall know more o' them anon . . . oh, all right then, they're Spanish soldiers from Cartagena, wi' arquebuses primed, d'yc see, and naked blades, preparing a camisado [which is not a highly-seasoned Catalonian stew, but a night attack, so called because they wore their shirts over their armour]. Eddication, by th' powers! But, mum . . .)

Prtzltntln buzzed through the silent temple passages and upstairs to a certain secluded balcony where, she had guessed, the Princess would be found. Sure enough, a feathered skirt was rustling in the shadows, and a liquid contralto was whispering: "Ai-ai, whatsat numbah? Ai-ai, Cuban rhumba," as the Princess, her tissues restored by a mammoth blast of chocolate which had reduced her pupils to the size of mill-wheels, undulated silently in an alcove where she could look down through a cunning screen at the vast Hall of Catzlotlbotzl far below, where a solitary but clcan-cut figure paced to and fro carelessly whistling "When you walk through a storm . . ."

Prtzltntln joined her mistress and glanced down cynically.

"Couldn't resist a last peek, eh? Well, make the most of it, 'cos the Banana Bunch are closing in. Two minutes, and counting . . ."

"Isn't he gorgeous?" breathed the Princess, starry-eyed. "That tawny hair . . . those shoulders . . . oh, God, if he turns that profile to the torchlight again, I'll freak . . . and I'm letting him go! I need my chocolate-injected head examined . . . couldn't the slavers lift him *after* the three days and nights? I mean . . . look at the way he moves . . . Oh-oh-oh . . ."

"He could scratch my back," admitted Prtzltntln, "but it's too late nów, all-highest. List!" From somewhere far below came the unmistakeable sound of a drowsy Indian sentry being sapped, and the figure in the hall stopped whistling, every nerve alert. "Get the alertness of those nerves!" hissed the Princess. "Hell, he's perfect!"

"Hist!" whispered Prtzltntln, and frowned, trying to think of a word ending in "ist" that meant "look". Baffled, she pointed, and the two women clung to each other and stared with bated breath. A door in the hall below had opened . . .

Captain Avery drew himself up. He had been kept waiting in this great gloomy place for several minutes, and Princess or no Princess, he was thinking impatiently, it wasn't good enough. And who came here, this unwashed half-breed with tangled locks sneaking furtively towards him with dubious intent? One of the temple staff? A cleaner, possibly . . .

"Evenin', mac," whispered the half-breed, with a snaggle-toothed grin. "Gorra light?"

He held up a half-smoked cigarillo, and the Captain relaxed, and made a polite token search of his pockets, since he was quite sure he hadn't a light on him . . . and out of the shadows leaped five grunting figures with clubs, sack, and ropes. Hi-jacked, thought Avery, too late, as something exploded on his skull, and it was pure reflex action on his part that sent two of his attackers sprawling ere he sank senseless with a murmur of "Sorry, I don't seem to have . . ." and was back picking primroses by the river's brim again.

The slavers bundled him up and were out and running with him in a trice, and far above the Princess of the Sun heaved a great sob and drooped in her feathers. "Gone!" she glooped, and listlessly plucked and ate a mango from her headdress. "The only man I ever loved, and I never even saw him conga!"

Prtzltntln regarded her with eyes of cow-like compassion. "Don't bear down, favoured child of the Sun God", she coaxed. "We'll get over it; he's just a rag and a bone and a hank of whatever-the-hell . . . and listen," she confided, "I've got something 'll blow what's left of your disintegrated mind." She stooped to whisper. "*Malted* chocolate dust . . . cray-*zee* about it!"

The slavers legged it through the jungly night, nor paused till they had reached a river and bestowed their precious cargo on their barge, which they warped hastily donwstream. Just in time, too, for the sound of marching feet and the smell of smouldering arquebus fuses was getting closer. See where the lights gleam in the undergrowth as the Spaniards close in on sleeping Cohaclgzln – but why? What's Cohaclgzln done? Cut to a jungle clearing where slaves stagger under the weight of three enormous sedan chairs, closely guarded by morioned pikemen. Two of the chairs were de luxe eight-slave jobs with ivory trim, and contained Don Lardo Baluna and his intended bride; the third sedan, a light sports model with two groaning carriers, contained Enchillada the Chamberlain. The Viceroy was all in gleaming black armour, his face alight with hideous glee as he stroked a live black mamba in his steel gauntlets. Meliflua (poor lady!) slumped gracefully in the height of night-jungle fashion – cloth-of-gold camouflaged gown, matching accessories, and a mosquito veil of priceless Mechlin lace. Dusky attendants fanned her and profferred cooling drinks which went unheeded.

"Hey, Excellencee!" Enchillada, having conferred with the military commander, was reporting, all greasy excitement. "We heet pay-dirt, I theenk! Thee scouts say we are approacheeng the los' city of Cohaclgzln, faymoos for gold, bloodthirsty natives, an' reepulseev works of art! Also, thee dumb bums don't know about wheels, even! Eet's the only los' city aroun' heer, so you bet your sweet bippy some of thee pirate fugitives weel 'ave taken refuge, you know?''

"Gold, you say?" lisped Don Lardo greedily. "Just what we need to finance my great crusade through the Indies! We shall fall upon it, put it to the sack, slaughter without ruth or pity – they make lousy slaves, anyway, and we haven't time to waste converting them to the True Faith!" His dentures wobbled alarmingly as he turned mad gleaming eyes on his lovely consort. "You hear, Meliflua angel, what hubby-wubby has in store for you? A whole savage civilisation to exterminate and cast down, not one stone left on another! Aren't you glad I persuaded you to come?"

Meliflua fluttered limp eyelids and gestured weakly. Persuaded, yet! For days and nights she had been toted along on this nightmare journey, with servants, portable dressing-room and bath, and even her own private collapsible four-poster in tow; this leering monster had sworn he could not bear to be parted from her for an instant, and had gloated about the carnage he would wreak for her amusement. And she was to marry this sanguinary loony? Santa Maria!

"Pliz, Don Lardo—" she began weakly.

"Lardo *honey*!" hissed the Viceroy, snapping his black mamba like a whip. "You remember, sweet Meliflua?"

"Ah, forgeev me!" faltered the bewildered hidalga. "Lardo honey, I mean. Thees Eendian town – couldn't we spare some of them, maybee? The leetle ones, an' the old pipple? Jus' for me – pliz?"

"Spare them?" Don Lardo goggled horribly. "Aahh – you mean for torture and burning at auto-da-fé? Why, that's terrific, cara mia! Brilliant! She's brilliant, I say – isn't she brilliant, you bastards?" he roared, lashing with his snake at the headquarters officers, who obediently chorused, "She's terrific – just like you!"

"Pass me a new snake, Enchillada," purred the Viceroy. "This one's gone all squishy and doesn't crack any more . . . All right, scum, what are you waiting for? Attack! Kill! Burn!

274

Throw discipline to the winds! They're endemonised heathen! Loot their temples, plunder their cellars, desecrate their altars in the name of the Father, Son, and Holy Ghost! We've got protection, I tell you – you'll all be absolved later, as soon as the accountants are through! On, in the King's name, for the glory of Spain!"

So now were enthusiastic cries of "Viva el sack and pillage!" and "Caramba, I can't wait!", and "Let's hear it for Lardo!" as the eager soldiery pressed through the jungle until in the baleful moonlight they beheld the ghostly outlines of step-pyramids and temples, and halted on the forest edge for a Pause for Suspense before the final assault. The soldiers bit their nails and the officers checked their watches, and a terrible silence fell on the scene – a silence that seemed to steal forward on the town like an ugly ghost, stifling even the light breaths of sleepers, muffling the heart-beats, the silence of approaching doom.

Black Sheba felt it as she prowled the deserted alleys, and stopped, rapier in hand, the sweat icy on her perfect spine. In the bed-chamber of the Princess, Prtzltntln sensed it, and shivered uneasily as she laid syringe and Choc-a-Toke capsules on the bedside table of her drowsy mistress; it penetrated even to the room where Vanity waited anxiously, wondering (1) was Avery in deadly danger, (2) if not, was the Princess showing him how the feathers worked on her conga skirt? Blood, his rascally instincts suddenly alert, stopped his pacing to listen, and Solomon Shafto, huddled in his rags in a corner, dreaming of dripping, suddenly sat bolt upright and croaked: "Voodle-de-oy-doy! Ole Sol smells garlic, adrift on the night air, wi' a curse an' dang it! The Dons be come! The damned Dons, I tell 'ee! Take ter the hills!" To confirm his diagnosis came sudden uproar of gunfire and musketry as the Spaniards stormed into the town, their morphological oaths mingling with the cries of the inhabitants who woke to find themselves beset by the forces of civilisation.

What followed was awful. The Spaniards rushed about

shooting and slashing, breaking windows, turning on taps, blocking drains in wanton fashion, and shouting "Wakey-wakey, you wogs! Stand by your beds for slaughtering, it's sack-the-city time!" Sheba in her alley was suddenly confronted by a mob of pike-wielding infantry who recognised her instantly with cries of " 'Tis the fugitive coon-lady! Seize her!" She turned at bay, and her bright steel sent two to their account ere the others bore her down, breathed all over her to the point of suffocation, and trussed her hand and foot before rampaging on to break more bottles, stove in the heads of casks, knock at doors and run away, and put the entire population to the sword.

Amidst the furore only the cacique Brasso kept his head. As soon as he saw that all was lost, he summoned a hasty meeting of community leaders in the temple, announced that the situation was in hand and that the Sun God's intervention on Cohaclgzln's behalf could be expected any minute, urged stout resistance, and promised that the Princess would issue an official statement shortly. Reassured, the citizens waited obediently to be massacred (which they were), while Brasso scooted to the royal apartments, where a distinctly woozy Princess was being tended by panic-stricken hand-maidens. Brasso informed them that they must convey their mistress to the secret VIP fall-out shelter beneath the great altar without delay.

"But, Keeper of the High Mysteries," faltered Prtzltntln, "her highness is stoned to hellangone and cannot locomote!"

"Just because she ain't fitted with handles don't mean she can't be carried!" snarled Brasso. "Up, up, an' away, girls!"

"But she will wish to share the fate of her people!"

"Twelve will get you seven she don't. Look, don't give me no grief, Beulah," warned Brasso. "She owes it to her people to survive, right? Man, who else is gonna be the repository of their culture an' traditions an' stuff? Who else is gonna carry on the dynasty?"

276

"What dynasty?" asked Prtzltntln, as the comatose Princess was borne hastily to the high altar.

"The dynasty she an' me is gonna found," chuckled Brasso wickedly. "Listen, don't knock this invasion – that ruckus out there is the priestly hierarchy getting theirs, along with most of the population. So they get thinned, so what? People, they're everywhere. But *we* survive, and when we come out, baby, we're gonna start this civilisation all over again, with Brasso top of the power vacuum, okay? Hurry along, ladies – and another thing, you can forget all this Sun God crap. That's out – it's King Brasso and the Sun Princess, in that order—"

It may have been a Spanish cannon-shot, or just wear and tear, but at that instant the gigantic statue of the Sun God toppled from its plinth and squashed Brasso flatter than a fluke. The hand-maidens screamed and swooned, but Prtzltntln rallied them, and they got the Princess below stairs and closed the hatch. (So it was that they alone survived the carnage, and no doubt emerged eventually safe and sound, for rumours still persist in the jungles of the Main of a lost all-female civilisation given to rhumbas and worshipping drinking-chocolate. But whether the legend be true no one knows, for Cohaclgzln's temples and pyramids vanished long ago 'neath the engulfing tropic forest, and no explorers have found it to this day, or pondered the mystery of the rejected wheel-prototypes which litter its silent courts and weed-choked plazas.)

Meanwhile, in the chamber where she and her companions were confined, Vanity was a prey to mounting consternation as the sounds of massacre and pillage drew nearer.

"Look, is my hair an awful mess?" she cried to Blood. "And this dress is a positive fright! Ah, what will our Spanish rescuers think to see a lady of quality thus reduced—"

"I can guess!" snapped Blood. "Ye're mighty confident they'll rescue us. From what I know of 'em they're a pack of

Papist rapists, and no way tender o' heretics, ladies or not. Listen, acushla, I can pass meself off as a left-footer, so I can, and if I give 'em a touch o' the pax vobiscums, and we pretend to be man and wife," he added with a meaning smirk, "then haply I may be able to preserve thy sweet person from ill-usage."

"Faugh! A distasteful subterfuge, and who needs it?" cried haughty Vanity. "Dagoes are remarkably civilised. Why, we had their ambassador's daughter in the Upper Fifth – Onions, we called her, a stuck-up minx with spots who sneaked about our vodka at the dorm feast, but that's not the point. Their officers will be caballeros who will show all courtesy to a lady of my station." She looked Blood up and down. "It'll be more convincing if I say you're my groom . . . Right, leave the talking to me."

And as the door crashed open to admit a pack of blood-drunk Spaniards brandishing reeking swords, the Admiral's daughter rapped sharply on a convenient table. "Pay attention! I am Lady Vanity Rooke, an English noblewoman held captive by these beastly savages. Where is your officer?"

A swarthy lout in a morion stopped brandishing to scratch his stubbled chin and scowl at her. "Eengleesh?" he demanded truculently. "You gotta passa-port?"

"Do I look as though I've got a passport?" retorted Vanity.

"So! An eelleegal eemigrant!" sneered the Spaniard. "Camarados, wee gotta buncha wetbacks heer! No passa-ports, huh? Hokay – you gotta any aneemal foodstuffs, uncook-ed meats, groweeng plants, raw vegetables—"

"Ar, plants, is it?" cried Solomon Shafto, hobbling forward, his knuckle to his brow. "Ole Sol's yer man, señor! Beddin'-out an' dung-spreadin' a speciality, wi' a ding-dang-diddle, but likewise herbaceous borders an' landscapin' o' cabbages, look'ee—"

"Hold your tongue, hobbledehoy!" grated Vanity, and to

the Spaniard: "I demand to be taken to your commander at once . . ."

". . . please," added Blood ingratiatingly, and the Spaniard scowled thunderously.

" 'Pliz', you say? You tryeeng to soft-soap Corporal Gomez, greengo peeg? Ha, I know-a yoor sort! You Eengleesh, you try-a to sneak-a into our country, try to take-a jobs from honest Spaneesh workeeng-pipple – like-a he wan's to be a cabbage-lan'scaper, the old-a bum, an' thee dame wan's to be a topless waitress, mebbe, an' you, wit' your clarkie moustache an' your 'Pliz', you want-a to set up as a peemp, I bet! You theenk," he roared indignantly, "we don't got cabbage-lan'scapers an' topless waitresses an' peemps of our own, who need-a the work, huh?" His followers growled menacingly. "You gotta nerve, greengo! No passa-ports, huh? Hokay—"

Vanity stamped with vexation, Blood protested, and Solomon grovelled, all at once, but Corporal Gomez silenced them with an angry gesture. "Yoo ask-a for eet, wetbacks! Hokay, I was joost a-goeeng to molesta thee dame an' then sleet all-a yoor throats – but now I feex you good! Yoo go beefore Don Lardo heemself, an' see how you like eet! Away wit' them, bravos!"

The hapless trio were hustled rudely out, into the smoking ruin to which the raiders had reduced Cohaclgzln. There were corpses everywhere, and Don Lardo had spent an enjoyable dawn reviewing the slaughter, and had returned with blood all over his boots to take part in a Te Deum and breakfast, and gloat over the huge pile of ornaments, jewellery, and native works of art before his pavilion. Cackling with glee, he had bounced up and down on the Princess's magnificent litter in full armour, a sight which had quite put Donna Meliflua off her toast and cereal and sent her shuddering to the refuge of her own pavilion.

But now a nasty shock awaited the Viceroy. It transpired that to their inability to design wheels the unfortunate

Cohaclgzlns had added a total ignorance of precious metals, for the vast heap of treasure glowing dully in the morning sun proved, on closer examination, to be not gold, but brass. Even the litter was made in Taiwan.

The Viceroy's rage was awesome. "They've cheated me, these aboriginal swine!" He shook steel fists to heaven and stamped his black mamba underfoot. "It passes belief! Honest conquistadores go to vast outlay and inconvenience to bring enlightenment to these vermin, expecting only a modest return to defray expenses, and what do we get? Junk!" He wheeled frothing on Enchillada. "I'll make them pay, por Dios! They'll feel my vengeance! Kill them! Massacre them all, the heathen reptiles—"

"But, boss, we jus' did," faltered the chamberlain.

"Are you trying to make trouble again?" blared Don Lardo. "Scour the woods! Look under beds! Discover trembling survivors – fool, whoever heard of a massacre where some old crone or village idiot didn't get overlooked? Find them! I want to see them slaughtered while I have my boiled eggs! And then I'll have her –" he pointed a passionate finger at Sheba, who stood smouldering defiantly between her guards "– crucified with the toast and marmalade. And a double orange juice and black coffee, damn you – but ha! Who are these?"

For Corporal Gomez and his three prisoners had hove in sight, and the Viceroy's gooseberry eyes widened alarmingly when he learned that they were English captives of the Indians, one of whom claimed to be the daughter of an English milord admiral, no less. Enchillada looked to see these heretics disposed of in swift and novel fashion, but to his amazement Don Lardo, after chewing his steel gauntlets in brief thought, suddenly contorted his features into a ghastly smile, and addressed Vanity in his most ingratiatory hiss.

"But how distressing! An English lady of quality, in the hands of these infidels! Dear madonna," he bowed his enormous armoured bulk, "I can only rejoice that Providence has made me the instrument of your deliverance. Pray be seated, and refresh yourself while you tell us what terrible misfortune led to your captivity."

"She's gotta no passa-port," announced Corporal Gomez, "an' the other two bums are a peemp an' a cabbage-lan'scaper—"

Don Lardo fractured his skull with a light backhand flick of his steel gauntlet and simpered ghoulishly at Vanity. "Forgive my peasant soldiery," he lisped. "Enchillada, wine for the lady – and have the corporal swept up. And now, madonna, we are all ears . . ."

(What's this? Don Lardo being *nice*? Ah, but you see, paranoid nut though he was, he still knew a heroine when he saw one, and the aristocratic breeding of this sculpted blonde in the velvet rags stuck out like a cauliflower ear. And what should a Spanish villain do with a heroine but lull her with honeyed words? It was part of their training, practically.)

As for Vanity, she had been through a lot lately, and to be kindly entreated, even by something that looked like King Kong with a stomach upset, had a disarming effect on her. Bewildered, she sipped the wine they gave her, and then briefly sketched the essentials of her adventures – how she had fallen into the hands of pirates, and then of Indians who would have sacrificed her but for the timely intervention of her fiancé, one Captain Avery, about whom she now expressed a touching anxiety.

"Avery? Avery?" murmured subtle Don Lardo. "Do I remember the name, Enchillada? No matter . . . since he is in the vicinity, our search parties will surely find him." He leered and poured more wine, and despite his Latin courtesy Vanity could not repress uneasy goose-pimples. Gosh, what a clock, she thought, but at least he's civil.

"Your father, the Admiral Lord Rooke," continued the Viceroy, "no doubt commands a fleet of ships . . . is he, ah, in Caribbean waters at the moment?"

"Alack, poor Daddy!" cried Vanity. "I last saw him in a rowing boat in the Indian Ocean, and know not wheresoe'er he may be!"

"We must pray for his safety," crooned Don Lardo, with his most charming smile, which would have curdled petrol. "And the pirates bore you from the Indian Ocean to New Spain – what an ordeal, for one so young and fair!"

"Oh, well, it was just a bit hairy now and then," admitted Vanity modestly. "Actually, Captain Pew was quite cute, in a Froggy sort of way – it was when he came ashore to bury his treasure that the Indians got hold of me—"

"Treasure?" Don Lardo's raised eyebrows crackled like kindling and his dentures rattled with animation. "Oh, he had a booty?"

"You can double that in spades!" said Vanity, and Blood, who had been listening uneasily, felt a wild foreboding. "Why, they must have robbed a bank! I mean, they had absolute scads of the stuff – gold, I warrant me, in vast shining heaps!"

"Which they buried? Why, its true owners will rejoice to have it restored, and be truly grateful to you, madonna . . . who knows where it is to be found."

"Who, me?" Vanity was round-eyed. "Gosh, I've no idea, I'm afraid – somewhere on a beach, not far from here, but I'm hopeless at geography! My man, Blood –" she indicated the Colonel who was mentally having pups, "– could probably find the spot . . . couldn't you, Blood?"

The Colonel's marrow froze as the gargoyle face of the Viceroy was turned in his direction. All this courtly Spanish grace hadn't fooled our Tom for a minute, and he was both apprehensive and sick as mud at Vanity's mention of the Happy Dan treasure, of whose location he had a very fair idea. Indeed, he had been dreaming of the day when (assuming he ever got out of this ghastly succession of crises) he might dig it up personally. That hope died before Don

Lardo's frightful regard, but Blood did his desperate best to play dumb – and Irish dumb, at that.

"Phwat's dat, y'r leddyship? Treasure, is ut? Sure, an' how would Oi be knowin', dat can't tell latitude from t'other t'ing? Faith an' begob—"

"Blood, eh?" The Viceroy's voice was silky smooth. "An appropriate name, I think. Enchillada, would you be so good as to send for four horses, and attach them, with stout cords, to this tall rascal's several limbs? Perhaps we can stimulate his memory – or madonna's." And with a sudden dreadful baying laugh Don Lardo thrust his face towards Vanity, who paled in panic. "No! No!" she fluttered. "What? Eh? Oh, golly –"

"Ha ha!" bawled the Viceroy in triumph, and springing to his feet he drummed his gauntlets on his breastplate. "I've done it again! Caramba, what genius! See, Enchillada, what good manners and Castilian subtlety can achieve! Instinct told me that if I wooed this peroxided heretic slut with fair words, she would spill something good! And what do I learn? Not only that her fool of a father is half a world away – which means one less enemy fleet to worry about – but that a vast treasure is available to finance my great crusade!" He strode up and down, clanging exultantly, his dentures flying out to be crushed 'neath his armoured feet. "You lot would have ravished her and butchered her buddies according to the book, wouldn't you? But not Lardo – I've got it here!" And he clashed his steel forefinger against his helmet. "That's why I'm a Viceroy and you're not! Now all we have to do is tear this lout apart between galloping horses and he'll sing like a bird! Sant Iago! I'll have *four* boiled eggs on the strength of this! Bring on the ponies!"

In a trice Blood had been flung down by brutal soldiers and neatly attached by wrists and ankles to four mettlesome chargers whose riders waited eagerly for Don Lardo's signal. The Viceroy was in a frenzy of self-congratulation, mitting his assembled troops who, under Enchillada's frantic cheerleading, flung up their morions in acclaim. Heedless of the tin hats which rained around her, Vanity fronted the armoured giant in fearless fury.

"Oh, base!" she shrilled. "So to impose on a lady in distress, with fair words and foul sticky wine! Well, I'd sooner have the new Beaujolais, so there! Of all the mean tricks, to wheedle information out of me unaware – and I thought you were a gentleman! Fie, you stinker! Know that I am a British subject – so's he, for that matter –" she indicated Blood, who was creaking slightly as the riders took up the slack "– and unless you release us with handsome apologies, 'twill be the worse for you!"

For a moment it seemed that Don Lardo would dash her to the ground with one sweep of his armoured hand, but a shower of falling morions impeded him long enough to regain his cool. He seized her proud chin 'twixt cruel metal fingers.

"Snarl at me, would you, Lutheran whelp! Aye, but I'll give you cause! When your fellow there has spoken his piece, and I have that pirate hoard for my war chest, you shall see how much protection your precious British crown can afford you – or any other of your heretic brood! For not only shall I cleanse the American seas of the pirate filth, but every foreign settlement with them – English, Dutch, French, Walloon, Scowegian—"

"Don' forget flags of convenience, Excellencee," put in Enchillada.

"All of them! Every vile interloper who does not acknowledge the sovereignty and supremacy of Spain!" bawled Don Lardo. "My fleets shall sweep from the Florida keys to the Amazon, my armies shall make rubble of your Limey, Frog, and Squarehead outposts, and no man, woman, child or farmyard animal shall remain! New Spain shall extend from Canada to the southernmost seas, and the tides that wash the Antilles shall be crimson with Protestant blood – which reminds me," he roared to the four horsemen. "Take the strain, and when I say heave—"

"Do your worst!" cried the indomitable Vanity.

"Wait your hurry!" thundered Don Lardo. "I'm not finished yet! Where was I? Ah, por los entrañas de Dios—"

" 'The Antilles shall be crimson'," prompted Enchillada.

"Right!" Don Lardo gloated down at his fair prisoner. "And when I sail on my great crusade of the Faith, to purge the New World of your northern corruption, I shall take you with me, proud Admiral's daughter, to afford me amusement on the voyage. You will make a piquant change from yon dusky charmer over the way—"

"One for odd days, one for evens!" chortled Enchillada. "Good thinking, boss!"

Even in her fraught situation, Vanity could not suppress a yip of astonishment as her eye fell on Sheba for the first time. " 'Tis she! Her! That woman who filched my Helena Rubinstein and had designs on my darling Ben! Where is he, you horrid wench?"

"You should worry," sneered Sheba. "We are not like to speak him this voyage."

"Nay!" cried Vanity frantically. "He's around some place, and will haste to my aid!"

"You'd like to think so, wouldn't you?" Sheba taunted, spiteful to the last. " 'Twas not your milky softness that he rescued from Dago dungeon! If he hastes to anyone's aid 'twill—"

"Stop them! Gag them!" screamed Don Lardo, his eyes rolling horribly as he clutched his temples. "Do something, Enchillada!"

"Can I say something?" Blood, taut in his bonds, spoke in an anguished voice.

"Yes!" shouted Don Lardo, recalled to the business in hand. "You can scream! – unless you reveal this instant where I may find the treasure trove! Speak, and I spare your miserable life – for the moment, anyway. Remain dumb, and you'll be a quintet! Horsemen, on your marks! Ready . . . get set . . ."

The riders steadied their mounts, and the spreadeagled Blood squawked as the ropes tightened. Don Lardo cackled fiendishly and swung round on Vanity. "Well, madonna, will he talk – or will you?"

"We will never submit!" cried Vanity. "I defy you! So does he! Listen to him, constant to the end! Go on, Colonel – tell him what he can do with his foreign threats!"

All eyes turned on Blood, who was twanging like a guitar string. A grimace which might have been of pain, or defiance, or resignation, or just wind crossed his tanned features. Then in a voice that rang clear, if somewhat strained, he spoke.

"If ye go back up the jungle trail for seven hours, ye'll come to the beach. There's a big palm tree, an' ye go left a couple o' miles, and there'll be bodies all over the place, because that's where Happy Dan's boys got their lumps from the Indians. Right, that's where ye start diggin' . . ."

Well, it's nice to know that all his hardships haven't warped Blood's instinct for self-preservation. Vanity may be disappointed in him, but at least he's still in one piece as Don Lardo, his dentures secured and his hapless prisoners in tow, sets off to dig up the pirates' treasure and then spread bloody ruin and destruction the length o' the Caribbean, by the powers! Aye, and who's to stop him? Our hero was last seen helpless i' the merciless grip o' slave-traders, our female leads are all in the clutches o' Bestial Villainy, Blood's had it up to here and can't be relied on, Solomon Shafto's barmy, the pirate fraternity are scattered and dispersed (Goliath probably hasn't even got a new leg yet), and poor old Admiral Rooke has spent the whole of Book the Second adrift in the Indian Ocean. Here, that's a bit rough; the old boy's due a few pages, isn't he? After all, he's a peer of the realm (and can probably make a ton of trouble if we neglect him much longer). So, knuckling our forehead apologetically, we shall butter him up with a chapter opening all to himself . . . aye, and more than a mere chapter, my lord, d'ye see, for here, by y'r lordship's favour, endeth the Second and Beginneth the Last Book of

THE PYRATES

BOOK
THE THIRD

CHAPTER
THE FIFTEENTH

he worthy and popular Lord Rooke came thundering ashore at Libertatia in a towering rage – and quite right, too. Since the pirate villains had set him cruelly adrift he had been sailing in circles (not his fault, mind, but that lubber Yardley's) and met with misdventures fit to curl his grizzled hair (for a full and luxuriant growth had his lordship, and those tales about his being bald beneath his wig were malicious focsle gossip). Aye, thanks to Yardley's bungling, the long boat with its loyal castaways had blundered around the Indian Ocean hitting reefs, splitting strakes, fouling oil platforms, and finally getting pinched by a Burmese coastguard for illegal fishing. His subsequent appearance in police court, confiscation of tackle, scathing remarks from the bench, sentence to death by the Thousand Cuts, and unfavourable press publicity, had worn the Admiral's patience thin. By the time he and his crew had filed through their shackles with the bosun's manicure set, tunnelled out of the condemned hold, overpowered the crew of a dilapidated junk, set fire to Rangoon, had a vitriolic argument with the harbour-master, and finally put to sea, his lordship's temper was beginning to boil; capture by Borneo pirates, slavery at the oar of a galley, escape by swimming down the crocodile-infested Papar river, and having to pay over the odds for passage west on a coal-boat, did nothing to restore his good humour, and by the time he and his whining followers had landed at Libertatia, where the coal-boat accidentally ran aground, the admiral was fit to bite lumps out of the pier. Nor was his temper improved by the discovery that all the pirates had sloped off to the Caribbean.

Like all other visitors to that port o' missing men, Rooke wound up in the establishment of Vladimir Mackintosh-Groonbaum, demanding transport at the top of his voice. Vladimir, who was busy calculating what Avery's annual income would be, with bonuses and graduated cost-of-living, by the time he was forty, surveyed the ragged but imposing admiral calmly and asked:

"Business or pleasure?"

"Both, damn your eyes!" bellowed Rooke. "Know, little shyster, that I command His Majesty's East Indies squadron, wherever the hell it is, and my urgent need is a sloop to the Cape, there to raise my powers and smite the Brethren o' the Coast. Business! Aye, and rare pleasure, split me, to hale those bloody rascals to Execution Dock!"

Vladimir shook his head sympathetically. "Sorry, mate, yer too late. My boy's takin' care o' them."

"Your *what*?" blared Rooke, bewildered.

"My boy. Cap'n Ben Avery", explained Vladimir complacently. "'E's prob'ly got most of 'em under wraps by now – well, 'e's bin gorn three weeks, 'asn't 'e? Bags o' time fer a fit young chap like him to pull the rug aht from—"

"AVERY!" bawled Rooke apoplectically, and shattered Vladimir's desk with a blow of his horny fist; timber and spilt tea flew amain. "That forsworn weasel! That renegade yard o' Brylcreem! He that betrayed us, the cowardly napkin-carrier, the smooth-sole purse-snapping pimp, wi' his Oxenford airs and his safety razor, damn him to hell! He'll be the first to go up in the air, by this hand! Aye, tarred and filleted and a-clank in chains 'neath high water mark, rot his patent-leather pointy-toed boots—"

"Beggin' yer lordship's pardin, but if I was you," interposed Vladimir frostily, "I'd watch me lip. That's slander, that is, afore witnesses – Gawd, I'll bet they can 'ear yer in Bombay! Nah, take it easy, stop turnin' purple, an' perpend." He raised an admonitory unwashed hand before the goggling admiral. "One thing at a time . . . or rather, three things . . ."

And so saying, he rummaged in the splintered remains of his top drawer and displayed before the other's stupefied gaze three dull crosses of undoubted gold, crusted with gems; in one shone the blue radiance of an enormous sapphire, the second was alight with the shimmering white of a splendid opal, and the emerald in the third rivalled a go-light for size and brilliance. "Why don't yer sit dahn, yer lordship," suggested Vladimir considerately, "an' I'll get the boy ter fetch yer a cup o' cocoa wi' somethin' in it."

Rooke subsided, giving a creditable imitation of a turkey in labour, and Vladimir continued. "Where'd I get 'em, you may be askin'? Well, I'll tell yer – where but from my client Cap'n Avery, wot you bin miscallin' so reckless." His gesture stilled Rooke's explosion of amaze and protest. "I dunno wot rags o' the gutter press you bin readin', milord," he added severely, "or wot malishus scuttlebutt 'as bin dropped in yore dainty shell-likes, but I'm 'ere to testify that Cap'n Avery, far from betrayin' anyfink, 'as bin flyin' rahnd the seven seas like an 'awk wiv a wasp up its frock, recoverin' bits o' Madagascar crahn faster'n I can enter 'em in me book. Oh, an' 'e's signed orf Akbar the Damned permanent, jus' by the way . . ."

Rooke couldn't believe it, of course – but there were the three crosses, and when it finally sank in the admiral's bellowings of disbelief turned to eruptions of delight. He punched the air, threw up the remnants of his hat, stamped around the room, and reduced a chest of drawers to matchwood in his glee – it was rather, reflected Vladimir gloomily, like having a disgruntled Firebeard loose on the premises. At last the admiral sank back, fanning his beaming brow.

"I'm all took aback!" he roared. "Sink me, that's a noble

lad! And I misjudged him! Nay, but I'll hear no evil of him after this! Why, that lying hellspite Sheba! She misled me a-purpose – damme, but she did! Brazen as monkeys, butter wouldn't melt, told me young Ben had ratted, never batted an eyelid! Women! By cock," he rumbled, "it makes ye wonder! And that sterling young feller has copped back three o' the crosses already—"

"Jus' like that. Prob'ly got t'other three by now, an' all."

"– and sent bloody Akbar post-haste to Hell!" Rooke shook his massive head in admiration, then grew more sober. "Mind you, he could do no less. After all, 'tis no more than making amends for losing the crown i' the first place. Dooced careless, that."

"'Arf a mo!" cried Vladimir indignantly. "You ain't 'eard nuffink yet, milord! 'E also rescued your lordship's daughter from 'ell of shame an' slavery—"

"Me daughter!" Rooke gaped in sudden recollection. "Little Vanity! 'Slife, I *knew* there was another score 'gainst those pirate villains! But rescued? Nay, where, sirrah? How? My darling child – where is she?"

"Well, nah," said Vladimir primly, "I look arter Cap'n Avery's business affairs, but 'tain't for me to pry into 'is private life, is it? Mind you, I did 'ear talk of a desert island, like," he added, reflecting guiltily that he hadn't bothered to have Vanity collected from Aves. Rooke started violently.

"An island? D'ye mean she and Avery ha' been on tropic isle together – alone, ha?" His brow darkened ominously and he took grizzled chin in mighty paw. "Gad's death! My little innocent . . . solitary, wi' a man . . . and she a tender virgin maid! Nay, here's food for thought, rabbit me!"

"Blimey, yore 'ard to please!" snapped Vladimir. "I wish it 'ad been one o' my bleedin' daughters – but they're all orphans, beggin' an' thievin' an' workin' the kinchin lay rahnd Aldgate Pump, wiv never a thought for their pore ole Dad, wot brought 'em up to the age o' three – an' four, in Gayleen's case." He sniffed and wiped away an oily tear.

"Ungrateful little barstids. Yore bleedin' lucky," he added resentfully. "I mean, I'm glad to be Cap'n Avery's agent, but I'd a sight sooner be 'is flamin' favver-in-law, wouldn't I?"

"Father-in-law?" Rooke went purple. "D'ye tell me the dog aspires to my daughter's hand? He – a penniless captain? A landless nobody – and she the daughter o' a peer and admiral and tennis captain o' Cheltenham Ladies—"

"You weren't!" exclaimed Vladimir incredulously.

"Not me, you fool, her!" roared Rooke. "Why, here's insolence! Why, the upstart rascal! Not," he admitted reasonably, "that he isn't a dab hand at recovering stolen goods and slaughtering corsairs, but dammit, I design her for a certain Duke's son!"

"Café society riff-raff!" scoffed Vladimir. "Not in the same class as my boy Ben. Look, guv, get realistic – it's an investment, see? I mean, you're not goin' to be short of a bob in yer old age if your daughter's married to that ball of fire, are yer? 'E's goin' places, is that boy – an' by the time 'e's finished toughin' up the Coast Bruvver'ood, 'e'll be laughin' all the way to the bank!"

Rooke's complexion faded to beetroot, and he plucked thoughtfully at a lip like a lifebelt. "D'ye tell me?" he said at last, and shook perplexed head. "H'm . . . I know not what to say . . ."

" 'Bless yer, my children' should cover it," said Vladimir. "You want to push this thing along, milord."

"Ye think so?" wondered Rooke, and frowned. "What the hell am I discussing my intimate family affairs with you for, anyway? What's my daughter's future to thee, shyster?"

"She's goin' to be my client-in-law, so to speak," said Vladimir. "I got a sort of avuncular interest. An' I reckon these two young love-birds need all the 'elp they can get from us older an' wiser 'eads. So while I continue to manage the business side, why don't yer lordship get yer fleet together – our boy's ragin' rahnd the Caribbean at the moment, beatin' the bejeezus aht of every pirate in sight, but I'm sure 'e'd be grateful for any assistance from 'is lovin' favver-in-law to be." Vladimir stroked his nose conspiratorially. "An' arterwards, if you was to report favourably on 'is conduck to the King an' Admiralty – well, it wouldn't 'urt 'is prospecks, would it?"

"I suppose not," rumbled the Admiral pensively. He eyed Vladimir shrewdly. "You see a bright future for the lad, ha? Harumph! A . . . rich future?"

"Stinkin' ", replied Vladimir. "The prize-money from this lot, 'e'll be able to buy 'arf Yorkshire."

"There's the mortgage on Torpedo Towers," mused Rooke. "And between ourselves, Vanity costs a packet . . ."

"Not any more, she wouldn't," chuckled Vladimir.

"Bigod, no – he'd have to support her! Well, the young must faces their responsibilities sooner or later . . ."

". . . an' repay the love an' care of elders wot guided their youthful footsteps."

"Thou sayest true, Master Pawnbroker! Why, have we not earned our repose?"

"You better believe it, squire! Slavin' over accounts –"

"Assembling fleets!"

"Sacrificin' our today for their tomorrer . . ."

"Mind you, that's what life's all about, I suppose. And they're worth it, bless 'em . . ."

"Ow, yerss, a lovely couple . . ."

The upshot was that Lord Rooke sailed for the Cape on the next tide, there to summon his fleet, and Vladimir, pondering their conversation, wondered if it was not time that he, too, shifted operations to his Caribbean branch office, there to keep a closer eye on his protégé. After all, hero though he might be, Captain Avery was a right mug in worldly matters, and would be none the worse of his agent's guiding presence, if only to count the prize money and outstanding Madagascar crosses which ought to be rolling in by now.

So where a lesser man (and they didn't come much lesser

than Vladimir, normally) would have kept a safe distance from the action, Master Mackintosh-Groonbaum put up his shutters, packed his bags, and took a through ticket to Port Royal, change for Nassau, Roatan, and the Mosquito Coast. He travelled first, since he was on his client's business, and consoled himself that it was all deductible anyway.

Now this happened on the very day that Avery and Sheba were escaping from Cartagena into Injun country, and Vanity and Blood were falling into the hands of the Cohaclgzlns. What has since happened to them, we know, but it may be as well to pause for station identification on some of our other characters, who haven't been heard from for a while.

Happy Dan Pew, for example, we left nursing his fractured heart and leafing moodily through Lesson One (je suis, tu es, il est, etc., poor devil) while he cruised dazedly towards Tortuga – thanks to his Vanity trauma he had forgotten all about joining Bilbo at Cartagena. Which was just as well, since when last seen Bilbo, Firebeard and Goliath were leaving the city at high speed, with Lardo's soldiers taking futile pot-shots after their canoe. Let's see where they went.

If you and I had been in their shoes (a horrid thought, when you condsider that Odor-Eaters had still to be invented) we would have continued downstream in top gear. But Bilbo reasoned coolly that his ship, the *Laughing Sandbag*, must still be lurking secure off the coast, since the Spaniards couldn't conceivably have found her yet. Accordingly he and his companions quickly beached their canoe and took to the woods, Firebeard carrying the woodenlegless Goliath as they struck out for the coast. A gruelling march it was, of a kind that nowadays would be attempted only with two-way radios, survival gear, nylon anoraks, and sponsorship by several sporting-goods firms, and even so would probably end in disaster and air-sea rescue. But those were the days when Morgan and Dampier and their crews were wont to plunge into trackless, fever-ridden jungle with a handful of salt and a cutlass, hack their unerring way to where the loot was, fight their half-starved battles against impossible odds, hack their way back again, and so home, thinking nothing of it. To Bilbo, who could read the stars as easily as a book, and carried his own radar in his head, the twenty miles to the sea were a mere irritating formality. Twelve hours' solid jungle-bashing, with Firebeard acting as a foliage-plough and Goliath singing 'Climb every mountain', brought them within sight of the sea; they were ripped and bitten and bloody from their ordeal, and virtually out on their feet (foot, in Goliath's case) with hunger, thirst, and exhaustion – but Bilbo had hit the coast within half a mile of their ship, and long before the guarda costas had peeped warily beyond Isla Baru, the *Laughing Sandbag* had slipped like a black phantom out to sea.

She prowled the shore for a few days, on the chance that Sheba might appear, and then sheered off to a convenient desert isle to careen, lay in wood and water, and have Goliath fitted with a new wooden leg from the local tree surgeon. (Bilbo had lost his toupee in the woods, and got the sailmaker to knit him a new one in secret, but it looked awful, and he had no choice but to wear his plumed hat permanently, which was a fearful nuisance in the tropic heat, particularly during the games of rounders and head-tennis with which the pirates beguiled their leisure.)

So now we know what Bilbo and Firebeard are doing (loafing, let's face it), and it is time to turn to sterner matters, for while we have been gathering in these lesser strands of our tale, Spanish devilment has broken loose, all unsuspected, behind our backs, and in the sneakiest possible way. 'Twas thus: ye mind how Don Lardo (out upon him!) vowed to launch a great campaign to sweep all right-thinking opposition from the Caribbean? Aye, says you, we mind – but would you believe that he's actually *got it under way already*, and us none the wiser? Never! says you, 'tis thing impossible – why, he's been fully occupied massacring Cohaclgzlns, and being beastly to Vanity, and offering to pull Blood asunder, and the like o' that. Aye, to be sure he has – but elsewhere his minions have been at their evil employs. Listen to this, and tremble:

Before sallying forth from Cartagena to hunt down our fleeing principals, the crafty Viceroy had sent a fast sloop scudding north to Santo Domingo of Hispaniola, wi' urgent commands to his governor there, Don Toro Molinos, to open the campaign with a sudden assault on the great buccaneer stronghold of Tortuga. Aye! So now – on the very morn when Lardo himself was digging up the treasure which Blood had betrayed, and gnashing his dentures exultantly; while Bilbo and Firebeard were lapping up the bread of idleness and pina colada on their careening island; while Happy Dan Pew was sailing along revising 'Une Promenade au Bicyclette' (and not making much of it); while Avery was being carried off ever farther by slave-traders; while Vladimir was joining in the keep-fit class on the games deck of his westering packet, and Admiral Rooke was trying to get his show on the road at the Cape – on that self-same morn a great red and gold fleet descended on Tortuga like a garlic thunderbolt, forced the rocky harbour of Cayona before anyone was out of bed, shattered its forts with broadsides, and stormed the buccaneer ships drowsing at anchor.

Pacing the gilded quarterdeck of his great galleon, the *Misconcepcion*, Don Toro Molinos twirled haughty moustache with lean swarthy hand emerging from a cruel froth o' priceless Mechlin lace, as he watched his guns pounding the hapless pirate ships, smashing buckets, severing washing-lines, damaging machines on the promenade, and generally creating havoc. Pirates were falling overboard, some only half-dressed and with their breakfasts untasted, piles of plunder awaiting inventory on the dockside were scattered by cannon-shots, floods of rum cascaded through the alleyways, and as he bounded from his office at the Filibusters' Co-operative and raced for the harbour, Calico Jack Rackham could see that much more of this and Tortuga would be closed for the season.

In a trice he had buttoned his pristine shirt, adjusted his head-scarf, dragged his sozzled crew from the haunts and hells, sent for the fire brigade, posted his will, and got sail on the *Plymouth Corporation's Revenge*. Plainly all was lost: Tortuga was aflame, Spaniards were pouring ashore in curled wigs with primed arquebuses, the harbour was a hell of burning hulls and wet buccaneers, Don Toro was quaffing a celebratory cup of rich Malaga on his poop before landing in person, and Rackham saw little point in hanging about. Wi' sailorly skill he warped his great ship through the inferno, its crew bravely manning the yards, sheets, tops'ls and ship's laundry, holystoning the scuppers, opening the bar, and even throwing things at their attackers; somehow she fought her way clear, with the loss of only her three masts and the bosun's wellingtons carelessly left on the afterrail. The crew hauled feverishly on the sweeps, and the sole survivor of the once-mighty pirate fleet escaped to sea, followed by a storm of chain-shot and canister and taunts of "Windy!" in Spanish. The overthrow of the Coast Brotherhood's great haven was complete, and Calico Jack, tight-lipped and with the daddy of all migraines coming on, could only flee to the safety of the Windward Passage.

He was not greatly cheered up when, two days later, he ran into the Tortuga-bound *Frantic Frog*, for Happy Dan was having one of his turns again, and lay on the hammock in the psychiatrist's berth whimpering about -oux endings. Taking overall command, Rackham put his crippled vessel in tow to the Frenchman, and ordered a course for his own private lair on the far side of the Caribbean, at the strange settlement of Roatan (of which more anon); there he would refit and retrench, pick up the latest news and some clean white shirts, send scouts to find how Bilbo and Sheba were doing at Cartagena (he's in for a nasty start, by the powers), and try to discover why the Dons were getting energetic all of a sudden.

Dark care sat heavily on the broad shoulders of the buccaneer chief as he brooded his way slowly south-westwards. He was used, was Calico Jack, to being the sheet-anchor of that wild fraternity, and never had he felt such a burden of responsibility as now, when catastrophe had overtaken the Brotherhood. Square chin in strong hand, he stood on his battered quarter-deck, listening to the rats playing in the bilges and the crew moaning through the rigging, and ever the same fateful question came to trouble his mind and make him grit his mighty teeth in near-despair: why, oh why the hell, he kept asking himself, hadn't he listened to his parents' advice and taken that office job with Somerset County Council?

Look, if Rackham thinks he's got trouble, he's not the only one. Things are in desperate shape all round. Why, at this rate it'll be Don Lardo who scoops the pool and goes sailing off triumphantly into the sunset on the last page, and God help the history of Western civilisation then. All right, you may say it all comes of leaving Avery in the hands of slave-traders through the whole of the last chapter; good point, and we agree it's time he started earning his corn again. But he's going to need a little help from his friends, and in especial, one – a rotund, ill-shaven, fatly furtive figure lately come ashore at that weird cesspool o' the Western Seas known as Roatan, where anything can happen and is just about to.

CHAPTER
THE SIXTEENTH

"I don't bleedin' believe it!" gasped Vladimir Mackintosh-Groonbaum in stricken incredulity. "It must be some other geezer."

He was at breakfast on his private verandah of the Roatan Athenæum Club – or rather, he wasn't, for the item in the broadsheet before him had caused him to leave untasted his dish of squid kidneys on breadfruit toast ("crisp wi' the fragrance o' your favourite focsle") and take a quick restoring draught from the pannikin of grog'n'orange at his elbow. He had arrived the previous night at this wide-open, lawless settlement which served as a great neutral clearing-house for the Caribbean, where honest traders rubbed shoulders wi' the scum o' the seas, where plunder was exchanged, contraband openly sold, plots hatched, government spies lurked, waterfront hells and merchant banks stood wantonly open day and night, and nothing was too wild or wicked – even tour parties were accepted. And before he had properly rubbed the sleep from his piggy little eyes or got over his galleon-lag, the paragraph on the classified page of the *Carib Curse* had smitten him like a falling belaying-pin. He goggled at it again:

FOR SALE: As new, one KING'S CAPTAIN, young, well-built, Double First, house-trained. Answers to name of Ben. One thousand doubloons, o.n.o. Write for brochure or apply in person, De Souza's Barracoon, Scupper Street. Hurry, hurry while stocks last!!!

"It can't be 'im!" muttered Vladimir. "Can it? Wot, Long Ben Avery, pride of the Senior Service, lettin' 'isself get put up for grabs in the slavery column? Never! 'E may be an officer an' gent, but 'e ain't that simple . . . is he? Oh, Lor'!" His little yellow jowls trembled in doubt, and five minutes later he was scooting along the colourful wharves, heedless of the raffish crowds of human flotsam who jostled him, accosted him, picked his pocket, offered to take his likeness, and plied him with postcards and Roatan Rock in five yummy flavours (tabasco, cinnamon, sandalwood, Reek o' Powder, and Bilge). In Scupper Street he obtained entry to the slave barracoon by flashing the complimentary voucher which the Athenæum gave to all its guests, and followed the shuffling turnkey through the foetid atmosphere of the foul underground pens marked "Sale Goods" where human cattle of every hue were packed in suffocating squalor. In the last chamber of all, marked "Special Offer – Not to be Repeated" he paused in horror, for there, alone, and chained by massy links to the floor, was the object of his quest – immaculately ragged, impeccably unkempt, radiating clean-cut fortitude through his five-day growth, Captain Avery rose with clanking courtesy to greet his visitor. His fine grey eyes widened with astonishment as the turnkey withdrew.

"My agent!" he cried. "Why, whence come ye?"

"Oh, unhappy sight!" exclaimed Vladimir. "Wot the empurpled 'ell are you doin' 'ere?"

"Preparing to escape," replied Avery in a cool whisper. "Know, small employee, that sundry nights agone I was trepanned from the temple o' Cohaclgzln by dastard knave who besought me for a light (aye, tho' he had matches and to spare, I warrant), and borne hither as probationary slave. The rotters," he went on grimly, "had me trussed secure, else had I escaped, yet all's for the best, for this night when I crash hence I shall take with me the many hundred sorry captives who lie in this vile barracoon, and if there happens to be a Spanish fleet attacking the town at the time, I and my fellows will mount bloody counter-assault, o'erwhelming the Dons and earning the gratitude o' the authorities, who will gladly confirm our freedom. That, according to what you told me, is the classic way of escaping from slavery, is't not?"

"Did I say that?" quavered Vladimir, bewildered. "But . . . but . . . supposin' there ain't a Spanish fleet attackin' tonight? I mean, yer can't tell, this time o' year—"

"Then I'll just take over the settlement by force," shrugged Avery, "and with my liberated band make haste to Cohaclgzln, there to rescue my betrothed, the peerless Lady Vanity, who lies captive o' heathen savages. You wouldn't have heard about that, though."

"'Old on a minnit!" Vladimir sank weakly on to a convenient pile of rusty shackles and mopped his brow. "I'm still not abreast. Why the 'ell," he demanded, clinging to essentials, "aren't you out there mollocatin' the Coast Bruvver-'ood? 'Ow come you've let yerself be took by slavers? I mean, it's not good enough, cap'n! You an' me gotta contrack, an' it don't say a dam' thing abaht yore goin' into domestic service—"

"How, sirrah?" Our hero's eyes knit and his brows glinted sternly. "D'ye presume to question? If fortune o' war deserts me for the nonce, 'tis no concern of thine! Besides, I'll be off and running as soon as I've broke me this chain, inspired the slaves to revolt, laid out the turnkey, and captured the local armoury. But to quiet thy importunities, and satisfy thee I have not been idle," he added carelessly, "cop hold of these." And from the ragged sash at his gracefully disordered waist he drew forth two Madagascar crosses, one enclosing a flashing diamond, the other a black pearl, and tossed them to the goggling Vladimir. "Now shut up a minute while I haul this ringbolt out of the floor."

But Vladimir was already speechless as he stared bug-eyed at the glittering trophies. Five out of six! Of course, Avery didn't know that Vladimir already had the crosses of Happy Dan, Firebeard, and Akbar, and the oily twister had no intention of telling him; keep the lad on his toes. So while Avery did a few yoga exercises and then began to heave amain to break his fetters, the agent gnawed his lip in silence, and then gave a deprecatory sniff.

"Well, that's two of 'em, I s'pose. Jus' two aht o' six, cap'n – we 'aven't been settin' the Seven Seas on fire, exackly, 'ave we? Gotta do better'n that, I think. Ah . . . which o' the bloody villains did you get these orf of?"

"Sheba . . . the . . . She-Wolf . . ." gasped Avery, heaving until his magnificent biceps creaked. "and . . . Black . . . Bilbo! Hah!" He paused, sighing. "Nay, I see I shall have to use both hands. Stand back, fellow, lest ye come to harm when I pull the floor up."

He laid hold again, but Libertatia's favourite pawnbroker paid no heed: he was calculating that the only cross now missing was the one held by Calico Jack Rackham, and he was confident that he knew exactly where it was. It was notorious that the prudent Calico, who believed in Post Office savings and Christmas clubs, forwarded all his loot to his voluptuous mistress and former comrade-in-arms, the celebrated Anne Bonney, who kept it safe on their shark-surrounded island retreat, not an hour's sail from Roatan. But how to obtain the cross from the formidable termagant, guarded as she was, and herself a notable sword-and-pistol dame?

"Oh, blow!" exclaimed Avery, who had been hauling prodigiously to an accompaniment of crackling concrete and clouds of dust; he had dragged up not only the ringbolt but the enormous boulder in which it was embedded. "I can't cart that lot around after me; I'll have to pound it to bits. Talk about slavery . . ." And of a sudden he checked, and wheeled on Vladimir, his rags aflap with inspiration.

"But of course! What need to labour towards escape, now

that thou'rt on hand, good Mackintosh-Groonbaum! Oh, by the way, your name is too much of a mouthful – I think I'll call you Mac. Unless you prefer Groon? No matter." He laid a hand on the shyster's grubby shoulder. "As I was saying, now that thou hast arrived so timely, thou canst *buy* me from these slave-traders, for I doubt not y'are well lined wi' funds. Why on earth didn't I think of it earlier!"

"Wozzat?" Vladimir started from his reverie, and blinked up at the eagerly-smiling captain. "Buy yer, did yer say? From the slavers?" His eyes owled in alarm. "Ooh, cap'n, I couldn't do that! Wot, me, dabble in slave-tradin'? Ow, my conscience wouldn't let me – it's immoral! Oh, that'd never do!"

Avery slapped his forehead in vexation. "To be sure, I never thought! Nay, forgive me, good Groon. I blush for my own lack of scruple. Thou art an honest fellow. Ah, well," he sighed, "I'll just have to bash my way out after all." And he began karate-chopping at the boulder, shouting "Hai!" Vladimir winced.

"'Old on a sec, cap'n," he pleaded, for Avery's proposal had sown a seed in his knavish mind, and he wanted time to think. "I couldn't buy yer, we agree . . . but I might be able to work aht somefink. I got contacts, see? An' we don't want you startin' a slave revolt unnecessary, do we, or strainin' yerself makin' an escape? Look – gimme a couple of hours, and I'll see wot I can do."

"Ye have a scheme, good fink?" cried Avery, a-quiver.

"In the bud," mused Vladimir, "in the bud. Lissen – you 'ang on 'ere – an' wotever 'appens, you go along nice an' peaceful, a'right? Do exackly wot you're told, 'owever unlikely, await directions, an' trust me, 'cos I think," he tapped his bulbous hooter, "I see daylight."

"Bravo, Groon! Nay, ninety per cent is little enough, I vow!" said Avery warmly. "Never fear, I'll abide thy stratagem, whate'er it be – and in the meantime, d'you think you could smuggle me in a razor, after-shave, and a complete change of kit, 42 chest, 30 waist, ruffled shirt and plain buckles?"

"Exackly wot I was abaht to suggest," said Vladimir unctuously. "Leave it to yer uncle. Turnkey!"

The jailer thrust in his villainous head, and swore at the sight of the ruined floor. "You bloody vandal!" he cried. "Next thing you'll be on the roof, I s'pose, throwin' dahn slates! Cripes, it's worsen 'avin' the I.R.A. on yer 'ands!" Vladimir waved him aside, and a few minutes later was closeted with De Souza the Slaver, a hook-nosed horror with a great whip coiled on his desk, and B.O.

"You wanta buy da Eengleeshman?" he croaked. "You crazy, he's a nut. Too much-a class, so who needs heem? It's like-a you try to sell a Gobelin tapestry in South Wales. I only took the bum for da prestige advertising." He glowered at Vladimir. "Go ahead, rob me. Laugh at my thousan' doubloons, an' offer me six hundred."

"Done," said Vladimir, "but I don't want 'im for meself, see? 'E's a gift, like, fer a lady o' my acquaintance. Nah, this is strickly 'twixt you an' me, see? I want him dolled up real nice, an' took across to Shark Island, wiv this presentation card rahnd 'is neck." And he scribbled on one of De Souza's labels and passed it across. The slave-trader gave a ghastly leer and chuckled.

"You weesh heem to be geeft-wrapped, eh? Heh-heh! I like-a your style, fatso. An' the recipient?"

"'E's to be delivered to Mistress Anne Bonney, from an anonymous admirer. An' mark," added Vladimir, "not a word to the boy 'imself. I want it to be a surprise to 'im, too." He smirked and winked, and De Souza bellowed with lewd laughter.

"Surprise, per Bacco! She will-a devour heem!" he roared. "An' Caleeco Jack ees away in-a Tortuga! When he come home he weel see a new slave on Shark Island, but eet weel be an old, trembling man weeth grey hair! Know what I mean?"

"I 'ad 'eard she was partial," murmured Vladimir. "But – mum!"

So now we see Captain Avery that same evening, clad in a clean ruffled shirt with crimson sash and dark breeches, his hair newly dressed, his chin shaved, his person a-reek with Eau de Portobello ("Morgan took Panama with five hundred men – and the Governor's lady with just a dab of Eau de P. Only five moidores the keg, or in the handy bucket size.") He is being rowed across the strait to mysterious Shark Island, reflecting that if this is how Vladimir organises escapes, he is indeed an agent beyond price. He breathes the scented night air, drowsing to the regular oar-beats of the silent rowers, nor marks the small boat that dogs their wake, a cable's length behind. At the Shark Island landing-stage, he is delivered into the care of a huge blackamoor in scarlet livery, who wordlessly beckons him to follow to the great white house bright with lights which nestles among dark groves of trees. Wondering, but with every confidence in his agent's arrangements, Avery follows – and beyond sight of the landing-stage the small boat creeps in among the mangroves, and a small fat figure scuttles ashore and is lost in the undergrowth.

Captain Avery now found himself bidden to wait in the spacious hall of a mansion of notable luxury. Silver candle-branches were reflected in the polished floor, furniture o' Master Gibbons abounded, as did priceless rugs and flying ducks, and on the walls, among the Van Dycks and Arthur Rackhams (work that one out some time) were group paintings of what looked like crews and their commanders, sitting with folded arms and loot piled before them, the frames labelled "Caracas '67" or "Nombre de Dios '71" and the like. On the spinet stood a portrait of a grinning, evil-featured foreigner in a head-scarf, inscribed: "A mon ami Jack, from his best pal at Maracaibo – Nau L'Ollonois," and signed with a ragged "X." Avery would have examined it, but just then he caught sight of himself in a mirror, and realised that his boat-cloak was decorated at the nape with a huge pink tinsel bow, from which hung a card. He glanced down to examine it.

It bore the slogan "Don't be a loser, shop with De Souza," and the written message: "A Present for a Good Girl – have fun!" The Captain frowned. It must be some code used by those whom Vladimir had employed to assist his escape – and at that moment, from the room into which the black footman had vanished to announce Avery's arrival, was heard a rich, honeyed contralto, laden with boredom and sex-appeal.

"A personal delivery . . . at this hour?", it drawled, sounding like a wanton Lady Bracknell. "Foolish Onslow, 'tis some tedious little salesman's ploy . . . one is fatigued, and does not wish to know . . . H'm? From De Souza's, and gift-wrapped? Nay, not another free sample? Heigh-ho, bring it in, then . . ."

Curious conversation, thought Avery, as the footman emerged and beckoned him – rather peremptorily, it seemed to the captain, but he strode into the room and found himself bowing before a red-haired Juno, lusciously overweight in a plunging silk gown, who was reclining on a sofa eating marshmallows and moodily studying a calorie chart.

You may have seen the picture, in Johnson's *Historie*, which shows Anne Bonney as a strapping virago in deplorable trousers and inadequate blouse, armed with cutlass, battle-axe, and pistols, one of which she is discharging at some unfortunate off camera. But that was ages ago, when she'd been a wild young pirate groupie racketing around with Calico Jack, scuttling ships, slitting throats, ravishing innocent youths, and styling herself "Ms." Nowadays the bra-burning buccaneerette had become an exquisitely languid young matron who ate far too much creamy food, dieted self-indulgently, read popular novels in bed, crammed herself into fashionable creations, and couldn't have roused herself to scuttle or slit a paper bag, although she remained passionately addicted to young men, innocent or not, because (she maintained) it took her mind off slimming.

The sudden advent of Avery, bowing his stalwart six feet two in sash and ruffles, caused marshmallow and calorie chart alike to slip limply from her fingers; she swallowed convulsively, and her sleepy green eyes and generous mouth parted in awed astonishment, slowly widening into a smile which, in a public place, would have led to her apprehension by the vice squad. Avery, poor simp, supposing her an accomplice of Vladimir's, took it for a polite welcome, and when she beckoned him closer he remembered his agent's injunction to do whatever he was told, and obeyed. Mistress Bonney, roused from her habitual ennui by this vision of masculine perfection, read the message on the gift card and couldn't believe her luck. Why, it was just what she'd always wanted.

"Gad's mercy, dahling," she murmured breathlessly, "and one really means, Gad's mercy! Wherever did they find you?"

"Lately, madam, in De Souza's barracoon."

"But . . . who sent thee – the dear, thoughtful people?"

Slightly puzzled, Avery replied guardedly. "One who is known to you, I think, ma'am."

"Well," purred the lady, "whoever he is, this certainly beats the hell out of Milk Tray." She took his hand caressingly. "And your name, dahling?"

Extraordinary woman, thought Avery, and hedged again. "Shall we say only that I am your most humble obedient servant, ma'am?"

"Well, of course you are, silly boy!" Mistress Anne uncoiled her plump stateliness from the sofa, and stood hand on hip, smiling hungrily. "And how obedient you're going to be, baby! Humble, who cares?" And she ran a playful finger down the opening of his shirt-ruffles, causing Avery to jump and go "Yeep!"

"Madam!" He was scandalised. "That's me in there!"

"Not madam, dahling . . . mistress. So hold still, rot thee, when she deigns to tickle. And be suitably grateful, understand?"

"Why, mistress then, if you like!" Another women's lib freak, evidently. "Indeed, I'll be deeply grateful if you will but give me directions—"

"Commands, dahling."

"Right. Fine. Commands. I'm easy, so we lose no more time in idle cross-talk, for I am all hot impatience to be doing, so for Pete's sake give your footman the gate, and—"

"What, saucy?" She stared, laughed sharply, and slapped him smartly on the cheek. "Mama gives the orders, dahling – remember?" Then to complete his confusion she slid soft hands about his neck and pouted teasingly. "Nay, look never adown, pretty fool, for I forgive thee, since 'tis a sweet impatience, and I'm all for it. Drift, Onslow," she added over her shoulder to the footman, who was sulkily reflecting that these honky studs had all the luck. "Oh, and Onslow – open an account with De Souza's for servicing and maintenance. Unless," she drawled at Avery, "you're under guarantee?"

Plainly she was off her trolley, unless this was more of their confounded code. "My agent is trustworthy," he hazarded, and Mistress Anne chuckled wickedly.

"We'll soon see about that," was her cryptic comment, and as Onslow withdrew she seized the captain in a hammer-lock and clamped her mouth on his with volcanic enthusiasm. He heaved manfully, but it was like resisting a rogue barrage balloon, and a strong, experienced one at that. Through his mind flashed a memory of being caught up in a wet mainsail during a hurricane, when he had saved himself by lying still and not panicking; he tried it now as they reeled about, glued together, until she pinned him on the sofa and broke the clinch, breathless but with a steely glint in her green eyes.

"Dahling," she panted, "less humility, and considerably more of that hot impatience you were advertising, or mistress is going to be rah-ther displeased—"

"But madam – I mean, mistress—"

"Damn your gorgeous hide, dahling, don't interrupt! Now, let's try again, shall we, and this time, obedient servant, one expects your best shot – or else. So . . ."

"Hold it!" Avery used his quarterdeck voice, and she quivered in sheer surprise. He struggled up. "Look – what gives? I am told at the barracoon (by one that I trust) that for my salvation I must do as I'm bid, ask no questions, and all will be well. So I look for directions – but am told nothing. I don't understand what you say, even less what you do – and frankly, it's pretty bizarre, if you ask me – or what happens next. Madam," he cried fervently, "or mistress – what am I meant to *do*?"

Anne Bonney's lips were parted in crimson bewilderment, her eyes pools of incredulous Crème de Menthe. She blinked.

"D'you mean . . . God help us! . . . you ha' never . . . ?" She gestured uncertainly with a white hand. "Never . . . had it . . . away . . . before?"

Had it away? Escaped from slavery, perhaps. Every trade had its cant, he knew.

"Why, never!" he assured her.

"But . . . ye protested all steamy impatience—"

"Well, dash it, who wouldn't? D'you think I like being bottled up?"

". . . and . . . you look to mistress for . . . instruction . . ."

"Lady, believe me, 'tis what I yearn for!"

Anne Bonney's lashes fluttered, and she fetched a slow ecstatic sigh that shook the sofa. She patted her glossy red tresses, and a strange excitement kindled in her wanton eyes.

"Oh, brother!" she murmured huskily. "One had dreamed o' this, since maidenhood – whenever that was. Talk about bonuses!" She felt delicious goose-pimples at the prospect: this answer to Messalina's prayer panting eagerly – and innocent. And she owned him, and Calico Jack wouldn't be back from Tortuga for ages . . .

"Thou sweet, gorgeous ignorance," she sighed, and fondly pinched his cheek. "Oh, and mistress was cross with thee! Nay, but we shall make all right, and school thee to our heart's content . . ."

"Prithee, let's go!"

"Ah, but softly, for 'tis not so simple." She gurgled voluptuously and flexed her imagination. "First, sit closer . . . closer, dahling, one isn't going to bite you . . . yet. Now, this hand about me, and t'other . . . so. Are you sitting comfortably? Then we'll begin . . . just do exactly as I do . . ."

Bewildering – but it gave our bemused hero something to cling to, in more ways than one. Obey orders, Vladimir had said, and it was the code by which Avery lived: broadsides or lady wrestlers, you did your duty, however improbable, and trusted Authority. So when Mistress Bonney's sweet lips closed on his, he kissed her back for all he was worth, which wasn't negligible, for he was Vanity-trained, and accidental embraces with Sheba and Meliflua hadn't blunted his technique. And oddly enough, he found it rather pleasant, nay, positively enjoyable – not like Vanity, exactly, and subtly different from Sheba and Meliflua . . . interesting, that. Of course, this lady was slightly older, with more . . . what was the word? Proportion? Generosity? What had that cad Blood called it . . . baaarroomph? Anyway, she was undoubtedly attractive, and most appreciative – tasted delicious, too, like a hungry mango, if one could imagine such a thing, and you felt you could go on eating it all day or all night or whatever time it was . . . oh, pity, she'd stopped, and was swaying with a slightly glazed expression, holding tightly for support.

" 'Strewth!" gasped Mistress Bonney reverently. "Ah . . . wow! And thou . . . a novice? Oh, dahling, thou'rt right, so right! We waste time indeed . . ." She lunged pneumatically against him. "Reach up behind and undo my top button . . . quickly, oaf!"

"But, madam! . . . to what end?"

"Dahling, don't tease! Mistress doesn't like it! To what end but to get the dress off, booby? Takes a shoehorn to get into the dam' thing! Oh, come on! . . . got it? Clever minion!"

He started back, fearing overspill as she rose abruptly, but to his relief she swayed tempestuously away to her boudoir door, pausing there to smoulder at him. "Mistress is going to slip into something loose, dahling," she drawled throbbingly. "Leave your things in yonder closet, and when mistress whistles . . ." she pushed her hair up and munched ardently in his direction ". . . break all records, is that clear?" She vanished into the boudoir.

He was nonplussed . . . ah, she was going to change, plainly so that she could conduct him to safety. And she was right; if stealth was required, he'd be better without this ridiculous cloak. He entered the closet, a small dim chamber off the other side of the drawing-room, and was casting the cloak aside when there came an urgent scrabbling at the shutter. He jerked it open, and the sweating face of Mackintosh-Groonbaum peered furtively in.

"That you, cap'n? Thank Gawd, I bin creepin' abaht everywhere—"

"About time!" snapped Avery. "I have been driven nigh hairless by thy female accomplice – couldn't you have found someone in their right mind? The woman's cocoa!"

"She ain't—"

"Don't tell *me*! You haven't had to go three falls with her – has she no sense of haste?"

"She ain't my accomplice, I mean!" Vladimir struggled over the sill. "Look, there's bin one 'ell of a balls-up", he lied earnestly. "Afore I could make arrangements to 'ave you enlarged, she bought you . . . as a slave, I mean. You bein' for sale, an' all. Well, I couldn't foresee that, could I?"

"Bought me?" Avery was staggered. "Why, a God's name?"

"I dunno. 'Ad a vacancy, prob'ly. But, cap'n, 'tis prodigious stroke o' fortune! Don'cher know 'oo she is?"

"Womanhood's answer to Black Kwango, the way she behaves." Avery was bitter. "Gad, she's got a cheek, buying a chap she doesn't even know! Well, she can forget it – we'll off smartly—"

"'Old on, cap'n, you don't cotton! She's Anne Bonney – former pirate wench an' paramour to Calico Jack Rackham! Don'cher see? This is 'is place, an' it's a stone ginger cert 'is Madagascar cross is in the 'ouse this minnit! We're in luck, cap'n!"

"You mean . . . I might employ the occasion to recover it?"

"'Ole in one," smirked Vladimir. "Funny ole world, innit?"

Avery stroked shaven chin, and got lipstick all over his fingers. "A rare opportunity, truly . . . but, how to find it?"

"Easy. Doth not she use it to deck 'er plump an' pleasin' bosom?"

"No." Avery gulped heavily. "I can vouch for that."

"Well, then, in 'er boo-dwar, among 'er fripperies. As 'er favourite an' pampered slave, you'd 'ave lotsa chances—"

"Who says I'm her favourite and pampered slave? Hardly met the woman!"

"Come, come, cap'n," leered Vladimir. "You'll get to know 'er."

"Bah! And how long would that take?"

"In the Biblical sense, abaht four minutes," said cynical Vladimir. "That ain't raspberry jam on yer clock, cap'n – she's bin tryin' to 'ave 'er lecherous way wi' you already, 'asn't she?"

"WHAT?" The scales fell from Avery's eyes, clanging through his brain. "Trying to . . . you mean, that in there, just now, she was giving rein to . . ." he quivered with outrage ". . . mucky passion?"

"I might ha' known you did biology at school," nodded Vladimir, and at that moment a soft, sex-laden whistle ululated through the gloom. Avery leaped like a stung whippet.

"That's her!" he cried, grammar forgotten, and Vladimir beamed and clapped him on the shoulder. "Go in an' win, my boy," he chuckled. "An' go through her jool-case arterwards."

"Not a chance!" Avery's voice grated like a grounded tanker. "Why, thou smut! Hast no shame? And I affianced to Lady Vanity! Even if I wasn't, I certainly wouldn't . . ." he blushed furiously ". . . misbehave . . . with this awful woman! Far too domineering, and red hair's a sign of bad temper. No, we must get the cross – but *that's* right out! Forget it! Think of something else."

Vladimir hopped in agitation. "Be reasonable, cap'n! Gawd, when I think o' the fellers who'd give up drink for the chance! Lissen – she's whistlin' again!"

"She can whistle till her toe-nails rattle," said Avery coldly. "The very idea!"

"But – she'll 'ave 'er blacks lookin' fer you in a minnit! We'll be nabbed, an' she'll do you over just the same!" Vladimir was almost in tears. "Do it the easy way, cap'n – for me!" And seeing Avery adamant, the little shyster fell to raging, and then hearing a third whistle, distinctly shrill, groaned and dug into his pocket.

"A'right then, you win! 'Ere, grab this! I brought it along, just in case." He thrust a small phial at Avery. "Take it! 'Tis butyl chloride, better known as Master Finn – used to shanghai silly sailormen an' zonk security guards. Slip that in 'er Ribena an' she'll drop like a factory chimney. Go on, cop 'old – find an excuse to ply 'er wi' drink . . . . I'll be 'neath the window, an' when she's flaked aht we'll turn the place over!"

Avery hesitated. "'Twill not harm her?" His eyes gimleted. "Or . . . arouse her . . . dark passions?"

"Don't be soft! She needs arousin' like I need an honest accountant!" Vladimir scrambled out of the window and Avery hesitated no longer; he shot into the drawing-room, slurped wine into a glass, added the knock-out drops, and paused. How to make her drink it, raging with impatience as she was? A whistle like a factory hooter shrieked from the boudoir. He pounced on the calorie chart and swanned in like a man deep in thought.

"Dahling!" Acid honey boiled from the darkness. "Does dahling have the teeniest inkling what happens to slaves who dawdle and keep mistress waiting? And od's bobs, hammer and tongs, you've still got your pants on!" Languid accent forgotten, it was the pirate wench spitting blood. "Now, hell rend thy mangy hide—"

"Sweet mistress!" he protested, contrite but puzzled. "Nay, pardon me, but I came on this . . . and pondering it, fell into reverie o' disbelief and dismay, for I do not well understand—"

"I'll dismay you, by thunder! . . . what's that?" From her tall white form dim-seen on the bed a naked arm shot into the moonlight, fingers snapping. "Give it me! 'Sdeath, 'tis my calorie chart!"

'I knew it – 'tis guide whereby ladies do adjust their adipose tissues! Ah, but why," he sighed cunningly, "why should my lovely mistress wish to put on weight?"

It chopped her anger across the windpipe. "Wish to put on . . . I? God ha' mercy! Are you mad?"

"If I am, 'tis you have maddened me!" he cried, suddenly fervid, and did a graceful kneel beside the bed. "Yet not so mad I can't tell delectable perfection o' shape when I see it! Aye, call me cheeky, but I say that to add one ounce to thy lissom lusciousness would be heresy! Ah, mistress, burn this trifle!" He twitched away the calorie chart. "Give up this mad idea of gaining half a stone – let other dizzy dames go ballooning around, but please – please stay sweetly slender as thou art!"

It would have convinced Tessie O'Shea she looked like Twiggy; with the moonlight on his profile and adoring eyes it caused Mistress Anne's wrath to dissolve like an election pledge. Lissom . . . slender . . . delectable perfection – she fairly purred. "Why, thou saucy rabbit! Judge my shape, will he? You're sure 'tis . . . enough?" She suddenly sat upright in the moonlight, vibrating triumphantly, and Captain Avery gulped, gritted his teeth, and tried to think of cold, solemn things, like church bells tolling . . . great big bells – no! Frosty nights, then, with pale full moons . . . round, glowing moons – Gad, even worse! Got to get a grip . . . swiftly he conjured up the wine cup between them, and spoke with an intensity that would have reduced the goddess Kali to molten toffee.

"If a mere slave may offer to peerless beauty a token of humility and love . . . why then, get this down you."

She took the cup, her green eyes sloppily moist. "Dahling, you shouldn't . . . a loving cup. Ah, sweet donation! Though y'are a naughty rogue to have kept mistress waiting," she added playfully as she raised it to her lips, "and if you're not starkers by the time I've drunk this, God help you!"

And ere he could stir she had gulped it and collared him lustfully, crying "grappling hooks away!", but even in that moment she went rigid, her eyes rolled, and with a stricken woof she fell back slowly, collapsing chimney-like from the base up, even as Vladimir had predicted. Before she hit the canvas Avery was at the shutters, and the little pawnbroker was tumbling in like a drunk gibbon, croaking: "'Ow's she doin'?"

"Stiffer than a plank." Avery was breathing hard. "And not an instant too soon. Right, Groon – do thou frisk the wardrobe and I the dressing-table."

They searched swiftly, Avery silent, Vladimir muttering "Gawd, the fings they wear nowadays – disgustin'!", and within ten minutes the floor was awash with shoes, dresses, frilly items, odd nylons, back copies of *Tortuga 'Teen*, bits of wire and pipe left in corners by workmen, used galleon tickets, laundry bills, and a set of embroidered table mats intended as a wedding present for Blackbeard Teach and his seventh wife, touchingly labelled "This time for keeps, eh, mess-mate – lots o' love, Anne and Jack," but with "Gone away – address not known" blue-pencilled on the outer wrapping. No Madagascar cross, though. Avery bit moulded lip and Vladimir swore.

"She can't 'ave swallered the bloody thing! Now, where . . . why, wot's amiss, cap'n?"

"This is a beastly business!" snapped Avery. "Going through her private effects like this . . . I don't know, it just seems sneaky, even if she is a bit of a shocker. I mean," he indicated a scarlet silk corset edged with black lace, "for all we know her mummy may have given her that!"

"Oddly enough, yer prob'ly right," said Vladimir, "but we can't afford sentiment! I mean – 'oo's cross is it? An' it's gotta be 'ere – she's bound to keep it by 'er!"

"What's this?" Avery was examining a parchment which had fallen out of a fashion sea-boot. "Ha, Groon – 'tis a chart! And new-drawn, too! Nay, but of what . . . ? why, 'tis of her bedchamber – this very room!"

"Once a pirate, always a pirate!" chuckled Vladimir. "Wot's it say, cap'n?"

"No soundings marked, but latitude and longitude, and all points plotted wi' rare skill." Avery glanced keenly round the great bedchamber, in which the candles they had lighted made a bright pool, leaving the farthest corners in shadow. "Aye – bed, chest o' drawers, vanitory unit and all, marked fair – and here directions writ! Stand by, Groon, and take course as I read!"

He began, and Vladimir ploughed off obediently: "East-nor'-east ten paces from ye window, then bear away due west wi' ye bed abeam . . . West, you idiot!" he rasped, as from dim recess came crash of falling china and a pawnbroker's anguished cry. "Bear up, man, or ye'll be caught in stays!"

"I am," whimpered Vladimir. "Them red an' black 'uns of 'er mum's; you should ha' hung 'em up. Right, cap'n!"

"Now west again, close-hauled . . ." Vladimir barked his shin and cursed in the gloom ". . . lest ye bark your shins on the commode, and tacking southerly, go under . . . what means that? . . . and so shall come hard by your goal . . . Groon? Where are you, man?"

"Under the bed", came the muffled reply, "bearin' ten degrees from the piss-pot, an' 'asn't bin 'oovered since the Flood!"

"Nay, 'tis impossible," muttered Avery, peering into the shadows. "Unless it's under the floor."

"Or in 'er mattress above me!" Vladimir's head appeared from under the four-poster. "That's it, cap'n! Where else?"

Hot on the scent they approached the bed, Avery averting his gaze from the stately nude slumbering rhythmically on the coverlet. Vladimir's eyes came out on stalks. "Gawd!" he gulped. "She's *real*! Cap'n, you're a gent – or an idjut, I'm not sure which. Anyways, you'll 'ave to lift 'er while I rummage."

So Avery gingerly lifted the buxom sleeper, and tried to imagine he was up to his neck in an icy duck-pond while Vladimir hacked and burrowed and raised a blizzard of feathers, gasping stifled progress reports from inside the mattress. Thank goodness they'd soon be out of the clutches of this dreadful woman – imagine really being owned by her! Avery shuddered, and wished he hadn't, for it set up a harmonic motion in his voluptuous burden, and he nearly overbalanced. Not that she was as heavy as he'd imagined; quite svelte, really . . . and probably a lot better than most slave-owners, if it came to that. She'd been amiable enough, when she wasn't being imperious and . . . and . . . *awful*, and she'd seemed to like him personally. Handsome woman; very like Mistress Gwynn, the actress, with that striking red hair . . . nice perfume it had. Lilac? Honeysuckle? He bent his face to the Titian head cradled on his shoulder, and inhaled . . . orange-blossom! Pretty, humorous mouth, too – what was it she'd tasted of again? Some fruit or other . . . Not orange, or pineapple . . . mango, of course. He liked mangoes, really delicious taste . . .

"Got somefink in 'er eye, 'as she?" said a voice, and in confusion Avery jerked his head up to find Vladimir eyeing him sardonically. Blushing, the captain would have explained, but the words died on his lips as the little shyster raised a hand in which something glowed like a bottle of port – a gigantic ruby, its crimson rays shaming the gilt cross in which it was embedded.

"Number three!" exclaimed Vladimir triumphantly, but inwardly he was gloating, Number Six, yippee! "I told yer we'd get lucky, didn't I? There it is – so now, if you've finished tryin' to guess Lady Godiva's weight, let's away wi' all speed!"

With guilty haste Avery replaced the drugged tomato on the ruin of her bed, and spread a coverlet over her lest she take cold in the dawn chill. For some reason, it seemed the least he could do; he felt a strange reluctance to leave so abruptively furtive; didn't seem polite, somehow.

"Here, I say, Groon, we've made the most ghastly mess of her quarters," he frowned. "Oughtn't we to tidy a bit – I mean, what's she going to think when she wakes up?"

"Why don't we sit on the edge of 'er bed an' wait to find out?" snarled Vladimir, one leg over the sill. "Fer Gawd's sake, cap'n! Wot the 'ell are servants for? Come on!"

But before Avery could reply, came a sound which froze him where he stood, while Vladimir gibbered and grabbed the shutter. Through the balmy tropic night came the crack of a shot – and then a rattle of musketry, and from far off the clang of a ship's bell and distant voices. Avery was at the window in a flash, and this is what he saw.

Through a gap in the garden trees the broad inlet between Roatan and Shark Island was clearly visible in the moonlight, and across the moon's bright wake on the water was gliding the black shape of a great ship, her spars stark against the pale night sky. Lights gleamed on her poop, and pinpricks of fire were at her rail – the crackle of reports followed, and now a long boat was pushing off from her towards shore.

"A ship!" Avery spoke without hesitation. "Who can she be?"

"Oh, the Mersey ferry, beyond a doubt!" cried Vladimir violently. "She's a bloody pirate, that's wot she is! Quick, cap'n – I got a boat beached! Let's scarper!"

But Avery's spirits had rocketed up past the hundred mark at this prospect of action. Shots, pirates, chaps in boats – this was more like it, and a sight better than grappling ardent redheads – well, it was a change, anyway. "If pirate she be, good Groon," quo' he briskly, "then I must know more o' her. Ye have the cross safe? Then haste away and wait for me. Shan't be more than a tick." He was off, a perfectly co-ordinated shadow gliding through the undergrowth, while Vladimir gnashed and implored and finally, for he was a realist, scuttled away to his boat. Nor, more shame to him, did he tarry; six crosses no waiting, and you can keep the ruddy Caribbean, was how he saw it, and who knows how many salt sea miles 'twill be ere we have the pleasure of his company again?

Meanwhile Avery was high-stepping stealthily for the shore, aware that up ahead more shots were sounding and voices swearing, and borne on the night-breeze was the sinister echo of rum-sodden music, for Vladimir's right – villainy's afloat again, wi' hanky round beetling brows and cutlass in horny fist, and who is this who comes galumphing through the bushes, fleeing for dear life, blind wi' panic? Whoever it is isn't going any place, for out of the shadows like a jet-propelled Nemesis rockets Fly-half Avery (Oxford U., Royal Navy, and Barbarians) to grass him wi' crunching tackle, and thereafter pin him to earth wi' steely whisper: "Who, sirrah? Whence? Whither? What's your hurry?" The stricken figure wheezed like a despairing air-cushion, subsided, and panted in surrender.

"I-wasn't-trespassin'-your-honour-an'-strike-me-dumb-

if-I-even-saw-a-rabbit-an'-wouldn't-ha'-touched-it-anyways-
for-amn't-I-a-landed-gentleman-meself – holy God!" exclaimed Colonel Blood weakly, "it's you!"

*Blood? Here? But he ought to be miles away on the
Main with Lardo and Vanity and the rest of the
Cohaclgzln Conservation Society, surely? Plainly
some matter o' great pitch and moment has occurred,
and must be looked to instanter, along with other
pressing matters, viz.: if Vladimir has absconded, how
is Avery going to get off Shark Island? What will Anne
Bonney say when she wakes up and finds her room
looking like Hurricane Susie? (These two questions
may be not unconnected). And what ship is that, what
o' Vanity, Sheba, et al., and whither do we go hence?
Let's ask Blood, says you . . . too late, Avery's 'way
ahead of us*

CHAPTER
THE SEVENTEENTH

o you mean to say," demanded Avery bitingly, "that you betrayed a vasty treasure to yon poultice Lardo, simply because he was having you pulled asunder by wild horses? Why, thou . . . thou . . ." He groped for words. "Thou twit! have ye no guts?"

"Happily, yes. I wouldn't have had if—"

"Faugh! Thou craven! Why, thou'd betray the . . . the Crown Jewels, I'll bet, if an old woman made faces at thee!"

"Do you mind?" Colonel Blood winced. "I once *had* the Crown Jewels, remember? And if some warder's interfering idiot of a son hadn't come home on week-end leave,"* he added bitterly, "I'd have 'em yet. I'll thank ye not to remind me of it."

"Oh." Avery frowned. "Sorry – didn't mean to turn the knife in the wound; just a figure of speech. Sorry, Blood."

"Och, forget it. It's just that I've got . . . feelin's, too."

"I know. Dashed thoughtless of me . . . but hang it, that's not the point!" cried Avery angrily. "Forget the Crown Jewels—"

"It wasn't me brought up the subject." Hurt sniff.

". . . the fact is you weaseled to that appalling Dago to save your own skin! Tchah! Pretty poor show, I'd say."

And he wrinkled his high-bred nose in disgust, which was

* True.

lost on Blood, since they were crouched in the pitch-dark interior of a hollow galoopa tree, where they had taken shelter so that Avery could be brought up-to-date, while in the dark undergrowth around their hiding-place buccaneers beat the bushes wi' cutlass blades, flashed gleaming lanterns, swore as they tripped over roots, wiped perspiring brows, and cried: "He'm gone to ground, skipper, belike! Aye, all hid snug an' solitary, d'ye see, burn 'im! C'mout, ye Irish tripehound, we know y're here!"

Colonel Blood shuddered, and whispered haughtily: "Weasel, nothing! I spoke up for the sake o' the woman I love, so there! To save her from mishandlement – aye, or worse. 'Lardo, ye great Spanish hog!' sez I. 'Ye may do your worst on me, but if ye lay a finger on that sweet saint, or offer to have her put in my place . . . well, faith, I'll just have to tell ye what ye want to know, bad cess to ye!' So on his promise to leave her be," the Colonel sighed, "I talked. Wouldn't you?"

"The woman you love?" breathed Avery. "Nay, that's different. Ah, Blood, I have wronged thee—"

"Not the first time."

"Nay, comrade, what can I say?" In the dark he sought to squeeze the Colonel's arm reassuringly, got hold of the wrong place, and evoked a muted squeal from his companion. "For thy true love's sake . . . that's something else. Ah . . . do I know her?"

Colonel Blood grunted painfully. "Bejazus, ye near ruined me! The lady . . ." He coughed deprecatingly. "Why, Lady Vanity, o' course."

The searching pirates assumed that it was the cry of some nocturnal creature; in fact it was Avery sounding like a leaky pressure valve. "Vanity?" he gasped. "My betrothed! Why, ye muckrake, wouldst lift defiling eyes to that divinity? Hast thou dared? Ha! Where's thy vile throat, that I may tear it out? Ah, I have it, scoundrel! Now, unsay those lying words, or—"

"That's my ankle!" snapped Blood. "Shut up, ye fool, or

they'll hear ye! And listen – ye can forget Lady Vanity. 'Tis up the spout ye are – and small wonder! D'ye think ye can fool about wi' Donna Meliflua, an' frolic in dungeons and long grasses wi' Black Sheba, an' make sheep's eyes and offer marriage to that be-feathered cooch-dancer at Cohaclgzln – God knows who ye've been hotly a-snog wi' since then," he added, and misunderstood the captain's guilty start. "Aye, tremble wi' remorse, Faithless Ben Avery! Anyway, Lady Vanity's given ye the door, an' small wonder—"

" 'Tis all vile libel!" hissed our Ben. "A chapter o' sorry misunderstandings, which I shall readily explain—"

"Dear lad," murmured the Colonel gently, "even if ye could, 'twouldn't make any odds. Rebounding, she loves another—"

"You? Don't make me laugh! Why, from the first she regarded thee as dog-meat!"

"Beglamoured by your outward showing, she did not mark my truth worth, no – at first. But since then I have been constant at her side – fightin' off Happy Dan Pew an' his sex-crazed apache dancers, preservin' her from Lardo, frontin' Indian hordes on her behoof, ever comforting her in her captivity, an' even now hazarding my poor self for her sweet sake. She knows me now for what I am," whispered the Colonel complacently, "and it's wedding bells as soon as we get home."

"You lie! It cannot be – she loves me, and I her—"

"The last thing she said to me," continued Blood remorselessly, "was: 'Dear paladin' – her pet name, ye understand – 'Dear paladin, I am thine now and always, and should ye go down the stank untimely in this thy noblest exploit, then shall I die o' grief, or drag out my weary days a maid.' Straight up, 'tis what she said."

(N.B. – Don't worry – he's lying, the snake. Vanity, tho' racked by jealous doubts anent Sheba, Meliflua, and so on, is true to our hero still. Blood's just trying to discourage the lad – gosh, he's rotten. End of N.B.)

Avery gave a stricken gurgle. Dear paladin! It rang true, in her dulcet voice – and if she believed all that stuff about Sheba and the girls . . . Was she indeed lost to him? And to Blood, of all men? Well, the brute had a moustache, of course, and if he'd been championing her through all perils . . . Anyway, no point brooding. He'd have to see – but if it was true, he'd give her a piece of his mind, the dear little Cheltenham half-wit. Oh, how he loved her! But to business . . .

"What happened," he whispered coldly, "after you weaseled to Lardo about the treasure?"

"After my reluctant disclosure, made solely to keep Lady Vanity from harm," said Blood coolly, "Lardo dug up the goodies and sailed wi' his Cartagena squadron for Octopus Rock, there to keep rendezvous wi' his Hispaniola fleet, which I'm told has been giving Tortuga big licks and reducing the Coast Brotherhood to scattered remnants. Thence shall Lardo, wi' full power o' forty galleons and soldiers a-swarm by thousands, sally forth to knock hell out of everybody, and 'stablish King Philip his power throughout the Americas."

"'Od's whillikins!" Avery's eyes flashed like police alarms in the dark. "The fiend! Then . . . our settlements – why, all honest folk, like the Dutch and Scowegians and . . . yes, even the French – stand in mortal peril!"

"That's what the wise money says," agreed Blood. " 'Tis a hell of a note, for now that the Brotherhood are off his back, and our King's ships but few, yon be-dentured loony may burn and rob, rape and mangle, conquer and enslave any which way he likes. He's got the ships, he's got the men, he's got the money too, to coin a phrase."

"Just let him try!" grated Avery, and sparks flew from his clenched incisors. "Nay, though I perish in the attempt, I'll wax his ass! I'll . . . but continue thy tale, man!"

"Well, Octopus Rock is where Black Sheba had her dreaded private castle; 'tis strong fortalice and cross-roads o' the Caribbean, and might ha' resisted any attack, but when its pirate garrison saw Black Sheba suspended in iron cage from Lardo's bowsprit, and the big ape himself hollerin': 'Pack it in, or we dunk thy dusky queen!' they were unmanned and threw in the towel. And Lardo, the hound, put 'em to the sword, every man, includin' even the Swedes and beef-cake boys from Sheba's indoor sports club. So there Lardo sits secure, waiting reinforcements, and Sheba hangs naked in her cage down a great black cliff o'er pool o' ravening octopi—''

"Not octopi. Sorry to interrupt, but it's Greek, not Latin. Octopods, octopod*es*, take your pick, but not octopi."

"O'er pool o' ravening octopusses, then!" snarled Blood. "And there she swings, mocked by lewd Spanish soldiers takin' pictures and offerin' her bananas through the bars."

"Rough," said Avery grimly. "Mind you, she's asked for it . . . but Vanity, man! What o' her?"

"Takin' no harm, for tho' Lardo would slake his evil lust wi' her, the presence o' his fiancée – what's her name, Meliflua? – cramps his style sorely."

"Ah, the sweet half-pint!" murmured Avery compassionately. "Doomed to marriage wi' yon walking disaster . . . but I'll save her yet—"

"I don't know ye need bother," said Blood. "The grapevine doth say that she hath o'ercome her maiden terrors o' Lardo, to the extent of refusin' to let him bring his snakes an' spiders in the dining-room, so it may be he hath bit off more than he can chew wi' the fiery young hidalga. Serve the big bastard right if he has."

"I'll be blowed! Good girl!" cried Avery admiringly. "But how did ye escape from such fell durance? And by what strange chance are ye here, and who be these who even now are beating the bushes for ye?"

"I'm glad ye asked that", said Blood. " 'Twas thus, on a night o' tempest and raging wind, as the surge lashed the base o' lonely Octopus Rock, heaving the Spanish ships in their rockbound haven, swinging the great cage in which Sheba huddled for warmth among old banana skins, rattlin' the dentures in Lardo's bedside bucket, and drivin' the Spanish sentries to seek shelter 'neath the battlements—"

"All right, all right! Skip the tourist stuff and get on . . ."

. . . High in the tower of the forbidding castle, in the spacious room which had once been Black Sheba's, Lady Vanity stirred uneasily in feverish slumber. She hadn't slept well since her arrival, and blamed the surroundings: the sable decor which Sheba favoured didn't help, or the row of stuffed Spanish heads which grinned high on the ebony panelling, or the disused Iron Maiden in which the pirate queen had been wont to hang her bath-robes and shower-caps; naught relieved the sombre ghastliness of the chamber save the Mr Universe calendar and a few of Master McGill's postcards from buccaneer friends which adorned the dressing-table mirror. The only good thing about the place, from Vanity's point of view, was the store of her own Helena Rubinstein cream which Sheba had pinched; it was some consolation, as Vanity dabbed it on before retiring, to think that her dusky rival was getting the salt-water treatment in her cage outside.

Yet more than her surroundings troubled the sleep of the Admiral's beauteous daughter, and not just Spanish cooking, either. "Ben, ah peerless Ben!" she murmured, and her dreams in which she spooned fondly with him at tropic taffrails were plagued by nightmares in which he ran, whistling lewdly, after dim shapes in leopard-skin tracksuits and conga skirts and a vague Spanish female in matador pants. But what was this? Before her very eyes stood the Castilian sex-symbol herself (not in matador pants, 'tis true, but in a pretty slinky cloth-of-gold peignoir with lace ruffles which must have cost a bomb), her dark hair down, a slim finger to her lips, and a candle in her hand. Behind her the door stood ajar, with three Spanish guards piled up on the threshold, snoring thunderously.

"Heest!' she warned. "They are droog-ed, but we moost

329

be silent as meeces!" She glided forward and regarded Vanity with sullen dark eyes. "Yoo are the Laydee Vanitee! Ah, I hate yoo! Yoo are so beeyootifool an' pale an' cold, an' – ah, caramba! eet ees too much! – yoo are a natchooral blonde!"

Vanity, golden tresses bemused, forget-me-not eyes aswirl, gave her lovely visitor a swift up-and-down. "Well, that's pretty steep! Certes, I'm beautiful, but *you* should complain, whoever you are – art dishy enough, I warrant!" She caught her breath as it flew past. "Golly, you must be Donna Meliflua! Ha! You and your matador pants, that did beguile my sweetheart, thou Benidorm snatch-artist!"

"I? Heh!" Proud tears sprayed from Donna Meliflua's lids. "I should be so loocky! I yam distract' weeth love for 'eem, your darleeng Ayveree – an' 'ee spurn my devotion, cast me aside – me, high-bred and allooring wheestle-bait of Castile, as you see me! Aside, I tell you, like an old boot! Only yoo 'ee loves, weeth your natchooral blonde 'air . . . Ha! Eet's not a weeg, ees eet?" she cried hopefully.

"Try pulling it," suggested Vanity, "and then start counting your teeth. But you say – he loves *me*? That he was blind to your attractions?"

" 'Ee onlee painted your 'ateful name on thee stern of my personal galleon, would you believe? *Glonde Vayinty* – weeth my own eyeses I see eet! An' oll through deener 'ee go on about you, an' call you beezer, Sooperwoman, light of 'ees life – an' me in my sexee-est manteella! I was seeck leesteneeng!" The lovely little face crumpled tearfully into gnash, and Vanity, albeit her heart was doing cartwheels at this glad news, was touched.

"Oh, poor kid! Gosh, I'm sorry!" She laid an impulsive hand on the hidalga's arm. "Well I know how he can enflame maiden passion, yea, to boiling-point – whether 'tis his godlike profile, or splendid physique, I know not . . . or his slow smile, his clear grey eyes, the dimple in his chin . . ."

"Button eet up, por favor!" sobbed Donna Meliflua, bouncing distraught on the bed. "I yam onlee hyooman!"

"Ah, fret not, sweet child," soothed kindly Vanity, "for I know Señor Right will come along, you'll see—"

"Oh, yeah? Take a look in thee Vicereegal suite some time! Señor Reepulseev, weeth 'ees snakeses an' black weedows an' 'ees 'orreeble teeth – forced on mee by crooel parentses!"

"You don't mean it? If my father had tried to pull anything half as grisly," mused Vanity, "I'd have bitten him on the leg."

"Ah, yoo Eengleesh, weeth yoor weemen's leeb an' deesco danceeng, anytheeng ees posseeble. Me, I yam stuck weeth Lardo, an' mus' make thee best of eet! Creesto!" She raised her eyes to heaven and spat. "Wheech reeminds me – yoor companion. Blodd? Blewed?"

"Colonel Blood?"

"Ah, Carnal Blodd. 'Ee moost eescape, at once. Thees verree night!"

"Escape?" Vanity's rosebud lips whiffled. "Is't possible? What, and convey me to safety? Oh, dearest Meliflua, let me embrace thee! Selfless child – thy tender heart has been moved by my plight, and would reunite me with my Ben! Gosh, that's white of you . . . I mean, considering you're the losing team, so to speak—"

"Ha! Leesen, vain Eengleesh rose," Mcliflua's fiery eyes crackled with disdain, "'tees not for thee or that ice-cold Ayveree 'oo spurn me that I yam concerneded! I weesh thees Blodd person to vamos, but 'ee lies een thee dungeons, een chains, an' I 'ave peenched the key from Encheellada's office –" and from the froth of lace at her bosom she hauled out a massive iron key, shuddering. "Boy, was eet cold! But 'ow to convey eet to Blodd, weeth soldiers everywhere? Onlee thee crayzee Eengleesh cabbage-lan'scaper . . . Shaff-tow, eesn't eet? . . . 'oo 'as been made slave een charge of thee castle pot-plants an' weendow-boxes, can pass safely, seence 'ee tends thee dungeon watercress, an' no one weel suspeesh heem. But I not spik Engleesh well enough, so yoo mus' tell 'eem." She raised a slender hand in caution. "Heest! 'E waits weethout!" And gliding to the door, she inserted two fingers in her mouth, and Vanity started at the eery blast which echoed up the vaulted corridor. There was a scurry of feet, and Solomon Shafto appeared, hopping nimbly over the drugged guards and knuckling his forehead bright-eyed to Vanity.

"Evenin', leddyship, an' oidle-doidle, sez you! 'Ell of a night, bain't it? Ar, chimbley-pots a-flyin', I reckon! Ar!"

"Steady on!" Vanity passed trembling hand o'er faultless brow. "Donna Meliflua – what mean ye? Blood to escape – but to what end? Don't tell me," she crisped, "that Irish smoothie has beglamoured thee, wi' his clarkie tash and winning tongue?"

" 'Ee ees nozzing to me!" shrilled Meliflua. "But 'ee must fly to warn the Eengleesh settlements that Don Lardo plans to destroy them weeth fires an' swords! There ees no time to looze!"

But . . ." Vanity was fogged. "Do you *mind*? I mean, as an Englishwoman I think it's perfectly ghastly . . . our colonies devastated, people massacred – no more cricket tours, or afternoon teas on H.E.'s lawn, or Mustique holidays – but you're Spanish! Why aren't you all for it? I ween," she added severely, "thou'rt pretty unpatriotic."

"Ah, caramba!" Meliflua stamped dainty foot in impatience. "I yam troo daughter of Spain, dedicate to glory of Castile an' Viva España! But eef Lardo make war on your pipple, what 'appen to my Papa's Eengleesh eenvestments? 'Ees sterleeng accounts? I tell yoo . . . they weel freeze them, those 'ereteec swine! Confeescate! Meelions lost! My Papa roo-eened! An' I yam onlee child," she added, her shapely nostrils pathetically a-droop. "So Lardo's schemes must bee scootled. Okay, tough – but Papa's forchoon weel be saved, an' no one weel ever know 'twas me, Donna Meleeflua Etcetera, 'oo pulled the ploog. So . . . Carnal Blodd must warn the Eengleesh in time. Tell Shafftow."

332

The flower of patriotic British womanhood needed no further urging. While Donna Meliflua idled by the window-sill, moodily dropping make-up jars on Black Sheba's cage far below, Vanity filled in the twitching Solomon Shafto on what must be done, and pressed the great key upon him. Solomon, agog to serve her, would have swallowed it for greater security, but Vanity wrested it from his eager jaws, and a moment later the ragged ancient was scurrying down-stairs, wi' watering-can and secateurs to lend colour to his errand, and the key concealed in his flapping beard. None hindered his passage through those gloomy vaults, past guard-rooms where torches guttered and sleepy sentinels yawned, until he came to the noisome watercress dungeon where Colonel Blood swung, suspended by chains round his ankles, crooning resignedly "Believe me if all those endearing young charms."

Hurried whispers i' the dark, groan o' key in rusty fetters, dull plosh as Blood dropped straight into a vat of mushroom fertiliser, stifled oaths, wet slurp of bemired feet across the flags, and stealthy sneak down dank corridor towards open postern. Beyond lay a narrow path skirting the storm-lashed rock to secluded cove where Meliflua, with forethought (and some artistic licence from the author) had caused a fast catamaran to be moored – but ere they won to the postern, an iron-bound door swung open, and guards in morions appeared, to yell alarm at the sight of the two figures, one ragged and wizened, the other plastered with muck, caught flat-footed in the torch-glare.

"Jail-break!" bawled the guards. "Clobber them!" But Blood was upon the foremost, wrenching rapier from the fellow's scabbard, and in a trice the corridor echoed to the clang o' steel as our Colonel beat a fighting retreat towards the postern, his blade whirling 'gainst three in the hands of his bearded pursuers. Before that leaping point, and the frightful pong of his befouled person, the Dons held back, until Blood's foot slipped in the mushroom-horror; he half-fell, and Spanish steel was about to spit him when it was turned by subtle parry of outflung water-can, and Solomon Shafto leaped between, brandishing his secateurs.

"Have at 'ee, hell-hounds, wi' a voom-vam-vimble an' be danged! Ha, Inquisition dogs, 'tis Secateur Shafto has 'ee at his point! Come, kiss my steel, vile thumbscrew-fanciers! Afoot, maister, an' down-derry-diddle, sa-ha!"

Shoulder to shoulder they retreated, the capering scarecrow and the reeking soldier of fortune; Spaniards fell before their steel and the flailing sweep of the watering-can, but more were coming, and e'en as they reached the iron wicket, a blade drove through Solomon's beard and he staggered, gargling. Quick as light Blood leaped through and slammed the postern; he heaved up Shafto bodily and sprinted along the rain-lashed path, but the Spaniards sallied after them and he turned in desperation to face the onion-gorged menace as it surged up the path with swords aloft and beards gloating. Solomon shuddered and slipped down on to the wet ground.

"What? Ha? How is't wi' you, old runt?" cried the Colonel. "Art foundered, or is't mere scratch?"

Solomon's eyes flickered, and a spasm of pain twisted the gnarled old face as he glanced back at the approaching Dons, and the secateurs fell from his failing grasp.

"Ha, maister! . . . nay, Ole Sol has took pesky thrust, d'ye see, an' . . ." He coughed weakly as his skinny hand gripped Blood's arm, and he forced a feeble grin. "Us . . . parts here, I rackon."

"Never say die, old joy!" cried the Colonel, moved even in this extremity. "I'll beat 'em back an' carry you!" But the old castaway shook his unkempt head.

"Nay, maister . . . us'd never make it, no'ow. Frapple-de doo . . . I be . . . an ole done husk, an' as things is shapin', 'tis odds I'll ne'er see Babbacombe again . . . ar, sweet Babba-combe, wi' drippin' hot from the sty! But you, maister – you'm young an' strong an' . . . sound o'limb. So," his faded eyes filled with tears, "you hold the buggers off while I get the hell out o' here!"

And with a galvanised leap he was off up the path like an electric hare. With an oath Blood slashed and hacked at the arriving Dons; the howling wind drove his stench into their faces, and they reeled back, choking. Blood fled, and reached the cove just as Solomon, gibbering with panic, got the catamaran under way; a frantic leap and Blood was scrambling o'er the gunwale even as Solomon flung the tiller into second, and they surged out of the cove and into the teeth of the storm . . .

"And then?" Avery's bated whisper echoed round the hollow trunk of the galoopa tree. "What next befell? What o' Solomon his wound?"

"Wound my foot!" scathed Blood. "The Don's point had been turned by the *Jobbing Gardener's Handbook* for 1654 in the breast pocket of the ould layabout's rags – an' him carryin' on like the last act o' Hamlet! Howbeit, we cleared cursed Octopus Rock, the Dagoes misliking to follow in the tempest, which drove us headlong two days. God," he shuddered, "what an experience! Two days in the company of that drivelling lunatic! Then we were becalmed, and lo! a distant isle, which the garrulous bum claimed to recognise, he having been marooned there years agone by Howell Davis. Who has my heartfelt sympathy," he added, with feeling.

"So we stood in, and there a great ship in the lagoon. Shafto climbs our mast, and 'What d'ye see, old gallows?' says I. 'Jolly mariners a-dancin' heel an' toe on the strand,' says he, 'to chirp o' pipe an' lilt o' small guitar, wi' a hey-ding-a-boogie.' 'Sounds all right,' says I, 'what more?' 'A gurt loon wi' a red beard practisin' press-ups,' says he, 'an' a swart lean fellow in a ribboned coat who lolls at ease in a deck-chair, attended by a timber-toed midget.' It seemed to me the descriptions were familiar. 'Turn this bloody boat round!' hollers I – but 'twas too late—"

"''Vast narrating!" Avery snapped his fingers. "Red beard . . . swart lean chap . . . timber-toed midget – d'you know, Blood, they sound familar to me, too . . . Great Scott!" He started up and hit his head a ringing crash. "It wasn't—?"

"It was. Help thyself to the coconut."

"Firebeard and Bilbo! Nay, then here's rare opportunity!"

"Not precisely how I put it meself."

"And they brought ye hither . . . and yonder fell black ship . . . the *Laughing Sandbag*?"

"As ever was. An' I can tell ye her accommodation for prisoners is pre-eminently lousy, especially when ye have to share it wi' a babbling nut like Shafto, and a faddle-de-bopple to you! If ever," Blood ground his teeth, "I hear the word 'dripping' again I may do something quite reckless . . . not that it didn't come in handy, mind you, for Shafto whined for it so oft that they gave him some from the galley, and when we anchored here I used it to slip me fetters an' bolt ashore. Speakin' o' which," he cocked his head, "the pursuit seems to have died down . . ."

But Avery's active mind was already pacing to and fro. "Right! I see the position, and what's to do. Phase One: I settle the hash of Bilbo and Firebeard for keeps, take over their ship, and warn our settlements about the Dons. Phase Two: I hie me to Octopus Rock, deliver my sweet Vanity and remind her that I'm her heart's desire and thou but vulgar passing fancy, put the skids under Lardo his vain dreams o' conquest, and slap Sheba in the cooler. Not necessarily in that order; we'll see how it goes. Phase Three: wrap up the remainder o' the Coast Brethren. Capital! A busy schedule, but I'm feeling pretty keen."

"Ye are, eh? Good, good . . ." Blood gave sardonic approval. "But no need to fret yourself over the Brotherhood, ye know; the Dons ha' settled them for you. On our voyage hither we fell in wi' two ships, one towing t'other – locked i' stinking lazarette, I but glimpsed 'em through a port, but by scraps o'erhead I gather they are sole survivors from Tortuga, where Lardo's galleons ha' minced the buccaneer fleet into tasty bite-sized portions."

"Nay! Who the dooce," cried Avery hotly, "do these Dons think they are? I was looking forward to that. Ah, well, I can still set about Fircbeard and Bilbo, and that wi'out delay. I've sat around long enough. You coming?"

Colonel Blood answered deliberately. "No-o . . . not coming, exactly – going, and that right speedily. To some sweet haven," he went on dreamily, "o' peace an' rest (if such there be, which I begin to doubt) totally devoid of Fircbcards, Bilboes, mad Frogs, black fiends, damned Dagoes, murthering Indians, Solomon Shafto, and above all," his whisper shook with passionate sincerity, "of heroical bushy-tailed duty-besotted supermen whose rightful place is in some remote and well-guarded home. Am I getting through to thee?"

"Perfectly!" snapped Avery. "So . . . thou'rt ratting? Again? 'Tis very well! I . . ." He broke off, sniffing. "Here, are you smoking?"

"Who, me? No."

"Somebody is. I smell smoke, distinctly."

"It's probably your ardour burning . . ." Blood stirred impatiently in the dark, then sniffed. "Bedad, y'are right! 'Tis reek o' fire—"

"As of wood-smoke! Nay, how should this be?"

"Don't look at me . . . oh, I see what it is!" Blood gave a light, hysterical laugh. "Our tree's on fire."

And it was. An idle pirate, fed up of looking for Blood, had sought repose 'neath the galoopa tree, and being unable to drop off for the racket of our heroes' whispering, had finally tumbled, and summoned his mates wi' gleeful stealth. For ten minutes the whole gang had been listening outside the refuge, cramming hankies in their mouths to stifle mirth and belting each other in the ribs. Then they'd decided to burn the tree down.

So now, as Avery streaked forth leopard-like, looking for someone to hit, and Blood stumbled after, coughing, they found themselves ringed in by blades a-glitter i' the firelight, and in the shadows sinister figures who roared with laughter, and having laughed, spake each in turn.

"So-ho, what dawcocks ha' we nesting here, bullies? A pretty brace, i' faith, and shall be plucked anon!" sneered Bilbo.

"Mais quelles oiseaux, slightly singed! Les jobards Anglaises, ain't it?" chortled Happy Dan Pew.

"Har-har! Belike, bedamned, an' good e'en to ye, cullies, an' which'll we fillet first, wi' a curse?" bawled Firebeard.

"Easy all, King's man – keep your hands up, and keep 'em empty," said Calico Jack Rackham.

Discouraging; no other word for it. Avery's schemes have caught their toe on the first hurdle, and Blood's only consolation as the jeering pirates bind them hand and foot is that there isn't much that can be done to him that hasn't been done already. Pretty worn, is our Tom. But stiffen the sinews! All's not done, and we haven't come 338 pages to have our Ben collapse wheezing in the straight, an' ye may lay to that. At least we hope not.

CHAPTER
THE EIGHTEENTH

e have it on the authority of Defoe (and who could doubt Desperate Dan for a moment?) that Anne Bonney once observed irritably of a lover, as he was dragged out to the gallows at dawn, that if he had fought like a man he need not have been hanged like a dog. Neat and pithy, and must have cheered him up no end, but the real significance of her remark at such a time has hitherto been overlooked by scholars, the dumb clucks. Not any more, though; we've spotted it: plainly she was not at her best first thing in the morning.

This is borne out by her reaction on waking up nude, cold, wi' coated tongue and a head like a burst cushion, to find herself lying on a mattress ripped to shreds, and her room in wild disorder. Her first bleary ecstatic thought was: Gad, that new slave is something else! – and then she realised that the Madagascar cross was gone, and that the smooth long rat must have slipped giggle-juice in her loving-cup. Her bliss evaporated in frothing rage – not only robbed, then, but *scorned*! Small wonder that Onslow, bringing prunes and poached eggs in response to her bellowed oaths, should have tottered out again with the breakfast tray wrapped round his head and the impresssion that her instant requirements were a pack of hounds, a horse-whip, and a cauldron of hot tar in the back yard.

Gripping her skull with both hands to prevent its flying

open, and mouthing rich sea-oaths, the unhappy redhead became aware of a distant clamour, and reeled to the window. Focusing with difficulty, she beheld on the sunlit reach beyond the trees three tall ships, which her experienced but glassy eye recognised as the *Laughing Sandbag*, the *Frantic Frog*, and (Gad's anchors!) the *Plymouth Corporation's Revenge* under jury rig – the big idiot was home, rot him! And then she realised that the garden was aswarm with pirates, trampling her croquet lawn and clock-golf layout, invading the barbecue pit, and close-packed in a noisy mob round the swimming-pool. There was Calico himself, with Bilbo and Firebeard and the snail-guzzler, all seated on barrels round the deep-end, regarding two pinioned figures who stood on the diving-boards, the nooses round their necks attached to the top platform. She started, reached for the brass-mounted telescope on her make-up tray, and homed in.

. . . A likely big rascal wi' black curls and pencil moustache . . . rather scrumptious, in a dirty-looking way . . . and the other – as the splendid Greek-god profile and lithe figure swam into her lens, Anne could not repress a cry of "Gotcha, you bastard!", and she was about to lean forth and, in a contralto which had hailed the fore-top ere now, instruct them to hold him down till she got at him – and then she bethought. Like anything.

If she denounced him for cross-snitching slave, last night's doings would be thoroughly aired, ripped mattresses goggled at, lewd conclusions drawn, and the scum o' the sea would cough delicately behind horny hands and give each other knowing looks. Oh-ho, they would murmur, at it again, is she? Not that she gave a hoot, normally; everyone knew, and dahling Calico had always been broad-minded – provided she was discreet. Ye-es, but he might be just a teensy cross if her latest attempted infidelity was flaunted before the crews of three notoriously gossipy pirate vessels . . . she found herself recalling how he had beaten Blackbeard at Indian arm-wrestling, and the thrilling night when he had flattened her iron-studded bedroom door with one blow of his fist (which had been holding her first husband at the time). No . . . it wouldn't be fair to embarrass dear Jack, definitely not. She'd better just forget about the Madagascar cross; it hadn't really gone with any of her outfits, anyway, and she could always tell him it had gone phut in the South Sea Bubble, or something. As to that gorgeous swine on the diving-board, who had passed her up, damn his impudence, *and* given her this monumental hangover, it was imperative that he should get his without delay, and without telling any bedtime stories, either.

Pausing only to swallow a pint of rum and seltzer, shudder, stare in the mirror, shudder again, repair her make-up, and fix her hair, Mistress Anne squeezed her way into a modish riding-habit o' turquoise nylon, donned a picture hat plumed au Mousquetaire, cursed the gremlins who were kicking holes in her cranial cavity, gulped four aspirins, summoned her chair, and sallied forth to enjoy the fun.

Meanwhile, it was all go at the deep end. The little Welsh pirate was laying it on the line passionately, while our heroes, noosed and attentive, waited to hear their fate.

"I'm not sayin' you can't 'ang these two non-union individooals yere – I'm just sayin', look you, that if you 'ang 'em *out of 'and* it'll be a flagrant contravention o' conference policy as democratically ratified by overwhelmin' block vote at the Port Royal Congress, innit?" The tiny Taffy brandished his rule-book. "Clause 2, sub-para 5 spess-ifickly states that when captives, prisoners, and/or hostages 'ave survived the ordeal o' Dead Man's Chest, then further disciplinary action at shop-floor level can on'y be implemented after affirmative vote o' the execcative council, see? 'Nother words, ye cannot 'ang 'em unless council sez so, an' it dun't matter a monkey's about yer show o' hands!"

Cries of "Cobblers!" "Stick it, the Welsh!" and "Order, order!" were stilled as Calico Jack pounded his cutlass-hilt.

"The council accepts Brother Aneurin's motion—"

"Wi' a curse!" bawled Firebeard, being awkward.

"That's an amendment!" squealed the little Welsh-man.

"Accepted wi' a curse, then," growled Rackham. "So, council o' captains must pass formal vote o' doom – 'tis all one, they swing in the end, and sing merrily all, sa-ha!"

"Jus' keepin' things reg'lar, like," said Aneurin primly, while the pirates roared: "Huzza! Tip 'em the Black Spot, cap'ns!"

But now Mistress Bonney's sedan had arrived, borne by stalwart blacks, and as she debussed and swayed oomphishly forward the assembly gave her gallant greeting, wi' sten-torian wolf-whistles and cries of "Ho for Red Annie, mess-mates all!" and "Hey, lady, you left your motor running!" which she acknowledged wi' languid grind o' hips. Rackham, not having seen her for months, bussed her fondly and set a barrel for her, Bilbo and Happy Dan made legs full courte-ously, and Firebeard lit his whisker-crackers, exploding in reeking welcome. The little Taffy offered her the minutes, which she waved aside.

"Taken as read, dahlings," she drawled. "Tho' one is. unacquainted with these . . . gentlemen." She gestured limp-ly at the prisoners, and introductions were hastily made by Rackham: "Cap'n Ben Avery, R.N., rot 'im; Colonel Tom Blood, cashiered . . . Mistress Anne Bonney." She inclined her head, Avery bowed superbly in his bonds (if she pre-tended non-acquaintance, not for him to bandy a lady's name), and Blood, despite his pressing anxieties, could not help noting that here was a well-built piece of all right, whose green eyes ignored Avery but warmed sleepily at Blood himself; she even murmured "Colonel . . ." in a way which spoke censored volumes. (No harm in making Avery realise he wasn't the only pebble on the beach, the handsome bastard, she thought spitefully. Not that much time would be left him for jealousy.)

"These two be for the see-saw, after formal vote o'

council," explained Rackham. "As to the fashion by which they die . . ."

Mistress Anne stirred an eyebrow. "No problem there, dahling, surely? A slight nudge, and let 'em dangle. We don't," she yawned elaborately, shooting a sidelong glance at Avery, "want them making a lot of unnecessary noise, do we? Not before lunch."

Cries of dismay arose from those who had been looking forward to slow fires, broken bottles, and bicycle pumps. Mistress Bonney shrugged, but plucked doubtful lip, and Avery, his razor mind instantly hep to her reasons for wanting him speedily despatched, hastened to reassure her. (He just oozed chivalry, our boy, and felt he owed her some amend for the state of her bedroom.)

"Mr Chairman," he baritoned meliflously, "let me assure madame – or should I say mistress? – that whatsoe'er form death takes, be it ne'er so lingering beastly, there shall be no untoward peep out of us."

"Is that right?" snarled the Colonel, but Mistress Anne was relieved. "One is beholden, captain," she purred. "Why, then, dahlings – let's fill up the pool with piranhas and slide the gentlemen down the chute, why don't we?"

Whoops of cruel glee and demands that the local aquarium should be contacted greeted this proposal, but Rackham waved them aside and addressed the doomed pair, Blood sweating large amounts, Avery wearing his noose wi' elegant composure, as 'twere à la mode.

"Bullies," quo' Calico Jack, "ye go clean to your long home. You, Ben Avery, for that ye swore vengeance on this Brotherhood, slew our mate Akbar, and wrested from our brethren Sheba and Bilbo two Madagascar crosses, knowing them to be hot ice, which doth make thee a receiver o' stolen goods." Roars of delight from the pirates, who hadn't thought of that one. "You," Rackham turned to Blood, "have just been a bloody nuisance from the start. So – ere the council damn thee both: hast aught to say?"

343

Blood could think of plenty, but gazing down on that evil, gloating company he thought, what's the point, and contented himself with an extremely vulgar noise. Polite clapping greeted this spirited statement, and Blood's stock rose several points. Avery, meanwhile, was choosing words that would sting – he mustn't appear to be pleading with these blighters, or have them think he minded dying, but by Jove he'd remind them how utterly lacking they were in sporting spirit and good form. Rotten thing to have to do, but if he didn't no one else would. He coughed modestly.

"I hate to bring this up, and I would ha' none think he owes aught to any," he remarked casually, "but I feel bound to point out that this council, which is about to vote us bootees o' cement, would be two men short if someone hadn't saved their lives at Cartagena. That's all. Talk among yourselves if you like." If his hands had been free he'd have blown lightly on his nails.

"Nay now, cully!" Bilbo was on his feet, all lean and sneering mockery. "Thyself did say, in Lardo's pesky dungeon, that 'twas but a moment's truce, and then red war betwixt us! So did ye cancel the debt! Ha, pull the other one, King's man!"

"Bloody cheek, by the powers!" howled Firebeard. "Saved my life, did 'ee – an' who carried thy mangy rat's carcase down them dungeon stairs, all tender lovin'-like, arter ye'd swooned at sight o' blood? Hey? Why, tear, scour, an' riddle thee for rank poxy ingrate!" He shook ham-like mottled fists. "We'm square, you an' me, an' hast the brazen neck to urge—"

"Urge nothing," said Avery coldly. "Forget it. Sorry I spoke. Should have known better—"

"You 'ad ter mention it, didn'cher?" Goliath the dwarf stumped forward on indignant peg-leg. "Cor, that's rotten, that is – at a time like this, an' all! Tryin' ter make people feel uncomfy an' mizzable! Reelly rotten!"

Murmurs of disgust arose from the pirates. "D'ye hear,

mates? 'Tis petty knave doth rake up old debts . . . Nay, what a slob! . . . Anything to get sympathy . . . Typical, trust the Navy! . . . Shame on ye, Avery!"

A faint glow mantled the captain's proud cheek. "Nothing of the sort! If conscience pricks it's your own foul fault! It shouldn't ha' needed mentioning . . . no, I won't shut up, Blood! One either has one's code or one hasn't . . . ha, what do I say? They're only a pack of pirates!"

The audience went berserk, swearing horribly and throwing cushions and programmes at the indomitable figure on the diving-board. Avery curled proud lip, and then Calico Jack flung up his arms for silence, a strange glint in his dark eye.

"Is that so?" quo' he. "Ye think ye're owed summat, ha?"

"Not in the least," clipped Avery. "But were I Firebeard or Bilbo (a perfectly ghastly notion, I agree), I fancy I should consult mine honour – if I had any . . ."

Firebeard ran screaming in circles and kicked his barrel into the pool; Bilbo, pale 'neath's tan, glared hate. Rackham nodded at Avery.

"So, bully? Pack o' pirates, is it?" He swung to the mob. "Mates – what be the first law o' the Brotherhood?"

That shut them up. Calloused thumbs leafed surreptitiously through Codes o' Conduct, wi' uneasy glance and whisprous doubt. "Dirty in thought word an' deed? . . . The proletariat is the material weapon o' philosophy, ha? . . . Don't ask me, where's that little Welsh git . . . ?"

Rackham spat. "I'll tell ye – it's 'Fair's fair'. So, get the Black Spots out an' let's get crackin'!"

Wow, the Black Spots! Here's sensation, by the powers – and while our Dynamic Duo watched wi' bug-eyed panic and cool disdain respectively, five ebony discs were laid on a barrel-head before the pirate leaders. "Aha, les petits Blobs Noirs!" giggled Happy Dan, and the tumult died as Rackham held up a disc to the prisoners.

"Now mark how a pack o' pirates deal. Thus we dooms our enemies –" and he slapped the disc on the barrel; it couldn't have looked blacker. "But if any among the council hold that a debt or favour be due to a captive, then may he vote to let him live – thus." He flipped over the disc, to show a reverse side of pure white. "Here be five o' the council – Cap'n Bilbo, Cap'n Pew, Cap'n Firebeard, Mistress Bonney, and myself. Each shall vote in turn – nay, patience, Brother Bilbo! All in due form, for our credit's sake; so let a brother stand by each captive, an' if the vote go foul for them, let 'em swing on the instant!"

Two hairy ruffians mounted the springboards and eagerly seized Blood and Avery, ready to launch them into fatal half-gainers when the time came. Rackham took his seat with Happy Dan and Firebeard on his right, Anne Bonney and Bilbo on his left. Avery glanced down at them wi' scorn in every ruffle of his shirt, but no hope in his gallant interior – Happy Dan's eyes were alight with epicene hostility and pure barminess, Firebeard was resting his red-fuzzed knuckles on the ground and emitting coughing growls, Rackham's face was impassive brown marble, Mistress Bonney's full lips were curved in mocking smile, and Bilbo was guzzling snuff wi' wolfish eagerness – his boots were probably giving him gyp, Avery reflected. All in all, not a happy sight for the boys (in fact Blood had his eyes shut, and was gurgling like a very old radiator).

In the deathly hush, Rackham spoke. "Cap'n Pew!"

"Qui? Moi?" Happy Dan flourished beringed hand, and his buckled shoes tapped a vengeful rigadoon. "Ah, par l'horloge sur le mur de l'école – je n'aime pas this Ayveree, 'oo 'ave slew le pauvre petit Akbar! Et le Paddy méchant, 'e play mauvais sur le plage, an' transform ma Fille Grande bouche fantastique into une scrubbaire peroxide!" He flung down his spot, black side up. "A la lanterne!"

"One-nil!" chanted the pirates, to the tune of 'Amazing

Grace', and Rackham pounded his hilt again. "Cap'n Firebeard!"

They had to beat the giant about his shaggy ears to make him realise it was his turn, so disordered was he in his resentful wrath. He glared on the twain from piggy eyes. "Belike!" he bawled. "Look'ee! Aye, an' d'ye see? I hate 'em both! They're honest men! Rip, tear, an' hammer 'em, sez I, King's man an' Mick alike!" He hurled his spot on the barrel so hard it split a stave – and there it lay. Two black spots.

"Ee-zy, ee-zy!" roared the pirates, and Rackham weighed his disc in his hand. "I said from the first ye was too good a man to lose, Long Ben – an' if my camarado Sheba was here, I know how she'd cast her lot. So, for all the good it'll do ye . . ." He laid his spot on the barrel, white side up – and Mistress Anne's green eyes narrowed, and she sighed a gentle sigh.

La, thought she, here's a turn-up. She and Calico Jack had voted the same ticket ever since she had placed her bloody, adolescent thumb-print timidly beside his on the New Providence manifesto telling Woodes Rogers what to do wi' his royal pardon. Against that, she burned wi' jilted fury against Avery, and he'd be safer silenced . . . on t'other hand, he'd kept quiet so far, and could any red-blooded man-eater worth the name put the bee on a creature so gorgeously edible? The Irishman wasn't bad, either, apart from being green in the face . . . oh, let Bilbo do it!

"Dahlings," she drawled, and smiled lazily on Blood, "you know one never could resist men with moustaches . . ." The disc fell from her plump fingers: two black, two white.

Wi' Rathbonian snarl Bilbo raised his disc, and from the pirate assembly burst a chant of "Bilbo, Bilbo, rah-rah-rah!". The ruffians gripping the prisoners prepared to heave, Goliath turned a cartwheel and snapped his fingers, Firebeard started striking matches in anticipation, Avery turned his best profile towards the audience, Blood wondered if chaps at Tyburn ever actually threw up – and Calico Jack Rackham, not leader o' men for nothing, look'ee, smiled grimly and . . . waited.

For Bilbo's lean fingers were fretting wi' his disc, and Bilbo's lean face shone wi' sweat, and Bilbo's black eyes burned. *Had* Avery been ahead on points that night at Lardo's palace? Nay, never – and yet might not men *say* he had been? What o' the winks and nudges and snide questions on chat-shows hereafter . . . " 'Twas pity, Cap'n Bilbo, thou never didst win decision o'er – plague take it, what was the rascal's name – Avery? Nor no return bout, neither . . . pray, sir, tell the viewers how that never came about . . ." Odd's pockets, he'd never live it down! Nay, more . . . if one aspired to gentle estate (as Bilbo did) and dreamed brave dreams of strolling arm-in-arm wi' the King's Grace at Newmarket, and chocolate wi' the Quality at Locket's, and spake, and dressed, and suffered excruciating shoon and bespoke head-doilies to that end . . . could one, wi' such genteel ambitions, damn wi' a spot a fellow swordmaster, rot him? Aye, and a gentleman born, too. What would Avery do in his place . . . ? And yet . . . Bilbo gnawed his disc in hesitation, laughed sneering laugh, and bared savage teeth as he took his revenge.

Never so tall and rakish he sauntered forward, took snuff, made play wi' lace kerchief, and grinned wickedly into Avery's calm grey eyes as he dropped his disc on the barrel-head.

"Now, prithee, captain, tell me," he lisped. "Who owes who?"

It was white side up. Three-two for the visitors, and no double-header today. Black Bilbo tossed his snuff-box to Goliath, swung round on red-lacquered heel, saluted the company, swept a bow to Mistress Anne, and strolled away, his bunions singing in triumph.

After that it ought to have been old pals' week, let bygones be bygones and be damned, wi' rum-sodden good fellowship among friendly enemies – but it wasn't. Once the verdict had sunk in, and the two captives had been released, as Brotherhood custom demanded, you might have expected back-slapping and congratulations, hearty jests, and much offering of pannikins and free advice about visas and galleon departures. Not a hope. The lower-deck pirates were thoroughly fed up at being cheated of their execution – it adds nothing to your enjoyment of buffet lunch to find that the man you'd hoped to see torn asunder by piranhas is standing next you wiring into salt-beef-i'-the-basket and rum Pimm's – and there were mutinous murmurs against the council, wi' dark hints that the old gang had been in long enough, it was time for new blood (preferably spilled), etc., etc., before the whole mob mooched off to the beach to get drunk and fall a-plotting.

Which left only our principals to dispose of the al fresco buffet on Anne Bonney's croquet lawn, and the atmosphere was strained. There was none of that polite chit-chat of oaths and blasphemies, enlivened occasionally by sociable clash o' steel and witty pistol-shot, which you normally got at a Shark Island picnic. Firebeard, infuriated at the verdict, had torn up a couple of trees before going off to sulk in the barbecue pit, barely picking at his roasted ox; Happy Dan, equally miffed, had suffered an attack of Liverpool accent and was lying down in a dim room; Bilbo, cockahoop at handing Avery the perfect squelch, was ruffling it insufferably at the swimming pool, doing high dives in a fleering, provocative manner; Rackham brooded apart on the Brotherhood's woes and possible mutiny; Blood, still barely out of shock after his ordeal, flirted automatically with Mistress Bonney, who in turn smiled with mechanical languor while seething inwardly because Avery hadn't so much as glanced in her direction, damn him! And after she'd tipped him a white spot, too – the detestable, magnificent swine who'd spurned, robbed, and drugged her. Was she, she wondered, losing her marbles as well as her touch?

And Avery? He was sicker than mud. To be spared – discarded, almost – by a set of despised villains! To be patronised, dash it, by Bilbo, of all people, with his ghastly taste in steenkirks and cheap aftershave and phoney Vauxhall accent. He'd have challenged the brute straight away – but how in decency can you challenge a bounder who has just saved your life? Besides, he was by no means certain that he could take Bilbo, rapier to rapier, and absolute though our Ben's courage was, he had his duty to think of: the British settlements to warn, Vanity to rescue, Lardo to shove down the pipe, Vladimir to find – and what to do about the Brotherhood whom he'd vowed to destroy, and who'd now morally disarmed him by not cutting his throat? Gosh, how troubles piled up! So he idled pensively on the putting-green, abstractedly sinking thirty-footers left-handed with one eye closed, and trying to ignore Bilbo who was doing hand-stands on the top board in his Lurex trunks.

Had the party lasted another twenty minutes in this atmosphere, it would have been the ultimate social disaster. For in that time Firebeard would have drunk enough to emerge from the barbecue pit, seeking sorrow, Happy Dan would have committed suicide at his inability to pronounce nasalised vowels, Avery's better self would have surfaced to the point where he offered to shake hands with Bilbo (which would certainly have led to bloodshed), Anne Bonney and Blood would have sought solace together in the rhododendrons, and Rackham would have caught them at it. Oh, and the pirate crews would have mutinied. And this story would have had a different ending, and ye may lay to that.

Fortunately, before any of these things could happen, the Spaniards attacked.

They always do – and it is arguable that they are acting not out of sheer badness, but from Castilian courtesy. Let the hero be facing sticky death, the heroine fleeing from a maddened ravisher, the cad on the point of telling all, the spy on the brink of discovery, the lovers about to quarrel, the mortgage to fall due, or the party to freeze over – and here they come, guns ablaze, banners streaming, trumpets blaring, and moustachios a-twirl, the dear old opportune Dons doing their stuff again, and everyone can forget their problems and pile in against the obliging common enemy.

It happened now, just as Anne Bonney was moodily viewing the piles of untasted canapés on the buffet and wondering if she could unload them on her plantation slaves for supper. A thunderous boom o' broadsides shattered the sultry afternoon, Avery dropped his putter, Bilbo did a startled belly-flop from the top board, Happy Dan awoke with a shriek of: "Nous sommes betrayed! Les voleurs sont sur nous!", Firebeard bit clean through his roasted ox, Rackham stroked shaven chin thoughtfully, Blood dived under the daybed, and Anne Bonney sighed contentedly – broadsides invariably meant visitors, so the canapés wouldn't be wasted after all.

And who should the visitor be, by the powers, but Don Toro Molinos, whom we last saw knocking big holes in the Brotherhood stronghold of Tortuga. Flown with victory, he had been cruising down to join Don Lardo at Octopus Rock when he had learned that the fugitive Rackham and two other pirate ships were heading for Roatan. (Don Toro got this news, of course, from a half-caste fruit vendor in a bumboat; as all students of romance know, they were the only reliable sources of information on the Spanish Main, and fleets of bumboats were specially maintained, manned by trained fruit vendors who had passed stiff examinations, like London taxi-drivers.)

So Don Toro had turned aside for Roatan to wipe up this last remnant of the buccaneers, and here he was, strutting his gilded poop and quaffing Charneco, what time his squadron swooped in like gulls to pound Roatan's forts to rubble, and his troops piled into boats, all hot for the loot of waterfront boutiques and delicatessens. And on nearby Shark Island the buccaneer crews took swift action in the face of this sudden menace – one mad rush and they were aboard their three vessels parked in the strait, cutting cables, casting off, setting sails, towels, pillow-cases and anything that might catch the wind, and roaring for their captains to get moving, a God's name, afore the Spaniards noticed them.

Their cries for leadership met with a mixed response. On the croquet lawn Bilbo was blasphemously trying to haul on his satin breeches without having dried his legs properly (yeegh!), Happy Dan was going glassy-eyed trying to say "ohn," "ahn," and "ehrn," through his nose (those nasalised vowels were really getting to him), and Firebeard was held up because, intent on clamping a cutlass 'twixt his teeth, he couldn't remember whether the sharp side went outermost or not. Two cool heads there were, fortunately: Anne Bonney calmly bade the servants place clean damp cloths over the canapés and refill the ice-buckets, and Calico Jack, having calculated that it must take the Spaniards a good hour to force Shark Island strait from the north, saw that there was just time for his ships to slip out by the southern end – but only if Happy Dan Pew could be rendered fit for duty wi'out delay.

This was vital, d'ye see, for while the buccaneers were never short of leaders of the Firebeard school, able to shout "Up and under!" and charge head-first through brick walls, they were always short of skilled seamen, and apart from Rackham and Bilbo, Happy Dan was the only captain present who could really handle a ship. When he was half-sane, that is; out to lunch, as he now plainly was, he wasn't fit to pole a punt, and with three ships (one of them jury-rigged) to manoeuvre out of that narrow channel, Rackham foresaw catastrophe. He ordered immediate emergency treatment for the wandered Frog, and while Goliath plied smelling-salts and the little Welshman sang 'The Ash Grove' in a vain attempt to charm the bugs out of Pew's steeple, Rackham, Firebeard, and Bilbo held urgent conclave – closely watched by Avery, his brain zipping like a computer in overdrive. Presently he sauntered up casually, lip a-curl and eyes glowing wi' contemptuous voltage.

"So, ye'll run, Master Rackham?" quo' he lightly. "British seamen will abandon their friends to hell o' Spanish sack, ha?" And he gestured airily towards Roatan, inadvertently burying his finger in the earhole of Colonel Blood, an anxious bystander.

Rackham eyed him full grim. "They ain't our friends – Roatan's a free port, payin' 48 percent to shareholders who make their profit floggin' our stolen goods and chargin' harbour dues that'd fright the Grand Cham. That," he jerked a thumb towards the gunfire, "is the risk they run."

"But ye ha' our good leave to die in its defence, bully," mocked Bilbo, and Firebeard raised two fingers and raspberried resoundingly.

"Unless . . ." Rackham's eyes glinted wi' sudden thought, "ye prefer to sail along o' us – as signed member o' the Brotherhood—"

"I'd sooner join the Maltese police force!" Avery freed his finger with a glugging noise. "But since ye won't fight, I've no choice but to sail with you – on a fare-paying basis, understand? For yon Spanish onslaught is but foretaste o' Don Lardo's design to sweep all non-Dagoes from the Caribbean, and I must bear speedy warning to Port Royal—"

"Sa-ha!" Rackham's shaven chin took another thoughtful fingering. "So that's why he drove us from Tortuga! Aye . . . but why should we risk our necks seein' you to Port Royal? The King's colonies is no pals of ours."

"Indeed, bully," Bilbo snuffed jauntily, trying not to wriggle in his wet pants, "shall we mourn if Lardo doth plunder fat Bristol planters and set merry torch to their sugar-cane? We owe naught to them – or to thee," he added, meaning it to sting, the cad.

"Aye, burn 'em all! They'm honest men!" bawled Firebeard. "Good luck to lousy Lardo, sez I, wi' a wannion, an' belike, an' nyah-nyah-nyah-nyah to thee, dandy-prat!"

Avery quivered wi' disgust. "You . . . cads! Nay, can rotters be so utter? Faugh! And tchah! I mean, I know you're bally pirates, but these are English settlements! Is that naught to thee? England? The old flag, free speech, honey still for tea, carol-singing i' the snow, little girls gathering primroses—"

"Guinness," put in Blood helpfully. "Meat pies. Brothels."

"Exac – Will you shut up, Blood? Look here, Rackham – can you stand idly by while Lardo wreaks red ruin on all decent chaps?"

"Decent chaps as builds gallows for us," said Calico Jack. "But belay that, King's man – for if ye did get warning to Port Royal 'twould do not a pinch o' good. There's but two leaky men-o'-war in Kingston Bay, a half-regiment o' invalids at Spanish Town, mebbe a frigate at St Kitts – an' no other help nearer than Port o' Spain or Providence. They'll not save the settlements, if Lardo sails, an' ye may lay to that."

"What?" Avery increddled. "I'll not believe it! No cover? Nay, 'tis not possible!"

"Ask the fruit vendors," jeered Bilbo. "They'll tell thee. Why d'ye gape, man? Wherefore should the King keep costly ships to guard his western outposts, when we o' the Brotherhood ha' ever been stout bulwark 'gainst the greed o' Spain? 'Tis not fear o' the Navy has kept Lardo and like wolves from the throats o' your Jamaicas and Carolinas – 'tis that we, the buccaneers, ha' kept the Spaniard his hands full this many a year—"

"Say it again, wi' three times three an' a curse!" bellowed Firebeard. "Aye, we'm the boys, by thunder!"

"And now we're broke – first at Tortuga, now at Roatan." Rackham shaded his eyes and looked north where the Roatan forts were burning. "So farewell an' adieu to the Americas for us – an' God help your honest folk, Ben Avery."

It shook even Blood, callous ruffian though he was – perhaps he remembered Cohaclgzln, and tales of other Spanish deviltry. But it acted on Avery like shot o' benzedrine; it was just what he had been needing for weeks – a hopeless cause, insurmountable odds, a sudden blazing inspiration, and a heaven-sent chance to start ordering everyone about. This, he realised, was hero time; his shirt-ruffles blossomed at the prospect.

"Farewell and adieu, ha? Don't make me laugh! Why, as ye stand, ye're in no case even to clear this island! Aye, scowl, villains – ye've a French skipper yonder who's in the Land of Nod and like to stay there – so ye need a commander o' proven sailorly skill, address, and character, able to hand, reef, steer, lay a course, fight a ship, quell a mutiny, keep a log in legible hand-writing, and see that the sharp end's pointing the right way at night. I even speak their beastly language", he admitted frankly. "In fine – you need me if you want to get the *Frantic Frog* out of that channel before the Dons are in among you."

Rackham, who had already reached this conclusion, took another scratch at his chin, glanced towards burning Roatan, watched as Goliath helped Happy Dan into a canvas jacket, considered the plight of the *Frantic Frog* with her alien crew wrangling hysterically about whose turn it was to go aloft, and didn't even bother to argue.

"We could abandon her," he said slowly. "But suppose ye conned her out for us . . . what's your price?"

"Bilbo," said Avery coolly, "you seem to be well in with the fruit vendors – what ships doth Lardo dispose at Octopus Rock?"

Startled, Bilbo went all slit-eyed. "Say . . . fifteen, ha?

Tall ships o' war. A round score, when Don Toro joins him . . ."

"But if, before then," cried Avery, his profile a-quiver wi' derring-do, "three stout ships, well handled and packed wi' reckless fighting men, were to fall all unsuspected on Lardo, they could so maul his fleet it would be in no case to harry the settlements for ages—"

"An' where d'ye get three stout ships, well handled and packed wi' reckless fighting loonies – as if I can't guess!" Rackham gestured angrily at the strait, where the pirate crews were beating the sides with pannikins and singing 'Why are we waiting?' with mounting urgency. "That's your price, ha? We'm to fight for you at Octopus Rock?" he rasped, and Avery nodded serenely.

Bilbo gaped, and smote his forehead in scornful amaze; Firebeard, when Avery's proposal had percolated, collapsed in helpless mirth, waving his hairy legs in the air and hooting. Rackham eyed our hero with grim amusement.

"Either ye're moonstruck," he growled, "or ye've a rum idea o' a bargain. For your mere two hours' pilotage, ye expect us to hazard our ships an' necks 'gainst odds o' five to one an' worse? Now, tell me, quiet-like, Long Ben – why should we, ha?"

"Fair question," approved Avery, "and I'll deal with it in a moment. But first, ask yourselves: why *shouldn't* you? I mean, what else have you got on offer? You admit your Brotherhood's kaput, you're out of a job, you're on your uppers, you can wander like Van der Decken till someone hunts you down and strings you up—"

"The world's wide, bully!" snarled Bilbo. "We're gentlemen o' fortune, and take our chance, damme! There's other oceans!"

"And better places for a funeral than Octopus Rock," said Rackham (but his glance at Avery was speculative and wary).

"Funeral?" Avery was amused. "With me in charge?

What funerals should there be but Spanish ones?"

"Oh, get knotted!" cried Bilbo, out of all patience. "To hear such braggart clack from you that but two hours ago stood mewling wi' a noose about your neck—"

"I'm still waitin' to hear," said Rackham quietly. "What's in it for us, Long Ben?"

"Well, it would be a jolly good thing to have done, for a start," said Avery warmly, "but if it's rewards you're after . . ." he paused impressively, "I can promise you the tops. The Big One. Wait for it . . . Free Royal Pardon, for all—"

Their hoots and oaths drowned him out; Firebeard begged him to stop before he, Firebeard, did himself a mischief. Even Rackham waxed derisive (but still with a thoughtful glint in his eye).

"Ye're sure ye could guarantee it? Maybe we's past pardon—"

"There's a man at my elbow who once stole the King's crown," cried Avery. "If he can get a pardon, and a royal handshake, anyone can!"

"Just hold on a minute!" protested Blood. "I'd have ye know—"

"Much good it's done him, too," scoffed Bilbo. "Look at him!"

"Pardon's the least of it, don't you see?" cried Avery. "What, for the men who'll have saved the Indies? Morgan got knighted for less than that!" He noticed Bilbo blink, suddenly thoughtful. "And look here, chaps – I know the King, and my future wife draws gallons of water with the Establishment; her old man's an admiral (whom you've met, actually). Why, ye'll be made men! I pledge my oath I'll get commands for you, Rackham, and you, Bilbo! For Firebeard . . . oh, gosh, we'll think of something, you'll see!" He paused. "And don't worry – I can take Lardo like a cup of tea. And you'll have saved your camarado Sheba at Octopus Rock."

Bilbo snarled and sneered, and Firebeard just lay there wheezing, but Rackham's shaven chin was rapidly developing grooves. Suddenly he kicked Firebeard upright, beckoned Bilbo, and the three went into a huddle. Fierce whispers and doubtful growls were heard, and once Firebeard roared: "I don't trust him – he'll shop us to the Maltese police, didn't ye hear?" At last they broke up, Firebeard scratching uneasily, Bilbo pale and fierce-eyed, Rackham grim. He stood arms akimbo before Avery, and looked him in the eye.

"Free pardon for all, includin' Sheba? An' your best endeavours for our fortunes?"

I'll be damned, thought Blood, for I don't believe it. Either I'm dreaming, or roguery's changed since I was a lad. And yet . . . while he wouldn't have trusted Bilbo or Firebeard a foot, he couldn't see Calico Jack as a breaker of articles. Avery, of course, would trust anybody, and gave his word on the spot. Rackham received nods from Bilbo and Firebeard, gave Avery another searching glance, and then held out his hand.

"Done," he said curtly, and glanced north again, where the cannonade on Roatan was slackening. "Best be away. The Frantic Frog's yours, Long Ben . . . camarado."

While the others hastened down to the beach, Avery in the lead shouting crisp commands in a perfect Sorbonne accent, Calico Jack strode up to the house to collect Anne Bonney – and was took flat aback, d'ye see, when she calmly informed him she wasn't coming.

"Dahling, you know one cannot abide ocean travel these days; one simply can't. Reek o' bilge and tar are for the young and active, and all that hearty yo-ho-hoing . . ." She reclined wearily and selected a violet cream. "One just couldn't survive—"

"An' ye'll survive here? Wi' Spanish fiends afoot to pillage, burn, an' rape—"

"They're hardly going to pillage or burn this charming mansion, dahling, are they? No, one imagines Don Toro –

that *is* the *Misconcepcion* out there making all that noise, is't not? – aye, well, Don Toro, being discriminating hidalgo o' Castile, will surely appoint this his personal quarters – Oswald's taking down the Brotherhood group pictures and that repulsive likeness of L'Ollonois, and we'll have King Philip his portrait i' the hall, the Pope in the drawing room, and that gold crucifix we looted from La Hacha—"

"But thyself, mad wench! Hast thought o' thy fate at the hands o' these pitiless ravishers?"

"Well, actually," smiled Mistress Bonney dreamily, "yes. Come, dahling, if you were Don Toro, striding in here all booted and dusty after a hard day's sack, in need o' refreshment and relaxation, well . . ." She stretched and pouted wantonly. "You wouldn't cast one out to the common herd – would you, now? After all, someone's got to sit at the other end of the dining-table . . . and that sort of thing . . ."

"But . . . you an' me, Annie lass! It's been twenty year together, fair an' foul – an' there be other islands, farther on—"

"And the Brotherhood's broke at last, Calico lad, and each must look to his own fortune, in his own way." She smiled up at him, and sighed, and held out a soft white hand. "We'll go no more a-roving, Jack. I'm home from sea, and too plumply idle to stir forth again – or to be carried off," she added, as he took a step towards the couch. "Nay, all courses part to westward; so kiss me, sweetheart – and let me hear ye laugh as ye go."

There was a long silence, while the big man all in white looked down at her, and remembered, and took her hand, smiling a little sad.

"A long time since ye called yourself 'me' and 'I'," he said softly, and stooped to kiss her and stroke the dark red hair.

"A long time since we broke the boom at Providence and stood out for Caicos Bank," she whispered, and kissed him again.

"And . . . ye're sure ye can deal . . . wi' the Dons?"

Mistress Bonney chuckled, purring. "When could one not?"

He went, laughing, calling back "Adios, bella camarado!" and so they parted as lightly as they had met so long ago. For a few moments she lay pensive, and at last heaved a little sigh, and summoned her butler and maid.

"Olives and sweet candies o' Peru in dainty silver dishes, Oswald, and a decanter of Madeira with the Murano cups; likewise candles o' scented wax, such as the Romish churches use, so shall our Spanish guest feel at ease." She waved languid dismissal. "Hebe, lay out the green brocade – la, wench, to be sure 'tis too tight, that's the purpose on't! Ah, yes – and a small stiletto for one's garter, in case one is expected to play hard to get. These macho Dagoes do so love to think they're taking one by storm. Heigh-ho . . ."

And settling back contentedly on her couch, Mistress Anne reached for another violet cream.

If only the guzzling nympho doesn't overdo the chocs, she could keep Don Toro dallying till the week-end – which wouldn't do our Ben and the boys any harm when it comes to the big show-down. You always knew they were going to get together, didn't you? O' course we did, sez you – aye, but can Avery trust the blighters, sez I? If it comes to that, can the blighters trust Avery? Oh, come on, really! What a question, at this stage of the story – can you see our hero doing Bilbo out of a knighthood? More to the point, will his scratch force stand a prayer 'gainst the vast might o' Lardo? Can he snatch Vanity, Meliflua, and Sheba unscathed from the Viceroy's loathsome clutches? Incidentally – where the hell is Vladimir? Did he catch the sloop shuttle out of Roatan before the Dons attacked? What o' – but we'll soon know, for here it comes, wi' a curse – the answer

to all questions, the payment o' all scores, as we lay
aloft, wear round, fall over, stagger up, and plunge
manfully into . . .

CHAPTER
THE LAST

loom hung in dank folds o'er the spectral castle on lonely Octopus Rock, gloom so thick, d'ye see, that it seemed to ooze through the battlements and drip down the sheer walls like treacle. No moon peeped through the lowering cloud-wrack, no faintest glimmer relieved the inky dark, save for the lanterns on the score of galleons riding in the rock-bound harbour, the guard-room lamp beaming above the grim castle gateway, the rays from a dozen crenellated windows in the massive keep, the flare of a match as a sentry had a crafty smoke, the whoof! of a chip-pan fire i' the cookhouse – oh, all right, the place was positively ablaze with light, and when the moon suddenly came out you could see for miles! Satisfied? It was still pretty dark in the corners, anyway.

Aye, but 'twas stilly night, wi'out wind (save in the great banqueting hall where Enchillada the chamberlain was making a right pig of himself on chilli con carne). No breeze ruffled the foetid waters o' the octopus pool beneath the great iron cage in which Black Sheba lay captive, nor whiffled the pale candle-flame by which Lady Vanity was gamely trying to pick the ponderous lock of her tower prison with a bent hair-clip, nor cooled the perspiration on Hattie McDaniel's brow as she ministered to yet another of Meliflua's screaming tantrums, nor rippled the black velvet waters far out to sea where – unless we're imagining it – dim shadows loom in the mirk, as of some dark presence drawing nearer, wi' faintest creak o' cord on timber, and on the air the thinnest whisper of that wild sea-march of long ago . . . no, it may be fancy, fading into silence over the face of empty ocean . . .

Aye, so haste we back to gloomy banquet-chamber, where Enchillada is on to the cheese and tacos, stuffing uneasily with piggy-eyed furtive glances at the table-head, where, throned in his great chair, sat the hideous Don Lardo, a nightmare figure in crimson silk which matched the ribbon round the scaly neck of the Gila monster purring on his lap. Enchillada didn't fancy the broody way the Viceroy was stroking his ghastly pet and rolling his dentures in awful contemplation, nor was he crazy about Lardo's occasional habit of crushing a priceless wineglass in his hairy paw, heedless o' the wine, blood, and broken glass which fell into his trifle. (Heedless, too, incidentally, of the matched sets of glasses which he and other seventeenth-century villains were forever breaking up in moments of crisis; snapped stems, broken bowls, shattered goblets, crockery all over the floor, they didn't give a damn, and never a thought for the butlers who had to clear up and order replacements.)

But crisis was there now, for suddenly the Viceroy broke the silence with a great blare of crazy laughter, swept the Gila monster aside, and sprang to his feet bawling:

"I'm getting married in the morning!"

"Deeng-dong!" yelped Enchillada sycophantically, stifling a guilty burp. "Terreefeec eemeetation, boss! Eef I'd 'ad my eyeses closed I'd 'ave sworn eet was 'Olloway! You wan' I should get Cugat an' thee boys for a seeng-song—"

"Silence, filth!" roared Don Lardo. "I'm proclaiming my nuptials, thou bloated worm! Tomorrow I wed Donna Meliflua – I'm fed up waiting, and what better way to beguile the time than by honeymooning with that sweet, innocent, tender bloom of maidenhood in these charming surround-ings?" He flung out a huge hand at the funereal walls where smoky torches flared, and slobbered crazily, his teeth popping out to bean the bewildered Gila monster. "Well, congratulate yourself, you lucky piece of putrefaction – you're going to be best man!"

"Gosh, Excellencee, I'm speechless weeth joy an' grateetude!" babbled the greaseball, grovelling at Lardo's feet. "Eet's great news, an' I'm so happee for yoo! Eet couldn't 'appen to a nicer tyrant!" He peeped up, hesitant. "Yoo . . . er . . . deecided not to wait until after we drench thee Caribbean in 'ereteec blood, huh?"

"Do I detect a reproach – a contradiction, even?" screamed the Viceroy, looming horribly. "Perhaps you'd care to repeat it to my Gila monster, when I've starved him for a week and sewn you up in a sack together, munch-munch-munch?" Then, as Enchillada gibbered and cringed, Lardo plucked him up by his fat neck, glared round as though for eavesdroppers, and grew frighteningly confidential. "Between ourselves, Enchillada – as Viceroy to rat – I burn with dark desires; the amount of unavailable nubile talent in this place is driving me crazy! Not only Meliflua, but that sleek spade in the cage and the luscious English peach upstairs!" He whimpered pathetically, his pale eyes gleaming. "It's not fair, I tell you – I daren't molest the captives before the wedding, or Meliflua might write whining to Daddy, and he'd cancel the match! Think of his fortune – lost to me!" He began to weep, mopping his cheeks with the chamberlain's scrubby head. "After we're married, it'll be different – I can go bananas with all three of them, and who cares? Anyway," he leered into Enchillada's sweating face, "dear child though Meliflua is, she needs a lesson such as only a wedding-night with me can teach her – criticise my snakes and spiders, will she? Wait till she looks under our marriage-bed!"

"Alleegators, huh, boss? Genius!" cried the terrified creep. "Say, does the luckee lady know that tomorrow's thee beeg day?"

"I told her before dinner!" cackled Lardo. "She swooned with joy, the sweet ecstatic little pigeon! Oh, I can't wait . . .

ceremony in the main dungeon, all hung in black crepe . . .
wedding breakfast . . . auto-da-fé in the afternoon . . . tea,
cream cakes, and crisps . . . feed the garrison defaulters into
the octopus pool in the evening . . . light buffet supper – and
then!" He swung the chamberlain round his head in mad
frenzy. "The bridal suite in an oubliette! Next to the torture
chamber! Mustn't neglect our work, even on honeymoon,
must we . . . ?"

Quick, let's leave Lardo's jolly stag night and plunge
down castle wall and cliff to the octopus pool, where Sheba's
grim iron cage swings creaking o'er murky waters a-swirl wi'
tentacled crawlies just waiting for the bolts in the cage-floor
to be slipped so that the occupant can drop in on them for
dinner. For a fortnight they've had nothing but the odd bit of
banana peel falling through the bars, and can't wait to sink
their beaks in the human dainty so tantalisingly close above
them – for these are man-eating monsters long since extinct
except in sensational fiction. But they're patient – like Sheba.

For two weeks the dusky demon has endured hell o'
blazing sun and lashing storm, sustained only by bananas and
rain water, enduring the make-up jars absent-mindedly dropped by Meliflua from Vanity's window, and the ribaldries of
brutal guards who ogled her undress and occasionally tried to
get fresh through the bars. Now she lies feigning sleep, with
every nerve alert, for she has caught the drift of that distant
sea-march on the night air, and instinct tells her it's now or
never, as through slitted eyes she watches the solitary sentry
lounging on the ledge beside which her cage swings, drowsing
as he puffs on his surreptitious cigarillo.

"Got a smoke for a nice girl, amigo?"

The sentry started at the throaty drawl. Two great amber
eyes gleamed at him in the moonlight, and a shapely black
form pressed ardently against the bars. "I'd do *anything* for a
couple of drags!" she hissed. "You can even have my autograph for your kid sister! Mmh?" And she pursed her lips
kiss-wise at him.

Caramba, thought the sentry, they don't build them like that in Barcelona . . . was this the wild hell-cat who had driven off his lewd advances with raking nails? He leaned forward to paw cautiously, but Sheba writhed back, purring, "Ah-ah, naughty – no smokee, no touchee!" and winked wickedly.

Well, we could have told him to pack in the nicotine habit on the spot, and holler for the guard, but being mere dumb peasant he reasoned that iron bars were protection enough, and held out his cigarillo, panting eagerly. Sheba caressed it from his fingers, inhaled luxuriously, bazoomed up against the bars again, he lunged leering – and fingers of black steel clamped on his throat, dragging him from the ledge to kick helplessly at empty air, her free hand plucked out his rapier, and grinning wolfishly into his empurpled face she slowly thrust forward. The sentry shuddered grotesquely, and with a hissed: "Come and get it, 'pussies!" she let him drop into the pool below. Splash, swirl o' blood-stained water, deep octopodal belch – and silence. That was the easy bit, thought Sheba.

The tricky part was to slip the floor-bolts while clinging to the side-bars with the rapier in her teeth, and then, when the floor swung down on its hinges, deluging the pool with used banana peel and leaving Sheba with nothing between her and the octopus-infested depths, to lower herself out of the cage at full stretch of her arms, feet cringing just above the water as she felt in horrid imagination the slimy touch of tentacles on her skin – then to swing out and up, snatching at the bars from the outside, clutching, slipping, clinging for her life, and then scrambling up the cage side to the safety of the roof. For a minute she lay panting and shivering, thinking six out of six for technical merit, but not more than four for presentation.

She gazed eagerly seaward, across the rock-bound bay where the Spanish galleons rode, but nothing moved on the dim water. Had she been wrong – no, she could feel it out yonder, and the sea-march was whispering in her ears. Wow, she thought, suppose it's – *him*, in person, hasting to my side! Or to the side of that blonde cream-puff up there who's been slathering herself wi' Helena Rubinstein like there's no tomorrow! Nay, it must not be! The sable sea-queen ground pearly teeth, her eyes blazed tawny sparks, and it took another digestive rumble from the depths of the octopus pool to recall her to her perilous situation. Time to get under cover – and where better than her own boudoir two hundred feet above, at the other end of the rusty, creaking chain from which the cage hung suspended? Little had she ever dreamed, in the carefree days when she had leaned from her casement, dropping debris, insults, and poisoned snacks on her own caged captives, that a time would come when she would have to climb up that dizzy height starkers, with her mouth full of rapier. With a wistful sigh the swart Aphrodite clenched the blade in her teeth, took a deep breath, flexed her lovely nostrils, and started up the chain, hand over hand . . .

With a startled squeak Lady Vanity jerked her bent hair-clip from the keyhole and sprang back. Someone was unlocking the door! For a wild moment she wondered if it was Meliflua, intent on a midnight feast – for since Blood's escape the dainty hidalga had been a frequent visitor, drawn despite her jealous rivalry by that sisterhood which links deb to deb, and many a snack o' sardines and cocoa had they shared, in giggling gossip, Meliflua discoursing of high jinks in the convent dorm, and Vanity describing how she had bundled the Roedean goalkeeper into the net, ball and all, in the last minute with the scores tied. They had also played Leviathan, Master Hobbes's fore-runner of Monopolie.

But it couldn't be Meliflua – there had been no sound of drugged sentries crashing to the floor of the passage. Who then? Blue orbs wide, rose lips parted, our heroine clasped her filmy robe about her, glanced in the mirror, adjusted a curl, flipped the betraying hair-clip deftly into a flower-pot, and recoiled as the door opened to reveal – Enchillada! And not just Enchillada, but Enchillada panic-stricken, with a proposition so bizarre that Vanity did a fluttering double-take.

"Me? A *bridesmaid*? I? Art surely loco, sir chamberlain, or legless quite! Why, whose nuptials – oh!" she gasped, discerning. "You don't mean Lardo is going to make Meliflua jump off the dock? Oh, the poor little twerp! How grisly!"

"You better believe eet, señorita!" chattered the plump chamberlain. " 'Ees excellence 'as commanded full rehearsal weetheen the hour, weeth you as bridesmaid an' me as bes' man – an' everytheeng's goeeng haywires! I 'ave no reeng, thee boss's weddeeng teeth are nowhaire to be foun', the Eenqueeseetion choir don't know thee words of 'Apple Blossom Time', and I theenk," he burst into tears, "thee Gila monstaire ees goeeng to 'ave pups! Oh, what shall I doo? Eef you fail me, I shall be blame', an' 'e weel fleeng me to the octopoodles!"

"But I can't be Meliflua's bridesmaid – I'm C of E!" protested Vanity. "Certes, you want a lady o' the Roman persuasion–"

"Een thees place?" wailed Enchillada. "The onlee other female creature ees that bloddy Gila monstaire!"

"What o' the blackamoor pirate – she who is so cruelly encaged over the octo-thingies, and serve her right? I don't know if she's a Catholic, but she'd look smashing in white –"

"A voodoo bridesmaid? Pleez, señorita, don' geev me a hard time – eet can onlee be yoo, an' oll ees arrange'. I 'ave priest can geev yoo crash course, special deespensations, confirmations, you name eet, you'll be shooteeng left-footed before breakfast –"

"Renounce my faith? Never! I'd sooner eat mud!" The dauntless English rose quivered to her full five foot five, hand outflung in a gesture that ordered St Augustine straight to the pavilion. "All right – so Daddy only goes to church at harvest festivals, and I'm sorry, God, for eating sweets at prayers and

368

reading Pooh in confirmation class – but never shall I bow the knee to idolatry, and chance it!" And she began to sing "Land of Hope and Glory" in a clear girlish soprano while the distracted chamberlain flung himself pleading at her feet.

"Pleez, señorita – onlee theenk, thee weddeeng woodcut weel bee een oll thee papers, an' you weel be recognise', an' Don Lardo weel 'ave to release you! But eef you don' play – 'oo knows yoo are 'ere? A 'orreed fate weel ovairtake yoo, an' yoor Papa an' friends noon thee wiseaire! Pleez, señorita, I beg – see, I smooch yoor tootsees een entreatee—"

"– make thee mightier yet!" concluded Vanity defiantly. "Stop it, you clot! What is it about my toes," she wondered, "that gets men going? Pew, Blood, and now you – jolly odd. But chuck it, fats, for I'll not yield to – but hark!"

From the corridor without came a rhythmic thumping of drugged sentries hitting the deck, the door crashed open, and on the threshold Meliflua paused dramatically, hair distraught and appearance streaming wildly. She saw Enchillada crouched in supplication at Vanity's feet, and immediately jumped to the wrong conclusion.

"Not yoo too?" she shrilled. "Thee greaseball ees proposeeng? Ah, keek heem een thee slats, proud Vanitee – geev heem a tooch of thee old Cheltenham bodee-slam, eesn't eet? Would that I could doo thee sayme to my persecutor, thee deezgusteeng Lardo, 'oo comes even now too claim me for 'ees bride! But I weel keel myself first—"

"Don't panic!" cried Vanity. " 'Tis but a rehearsal, and if the main event depends on having me as a bridesmaid, Lardo can scratch it off his card right now! Get that, Enchillada? Then hie thee to thy vile master, and tell him—"

"Tell heem yoorself!" moaned the chamberlain. "Leesten!"

From the depths of the castle boomed a crazy brazen voice, echoing up stone stairway and along vaulted passage, loosening plaster and shaking the very walls; the Mr Universe calendar fluttered at its moorings, and one of the stuffed Spanish heads fell off the panelling.

"Enchillada!" it (the voice, not the stuffed head) bawled. "Where are you, corpulent vermin? I'm waiting, Enchillada, for you and that heretic slut! To say nothing of my bride, my wedding teeth, the 'Apple Blossom Time' sheet music, and a vet for the Gila monster! Forty-five seconds to rehearsal, Enchillada – which is about twice as long as you'll take to fall screaming from the battlements if I have to come looking for you! Forty seconds and counting . . ."

Wi' shuddering sob Meliflua slammed the door. "I moost 'ide! Ah, conceal mee, Vanitee carissima! 'Ee may not theenk to look for mee 'ere—"

"Nay, why should he, wi' a passageful o' stoned guards outside the door!" snapped Vanity. "Stay! Could we revive them, think you, and send them about some errand – what didst zonk them wi', child?"

"'Ow doo I know? Some droog wheech my maid get from 'er pushaire – streekneen she call eet . . ."

"Golly, that's torn it! We must both hide – nay, such castle as this must ha' hidden passage, priest's hole, whatever! Thou, Enchillada—"

"Pleez, señoritas, eet's no use! Eef yoo deefy heem . . . ah, Jesus Maria, 'ee ees comming!"

"Time!" boomed the distant brazen voice, wi' hideous peal o' laughter. "Prepare for take-off, Enchillada!" Then he was bawling commands, and they heard the menacing tramp of guardsmen hastening to follow their dread master as he came ravening upstairs in search of his prey.

Meliflua shrieked with dismay. "All ees losted! Ah, but 'ee shall nevaire possess mee! Eet's sooeecide time – I shall fleeng myself from thee weendow onto thee crooel rocks below, an' cheat 'eem of 'ees loathly tryoomph!" She streaked to the window, leaped to the sill, and stood poised, holding her nose for the jump, ere Vanity could stop her. "Farewell, sweet Vanitee!" she enunciated with some difficulty (and if you think we're going to attempt a nose-blocked Spanish accent you're mistaken). "Adios, and may yoo find 'appeeness weeth yoor yummy, deevine, scroomptious Ayveree! Ah, Ben, mi amore, I shall nevaire – eek!"

The lissom figure tottered on the sill, gaped downward, and sprang back into the room like a startled budgie, great dark eyes wide wi' amazement.

"Vanitee!" she squeaked. "Thair ees someone climbeeng up thee chain to yoor weendow!"

Which is as climactic a moment as we could wish to zoom out and away from Octopus Rock, leaving Vanity and Meliflua clinging to each other as they gaze down from the sill at the dim form writhing up the creaking chain out o' the dark depths – and if they'd just happened to look straight out instead of down they might have seen more matter for a buccaneer midnight, by the powers, for far out on the dark water something *is* moving indeed – it wasn't our imagination, d'ye see? – nay, those tall black shadows on the face o' the deep are things palpable and charged wi' menace, surging in towards Octopus Rock from out of the tropic night, and ye may hear the wild sea-march singing through their shrouds as they come – one, two, three great ships wi' canvas spread but nary a light among them, save the faint glow at the binnacle o' each, where stoop the tight-lipped commanders, their eyes fixed ahead to scan the stark outline of rock and castle a bare half-league away, and the dark loom o' the harbour-mouth through which glitter the lights of the Dons at anchor.

Aboard the first ship . . . a whispered exchange by the wheel.

"Right, capting – got everyfink? Rapier, brace o' barkers, dagger, snuff-box, clean kerchief (I'm carryin' a coupla spares), deodorant, an' a buckshee wig just in case. 'Ow's the one ye got on – stuck dahn a'right?"

"Gummed to perfection, halfling – nay, but my cursed

boots do pinch exquisitely, ha! Haply we'll find replacements o' rare soft Cordovan neat's hide in Lardo his wardrobe – dead men's boots they shall be, Goliath, when I ha' sped that monstrous bastard to's last account!"

"Attaboy, skipper! 'Ere – think we can pull it orf, though?"

"Aye, can we, imp! Codso, shall be such exploit this night as shall live in sea-history – when they clink their cans on Plymouth Hoe and Severnside, and talk o' Drake at Nombre, Morgan at Maracaibo, and Flynn i' the Warners' tank, then shall they also roar a rouse for Black Bilbo that led the storm o' Octopus Rock, sa-ha! Aye, zooks – the deadliest blade o' the Brotherhood, they'll say, and the best-dressed . . ."

In the hold o' the second ship . . .

"Easy, old 'un, wi' they matches! There's forty ton o' powder close-packed about us, d'ye see, an' it ain't non-inflammable!"

"Forty ton, Calico, ha? Har-har! Enough to light my crackers, by the powers, wi' a curse, belike, an' damn-all, say I! Aye, an' to blow the Dagoes to hellangone – so shall they speak o' the harbour at Octopus Rock as 'Firebeard's Beard', look'ee, that flamed an' roared an' consumed bloody Lardo an' every bottom o' his cursed fleet!"

"Nearly, old son, nearly . . . but hark'ee now – when thy fuses be lit, an' this old *Revenge* has driven to the very heart o' the Spanish squadron, then every light above-deck must gleam of a sudden, an' thou and the lads blaze defiance at the Dons, so shall they bring their ships close about to grapple an' board—"

"– an' when *Revenge* doth blow her forty ton, 'twill hoist the buggers nigh to Kingdom Come – rat, burn, damn, an' devour me else! Aye, shall have an auto-da-fee o' their own! But . . . when they be all flamin' in glory, an' we victorious . . . then, Calico brother, we take pardons, ha . . . ? An' swallow the anchor like bonny Anne? Sure, 'twill be strange, that . . . wi' a curse, an' belike, d'ye see . . ."

"Aye, strange, old rogue. So . . . see's thy hand, camarado . . . an' good fortune . . ."

"An' thou, messmate! An' damn all Dons an' honest men! Har-har!"

While aboard the third ship . . .

". . . so there's no call to get all la-de-da wi' me, Blackleg Avery! I'm tellin' you the execcative totally an' arbitrarily exceeded their powers in givin' command to a non-union individooal, an' unless yore pree-pared to sign this applecation for a temp'ry probation'ry card, I shall be forced to black this entire operation, see—"

"A fig for thy card, sirrah! What, in five minutes we'll be at grips wi' the cursed Dons! Steer small, quarter-master! No smoking forrard! Bosun, take that man's name! Now, look, *you* – I've explained that as captain I'm part of management—"

"An' therefore confined to poop operations, an' not entitled to engage in tradesmen's activities, to wit – boardin', cuttin', thrustin', swingin' on ropes, dischargin' firearms, stormin' fortifications, lootin', pillag—"

"Don't be ridiculous! I'm the hero! Stand by, men – and when I cry 'Grapnels away!' I want to see good clean throws wi' bags o' follow-through! Ready, Trumpeter Korngold . . . ? *Will* you get off my quarter-deck, you Welsh pest?"

"Oh, a lock-out, is it? Comrades, we got a right fascist yere! Right, boyo, I'm not comin 'ead-scarf in 'and to you, so—"

"Hit him, Blood, will you? Thanks. Right, chaps, any minute now . . . all set, pikes? Ready, rapiers? Stand by, cutlasses! Quiet, please . . . settle down, everyone. I want this done in one take, remember, so when I shout 'Action!' . . ."

We can't deny him a close-up – there he is, for almost the last time, one hand on the rigging, profile cleaving the night air, spray dashing against smiling teeth, keen grey eyes and shirt-ruffles dancing in unison. He flourishes gallant blade to his followers, who skip hurriedly back out of harm's way, laughs wi' carefree confidence as he pops a Sea-Legs pill 'twixt eager lips, and claps Blood on the shoulder – possibly out of comradeship, but more probably to make sure he doesn't sneak off at the crucial moment.

For now they're rocketing in on the last lap, *Frantic Frog* and *Laughing Sandbag* to launch their crews in surprise assault on the castle, d'ye see, while the *Plymouth Corporation's revenge*, a floating bomb with a skeleton crew, will add to the general gaiety by exploding amongst the close-packed galleons. A mighty hazard, says you, they want their heads examined – which they undoubtedly did, just like Piet Hein and Pierre Le Grand, and Howard and Drake with their improbable fireships at Gravelines, and Morgan with his crazy stratagem at Maracaibo, and all those other mad adventurers who apparently couldn't count, and whose ghostly outnumbered men-of-war and caravels and longships hung like wraiths on the heels of the buccaneers gliding in towards Octopus Rock . . .

" 'Oo can it bee?" cried Meliflua, window-hanging breathlessly as the chain creaked and swung with the approach of the mysterious climber. "A boorglar? A hyooman fly? Ah, Vanitee – per'aps eet's some gallant offeecer from the galleons 'oo 'as seen yoo from afar, and ees climbeeng mad weeth love for yoo – an' 'ee weel rescue us een the neeck of tyme!"

"Oh, don't be so soppy, Meliflua!" blushed Vanity. " 'Tis far more like to be someone who's been gated, sneaking in after breaking bounds. I mean, who could fall in love from that distance – he couldn't even see me!"

" 'Ee coold, I say!" stamped Meliflua. "Weeth a telescopp, eezy!"

Their speculations were interrupted by a thunderous din as of eleven zinc baths toppling in the corridor without, followed by a metallic pinging not unlike a pin-table – noises which the terrified girls instantly diagnosed as a Viceroy in full ceremonial armour tripping over a pile of drugged guards, his false teeth flying out and rebounding from stone walls. With a shriek of alarm Enchillada dived beneath the bed, and Vanity sped to the door and shot the bolts home only an instant before some massive object (Don Lardo's skull, in fact) crashed against the panels. The great door creaked and shuddered as he beat on it with steel gauntlets. (In case you're wondering why Don Lardo should be armed cap-a-pie for a wedding rehearsal, it was because his family always got married in full martial panoply, a quaint custom dating back to the Crusades, when Starko Baluna, first of the line, lost his spanners at the Siege of Acre . . . but it's rather a long story, and the fact is we want Lardo in armour for this scene anyway.)

"I know they're in there!" he bellowed. "Enchillada, you maggot, what have you done with my betrothed! Is this your idea of a stag-night practical joke? I know your zany sense of humour, you mad barrel of fun, you! Well, I'm not a bit angry," he screamed, tearing great lumps of wood from the door, "and if you open up we'll say no more about it – at least, you won't, because I'm going to nail your tongue to the back of your head!" The door shuddered on its hinges, and the helpless girls did another panic-stricken cling.

"What can wee doo?" moaned Meliflua. "Hey – coold we take Enchillada 'ostage, an' threaten too cott 'ees throat unless they promise us transport to Panama?"

"That'll send Lardo scurrying!" cried Vanity sarcastically. "Ah – they are taking axes to the door! Quickly, Onions – to the chain, outside the window! If someone can climb up, perchance we may clamber down! 'Tis perilous chance, but our only hope—"

A dreadful throaty chuckle cut her short. "Feel free – the chain's empty at the moment. After you, ladies!" And with a mocking gesture of invitation Black Sheba slipped over the sill, rapier in hand. Meliflua clutched flawless brow, but Vanity was equal to this new crisis, and made an instinctive grab for the one remaining pot of Helena Rubinstein on the dressing-table. Sheba snarled, and flung her sword wi' diabolical nicety, pinning the English girl's sleeve to the timber.

"Hands off, honky!" Sheba bounded to the table, jerked free her rapier, and with a malicious chuckle tossed the precious goo-pot through the window. Vanity wailed with dismay.

"Oh, spiteful – 'twas the last o' discontinued line!"

"Who needs it?" Sheba thrust out her lovely ebony chin. "Two weeks I rotted in yon foul cage – yet mark my complexion its creamy softness, its warm glow o' vibrant tissue! Saw ye ever such satin perfection, ha?"

Vanity marked, in wonder. "Why, 'tis true! Nay, but to what . . . ?"

"To what but Dame Nature's own abundant oils and vitamins!" crowed the sea-queen. "Mashed banana, sparingly applied twice daily, and laved clean wi' pure rain-water – so a pox on their apothecary gunge! Aye, and not for facial beauty alone!" She pirouetted, gleaming nudely. "How's that for all-over skin tone?"

"Terrific! . . . but, Dark Medusa, we are beset! Don Lardo rages without, intent upon our shame! Aid us, for pity's sake!"

"Good luck to him!" mocked Sheba, rummaging for clothes in the wardrobe. "He can have you and welcome – and yon green-sick Spanish pansy, too! 'Twill be his last fling afore the Brotherhood lowers the boom on him!" She was whipping on shirt and breeches o' familiar scarlet, chuckling wickedly as she drew on her long boots. "Take comfort from that, dainty Vanity – thy ravishment shall be speedily avenged!" She sped to the mirror and tried on a picture hat wi' a green plume, adjusting it doubtfully.

"Captivitee 'as driv' 'er mad!" cried Meliflua. "Black fool, 'oo ees goeeng to doo any avengeeng once that door ees down? Enchillada, under thee bed, maybee?"

"Lardo'll give you the works as well as us!" urged Vanity. "And that colour combination stinks, incidentally."

"Ha?" Sheba glared at the mirror. "What's wrong wi' green?"

"Clashes like maracas – if you can't match the red, forget it. Right, Meliflua? Ah, see where the door splinters!"

Sheba, with an oath, tried a yellow plume, biting her lip. "Nay, 'twill have to do!" She snatched up her rapier and leaped cat-like towards the door. "Get a blade, fool, if ye would save your milky hide – from the rack yonder! Canst use a tuck, ha?"

"Oh, gosh, sorry – didn't take fencing at school. Haven't got a hockey stick, have you?"

"Jesu! And ye think yourself fit mate for Long Ben Avery! The chest, then – pistols and shot! Haste, wheyface – if we can hold them off, the Brotherhood shall be here anon – I've had their sea-drums in my ears this hour past, I tell you! Speed!"

Little though she had expected to find herself embroiled in such boudoir battle, Sheba was raring to go; she whirled a satin hanging round her left arm, and as an axe-head bashed a great hole in the upper door and Lardo's frightful clock appeared, agrin wi' bestial fury, the dusky wild-cat yelled with glee and thrust like striking snake, ploughing a great gash in his cheek; howling, the Viceroy recoiled, but a rush of his followers beat down half the door, and furious clang o' blades followed as Sheba held them in that narrow space, thrusting, leaping, taunting, and doing some neat matador work with her satin shield. Vanity scrambled for the pistols, and presently the chamber was a-reek wi' powder smoke and booming with discharge as she blew holes in the floor, ceiling, and dressing-table mirror, while Meliflua lent valiant support by climbing on a chair to spot targets and shout out the ranges and elevations to the blonde pistoleer.

"Take 'em alive!" hollered Lardo from the back of the

press, dashing gore from his face with his steel gauntlet. "Yuggh! Blood! *My* blood! God, if she's ruined my looks I'll roast her alive! On, on, you scum – bring out my bride unscathed and you can have a gang-bang with the other two! Down with them, sort them out, or we'll never get this wedding rehearsal under way! Laggards! Cowards! Have at them – they're only a pack of frustrated feminists!"

His men flung themselves reluctantly into the half-blocked doorway, to meet the triple threat of Sheba's dazzling point, Vanity's artillery (she was getting the range now, and several shots hit the wall within yards of the doorway, one even grazing the lintel), and the hail of missiles which Meliflua, screaming with rage, was hurling from the dressing-table. Skilled from infancy in hitting a running Hattie McDaniel with anything from wooden blocks to Dinky toys, the fiery hidalga rained scent-bottles, brushes, and make-up jars on her countrymen with devastating effect; shrieks of the stricken mingled with cries for stretcher-bearers and impassioned peace slogans as the threshold became a shambles of blood, hand-cream, and Chanel No 5.

But it couldn't have lasted. Sheba's steel strength, weakened by a fortnight on bananas (whate'er their cosmetic properties, they just don't provide the roughage) was flagging; panting magnificently, she lunged to bury her point in a Spanish torso, felt the blade snap, and fell back wi' a defiant sob and a sword four inches long; Vanity, startled off her aim, shot an opponent plumb between the eyes; Meliflua was reduced to hurling the Mr Universe calendar. It was the end! Beauteous but beaten, our indomitable trio had had it; with howls of gloat the brutal soldiery, urged on by the unspeakable Lardo, gathered themselves for the final rush . . . heavens, can nothing save them? Of course it can – listen! Aye, in that fatal moment of defeat and despair, they heard it, borne from afar through the night air on wings of hope and triumph – the gathering rumble of the Warner Brothers' fanfare, and on its heels the stirring double flourish of the Korngold trumpet: woooomph-tara-tee, tan-tara, tan-tee-tan-tan-tarraaah! followed by the thunder of broadsides as the *Frantic Frog* and *Laughing Sandbag*, heeling out of the sea-mist, poured their storm of shot and flame into the harbour fort and the sea-gate of the castle itself. The tower shook to the fury of the cannonade, twice and thrice repeated, and as it died echoing away came a sound even more terrible, as of hordes of desperate, cutlass-waving ruffians swinging recklessly to and fro in the rigging, pouring wildly in and out of hatches, leaping from the bulwarks, screaming with shock as they landed in shallow water, and finally storming up the beaches yelling that dreaded buccaneer war-cry wherewi' Spanish mothers were wont to fright their babes: "You go ahead, Jack, I'll beach the boat!"

The Spanish garrison were taken completely unawares. They always are; it's part of their training. They responded perfectly; while the officers leaped from their chairs, overturning their wine-cups, the men gaped blearily, a sergeant in a morion ran about shouting "Andalusian rhubarb!," and a small drummer began an impersonation of Buddy Rich in ill-fitting tights. In seconds, stairs and doorways were jammed with men in helmets carrying pikes, while a file of arquebusiers knelt down in agitation and opened fire at a blank wall.

Into this brilliantly-choreographed chaos the buccaneers swept like a tidal wave – and guess who was at their head, in white shirt and ruffles, lithely skewering everything in his path, pausing only to point wi' muscular forearm and cry: "On, on, my lads! Feet-feet-feet, School – now let it out!" before bounding sideways on to an outside staircase to trip a couple of sword-waving idiots coming down, pink a third (who gets to do a slow artistic death-roll into the courtyard), pause for a grimly smiling profile shot in shadow, and then plough upstairs in search of Vanity.

Down at the sea-gate Bilbo was in equally spectacular form, making kebabs of three foemen in quick succession, and fleering elegantly while performing the showy trick of taking snuff and discharging a pistol with one hand simultaneously – the least lapse of concentration and his opponent would have been struck by a pinch of Best Rapparee while Bilbo got a pistol ball up his nose, but the filibuster captain managed things to perfection; the Don went down, Bilbo fluttered kerchief to nostril, Goliath squealed admiringly "Four in a row, boo-boom!" and the men of the *Laughing Sandbag* o'erwhelmed the gate in celebration. At the same moment the harbour fort succumbed to an excited flood of pirates in striped jerseys and red pom-poms yelling "Vive la différence!", and headed by the gallooned and prancing figure of Happy Dan Pew – a restful sea voyage and course of strongly-voiced consonants had restored him to comparative sanity. His nasalised vowels and sweeping épée drove the Spaniards like sheep, he prattled with fluent confidence of prefixed verbs and mesures thermométriques, and when he slashed down the Spanish flag with an exultant cry of: "I have reason, me!" his Gallic followers wept for joy, and only the more cautious spirits felt he was tempting providence.

Down in the harbour itself was sheer panic. The crews of the galleons lined the rails pointing and holding on to the shrouds in disorganised fashion, while their superiors stood open-mouthed on their poops, fists on hips, crying "Caramba!" "Valencia!" and "Granada!" in well-bred amazement. And as trumpets blared and orders were shouted, none marked the black shape o' the *Plymouth Corporation's Revenge* gliding into their midst like very shadow o' doom – until all its lights went on at once, and it hove to, blazing like Blackpool front, while its skeleton crew leaned over the side sounding rattles, deflating poo-poo cushions, waggling their fingers beside their ears, and waving intimate garments at the Spanish ships. Firebeard was conspicuous with his exploding whiskers and lewd gestures.

"Har-har, Dagoes!" he bellowed. "King Philip's a fairy,

d'ye see? Notts Forest one, Real Madrid nil, belike! Latins are lousy lovers, wi' a curse! Har-har!"

Enraged, the Spanish captains instantly ordered their ships to close on the insolent intruder, and in a trice half the squadron was close-packed round the pirate ship, while the skeleton crew were nipping smartly down to a jolly-boat 'neath the stern, Firebrand landing head-first (wi' a wannion), and as the unsuspecting Dons flooded aboard, the jolly-boat scooted for safety as hard as it could row, with Calico Jack at the tiller.

High on a stone staircase in the castle, Avery was disposing of a platoon of sword-waggling opponents when he heard the cataclysmic boom of the *Plymouth Corporation's Revenge*'s explosion. Pausing in his parry of five simultaneous thrusts, he had time for a hearty chuckle ere swinging to safety via a conveniently-hanging curtain; with a flick of his wrist he thrust a chest of drawers down the steps, sweeping his enemies away in confusion, and hastened to an embrasure from which he could look down on the panorama of courtyard and harbour, and tot up the score.

Despite the good write-up we've been giving the buccaneers so far, it wasn't a totally satisfactory picture that met the captain's clear, grey-eyed gaze. True, the harbour was a roaring sea of flame, with half the galleons burning in a veritable holocaust of special effects, but the other half were making tracks for the harbour entrance in good order, and blasting holes in the *Laughing Sandbag* and *Frantic Frog*, which the pirates had carelessly left untenanted when they stormed ashore. Making a mental note to have someone on a fizzer for that dereliction of duty, our hero switched focus to the land-battle, and his knuckles beat faster and his ruffles rose in alarm as he saw that the buccaneer attack was running out of steam. (Here, that's bad.)

To the untrained eye it was the usual torch-lit mêlée of bodies heaving lethargically to and fro, but Avery could read the tell-tale signs – Spaniards were falling screaming from the walls at far below the standard rate, no pile of surrendered weapons was visible, the music was nowhere like reaching a triumphant climax, cries of "Quarter!" were just as frequent in English as in Spanish, and – his lips tightened in anger – several knots of pirates had fallen out for a quick smoke and, in one sheltered corner, a surreptitious brew-up. Wi' muttered exclamation he was about to rush down and turn the tide single-handed, when his marrow froze and his hair congealed as from somewhere overhead there echoed the shrill wail of a woman – whether in agony, danger, disappointment, or screaming tantrum he could not tell . . .

It's always difficult, with battle finales, to keep tabs on all the principals, and while the lads have been doing their thing we have lost track of events at the top of the tower, where we left les girls on the point of capture by Don Lardo's crew. The Spaniards were about to barge in, you recall, when the pirate onslaught froze the scene – then it all happened. Sheba leaped to the panelling, pressed a button, and vanished into a secret passage with a sharp click, Meliflua swooned and was dragged out to the cruel embrace o' beastly Lardo, Vanity screamed, and Enchillada (who'd learned a thing or two in his career as a court functionary) shot from beneath the bed like a flying profiterole, and with a squeal of "Too thee bathroom!" pointed the way to sanctuary for our heroine. Vanity got inside just in time to see him vanish behind the shower curtain; then she had slammed the door in the Spaniards' faces, the 'Engaged' sign shot up, and with all hell breaking loose outside the Viceroy ordered his men downstairs to lend the garrison a hand.

Fine – that's Vanity out of harm's way, and the stage is set for Lardo and Avery to run into each other somewhere on a lonely stairway or in a great shadowy torch-lit hall, exchange long, slow, burning looks – revoltingly contorted and deep-breathing hatred on one side, steely-eyed and grim-smiling resolution on t'other – bandy remarks like "So, English dog – you'll yap defiance at the finest swordsman in Spain, will you?" and "All right, Lardo, we'll see if your blade's as nimble as your tongue – I've no doubt it's cleaner," slash a few candles in half, and get down to business.

Sorry, that's not what happened. Avery, hearing that piercing shriek (Meliflua coming up for air, actually), was making for the stairs like a frenzied whippet, but got caught up not with Lardo but with a spare bunch of guards – the ones who are forever emerging at the double from archways and passages with shouts of "Ha! Jumble!" whenever the hero is operating solo in the enemy HQ and needs some time to himself. So it was back downstairs again for our Ben, wi' thrust and parry and flying furniture, while Lardo, wi' his limp and lovely burden . . .

He wasn't the best swordsman in Spain, or even in Madrid W1; huge, ugly, disgustingly strong, yes, but strictly Fourth Division when it came to stamp and slash, sa-ha! And he was chicken, too; one quick look from a window at the carnage beneath, and he was making for the backstairs, with Meliflua in a fireman's lift, his one object to scuttle out the back way, get aboard his private flagship, the *Santa Umbriago*, which was round the corner in a secluded creek, and make for the tall timber. For aboard the *Santa Umbriago* was all his loot, including the multi-millions of Pew's treasure in used gold coins – that fabulous hoard which Blood had betrayed, ye'll mind.

And speaking of Blood, you haven't noticed him laying on i' the thick o' the fight, have you? Not we, says you, blinking – where on earth . . . ? Even so, says I, step this way . . .

Deep in the gloomy bowels o' Octopus Rock, where walls dripped and all manner o' uggle lay underfoot, two figures stole through the odorous dark of the watercress dungeon, and paused in indecision where dim-lit passages converged. Hark 'ee . . .

"Come on, ye ould idiot – ye were down here long enough to grow fins, so ye must know the way up! Take a cast about, rot ye, an' if ye land me in another tub o' mushroom dung I'll lose me temper, so I will!"

"Oidle-de-dang-doo! Thataway, ha? . . . nay, p'raps not . . . or by yarnder stair, eh? Ar, mizzle it! ole Sol be confazzled, maister, d'ye see? 'Tis shortage o' drippin' – ar, sweet, nourishin' drippin' – as do blunt the senses keen, so it do . . . So whither, ha . . . ? Let's lay aloft on this tack, wi' a baddle-de-bop . . ."

Blood and Shafto, by the powers! What should this portend? Easy. Blood, misliking hard knocks, yet eager to show well wi' Vanity in the last act, had sloped off like the skunk he was when the pirates first landed, and with Shafto as guide had entered by the familiar postern. For Shafto, ye mind, knows where our heroine is confined, and for promise o' rich reward he has engaged to conduct knavish Tom thither, Blood's reasoning being that if he's the first Marine to land, the Admiral's daughter may yet be his. Devious type, isn't he? So up they steal, past echoing empty cells, on those fatal backstairs – and we know who's on his villainous way down, don't we . . . ?

They met with mutual yells of alarm – the hideous Viceroy had retained two trusted thugs as bodyguards, but Blood and Shafto had no time to reckon odds, let alone flee. It was swords out and get stuck in, Blood's rapier and Solomon's gardening implements 'gainst the three Spanish broadswords, while Meliflua assumed the classic pose for spectating heroines, one hand clasped to muslin brow while the other plucked her marble fichu.

Brawl right murderous ensued, for Lardo, armoured and berserk wi' panic, was lethal as a rogue steam-roller, bawling and clanging as he unleashed savage swipes which would have cloven our twain in two (or vice versa) had they been less nippy. Blood, parrying desperately, was beaten back by sheer weight, and as Lardo closed with him a thug let drive at the Colonel's undefended flank – but swish-thunk! came a high-heeled stiletto, flung wi' unerring aim (well done,

Meliflua!) to pierce the rascal's sword-arm. As Blood broke free, Solomon's secateurs found a gap in the second thug's guard, Blood completed the good work wi' punta rinverso olé! and a hack on the shins, and Lardo, the yellow hound, pausing only to scoop up case containing credit cards and traveller's cheques, snatched Meliflua under one huge arm and legged it incontinently, with the Irish adventurer and the ragged galoot in hot pursuit.

Lardo boobed. Fleeing regardless, he was making for the front of the castle, and his mad rush carried him out on to a balcony overlooking the flaming harbour; trapped, he turned at bay, his nightmare features glaring horribly, and as rapier and secateurs drove in for the kill, the craven Viceroy sank to the pits of caddish behaviour. His steel fingers closed on his lovely hostage's slender throat, and his dentures gnashed in fiendish threat.

"Back! Back, I say – or the frail gets hers! Another step, and bye-bye vertebrae!"

"Uulngh!" gasped Meliflua piteously. "Hoidle a-gling!" cried compassionate Shafto. "Pack it in, Lardo, and I'll try to get ye off wi' 99 years!" shouted Blood, white-lipped, but the Viceroy gibbered wi' mad laughter, and his free hand sought the great rusty chain which hung hard by the balcony down the sheer castle wall to Sheba's cage far beneath. One step and his foot was on the iron links.

"Stay me at your peril!" he snarled. "Once aboard the chain I'm immune as I scramble down to safety – for if I fall she falls with me, to manglish death! Ha-ha-ha, I've scored again! Pass me that case of traveller's cheques, Irish lout, and then turn to the wall and count a hundred! And no peeking!"

Tense as an E-string, Blood edged forward, took the case on his sword-point, and cautiously extended it. Straddled 'twixt balcony and chain, but hampered by Meliflua as they hung o'er the dizzy drop, Lardo opened mailed hand to receive it – and with a mad yell of "Froodle-me-zip!" Solomon suddenly flung his deadly watering-can. Straight as an arrow it sped, clanging resoundingly on the back of Blood's head – he reeled, the case fell, Lardo grabbed at it, Meliflua slipped from his grasp and landed, decoratively asprawl, on the balcony coping, Blood lunged and seized her, the Viceroy swung out and away on the chain, howling with rage, the tiny rivets on his steel gauntlets popped free under the strain of clutching the rusty links – plink-plink-plink-plink! – the metal glove came apart, and with a hideous scream the massive armoured figure fell, turning over and over, growing smaller and smaller as it plunged down at 32 feet per second per second into the gloomy depths. They waited breathless, Meliflua swooning in Blood's arms, Solomon chewing his beard and counting, until from far below came the ultimate almighty clang and splat! Fearfully they peered down and beheld the octopus pool a-churn wi' horror, and thereafter the tentacled denizens scrambling out with octopodal noises of disgust, and slithering hastily across the rocks seaward. But of infamous Lardo naught remained, save shattered dentures on the pool's rim.

Ye may think, belike, that with Meliflua snuggling up to Blood a new romantic attachment is imminent – after all, he's plucked her from grisly fate, and she's unattached. Sorry again – Blood isn't privy to her old man's bank balance, and anyway she's too young for him. Disposing her decently on a convenient couch, Tom is hot-foot upstairs again to find Vanity, while Solomon clambers nimbly down the chain to retrieve his fallen watering-can, which had ricochetted from the Colonel's skull into the void.

But what's happening down below, anyway? Faith, but we're in desperate case, for the sheer weight of numbers of the damned Dons is like to turn the scale, d'ye see? The buccaneer detachments, their first fury spent, are barely holding their own against vasty odds as the battle rages across the great courtyard and round the sea-gate; the Spaniards, heartened by the rumour that their leader, Don Lardo, has met a timely end, have got their heads down in a really splendid shove, and the pirate pack is like to be heaved off its feet, look'ee – ah, them breaks in training, they crafty smokes when all was going well, we'm paying for them now as the Dons wheel and take in an inspired foot-rush, and the tide of battle rolls inch by inch towards the great sea-gate with its looming portcullis, fit scene for desperate last stand by the ragged rabble as the Dons press in on them, wi' a curse. But they're going game.

Black Bilbo, his shoddy finery cut to ribbons, his boots pinching like bedamned, fights like a lean fury in the front rank; beside him capers Happy Dan, plying lively blade and hissing his vowels through clenched nostrils, with no trace of diphthongisation; Goliath, his leg in splinters, lies gnashing tiny teeth and biting every Spanish ankle in sight; Firebeard, up from the harbour, his beard a charred wreck, plunges into the mêlée roaring and reeking; Calico Jack spits again on his horny hand and swings ponderous cutlass; Solomon Shafto, his secateurs snapped off short, lays on with watering-can and pruning-knife – and still they give slow ground, the battered remnant of the once-mighty Brotherhood, their backs to the sea where the unscathed Spanish galleons are wheeling leisurely towards shore, preparing to rake the retreating enemy with grape and so make an end. Let's face it, the buccaneers are right in it, up to here.

Nay – but this can't be! says you. What, wi' vile Lardo slain, Vanity and Meliflua preserved miraculous, Sheba taking care of herself somewhere, and the lads but a moment since within an ace o' glorious victory – it cannot go sour at the last, ha? Can it not, says I? We warned you from the first, remember, that this was no ordinary tale; happy endings are well enough for the last pages of romance, or the closing reel of spectaculars . . . but this is not Hollywood. This is Octopus Rock.

Even Avery frowned in vexation as he dropped from an embrasure on to the sea-gate wall. He had disposed of those inconvenient guards upstairs, and now sped nimbly along the wall, dusting off stray Spaniards, launched himself at a torch-sconce, and with a series of trapezish swings, dropped into the midst of the buccaneer force as it beat its fighting retreat in a choking haze of powder-smoke and recriminations. Heedless of the din of battle, the crash of shots and clash of steel, the gloating yells of the Spaniards and the appalling language of the pirates, he demanded situation reports from his commanders. He got them.

"We'm beset, d'ye see!" bellowed Firebeard. "Took fore an' aft, burn, rot, and sink them sneakin' Dons! I despise 'em! They ain't even honest men, dammem!"

"C'est un fact, morbleu!" chortled Happy Dan, executing a neat pas seul and unseaming a passing Spaniard. "Mais que voulez-vous? C'est la vie! Ha, what do I say, me? Ce n'est pas la vie at all . . . c'est le mort!"

"And no gainsaying!" growled Calico Jack, his fine white threads begrimed with powder-reek. "We ha' bit off the inch too much this v'yage, Long Ben, and there's an end to't."

"So shall ye have your way at last, King's man!" jeered Bilbo, leaning panting on his black rapier. "An end to the Brotherhood – well, ye ha' led us to it! Die all, die merrily!"

"Absolute rot!" cried the undaunted Avery. "Why, we haven't even started – so what I want to see is a good deal more effort and less of this defeatist croaking! Why, all we've got to do is knock the stuffing out of these blighters – or even half of them, and the rest will pack in, you'll see! Vive la France, Happy Dan! Give 'em the message, Firebeard! Goliath, you're doing extremely well – carry on gnashing! All right, Shafto, settle down! The rest of you, get stuck in, and hip-hip-hurrah!" But as the buccaneers roared their derision and fought tooth and nail with their onrushing foes, our hero's jaw tightened with an audible creak, for he could count as well as the next man, and unless he was mistaken, the end was near.

"Bilbo," he said quietly, "just for the record – you're the best swordsman I've ever seen."

"Indeed, cully," drawled exhausted Bilbo, "I verily believe I am. For, see thou – I have never met my master." And he grinned his most vulpine grin, and nodded to Avery. "Only my match."

And with that he laughed and plunged into the fight, his black blade darting, and was lost to sight.

"Rackham," said our hero, his sturdy chin a-quiver with manly apology, "I may have goofed after all. Sorry about the pardons."

The big man nodded, with an odd, slow smile. "An we never claim 'em, camarado," quo' he, "yet shall we have our quittance here, one way or t'other."

And that, as the tide of battle surged around the sea-gate, should have been it . . . but of course it wasn't. For as someone protested a couple of minutes ago, we haven't come four hundred pages, near as dammit, to have everything fall apart in the last chapter – nay, there's card to play yet, and here it comes, for even as we glance fearfully seaward, to watch the Spanish galleons standing in, ports up, guns out, stately grandees pacing the poop, linstocks smoking as their gunners prepare to sweep us all to blazes wi' langrel and canister, we're all took aback to see that there's summat amiss wi' the Dons, ha! They veer, they yaw, their sails buckle, they bump into each other in confusion, some of them are even caught in stays – and ashore, too, their troops give ground, gesticulating in dismay and starting to run in circles, while from the beleaguered buccaneers goes up a great ringing cheer, head-scarves are flung into the air, timbers are shivered, out come the baccy and rum-flasks, Solomon Shafto dances above the sea-gate, skinny finger outflung to seaward . . . and Calico Jack stares long and hard, bright-eyed, before taking chin in hand and beckoning Bilbo and Firebeard aside . . .

For yonder, coming up with the sunrise, the Union Flag a-flutter in the dawn breeze and the strains of 'Rule, Britannia' sounding soft and steady across the track of the morning, a great double column of stately men-o'-war is ploughing over the sunlit sea, and from the erratic course they're steering it can only be Admiral Lord Rooke and his fleet, arriving in the nick of time – aye, he got the show on the road after all, the stout old salt, and well pleased is he as he stumps his quarter-deck, scratches his grizzled head, and congratulates his sailing-master, Cap'n Yardley, on having navigated them so skilfully to Port Royal. It isn't quite the Jamaica coastline as he remembers it, but of course memory plays strange tricks . . . h'm, seems to be a fire in the harbour, and a fair bit of Spanish shipping about. Odd, that.

"Firing salutes, too," he remarked approvingly, as smoke billowed from the guns of the nearest galleon. "Well, that's courteous. Damned careless, though," he added, as a red-hot shot ploughed a smoking furrow in the deck and blew the stern-rail to pieces. "You there, sir, Don Whatever-the-hell-your-name-is!" he bellowed at the approaching Spanish ships, "don't ye know to take the goolies *out* o' the guns afore ye exchange compliments? We might ha' taken a mischief—"

His protest was lost in a crashing broadside which battered his flagship from stem to stern. The Spaniards, recovering from their momentary confusion at the sight of the British fleet, had seen that a quick, sneaky Castilian strike was imperative, and quickly turning their vessels round, were advancing to battle with guns blazing and trumpets sounding, silver sails a-gleam, red and gold banners streaming, and their commanders hurriedly quaffing last-minute cups of Malaga and wiping their moustachios. Promptly the British tars sprang to action with cries of "Belike!" and "D'ye see?", urged on by their commanders, and none more stentorian than Admiral Rooke as he blinked at the shambles of his poop, stepped smartly aside to avoid a falling mizzen-mast, and demanded thunderously:

"Damn you, Yardley! Are you *sure* that's Port Royal?"

Equally prompt was the action ashore. As the two mighty fleets met with crashing broadsides and billowing smoke, in which they searched vainly for each other for several hours, the contending parties on Octopus Rock reached an un-spoken truce, each reasoning that there was no point in sweating away fighting when the issue was plainly going to be settled by the warships. So the Spaniards prudently withdrew to the castle, locking the doors and peering uneasily out of windows, while the pirates dug in on the beach with cries of: "Get your heads down! Let the Navy take the strain!" much to the disgust of Captain Avery, who protested furiously that while their countrymen were doing the dirty work, the least the pirates could do was line the water's edge and cheer. No one paid him a blind bit of notice.

And while they are all thus gainfully occupied at Octopus Rock, let us take wing for just a moment, far across the broad Atlantic, and see what was happening on that very day in far-off, peaceful old England, whence we weighed anchor so many pages ago . . .

Master Samuel Pepys sat in his fine office at the Admiralty, massaging his Akeing Hedd and deciding that he didn't feel at all well. Last night had been bad enough; he'd been bored stiff admiring Mr Evelyn's collection of pressed leaves and listening to his ghastly poetry, and then he'd been unwise enough to sit up late with Captain Cocke, "drunk as a dogg", hearing some juicy scandal about Lady Robinson. And this morning, when he felt fit for nothing beyond quietly record-ing those events in his diary, had come this appalling little stranger, bearing Bigge Trouble, the evidence of which was spread on the Secretary's table. He stole another uneasy glance, and shuddered – yes, they were still there: six col-oured sketches of six priceless jewels . . . opal, sapphire, pearl, diamond, emerald, and ruby, each depicted in a gem-encrusted cross of solid gold.

"Whence," croaked Master Pepys unsteadily, "had ye these?"

"Would you believe," asked Vladimir Mackintosh-Groonbaum earnestly, "that them pictures was delivered anonymous at my lodgin's, wi' instructions to bring 'em to yore good self?"

"No," snapped Pepys, "I wouldn't. And let me tell thee, sirrah, whosoever thou art, that if I order thy arrest on suspicion of possessing stolen goods – to wit, the Madagascar crown from which these sketches were made – it shall avail thee naught to tell my Lord Jeffreys it fell off the back of a sedan chair. He's heard that one before—"

"'Aven't we all?" chuckled Vladimir, no whit abashed. "So let's get practical – for I see, Master Secretary, that yore not one to beat abaht. So . . . we ain't bugged 'ere, are we? No coves wi' ear-trumpets at the panellin'? Good, good, can't be too careful. Well, nah . . . 'twixt ourselves, I *might* be able to lay 'ands on the originals – those six pieces o' the Madagascar crahn which was so misfortoonately lost as a result o' Admiralty negligence, but which 'ave now bin recovered thanks to the sterlin' efforts o' my client, Cap'n Benjamin Avery, R.N.—"

"Avery? Sterling fiddlesticks!" yelped Pepys. "Gad's life, he lost the damned thing in the first place!"

"Through no fault of 'is own," countered Vladimir promptly. "Consider the facks. It wasn't Cap'n Avery's bright idea to 'ave this priceless diadem entrusted to a single messenger (albeit a distinguished officer) wivaht proper escort, was it? It wasn't 'is fault that the crew o' the *Twelve Apostles* – a King's ship, mind – included some o' the bloodiest buccaneers that ever wrung salt water aht o' their socks, was it? It wasn't 'is fault the ship was hi-jacked by pirates, was it? An' it wasn't 'is fault the crahn was betrayed by one Colonel T. Blood, who is not only a well-known jool-snitcher but is also –" Vladimir tapped his bulbous nose knowingly "– a former acquaintance of a certain royal personage 'oo is always notoriously short o' cash." Vladimir shook his unkempt head solemnly. "Admiralty negligence, did I say? Some might 'ave another word for it, mightn't they?"

Master Pepys discovered that his Hedd was Akeing worse than ever, and that he was starting to sweat most uncomfortably.

"But fret not," continued Vladimir smoothly. "My client 'as instructed me to restore the jools, as an earnest of 'is unremittin' zeal for 'Is Maj.'s service – which 'e continues to do, incidentally, by riddin' the Western Seas o' the pirate scourge, for which I doubt not 'e shall presently receive rich reward an' fulsome honner from said Maj. 'E's goin' to be front-page stuff," added Vladimir impressively, "my boy is."

Master Pepys fought for speech. "But . . . but why, then, have ye not brought the Madagascar crown itself, 'stead o' these trumpery drawings?"

"Well . . ." Vladimir pursed his lips judiciously. "I 'ad to take precautions, didn't I? An' it did occur to me that you might like the jools returned private-like, wivaht embarrassin' publicity. I mean," he leered confidentially, "we wouldn't want the facks I mentioned jus' now to become common gossip, would we? If they did – well, at best the Admiralty'd get egg all over its face, an' at worst," he sighed anxiously, "there could be an 'ell of a scandal, reflectin' even on yore good self, to say nuffink o' the geezer wiv the long wig an' spaniels. Ow, we *know* it was all jus' bad luck an' coincidence, but malishus tongues bein' wot they are . . . anyways, I thort you might like the jools back confidential, no questions arsked. Worth everyone's while, I should think." He blinked and beamed greasily.

Ha! thought Pepys, blackmail! And this oily little knave was right – it *could* look like some infernally complicated plot, especially with that rascal Blood involved . . . the King's honour . . . Pepys's own reputation . . . He gulped, and glared at Vladimir. "Did Avery put you up to this?"

"Perish forbid!" exclaimed the fink indignantly. "Wot kind o' clients d'you think I got? Between ourselves, 'e wouldn't care for this one bit, decent lad that 'e is, but," he smirked virtuously, "I gotta do my best on 'is be'alf, ain't I?"

Master Pepys ground his teeth. "How much?" he demanded.

"Well, nah . . ." Vladimir settled himself comfortably. "There oughta be a knight'ood, right? An' a Civil List pension . . . say two thahsand a year? An' the deeds to a nice little property . . . oh, somewheres abaht Chelsea, or Richmond. Yerss, that'd be fav'rite . . ."

Master Pepys took a deep breath. "You'll want it in writing, I suppose?" he grated. "Aye, very well."

"Good! Right," said Vladimir contentedly, "that's me taken care of. Nah, for my boy . . ."

His boy, at that moment, was having an incredulous confrontation with Colonel Blood on the beach at Octopus Rock.

"Locked in the *what*?"

"In the bathroom," snapped Blood.

"My sweet Vanity, confined i' Spanish closet?" cried Avery in anguish. "Nay, 'tis fiendish refinement o' cruelty, even for Dagoes! To prison a tender maid in their foul tropic convenience—"

"She wasn't prisoned," said Blood, who seemed to be in a bad temper. "Accordin' to a fat little greaser who was tryin' to crawl up the ventilator shaft, she had took refuge when Lardo an' his gang besieged her bedroom wi' intent to ravish her an' Donna Meliflua – hell of a mess, blood an' setting-lotion all over the shop. Fortunately," he added carelessly, "I was in the vicinity an' dealt wi' Lardo an' his rascals. Och, there were four or five o' them, but ye know my old style – back to the wall, give 'em the old imbroccata, one-two—"

"But Lardo, man? What o' him?"

Blood shrugged. "I just defenestrated him."

Avery went pale, wincing. "Gad, but you're ruthless! Will he recover?"

"From two hundred feet up, are you kidding? He didn't even bounce. But for all the thanks I got," Blood went on bitterly, "I might ha' saved my labour. For what says my Lady Vanity, when I knocked on the privy door wi' the tidings that I had braved all hazards to win to her side, demolishin' Dagoes right and left? Did she even say thank you? Did she hell-as-like! 'Where's my Ben?' were her first words as she issued forth. 'Downstairs', says I, 'givin' his well-known impression o' Louis Hayward, wi' never a thought for your sweet self – but fret not, acushla, I'm here, your faithful Tom to rescue you and lay me heart at your feet.' Did she swoon gratefully on my breast, though? She did not. 'Heavens!' says she, 'he mustn't see me like this, I'll have to change! Oh, look at my hair! And is he well? How's he looking? Ah, but how thoughtful of him to send you ahead, Colonel; so like him, dear considerate Ben!' An' me wi' ensanguined blade and my shirt thrust through in four places! Women!" The Colonel snorted with disgust, and fell to sulky brooding.

Avery's spirits had rocketed at this recital, but now he laid a sympathetic hand on the Colonel's shoulder. "What else did you expect?" he wondered. "Some fellows ha' it, some ha' not. I ha', you ha'nt. That's all there is to it. But she is safe, and awaits me in the castle yonder? Nay, I am afire to hasten to her – and shall presently, once Rooke has got the lead out of his pants and come ashore. What's keeping him?"

For things have been moving while we've been away with Pepys and Vladimir; the great sea-battle between Rooke's squadron and the Dons has run its inevitable course, and if we didn't show it to you in full, well, we have to keep an eye on the budget, and you didn't miss much anyway. The fact is they blazed away all day in blinding smoke, only to find after it had cleared that they had been facing in opposite directions, wasting their shot on empty water. At which point the Spanish admiral had come to his senses, realising that since he didn't outnumber the British fifty-three to one he was in a position of historical futility, with nothing for it but to strike his colours, his forehead, and his subordinates before surrendering wi' courtly foreign grace to a bewildered Lord Rooke, whose annoyance at being hundreds of miles off course vanished when he discovered how opportune had been his accidental arrival at Octopus Rock.

The Dons' capitulation had been the signal for a corresponding armistice ashore, where the Spanish garrison had mooched out sullenly from the castle with rather grubby white flags; Avery had received their surrender and set them to tidying up under the buccaneers' direction while he hastened down to the beach to welcome Rooke ashore in the big reunion scene. This was somewhat delayed, since his lordship was still in a state of confusion after his unlooked-for victory, with his great cabin full of bowing grandees offering him their swords and demanding separate berths as prisoners of war, and Cap'n Yardley at his elbow protesting that it wasn't his fault they'd strayed off course, it was these blasted Admiralty charts, d'ye see, and he'd always said they should never ha' gone metric . . .

Meanwhile Captain Avery, all eagerness to report to his superior, waits on the beach, where we have just seen Blood bringing him up-to-date on events in the castle – for it's been such a busy day, what with sea-battles to watch and surrenders to receive, that conscientious Ben hasn't had a minute, not even to seek out his lady fair. Now, reassured that she is in good shape, he is feeling pretty bobbish, unlike Blood, who is cheesed off to yonder. They stand side by side in the gathering tropic dusk, looking out across the dark waters towards the British and Spanish ships still sorting themselves out after their battle, wrapping up their sails and trying to find their anchors; over in the harbour the exploded Spanish ships have burned themselves out, the captured garrison have been locked up for the night with their tacos and tortillas in the castle out-buildings, and the weary buccaneers appear to be settling down at a respectful distance to a little light rum and music round their camp-fires. The soft strains of a chanty drift on the warm evening air, the moon is rising like a silver ghost – and suddenly we realise that this is the finale coming up, for 'tis all over, look'ee! Aye, virtue has triumphed at last, villainy has been given the heave, Rooke will be falling headlong ashore any minute full of bonhomie and congratulations, the pirates will get their pardons for services rendered, and e'en now Vanity in the castle is putting the last touches to her make-up for the moment when she and handsome Ben will hasten to each other's arms in slow motion to a thunderous crescendo of violins. And that'll be it.

No wonder Avery wears an expression of smug nobility, a pleased smile touching his chiselled lips, hand elegantly rested on placid rapier-hilt; even his ruffles stir complacently in the night breeze.

"I tell thee what, Colonel," he observes contentedly, "I'm feeling not bad. Who says all doth not come up roses? Here's mission accomplished, duty done, honour restored, sweet Vanity to be claimed presently, young Meliflua delivered, Lardo clobbered (pity I didn't fix his waggon personally, but you seem to have done a competent job), Spanish devilry foiled, our settlements saved, the Coast Brethren under wraps, and a golden future ahead. I wish I knew where that blighter Mackintosh-Groonbaum has got to," he added, frowning. Little does he guess. "But that's a trifle, and shall not mar my merited satisfaction."

"Hip-hoo-bloody-ray," grunted moody Tom. "Fine for some – what's in it for me, after all I've been through, eh? Who saved Meliflua, slipped it to Lardo, and looked after your hoity-toity piece, will ye tell me? But you finish up wi' the girl, the credit – an' the profit, devil a doubt! Great! Congratulations!"

"Little beef hast thou!" retorted Avery warmly. "After the way you've carried on – renegading, chickening out, betraying, making passes, and generally behaving like rascal stinkard. All right, ye ha' done some service – reluctantly – but let me point out that as anti-hero you ought by rights to be stiff and stark at this stage of the story—"

"Burn your impudence!" cried indignant Tom. "Who says so?"

"You know perfectly well," said Avery coldly, "that you should ha' perished in the final assault, making proper amends for sundry villainies. Struck down by a chance shot, say, or stabbed in the back by someone like Sheba in a fit of passion – by the way, I haven't seen her since we landed, have you?"

"No, an' it can stay that way!"

"Odd, that," frowned Avery. "I'd have thought she and the other pirate rogues would have been sidling up by now, knuckling their foreheads and reminding me about their pardons. However . . . yes, Blood, by all the canons you should have bought your deserved lot, and died in my arms, making repentance in tones right piteous, smiling last rueful smile and begging me to take the news to your dear old mother in Wicklow—"

"Galway, rot ye!"

"Naturally, I'd have forgiven you, and said I could ha' spared a better man – although I can't think of one offhand – and doubtless ere Vanity and I walked off into the sunset she'd have been soft enough to drop something on your grave – a glove, an old hair-grip, a tear, even. As it is," said Avery censoriously, "since you hadn't the decency to die in character, here you are, all in one inconvenient piece, and we'll just have to make the best of it, I suppose—"

"Right, that did it!" roared Blood, and yanked out his sword in a fury. "I've just about had it up to here wi' you, Captain Benjamin Smartass – aye, wi' you and your six foot two of nose-in-the-air park-saunterin' blow-waved ruffle-shirted public-school poncin' airs an' graces! I should ha' blitzed you on the *Twelve Apostles* or on Dead Man's Chest when I was sentimental mug enough to take pity on your

Dartmouth College ignorance, so I was! So I should ha' died, eh? Right, me bucko, here's your chance! Pluck out your iron!"

"Frenzy," snapped Avery. "Rhodomontade. Middle-aged spread."

"Oh, I'll give you middle age – permanent! On guard, ye great long streak o' wind an' water!" He flourished furiously.

"Oh, calm down! And be careful with that thing—"

"Nervous, are ye? Here's the cure, then! Draw, ye gallery-playin' jackanapes – or d'ye need a female audience to show off to? Is that it?" sneered the raging Colonel.

"Show off?" cried Avery, stung. "Nay, now you've gone too far! On your head be it, then!" And he whipped out his rapier, meeting Blood's lunge. The blades clanged – is this where Blood finishes up à la Rathbone, you ask, with the surf washing through his curls? Not a bit – a few passes and Avery had jumped back, lowering his point in angry disdain.

"Oh, pack it up!" quo' he. "This is just too silly for words. I can't fight you . . . not after . . . not at this stage of the game . . ."

"Oho!" crowed Blood. "An' why not, ha? Pangs o' conscience, is that it? Because ye know ye'd never ha' got this far wi'out me? Hey?"

"Nothing of the sort! It's just that . . . well, for one thing, suppose there was a sequel, you'd have to be in it, wouldn't you? And what the blazes do *you* want – can't you see we're busy?"

This last was addressed to a small fat figure in prisoner-of-war garb who had come scampering down the beach, and was now cringing obsequiously at Avery's elbow. It was Enchillada, doing a Uriah Heep. Avery glared sternly.

"You're Spanish – why aren't you in prison?", he demanded, and the oily chamberlain fawned nervously.

"Pliz, excellent 'ereteec señor! I got parole, honest! Thee beeg pirate in thee white threads, 'e geev me thees –' he held out a sealed note "– an' say I mus' breeng eet to you, at moonrise, not beefore." As Avery took the paper, puzzled, Enchillada scuttled away, and Blood, curiosity getting the better of his recent anger, came forward for a peek.

"From Rackham?" frowned Avery. "Nay, what should this be?"

"Probably a loyal address to the hero o' the hour," said Blood sarcastically. "Or a whip-round to send Firebeard to university. What's it say?"

Avery broke the seal, turned the paper to the moonlight, and read aloud the following:

To Cap. Ben Everie, R.N., wi' all despatch.
Honnered Sir (and Camarado).

Wee want noe Pardones, nor ever dyd. Wee sayled wi' you for oure owne purposes onlie – viz., that in takyng Octipusse Roacke and o'erthrowing the Dons, soe we myght cum to possession of Lardo his Greate Treasure, the whych was Pyrate Monies i' the first place, soe are wee entytled.

Thynke itt not amiss that wee looke to oure owne Profitt and trust nott to th'Admiral's bounty to rewarde us fyttyngly. Heard ye ever o' Ben Gunn, that was wi' Flint and John Silver and Billie Boanes and Hands and Merry and others o' the pyrate brig Walrus, that buried a greate bootie on a Certaine Island? Whereto in later yeeres came sundrie Gentlefolk, and digged upp the bootie, whych was nott theirs, surelie. Yett they enjoyed itt, and hadde rich use of itt, whiles Silver and his felloes (that had beene at the Paines of earning itt) got Naught, sayving a pittance to poore Ben Gunn that the Gentries gayve him as 'twere a Dole or Charitty. Now was this just, think ye? But 'tis ever the waye.

Soe wee thynk to Mend our owne Fortunes as chance serves, nor trust to noe Pardones. And if ye looke presentlie o'er the loom o' the land, shalt see us at oure sayling. Come nott agaynst us, King's man, for wee goe south o' the setting sun to those other islands farther on, but gette ye to youre Ladie, and to that Fayme and Fortune whych wee doubt not ye shall fynde.

Adios, camarado, and when the sun is over the foreyard – forget nott thy foes.

Sygned this night, wi' all good fellowship an' be damned.

Jno. Rackam. Jas Bylboe the Blacke. Fyrebeard, hys mark. Le Chevalier H.D. Pew. And the companie.

Post-scriptum – wee clayme the Pardone for oure Camarado Sheeba, that sayles nott with us, having some enterpryze of her owne.

A strange keening noise like a deflating football issued from Captain Avery. He stared at the missive, at Blood, and finally up towards the sea-gate, where the buccaneers had been singing round their fires. The fires still twinkled in the dusk, but all was silent, save for the Spanish prisoners snoring and champing in their lock-ups. Avery clutched his head.

"The bounders!" he cried. "Oh, the ingrate, forsworn rotters! After all I've done for them! Why, dash it, Blood, they're just a gang of thieving pirates – that's two million quids' worth of government prize money they're pinching, not just any old loot! Well, they're not getting away with it – come on!"

He legged it along the beach and up on to a small headland where he could look clear across the harbour to the open sea beyond, and as he gazed, with Blood panting at his elbow, out from the lee of grim Octopus Rock a tall ship was gliding over the moonlit water, with creak of cordage and distant sound of triumphant revelry – hang it, he could even hear Firebeard blundering about roaring "Har-Har!", and Goliath's shrill piping voice, and a babble of French irregular verbs, and Solomon Shafto gibbering crazily o' dripping unlimited, and on the poop, unless his straining eyes deceived him, an elegant black-coated figure, d'ye see, and another massive in calico white. And as the vessel heeled under the night wind that filled her sails, the tumult and cheering were blending into such a song as the Brotherhood sang when they went down to the sea – a sinful, ranting chorus, by the powers, all about dollars spinning, and drinking at an inn, and dying in their boots like old bold mates o' Harry Morgan, and laying 'em board and board, and swimming in rum to Kingdom Come; a godforsaken wanton singing, and ye may lay to that.

"'Tis the *Santa Umbriago* right enough!" cried Blood. "Don Lardo's great treasure ship – wi' a fortune in her hold."

"Those blighters," quo' Avery, gritting from incisors to molars, "will be singing another tune presently, and it won't be 'Happy Days Are Here Again', I warrant ye. Run out on me and a royal pardon, will they? We'll see about that! What, shall I not hunt them down, wheresoe'er they venture, and bring all to book, and chance it—" He was interrupted by a hand laid on his arm.

"Easy, boy," said Colonel Blood. "Prithee hold on but a moment. Ye'll mind," said he weightily, "that on Dead Man's Chest I said I'd stand by ye an' see ye through the wickedness o' the world, wi' sound advice and good counsel?"

"Ha! We know what came o' that! First crack out of the box you were chummying up to my betrothed and oozing off with Akbar's cross and—"

"Tut-tut," reproved Blood. "Mere trifles – this is your Uncle Tom talking, for your own good, and I'm tellin' you—" he nodded in the direction of the treasure ship, standing out now to the open sea. "Let 'em be. Forget it. Not because 'twould be perilous pursuit, or revenge too dearly bought, but just for your own peace o' mind hereafter. Never mind what we were debatin' a minute since, whether I'd been of service to ye or not; that's no matter. But ask yourself," and he looked our hero in the eye, "where would ye ha' been without them?" He nodded again towards the *Santa*

Umbriago. "Not on Octopus Rock, and all well."

Avery blinked, and a thoughtful frown crossed his hand-some features. Conflicting emotions traded punches in his finely-tuned brain. He glanced at the distant ship, and gave a sharp intake of breath as a faint 'Har-har!' floated across the water. He sighed heavily – but what he would have said we'll never know, for at that moment a silvery soprano was calling his name, and he was wheeling round like a pointing gun-dog to gaze enraptured towards the castle.

There she was, framed in the gateway, a shining vision in cloth of silver, blonde hair elegantly shampooed and set – she'd had all day to get glamoured up, and had made the most of it. Now, as her sparkling eyes discerned the distant figure of her lover, her voice tinkled again like a crystal chandelier in a high wind.

"Ben! Ah, Ben, darling! Where on earth have you *been*? See, 'tis I – thy Vanity!"

"Vanity!" Avery's ecstatic baritone quivered with long-ing. "My own! Hang on, beloved, I'll be right—"

"Capeetan Ben! Ah, eet ees yoo indeed! Ah, caro mio, eet ees I, Meleeflooa! You 'ave com' back for mee!"

Avery, on his mark and about to bound towards the castle gate, checked as though hit by three wing forwards. From a sally port in the castle wall, hidden from Vanity, a small and dainty figure was tripping down a flight of stone steps, waving as she came. Even at that distance he could see the love-light suffusing the face of the beauteous little hidalga. But there was more to come.

"Barracuda!" The throaty, exultant contralto throbbed through the tropic evening, and he turned in disbelief to see a magnificent figure in a leopard-skin track suit sashaying across the rocks. (Sheba always kept a spare leopard-skin track suit in the secret passage, for just such emergencies as this.) Beneath her plumed picture hat he could see the brilliant gleam of teeth as she strode towards the little hill on which he stood. "Barracuda – at last!"

Captain Avery did a stricken triple-take of the gorgeous trio advancing on him from different directions. By his calculation, if he stood rooted (which seemed likely) they ought to arrive simultaneously, in approximately sixty seconds. Hero that he was, his classic features went distinctly pale.

"Oh, lor'!" he said.

"As ye said yourself," murmured Blood sardonically, "some fellows ha' it; some ha'nt. An' the best o' British, brother!"

"Blood!" Avery seized his arm. "Tom – don't go! I need thy sound advice and good counsel! What am I going to do? I mean . . . most embarrassing – what'll I say? You're a man o' the world, Tom old chap – couldn't you take at least one of them off my hands, dash it all? Not Vanity, obviously, but . . ."

"The trouble is," said Blood apologetically, "I don't speak Spanish all that well – and as for Black Beauty . . ." He shivered. "Besides, I've had this fancy to slip down to Roatan an' pay me respects to Mistress Bonney – more my style, d'ye see?" He patted the distraught captain on the shoulder. "Sorry, ould joy, but ye're on your own this time. Tom Blood bids ye good luck an' good-bye."

"Recreant!" cried Avery. "Ha, false to the last!" He braced himself, took a deep breath, and turned with dauntless bearing to meet them, arms outspread to Vanity, a glad smile on his lips. Perhaps if he pretended the other two weren't there . . .

Colonel Blood walked down the hill towards the beach, whistling softly to himself. One backward glance he took, as the sound of female voices carried down to him, and then he was striding across the sands, and far out on the shining sea the tall ship was standing away down the moon's track with all her canvas spread, and very faintly across the water he could hear the pirates singing.

> *Farewell and adieu to you*
> *Fine Spanish ladies,*
> *Farewell and adieu to you*
> *Ladies of Spain . . .*

And for all I know, they may be singing still.

AFTERTHOUGHT

lert readers may have noticed that in THE PYRATES occasional liberties have been taken with history, geography, seamanship, haute couture, French, archaeology, and even logistics – try sailing a small boat from Madagascar to the Isle of Aves and back, and see how long it takes. For this no apology is offered; you were warned on page 13. But where real historical figures have been press-ganged into the story, and used without scruple as the author thought fit, it seems only fair, now that it's all over, to set down the brief truth about them. Not the great names, like Charles II and Mr Pepys (although it should be noted that the Duke of York, later James II, and Paterson the blacksmith *did* represent Scotland at golf against two gentlemen of England – and won), but those lesser-known folk whose names have receded into the shadows of history.

For example, there was a real Long Ben Avery (or Every, or Everie, and his Christian name may have been Ben or John or Henry), who came from Plymouth and is said to have been a naval officer before leading a mutiny and turning pirate in the 1690s. He was nothing like as splendid as our Ben, and probably not even mildly heroic, but he was the most celebrated sea-rover of his day, the subject of a play and a novel and countless broadsheets. For Long Ben Avery, now forgotten, set a world record which has never been broken: he committed the richest single crime in history. This was the seizure of the Great Mogul's treasure ship (and according to romantic tradition, of the Mogul's beautiful daughter – shades of Donna Meliflua), and since this one prize was worth close to half a million sterling of his day, it ranks far ahead of such petty larcenies as the so-called Great Train Robbery, the Brinks armoured car job, and even the recent Conduit Street gem theft (which involved, curiously enough, some Mogul jewellery).

This spectacular coup won Avery a fame far greater even than that of his notorious contemporary, the unfortunate Kidd (who was not much of a pirate, really), but he got little good out of it. The story runs that he was cheated of his spoil by Bristol merchants and died impoverished, like Israel Hands, that other real pirate whom R. L. Stevenson plucked from Blackbeard's crew and immortalised. Avery is said to be buried at Bideford; a hero he may not have been, but he provided a splendidly romantic name which it would have been a pity to neglect.

The same is true of John Rackham (d. 1717) a fairly small-time sea-thief of the New Providence fraternity, whose nickname Calico Jack is pure deep-sea poetry, and entirely fitting for a pirate whose history was bizarre even by filibuster standards. It was his misfortune to fall in love with Anne Bonney, the illegitimate daughter of an Irish attorney; Rackham took her to sea disguised as a man, no doubt to avoid any objections from his followers, but unfortunately the lady was of a wanton disposition, and made advances to a handsome young member of the pirate crew – who proved to be another disguised female, Mary Read, former trooper in the British Army and lately landlady of the Three Horseshoes inn at Breda in Holland. She, in turn, had fixed her affections on a (presumably) male pirate in Rackham's following, and even fought a hand-to-hand duel on his behalf, killing her opponent.

At about this time Rackham took to drink, which is

hardly surprising, and when the pirate ship was finally cornered by a King's vessel, he and his fellows shirked the action, leaving the Mesdames Bonney and Read to put up a spirited fight alone. Taken to trial in Jamaica, Anne and Mary escaped the gallows by pleading pregnancy, and although Mary subsequently died of gaol fever, Anne appears to have been eventually reprieved. Rackham was hanged on Gallows Point, Port Royal.

This is the received story of Calico Jack and the women pirates, and no fiction-writer in his senses would accept it as a credible plot for a moment. But the one difficulty about dismissing it as far-fetched nonsense is that, so far as can be judged from the evidence, it appears to be true. Records of the trial are said to exist, and no one has ever cast convincing doubts on the detailed account given in Defoe.

Of the other principals in THE PYRATES, Firebeard is loosely based on the famous Blackbeard Teach of Bristol, that extravagant monster who, if the extract from his journal quoted by Defoe is authentic, must have been one of the most brilliant prose stylists of the Augustan Age. It demands quotation again:

"Such a Day, Rum all out – Our Company somewhat sober – A damn'd Confusion amongst us! – Rogues a-plotting – great Talk of Separation. So I look'd sharp for a Prize – such a Day took one, with a great deal of Liquor on board, so kept the Company hot, damn'd hot, then all Things went well again."

Fifty-four words to paint as vivid a picture as any in the English language.

Happy Dan Pew was vaguely inspired by two French buccaneers, the mad Montbars who was known as the Exterminator, and the abominable Nau L'Ollonois; Bilbo is Basil Rathbone playing a raffish Captain Hook; and Sheba is a Dahomey Amazon with echoes of Lola Montez, Queen Ranavalona, and a pantomime principal boy.

But they are pirates for fun; the real Brotherhood of the

Coast, that astonishing fraternity which grew in a generation from a few woodsmen and hunters ('boucaniers') into the strongest mercenary fleet ever seen, is a serious subject, and this is not really the place to write about it. The story of how, under leaders like Morgan, whose genius might have won him a place among the great captains, the buccaneers shook the power of Spain and helped to plant their countries' flags in the Western seas, can be found in the histories listed in my bibliography; sufficient to say here that, bloody ruffians though they were, they gave to piracy a kind of stature, and played an often underrated part in the making of the New World.

Which brings us finally to Colonel Thomas Blood who, if he was never a pirate, was pretty well everything else – soldier, rascal, secret agent, Justice of the Peace, perpetual fugitive, Fifth Monarchy Man, hired assassin, Covenanter, conspirator, confidant of royalty, occasional medical practitioner, and jewel thief extraordinary. He is rather better documented than the other real-life ruffians whose names I have appropriated, and even more eccentric. He seems to have spent much of his life on the run, following plots and crimes which invariably went wrong, for while he was an adventurer of great ingenuity and tremendous style, the execution of his schemes was often marred by an over-elaboration bordering on lunacy. Not many adventurers, planning to seize Dublin Castle, would have tried to divert the guards by hurling loaves of bread at them, in the hope that while they scrambled for the food, Blood and his associates could sally in and seize the fortress. And only a perverted artist, bent on the fairly straightforward task of assassinating the Duke of Ormonde, would have tried to do it by carrying his victim on horseback to Tyburn with the intention of hanging him from the public gallows.

Blood's most celebrated exploit, the theft of the Crown Jewels from the Tower of London, he undertook disguised as a clergyman, and very nearly got away with it; apprehended, he demanded audience of Charles II, and emerged with a pardon and a reward, which caused some comment at the time and remains unexplained to this day.

That Blood was deep in political intrigues is certain, but what his exact relations were with the King (and the Duke of Buckingham) it is impossible to say. It seems unlikely that he won Charles's favour by confessing that he had once been hired to murder the King while the latter was bathing at Battersea, but had held his fire out of sheer loyal awe; possibly the Merry Monarch had a fellow-feeling for such an intrepid and charming rogue; but the most probable explanation for Blood's immunity is simply that he knew too much, and bought his freedom with the promise of silence. In the end, after a lifetime of adventures, escapes, pursuits, disguises, and hand-to-hand encounters, he died of natural causes in 1680, aged about 62 – and after his funeral at Tothill Fields they dug the body up again just to make sure that the nimble Colonel was dead at last.

INFLUENTIAL
BIBLIOGRAPHY

Pirates and blue water took hold of me in childhood, and show no sign of letting go fifty years later. It started with tuppenny bloods and boys' annuals, and continued through those splendid Hollywood epics of the 30s and 40s and the works of the great historical novelists (Sabatini was my hero then, and still is) to the original sources, among them the memoirs of buccaneers themselves. One result of all this mingled reading and watching and dreaming is the foregoing fantasy, written for the fun of it, and since it grew from so many influences (some of which had nothing to do with pirates at all) and since I am a compulsive foot-noter anyway, it seems right to set them down.

They are a mixed bag: what, you may ask, has Lord Macaulay got to do with an anonymous writer for the *Wizard* (or was it the *Skipper*?) and with Michael Curtiz, film director? Simply, one of them gave me an unforgettable picture of Restoration England, another introduced me to the dreaded maguay plant (by the powers!), and the third put Errol Flynn and Basil Rathbone rapier to rapier on a rocky seashore. And so on, with all the rest. They are not to be held responsible for my mad fancies, but I owe them my admiration, gratitude, and abiding affection.

Adventure, Hotspur, Rover, Skipper, Wizard (D.C. Thomson publications)

BALLANTYNE, R.M. – *The Coral Island*
    Martin Rattler

BARRIE, J.M. – *Peter Pan*

BURNEY, James – *History of the Buccaneers of America*

Collins' French Primer, volumes 1 and 2

DAMPIER, William – *Voyages and Discoveries*

DEFOE, Daniel – *Robinson Crusoe*
    Captain Singleton
    The King of Pyrates
    A General Historie of the . . . Most Notorious Pirates (as Charles Johnson)

DELL, Draycott M. – *Ghosts of the Spanish Main*

DIAZ, Bernal – *The Conquest of New Spain*

Dictionary of National Biography

DOYLE, A. Conan – *Tales of Pirates and Blue Water*

ESQUEMELING, Alexander – *The Buccaneers of America*

EVELYN, John – *Diary*

FARNOL, Jeffrey – *Adam Penfeather, Buccaneer*
    Black Bartlemy's Treasure
    Martin Conisby's Vengeance
    Winds of Fortune

HAKLUYT, Richard – *Voyages*

MACAULAY, T.B. – *History of England*

MARRYAT, Frederick – *Masterman Ready*
    Mr Midshipman Easy
    Peter Simple

The Newgate Calendar

Notable British Trials – The Bounty Mutineers
    Captain Kidd

PEPYS, Samuel – *Diary*

PRESCOTT, W.H. – *History of the Conquest of Peru*

ROGERS, Stanley – *The Atlantic Buccaneers*

ROGERS Woodes – *A Cruising Voyage Round the World*

SABATINI, Rafael – *Captain Blood*

The Chronicles of Captain Blood
The Fortunes of Captain Blood
The Black Swan
The Hounds of God
The Sea Hawk
The Sword of Islam
SMOLLET, Tobias – *The Adventures of Roderick Random*
STEVENSON, R.L. – *The Master of Ballantrae*
Treasure Island
SWIFT, Jonathan – *Gulliver's Travels*
TRELAWNEY, E.J. – *Adventures of a Younger Son*
TAYLOR, W.F. – *Shirwah the Corsair*
VANBRUGH, John – *The Provoked Wife*
The Relapse
WAFER, Lionel – *A New Voyage and Description of the Isthmus of America*
WALKEY, S. – *Rogues of the Roaring Glory*
YOUNG, Gordon Ray – *Hurok the Avenger*

Motion Pictures
Treasure Island (1934)
Captain Blood (1935)
Drake of England (1935)
The Sea Hawk (1940)
The Black Swan (1942)
Captain Kidd (1945)
The Fortunes of Captain Blood (1950)

To all of which must be added:
The music of Erich Wolfgang Korngold, Alfred Newman and Dr Arne
The poetry of John Masefield, Alfred Noyes, Henry Newbolt, Lord Byron, and Rudyard Kipling
The singing of Peter Dawson
The drawings of H.M. Brock
and the songs and shanties that sailors used to sing.

G.M.F.

413

Fiction

☐ **The Chains of Fate**	Pamela Belle	£2.95p
☐ **Options**	Freda Bright	£1.50p
☐ **The Thirty-nine Steps**	John Buchan	£1.50p
☐ **Secret of Blackoaks**	Ashley Carter	£1.50p
☐ **Hercule Poirot's Christmas**	Agatha Christie	£1.50p
☐ **Dupe**	Liza Cody	£1.25p
☐ **Lovers and Gamblers**	Jackie Collins	£2.50p
☐ **Sphinx**	Robin Cook	£1.25p
☐ **My Cousin Rachel**	Daphne du Maurier	£1.95p
☐ **Flashman and the Redskins**	George Macdonald Fraser	£1.95p
☐ **The Moneychangers**	Arthur Hailey	£2.50p
☐ **Secrets**	Unity Hall	£1.75p
☐ **Black Sheep**	Georgette Heyer	£1.75p
☐ **The Eagle Has Landed**	Jack Higgins	£1.95p
☐ **Sins of the Fathers**	Susan Howatch	£3.50p
☐ **Smiley's People**	John le Carré	£1.95p
☐ **To Kill a Mockingbird**	Harper Lee	£1.95p
☐ **Ghosts**	Ed McBain	£1.75p
☐ **The Silent People**	Walter Macken	£1.95p
☐ **Gone with the Wind**	Margaret Mitchell	£3.50p
☐ **Blood Oath**	David Morrell	£1.75p
☐ **The Night of Morningstar**	Peter O'Donnell	£1.75p
☐ **Wilt**	Tom Sharpe	£1.75p
☐ **Rage of Angels**	Sidney Sheldon	£1.95p
☐ **The Unborn**	David Shobin	£1.50p
☐ **A Town Like Alice**	Nevile Shute	£1.75p
☐ **Gorky Park**	Martin Cruz Smith	£1.95p
☐ **A Falcon Flies**	Wilbur Smith	£2.50p
☐ **The Grapes of Wrath**	John Steinbeck	£2.50p
☐ **The Deep Well at Noon**	Jessica Stirling	£2.50p
☐ **The Ironmaster**	Jean Stubbs	£1.75p
☐ **The Music Makers**	E. V. Thompson	£1.95p

Non-fiction

☐ **The First Christian**	Karen Armstrong	£2.50p
☐ **Pregnancy**	Gordon Bourne	£3.50p
☐ **The Law is an Ass**	Gyles Brandreth	£1.75p
☐ **The 35mm Photographer's Handbook**	Julian Calder and John Garrett	£5.95p
☐ **London at its Best**	Hunter Davies	£2.95p
☐ **Back from the Brink**	Michael Edwardes	£2.95p

☐	**Travellers' Britain**	⎱ Arthur Eperon	£2.95p
☐	**Travellers' Italy**	⎰	£2.95p
☐	**The Complete Calorie Counter**	Eileen Fowler	80p
☐	**The Diary of Anne Frank**	Anne Frank	£1.75p
☐	**And the Walls Came Tumbling Down**	Jack Fishman	£1.95p
☐	**Linda Goodman's Sun Signs**	Linda Goodman	£2.50p
☐	**Scott and Amundsen**	Roland Huntford	£3.95p
☐	**Victoria RI**	Elizabeth Longford	£4.95p
☐	**Symptoms**	Sigmund Stephen Miller	£2.50p
☐	**Book of Worries**	Robert Morley	£1.50p
☐	**Airport International**	Brian Moynahan	£1.75p
☐	**Pan Book of Card Games**	Hubert Phillips	£1.95p
☐	**Keep Taking the Tabloids**	Fritz Spiegl	£1.75p
☐	**An Unfinished History of the World**	Hugh Thomas	£3.95p
☐	**The Baby and Child Book**	Penny and Andrew Stanway	£4.95p
☐	**The Third Wave**	Alvin Toffler	£2.95p
☐	**Pauper's Paris**	Miles Turner	£2.50p
☐	**The Psychic Detectives**	Colin Wilson	£2.50p
☐	**The Flier's Handbook**		£5.95p

All these books are available at your local bookshop or newsagent, or can be ordered direct from the publisher. Indicate the number of copies required and fill in the form below   11

....

Name..
(Block letters please)

Address...

_____   _____

Send to CS Department, Pan Books Ltd, PO Box 40, Basingstoke, Hants
Please enclose remittance to the value of the cover price plus:
35p for the first book plus 15p per copy for each additional book ordered
to a maximum charge of £1.25 to cover postage and packing
Applicable only in the UK

While every effort is made to keep prices low, it is sometimes
necessary to increase prices at short notice. Pan Books reserve
the right to show on covers and charge new retail prices which
may differ from those advertised in the text or elsewhere